The Titus Chronicles
Viking
Book 2

By R.W. Peake

Also by R.W Peake

Marching With Caesar® – Birth of the 10th
Marching With Caesar – Conquest of Gaul
Marching With Caesar – Civil War
Marching With Caesar – Antony and Cleopatra, Parts I & II
Marching With Caesar – Rise of Augustus
Marching With Caesar – Last Campaign
Marching With Caesar – Rebellion
Marching With Caesar – A New Era
Marching With Caesar – Pax Romana
Marching With Caesar – Fraternitas
Marching With Caesar – Vengeance
Marching With Caesar – Rise of Germanicus
Marching With Caesar – Revolt of the Legions
Marching With Caesar – Avenging Varus, Part I
Marching With Caesar – Avenging Varus, Part II
Marching With Caesar – Hostage to Fortuna
Marching With Caesar – Praetorian

The Titus Chronicles – Eagle and Wyvern

Caesar Triumphant
Caesar Ascending – Invasion of Parthia
Caesar Ascending – Conquest of Parthia
Caesar Ascending – India
Caesar Ascending – Pandya

Critical praise for the Marching with Caesar series:

Marching With Caesar-Antony and Cleopatra: Part I-Antony

"Peake has become a master of depicting Roman military life and action, and in this latest novel he proves adept at evoking the subtleties of his characters, often with an understated humour and surprising pathos. Very highly recommended."

Marching With Caesar-Civil War

"Fans of the author will be delighted that Peake's writing has gone from strength to strength in this, the second volume...Peake manages to portray Pullus and all his fellow soldiers with a marvelous feeling of reality quite apart from the star historical name... There's history here, and character, and action enough for three novels, and all of it can be enjoyed even if readers haven't seen the first volume yet. Very highly recommended."

~The Historical Novel Society

"The hinge of history pivoted on the career of Julius Caesar, as Rome's Republic became an Empire, but the muscle to swing that gateway came from soldiers like Titus Pullus. What an amazing story from a student now become the master of historical fiction at its best."

~Professor Frank Holt, University of Houston

The Titus Chronicles – Viking by R.W. Peake

By R.W. Peake
Copyright © 2021 by R.W. Peake

Foreword

I suspect that I'm far from alone in saying that the last year, plus the first few months of 2021, have been a challenge for me, as I'm certain it has been for most, if not all of you, my readers. In my case, however, I didn't begin feeling the effects of what has been the most disruptive event of our lifetime until relatively recently, or at least, I wasn't aware of them until recently. I am, by nature, something of a solitary person; I am the only child of a single mother who, because her job as a professional symphony musician made for odd hours, particularly nights and weekends, I found myself alone a great deal. Because of that, I became accustomed to my own company, and have been able to entertain myself for as long as I can remember. It's not that I'm anti-social, it's just that I never seemed to require the level of human interaction that many, if not most, people require...or so I believed.

But, beginning a few months ago, I began realizing that, in fact, I *was* missing human connection. Not as much in terms of friendships and missing seeing relatives, although it's been incredibly difficult not having the opportunity to be in physical proximity to my only child, my daughter, prior to her and her husband finally achieving their dream of returning to London and the United Kingdom, where they spent the first seven years of their marriage. We've gone this long without seeing each other before, but now there's an added element that, while we don't talk about it, also can't be denied because it's always there, lurking in the background, the idea that we may never see each other again. And, without going into detail, I have two autoimmune conditions, one of which has already done its best to kill me a couple of times, and I have to admit that, when the pandemic first hit and they started talking about vulnerable people, specifically those over sixty and with even one, let alone two autoimmune diseases, it was with a fair amount of shock that I realized, "Holy crap...they're talking about ME!" Despite dealing with these issues for a couple decades, and my close calls, this is the first time I ever thought of myself as "vulnerable."

It's a consequence of our daily reality, with the stories of emotional farewells to loved ones via FaceTime, or even worse, over the phone, and while it's easy for us to ignore these stories when they rarely happen, they've been a daily feature of the lives of all who have stayed at least nominally engaged in the larger world. It's a steady drip, drip, drip of heartbreak and loss, but it was one that, at least in my mind, I had been able to compartmentalize, at least until recently.

What I realized was that what I was missing were the mundane acts of human interaction; going to the store and listening to the same clerk make the same joke to a regular customer, simply being able to smile at someone when you pass by each other, make some comment about the weather, or talk about the Seahawks, my adopted team. When I first relocated from the fourth largest city in the country to a town of less than ten thousand here on the remote Olympic Peninsula, when someone engaged me in conversation while standing in line and they would ask how my day was going, for example, my first reaction was invariably, "Why do you want to know?"

And, being completely honest, I still do get irritated when the cashier and the customer ahead of me spend a couple minutes catching up because they have known each other for years...but I don't get nearly as irritated as I used to, and this was something I realized that I was missing, much to my surprise. There's security and comfort in these everyday exchanges; at least, that's proven to be the case for me, and these last fifteen months (and keep in mind that I live about fifty miles as the crow flies from Ground Zero for COVID-19 in the U.S., and Washington was one of the first states to initiate a complete shutdown, and is one of the slowest to open back up) have been anything but mundane and routine. And, if I'm being completely honest, I view the pandemic in much the same way I viewed 9/11; I vividly recall being called to a company-wide meeting on that day, where our CEO told us to go home and hug our families, and I turned to a coworker to say, "This has changed our lives in ways we don't even know yet." That's how I feel about this event; we're never going back to the normal world of 2019; we're going to have to learn to adjust to a new normal. What that means remains to be seen.

However, there's been one thing that has sustained me through this period, and that's you, my readers, and my desire to keep telling the stories of what has now become a multi-generational family of warriors. For the reasons I mentioned above, this has proven to be one of the most challenging books

I've written, but I suppose it's a testament to my stubbornness if nothing else that I simply can't leave a story untold, at least not anymore. For more years than I care to remember, I was a *great* starter of stories; I have easily a dozen stories that I've started (though none of them are historical fiction) and then put down for one reason or another. It wasn't until 2006, when I wrote what is actually my first novel that I won't be publishing for a few more years, and actually completed it that I was able to say, "I am a writer," and it's something that I tell all aspiring authors. Until you *finish* something, and I mean whether it be a short story, or a novella, or a full-length novel, you can't consider yourself a writer, in my humble opinion; you're a dabbler and a wannabe. Once you complete that first work, then you can think of yourself as a writer; until you've got something published, you can't call yourself an author, and until you get positive feedback from readers who aren't called "Mom," or "Dad," or some other title that indicates they have a rooting interest in your success, you can't call yourself a successful author. And, thank God for you, the readers who have taken Titus the Elder and all of his progeny to heart, I can say that I meet the criteria for all of the above, and I will *never* take that for granted.

What it also means, at least in my case, is that I simply can't leave a story unfinished, not anymore. It's like a deep itch inside my brain that can only be satisfied by completing it, even if it's a struggle because of external factors. Hopefully, we will never face anything like 2020 and all that came with it again.

As always, thanks to my editor Beth Lynne for catching my many errors (especially my continuing inability to remember when to use "lie" and "lay"), and understanding what I am trying to say even when I'm not sure. Also, thanks to Laura Prevost for being able to interpret what's in my head into a cover image that hopefully conveys the essence of the story.

And with that, I hope that y'all enjoy *The Titus Chronicles-Viking*.

Semper Fidelis
R.W. Peake
April 6, 2021

Historical Notes

"A.D. 882. ...and the same year went King Alfred out to sea with a fleet; and fought with four ship-rovers of the Danes, and took two of their ships; wherein all the men were slain; and the other two surrendered; but the men were severely cut and wounded ere they surrendered."

~Bede- Anglo-Saxon Chronicles

It's a truism that every student of history, amateur and professional, knows; history is written by the winners. This is the genesis of what is now *The Titus Chronicles-Viking*, a relatively innocuous entry for a year that was not nearly as momentous and event-filled as 878, or 885 and beyond. My purpose in choosing 882 as the year we return to Titus of Cissanbyrig's story was mainly for purposes of the narrative, thinking that an eight-year gap or more would require far too much explanation. However, as I began thinking about how to construct this next chapter in Titus' life, I also began to think about something that I have employed in my other books, particularly about Titus the Elder and his time under Gaius Julius Caesar during the Gallic War and the Civil War with Pompeius Magnus, where an eyewitness to the history that we know has a different perspective than what ends up in the historical record.

And the more I thought about it, the more I began wondering about this episode as it pertained to the larger situation, specifically the peace between the Saxons of King Alfred and the Danes loyal to Guthrum, the self-styled King of East Anglia, or the Danelaw. Four years into the Treaty of Wedmore, from the contemporary chroniclers like the Venerable Bede and his *The Anglo-Saxon Chronicles*, who I use as one of my primary sources, by and large, things were peaceful between the two adversaries. Certainly there were raids that originated from within the Danelaw, mostly into neighboring Mercia, but it's clear that both Alfred and Guthrum, undoubtedly for different reasons given later events, were interested in maintaining the peace. Consequently, it was in their mutual interest to avoid being seen as the aggressor at this point in time.

As I've mentioned before, being an author of historical fiction who tries to hew as closely to the primary source material as possible is a sword that cuts both ways; in some ways it can be constraining, but in other ways it allows the author to either speculate, or completely fabricate a smaller event for the purposes of telling what they all fervently hope will be a compelling story for their readers. In this case, I decided to speculate, both on where these Danish raiders came from, and in direct contradiction of Bede's account, the number of ships that Alfred encountered, and defeated. While I won't go into much detail, I concluded that, given the political context of the moment, it wouldn't have been in Alfred's interests to let it be known that this was a larger incursion, consisting of a higher number of Danish raiders, and Bede himself only refers to these raiders as "Danes" and not "Guthrum's Danes" or "Danes from the Danelaw" or something of that nature. While it's also speculation, it's not much of a stretch to think that there were high-ranking noble Saxons who weren't happy with what they likely would view as Alfred's appeasement of the pagan Danish and Northmen invaders; having a more potent force of raiders would have given them fodder to agitate against Alfred's policy of maintaining the peace with a people who, even by the standard of the day, were aggressive invaders of other lands. In fact, I strongly suspect that there was a contemporary viewpoint that we Americans are familiar with from our own history with Native Americans: "The only good Dane is a dead Dane."

So, if I'm Alfred, what would I do? That's essentially what I do with all of my characters, keeping the context and values of the time period in mind, and my speculation is that Alfred would have wanted to minimize the impact of this Danish incursion, reducing it to more of a minor nuisance. However, I also believe, and in this I can point to later events, that this was also Alfred's attempt to negate the one strategic advantage that the Northern invaders held over the Saxons, and that was their mobility at sea. This episode also supports the latest scholarship that Alfred already had at least something of a naval arm, prior to the popularly accepted belief that he was the father of the Royal Navy by ordering ships specifically designed to defeat the Danish longships in 897 CE. However, I also make the supposition that the reason Alfred commissioned the construction of ships specifically designed to combat the superior design of the Danish longships stemmed at least in part from his dissatisfaction with the ships that were at his disposal. While I don't believe this is much of a stretch, I also have learned that it's highly likely there will be readers better versed in this subject than I am who would argue that it is, and I ask forgiveness from them in advance.

Why is a story about a young Saxon warrior titled *Viking*? Because as I learned some time ago, the term "Viking" that we use today to describe the raiders from Scandinavia was essentially a word describing their actual *activity* of sailing to foreign lands to attack and plunder them. The Danish raiders in this story were participating in "viking"; they were *not* "Vikings" which is why I chose this title.

As always, there is a mixture of historical and fictional characters, and as I did in Volume I, I use the term "Ealdorman" a bit loosely, specifically as it pertains to Lord Eadwig of Wiltun, who in the story might technically be a Thegn, but is a "super" Thegn, and given that after Wulfhere, the Ealdorman of Wiltscir (in keeping with my practice, I use the Old English spellings for locations like shires and rivers) vanishes after he either sided with Guthrum or, what appears most likely, to have sat out the Battle of Ethantun, I was unable to locate the name of the Ealdorman of Wiltscir for this period of time; only in the 890's does Aethelhelm's name come up as the Ealdorman of Wiltscir. Until that time and in my story, Eadwig will essentially rule as Ealdorman, if only in practice and not name. None of the Danes, aside from Guthrum of course, are based in the historical record. On the Saxon side, Mucel and Eardwulf return, and Cuthred of Hampscir and Odda of Devonscir are real; what is not so clear is whether Sigeræd of Cent is or not. The truth is that I found arguments on both sides, so at the moment, he is an Ealdorman with a question mark behind his name.

Stanmer is a real place, and was the site of a monastery, which I discovered using what has become an indispensable resource, *An Atlas of Anglo-Saxon England*, by David Hill, as is the village of Hamsey, upriver from modern Lewes on the Ouse River. Also, according to Google Earth, there is in fact a stretch of sandy beach directly south of Stanmer. Romney is also a real place, although the village of Romney of Alfred's time, on the River Rother and located in a loop of the river called The Great Estuary, near the better known town of Rye, which became one of the Cinque Ports, suffered the fate of having its port silted up by The Great Storm of

1287. There was also a port at Lydd as well as Rye, but I chose to use Romney because of an article I read in *Archaeologia Cantiana*, Vol. 65 1952 that indicates that it was more important during Alfred's time than the other ports that have survived longer. Now, there is an Old Romney and New Romney, "New" being a relative term, since New Romney is mentioned in the Domesday Book along with Old Romney, but at the time of the story, there was just one.

As far as the Danish curse words, I found the website "How To Curse In Norse" extremely helpful, while the training for shipboard combat is strictly of my own invention, and is again based in the idea, "How would I try to train men without having half of them drown?"

Finally, I make mention of a ford across the Temese (Thames), at Lambehitha, or modern-day Lambeth, and I base my mention of it on the long-held belief that there was a ford at this location dating back to Roman times. Granted, today, it's impossible to imagine such a thing, but the modern Thames and the Temese of the First Century and Ninth Century respectively, would bear little resemblance to each other now that the river has been dredged and remade over the centuries.

Table of Contents

Chapter One

In the early months of the Year of Our Lord 882, Titus, formerly known as Titus of Cissanbyrig but now more commonly known locally as Titus the Berserker, was eighteen years old, standing three inches over six feet tall, weighing more than sixteen stone (224 pounds), all of which was muscle. He now had a full mustache in the Saxon style, and he had let his hair grow to shoulder length, which he wore in a braid at moments like this, standing in the yard of his Lord, Otha, as he faced another of Otha's retainers, Uhtric, who also happened to be Titus' best friend and brother-in-law. Each of them held a shield and a wooden sword, while Uhtric was wearing a helm with a mail fringe and Titus was bareheaded, although this was by choice.

"You know you haven't beaten me in six months," Titus taunted Uhtric, but Uhtric was as quick with his tongue as he was with his *seaxe*, reminding his much larger friend, "It took you two years to beat me for the first time. I'm just letting you catch up. But then..."

Uhtric did not finish because he was lunging, aiming the rounded point of his wooden sword directly for the slight gap he had spotted in Titus' defenses when his younger friend had become distracted by their banter. At least, this was what Uhtric had believed, but even in the eyeblink of time between launching his thrust and seeing Titus' shield already in position to block it, he thought, He fooled me again. Fortunately, although Titus knew Uhtric's style of swordplay, Uhtric knew Titus' as well, so that his own shield was already moving, but as often happened, despite blocking Titus' counterthrust, Uhtric was forced to move his feet to keep them under him as he reeled backward from the sheer power.

"Do you always have to do that?" Uhtric complained, which made Titus laugh, although he was also moving forward to keep his pressure now that he had Uhtric backpedaling.

For the span of several heartbeats, the pair were seemingly

content to strike each other's shield, but while the sounds were similar, the cracking sound that was made every time Titus struck with anywhere near his full strength was sharper, and louder. However, Uhtric was not fooled by this seeming complacency on Titus' part, and he muttered a curse when a drop of sweat ran down his forehead and into his eye, the sign that Titus was wearing him down. As proud as Uhtric, son of Wiglaf, was of his brother-in-law, Titus' seemingly limitless need to prove his dominance over others could be quite trying, and right now, Titus was being insufferable. Nevertheless, he also knew better than to make a deliberate error to end the bout, because this only angered Titus, and even if the sparring session was over for the day, he would not forget and would express his irritation with a heightened effort the next time. With increasing desperation, Uhtric offered a combination defense of shield and footwork, backing up though not allowing himself to be pinned against the stack of sacks and wooden crates that outlined three sides of the square, with the barn wall the fourth. The end was inevitable, however, and it came when Titus made a feint that drew Uhtric's shield out of position, then with a quickness that only seemed to increase every year, he launched a thrust that struck Uhtric in the pit of his stomach. Even with his mail shirt and not one but two padded shirts, the air was driven from his lungs in an explosive gasp, and he immediately dropped to his knees.

Before he had regained his breath, a hand thrust into his vision, and he looked up into Titus' grinning face, but while he accepted it, as Titus hauled him to his feet, Uhtric managed to get out, "I really don't like you sometimes."

This made Titus laugh, and he replied cheerfully, "You don't have to like me, but you have to love me. I'm Wiglaf's uncle! If I told him that you don't like me, he would be very upset."

The mention of Uhtric's son, who was approaching his third birthday, made his father smile, as Titus knew it would; besides, Titus was speaking truthfully. As trying as it was at times, Uhtric felt a connection with Titus that went beyond familial bonds and was strengthened by his gratitude that Titus' oldest sister Leofflaed was his wife and was almost due with their second child. All in all, Uhtric thought with satisfaction as he and Titus shared a dipper of cold, clear water, the years since Ethantun, when a raw but immensely strong fourteen-year-old son of a *ceorl* had walked all the way here to Wiltun from Cissanbyrig to join the *fyrd* and who now stood next to him, had been some of the best years of Uhtric's life. Unfortunately, these years of relative peace, as the peace treaty struck between King Alfred and the King of East Anglia, Guthrum, or as he insisted being called now, Aethelstan, took hold and solidified, had not been viewed with pleasure by everyone, and at the top of that list was his brother-in-law. Uhtric knew that Titus had been growing increasingly restless, but that was the least of Uhtric's concerns about him; he had also become increasingly combative, always spoiling for a fight, and it did not matter with whom. Of course, this was to be expected to a degree for any warrior in the employ of a Thegn like Lord Otha, but Titus was becoming increasingly difficult to control, and Uhtric and Otha had had more than one discussion on what to do about the young man. Right now, thankfully, Titus seemed in a cheerful mood, which Uhtric knew stemmed from the fact that he had just defeated him, something that did not make Uhtric happy in the slightest, but he reckoned it was a small price to pay.

"Have you attended to the mares yet?"

While Uhtric knew the question was not aimed at him, he turned about with Titus, seeing their Lord, Otha, approaching, a bucket in each hand.

"Er, no, Lord," Titus mumbled, suddenly back to a stammering teenager.

"How many times have I told you that sparring only comes after finishing your work?" Otha snapped, then pointed to the barn. "Get in there, boy. You've got work to do!"

The fact that Lord Otha called him a "boy" was the most potent signal to Titus that the Thegn was truly angry. And, despite Titus' size, strength, and growing prowess, his respect for Lord Otha was based as much in fear as it was in what Titus would have scoffed at if he had been forced to describe it as such, but was actually love of the kind a boy feels for his father. Although the fear was also of a physical nature, as Titus had grown and matured, he had grown less fearful of what Otha could do to him in the sparring ring while becoming more concerned with not wanting to disappoint the Thegn. It was never spoken of between them, and in fact it had been Otha's wife Wulfgifu who had seen the bond between her husband and this overgrown boy develop.

"He looks up to you like a father, Otha," she had said one night in bed about six months after Titus' addition to her husband's retinue, after enduring listening to Otha grumble about the youth because he had spilled a bag of oats, even while acknowledging that the boy was going through a growth spurt and learning how to handle a body that was even larger than it already was.

This had never occurred to Otha, who looked over at his wife in surprise, but he saw that she was serious.

Still, he shook his head, frowning as he replied, "I don't think so, wife. Although," his tone turned thoughtful, "I will say this. That boy's father is a foul bastard for treating Titus the way he did. He's a fine boy, and I think he has the makings of a good Saxon man, maybe even a great man."

"And a Thegn one day?" she asked him teasingly.

"I should never have told you he said that," Otha grumbled, but with a smile on his lips. "And," he allowed, "there's nothing wrong with being ambitious. No," he sighed, "the trick is going to be to not let his prowess as a warrior go to his head to the point that's all he becomes."

Over the course of the next four years after this conversation, Otha had learned that his wife had been right, something that he had been forced to admit, much to her delight. What he had not said, ever, was that his feelings for Titus had developed into more of a father figure than a liege lord, although Wulfgifu had not been fooled, but she was wise enough to know not to bring it up. And, now that Titus and Isolde had had their falling out, and she was being courted by another man, both husband and wife were as worried about Titus as Uhtric and Titus' sisters were.

What tormented Titus was that he knew that everything that had happened between him and Isolde was his fault, and that he had essentially driven her into the arms of Hereweald, the son of Hereweald, who served as the master blacksmith serving Ealdorman Eadwig of Wiltun. Although Hereweald was not Titus' height, nor as broad across the shoulders, like most sons of smiths who followed their father in trade, he was immensely strong in his own right. He was not a warrior, but he had stood in the shield wall as one of Eadwig's *ceorls* at Ethantun, and although he had not done anything noteworthy, he had been there and acquitted himself well. That, at least, was what Isolde had told Titus when she first casually mentioned his name on one of Titus' visits to her father Cenric's holding on the opposite side of Wiltun from Lord Otha's estate. And, much to Titus' distress later, he had been dismissive of Hereweald for the simple reason that he was not only not a warrior, he clearly had no desire to be one. Still, Titus was honest enough with himself to privately acknowledge that it was almost entirely his fault. Titus was also aware that his behavior was becoming a problem, not just for himself but for Lord Otha as well because, as Otha had reminded him more times than he could count, what Titus did in Wiltun reflected on the Thegn as much as it did on himself. If he had articulated it aloud, what Otha, Uhtric, and his sisters would have found odd was that, while Titus had tried to hate Hereweald, he just could not maintain it for any length of time, because Hereweald was just so...likable. Oh, the smith's son had certainly been nervous once the news got out, and it had been Cenric himself who came to Otha's farm to deliver the news to Titus. Their relationship, which had been friendly, one where Cenric had openly encouraged Titus to court his daughter, had soured, although while Titus did not know it, the *ceorl* now viewed the whole business with as much sadness as anger by this point, because he had seen how Titus and Isolde had felt about each other, and how his daughter would come alive whenever she saw Titus approaching, wearing an almost identical expression. On that day months before when Titus' life had so dramatically changed, Cenric had done his best to maintain a cold and aloof demeanor, and in the beginning, it had been easy since he was still angry at Titus.

"I have to do what's best for Isolde, Titus," Cenric had told him. "And what's best for her is that she marry someone other than you. Not," he added quickly, "yet. I still need her help with the boys. But...soon."

They were standing in Otha's hall, and Titus was so distracted that he barely noticed how Otha had quietly summoned Uhtric, Hrothgar, and Willmar, three of the other warriors sworn to Otha who were also Titus' closest friends, and all of them were watching him carefully, each having seen examples of what Titus was capable of when he was truly angry. In the aftermath, as Cenric rode back to his farm, he acknowledged that *that* would have been better, to see Titus in a rage, than what he was confronted with, a devastated young man with a broken heart.

Only Titus would know the effort of will it would take for him to maintain his composure when his world collapsed, but he surprised even himself when he heard himself say calmly, "I understand, Cenric. This is all my fault anyway." A lump that felt as big around as his fist lodged in his throat, yet somehow, he managed, "Please extend my apology to Isolde...and whoever she chooses to marry. I wish them both a long and happy life."

In that moment, Cenric's dominant thought was that Titus did not look angry; he looked...shattered, and the sight of the young man's anguish dissolved a great deal of the antagonism Cenric had been holding against Titus. In fact, he realized, this was what Isolde had looked like when she came to me to tell me that she and Titus would never marry, nor could they even remain friends because of her sense of hurt and betrayal. As far as Titus, the concerns of those around him about his behavior had begun that day. What would have shocked, and worried, them was that Titus was acutely aware that he was on the bare edge of losing his control, and that his actions in the preceding months had created many problems for Otha as the Thegn struggled mightily to both keep a tight rein on Titus and, most importantly, his transgressions a secret from Ealdorman Eadwig, yet despite being aware that what he was doing threatened the future he envisioned for himself, Titus himself seemed powerless to stop what he was doing. More times than he could count, he was beset by the thought, I *want* to destroy myself, which was always followed by an almost overwhelming sense of shame. It had been a stupid, reckless thing to do; indeed, he had known it at the time, but when Aslaug, the daughter of Wulfnod and his Danish wife, had sent a signal that the flirtatious banter the pair had been exchanging on market days when she worked at the stall selling the cloth her father sold was not enough, because of what had taken place between him and Isolde, she found in Titus a willing accomplice. Oh, he had known that Aslaug had a reputation for being a girl who would lead a man on by allowing them to fumble with her tits and even provide relief with her hand—over the trousers, of course—and in fact, it had been Isolde who had warned him.

"You know," she had said matter-of-factly one day when they were walking about Wiltun hand in hand before their argument, "you need to be careful with Aslaug. She's got her eyes on you."

Titus had laughed this off because, at least at this moment in time when Isolde had broached the subject, he had not even entertained the thought of doing anything with Aslaug that might get back to Isolde.

"You have no cause for worry," he had assured her. "She might have eyes for me, but mine are set on you and you alone."

He had been quite proud of that, and he could see that she was pleased, giving him one of her smiles that always made his knees go weak. Aslaug was pretty enough; it was held by the boys around the same age that only Isolde was prettier among the girls around her age, and it would only be with the clarity that comes with hindsight that Titus would know how much of a role that consensus had played in Aslaug's actions. More times than he could count, Titus would find himself standing in the stable as he mucked them out, or working with one of the horses on a long lead as he got them accustomed to his scent and thinking, If only we hadn't had that fight. A fight that, Titus now understood, he had instigated because of his constant need to impress others, particularly Isolde. Not uncommonly for people their age, much of their time together was spent daydreaming about the future, and while they never spoke of it openly, they both knew that they were including each other.

It began innocently enough, as Titus boasted, "One day, I'm going to be one of King Alfred's personal bodyguards. The

Danes will shit themselves when they hear my name!"

This was hardly the first time he had uttered this, but for some reason this time, Isolde was not in the mood, and he missed the warning in her tone as she demanded, "Is that all you ever think about, Titus? How great a warrior you want to become?"

He had looked down at her in surprise, but though he did not know why, he could see his words angered her more when he said, "What else is there?"

They had been walking, and this caused Isolde to stop in her tracks to stare up at him incredulously. "What else is there?" she echoed with disbelief. "*Everything*, Titus! A home, a family, children, peace, contentment...*life*," she finished, clearly frustrated.

If he had only recognized the signs, except that now Titus felt a stirring of anger at what he saw as Isolde belittling his dreams.

"That's fine for a *ceorl*," he snapped. "For someone who wants to spend their entire life behind a plow, working from dawn until dark as they wither up and die inside! A warrior," Titus said loftily, "is above that." This was bad enough, but he compounded it by saying smugly, "And you should know that I want more than just...that." Before he could stop himself, he said contemptuously, "I will *never* be just a farmer."

"My father is a farmer," Isolde replied quietly, and despite his ire, Titus was certain that she had never been as beautiful as she was in that moment, her face tilted up to look him in the eyes, her own glittering with unshed tears.

"I'm not talking about Cenric," Titus protested, but he knew how lame this sounded, giving an internal wince at the words. "Your father is a brave, good man, Isolde. You know how I feel about him!"

"I do." She nodded, and for the span of a couple heartbeats, Titus thought the moment had passed, that they would resume walking. It was only later as Titus replayed this scene in his mind that he understood they had stopped in the middle of the market, and more crucially, directly in front of Wulfnod's stall. Where, he thought dismally once it came back to him, Aslaug was standing watching...and listening. Isolde continued, "But,

Titus, what kind of life are you offering me? Eh?"

"A life with a lot more money than we would ever make from a farm!" Titus countered, the anger growing. "A life where you would be in the company of the King and his court!" Realizing he was growing too loud, he had lowered his voice. "You know how many women would love the chance at that? To be at Wintanceaster and part of the royal party?"

"And spend every moment worrying whether I'm going to see you brought home as a corpse?" Isolde shot back, clearly every bit as angry. "Not knowing when you walk out the door if I'm ever going to see you again?"

Perhaps if she had not said that, Titus would think, perhaps if she had not openly questioned his abilities because, like so many youths of his age, the idea that he might die and might be defeated was foreign to him.

Adding to his anger, Titus was also truly baffled at what he saw as Isolde's obtuseness, and this was what caused him to warn, "You know, there are plenty of women who would love to have that kind of life!"

He knew instantly that he had erred, the blood draining from her face, but with a visible effort, Isolde drew herself erect, and her voice was as cold as he had ever heard it.

"Then maybe you should find one of those women," she said quietly.

Before he could respond, she spun about and walked away, leaving Titus in a state that was almost equally composed of anger, bemusement...and fear. However, it did not take long for Titus to convince himself that he was the wronged party, that it was Isolde who had been unreasonable, meaning that it was almost inevitable that he found himself in one of the two alehouses in Wiltun, The Boar's Head, using some of his hoard of silver to get roaring drunk. The results that night, and ramifications from them, would end up haunting Titus the Berserker for some time to come.

She had been waiting for him, outside the alehouse, when he came staggering out, and while he had been drunker than he was that night, he had not been in the muddled state of anger, confusion, and worry that he was then. And, even worse, she had made him jump, but it was the startled squawk of surprise that had made Aslaug laugh.

"Well, Titus the Berserker," she had called out mockingly, using the shadows to her advantage, "you don't sound so fierce now!"

Hearing, and recognizing, her voice had actually angered Titus, and he growled, "You step out of those shadows, and I'll show you how fierce I am!"

As drunk as he was, Titus recognized his error immediately, and Aslaug did not hesitate to obey, giving a throaty, husky laugh as she walked up to him until there was barely a hand's breadth between them.

"Well?" she challenged him, her full lips curved up into a smile that inflamed Titus as much as it angered him, as if she knew some sort of secret about him. "Here I am. What are you going to do...Berserker?"

As she sometimes did, Isolde had chosen to spend that night with her best friend, Cyneburga, the only person in the world who knew everything about her and her feelings about Titus. Cyneburga's father Cynebald was one of the three bakers in Wiltun, which meant that their family rose early, and while both girls were tired from staying up through the night as Isolde poured her heart out to her friend, Cyneburga had her duties to attend to, while Isolde knew that she would have to hurry to her father's farm to be in time to rouse her brothers, as she was now the woman of the house since her mother's death several years before. She also knew that this was why her father had never been in any hurry to see her marry, which, since she had known who she wanted to marry from almost their first meeting at Lord Eadwig's estate when the Ealdorman was gathering the Wiltun *fyrd*, did not bother her at all. This was how she found herself hurrying down the muddy street where the stable owned by Eastmund, the town hostler, was located. She had heard from other young townspeople that this was a favored spot for secret trysts, but she had never given it any thought until, as she turned the corner, the door opened and Aslaug stepped out into the early dawn. Both of them froze...but then Aslaug smiled, although she did not say anything, instead turning about and walking away, her hips swaying in a manner that seemed to taunt Isolde. Regardless, she could have continued on her way, following behind Aslaug, who had just turned the corner to head in the direction of her father's house, but despite a part of her screaming to do that very thing, Isolde found herself walking slowly to the stable door, which was slightly ajar, though not to the point where she could just peer inside.

Putting her hand against the door, Isolde stood there for what seemed like a full day, arguing with herself that she needed to hurry home, that the boys would be rising soon and would be hungry, but like her feet, which seemed to have a mind of their own that led her to this spot, her hand pushed against the door. There was just enough light outside now that she did not have to step into the stable to see inside, because the huge pile of hay that served as not just the source of feed for the animals inside, but as the bed for the trysts of some of the young people of Wiltun was directly across from the stable door. The figure lying in the hay was turned away from her, but it was the size of the body that wrenched the moan of pain from Isolde, which in turn caused Titus to stir, rolling over and blinking in bleary surprise. It was the first time Isolde had ever seen him naked; later, she would be ashamed at how, in her moment of disgrace, she was also aroused at the sight that she only barely admitted to herself she had fantasized about more hours than she could count. Titus, however, was slow to recognize not only who it was standing there, but the meaning, although he did grab his tunic and pull it on, then got to his feet. At least, that was what he tried to do, but he was still drunk, and he fell backward into the hay.

It was his chuckle that loosened Isolde's tongue, her voice cold. "I'm happy to see that you enjoyed yourself, Titus."

The sound of her voice sobered Titus up immediately, so this time when he scrambled to his feet, he managed to stay upright, but Isolde had already turned away and disappeared.

Racing outside, he called out to her, "It's not what you think, Isolde! I swear it on the cross!" Isolde did stop, turning to face him with her arms crossed, but said nothing, and Titus hurried on. "I had too much ale, and I didn't want to go back to Lord Otha's in the dark, so I..."

"I saw her, Titus," Isolde cut him off, surprised that her

voice sounded so calm. "I just saw Aslaug leaving the stable."

"I...I..." Titus stammered, but could not seem to get anything else out.

For her part, while Titus seemed unable to speak, Isolde seemed unable to move, and in the back of her mind, she dimly realized that she was waiting desperately to hear something, *anything* from Titus' lips that would give her something to which she could cling. It was something that neither of them would ever know, how aligned their thoughts were in that moment, each of them urging the other to rescue the both of them.

It was Isolde who realized it first, that there was nothing coming, so without another word, she spun about and fled down the street, not noticing it was in the opposite direction of her farm, leaving Titus to stand there helplessly, mouth hanging open, yet with nothing coming out of it.

Still, although he was shaken, he was also young, and even more confident than other youths his age, and from the recesses of his mind, a voice assured him, "She'll be back."

And, by the time he returned to Otha's, he had convinced himself that not only was this true, that it was almost guaranteed that it would be Isolde who would show up at the Thegn's estate, begging his forgiveness for her presumption in thinking that he had actually done something wrong.

By the time a week passed, Titus realized that Isolde would most definitely *not* be showing up at Otha's and asking Titus to forgive her, but it still took him three more days to work up the courage to approach Uhtric, the only person he trusted to keep his mouth shut and not tell the other men, although he knew that he would have to endure some sort of mocking from his brother-in-law before Uhtric gave him sound and sober advice. He was completely unprepared for Uhtric to be angry with him, although he quickly determined that it was unfeigned, but even worse, Uhtric had already known and, in fact, had been waiting for Titus to come talk to him.

"She deserved better from you, Titus," Uhtric had snapped.

"But," Titus gasped, "how did you know?"

"Because *everyone* knows," Uhtric had replied scornfully,

but this did not help Titus in the slightest, and he repeated, "But how?"

"How do you think?"

It had not been Uhtric who asked this, but Leofflaed, and before he could stop himself, Titus groaned aloud; as bad as facing Uhtric was, his sister was an even worse proposition, but he still had no idea.

"It was that...*witch* Aslaug." Leofflaed spat the name. "She was in the market the next day telling the other girls that you were taken and belonged to her now!"

"*What*?" Titus gasped, shaking his head in disbelief. "I never said anything about getting married!" Suddenly, he was struck by a sickening thought that forced him to add lamely, "At least, I don't *think* I did."

"That's not what she said," Leofflaed retorted, then in a marginally softer tone, added, "although I will admit that she hasn't talked about it since."

"There you are, then!" Titus said in a tone composed in equal measure of triumph and desperation. Slightly inspired, he argued, "Have you ever heard of a woman who's just been betrothed talking about anything else?"

He had not meant it to be funny, but Uhtric gave a sharp cough, and when Titus glanced over at him, his brother-in-law was suddenly looking at the ground, wearing an expression that he knew meant that Uhtric was fighting a laugh. Leofflaed did not find it humorous in the slightest, or at least she tried to portray this, scowling first at her brother then her husband before one corner of her mouth twitched upward.

This moment of levity did not last long, however, and Titus asked miserably, "What should I do?"

"You should have gone to Cenric's farm and begged Isolde's forgiveness the day after it happened, Titus," Leofflaed said quietly. Then she shrugged. "Now? It might be too late."

"But why?" Titus cried out, but despite the fact that he was certainly confused, deep down inside, he was not surprised when Leofflaed answered in her most sympathetic tone to that point, "Because you broke her heart, Titus. A woman *may* forgive, but she will never forget that."

To his credit, Titus did not hesitate any longer, leaving

immediately on Thunor at the canter to Cenric's farm. He was met, however, by Cenric who, having seen Titus coming, had hurried down the short track that led from his farm to the main road to intercept the younger man. The fact that Cenric was carrying a pitchfork caused Titus to draw Thunor up, although the *ceorl* had only been forking hay into the stalls for his animals, and the pair closed the distance between them cautiously, until they were about a dozen paces apart. Titus took advantage of the height atop Thunor to look over Cenric's head to examine the farmhouse first, then seeing no movement there, turned his attention on the barn, but while he caught sight of a darting figure that ducked back inside, although he could not identify which one, he could tell by the size that it was one of Isolde's brothers, and it was Cenric who broke the uneasy silence.

"Titus," he said, foregoing the customary greeting, but when he said nothing more, it forced Titus to respond.

His cause was not helped by the sudden flare of anger at what he took to be rudeness on Cenric's part, it not occurring to Titus that Isolde's father may have been at as much of a loss about what to say as he was in that moment.

This was why, without having any intention of doing so, he demanded bluntly, "I need to speak to Isolde, Cenric. Where is she?"

"She's in the house," Cenric replied calmly, and it was his tone as much as the words that ignited in Titus a flare of hope, which only lasted long enough for Cenric to say, "But she doesn't want to see you, Titus."

"But it's important!" Titus insisted, but when he began to swing down off his horse, Cenric suddenly shifted his weight while dropping the pitchfork down in a subtle but unmistakable move that froze Titus in what was, being honest, an absurd position, with one leg dangling up just above the saddle.

Titus was not armed, although that did not matter, and he was grimly pleased to see that the *ceorl* was equally aware of this reality, yet he also experienced a pang of sadness that things had come to this. Even before he had fallen in love with Isolde, Titus and Cenric had had a good relationship, despite the fact that in the first hours of their association, Cenric and another

14

ceorl, Heard, who had been on guard duty the day that young Titus had left his childhood home of Cissanbyrig to join the *fyrd* called by King Alfred, this had decidedly *not* been the case, the two grown men administering Titus a beating at the order of Otha. Titus had answered the *fyrd* in direct disobedience of his father Leofric, a *ceorl* with the minimum of one hide of land to be considered a free man under Saxon law. Although the older man never spoke of it, Titus knew that Cenric was fond of Titus, and the prospect of having Titus as his son-in-law pleased him, and not just because of how Titus had distinguished himself during the campaign against Guthrum who, after his defeat at the Battle of Ethantun, had been adopted by the victor, King Alfred, and had taken the Saxon name Aethelstan. Now the pair faced each other, neither of them speaking for a long moment.

Finally, more to break the unbearable silence, Titus asked miserably, "Do you think she'll ever forgive me, Cenric?"

He did not show it, but it took an effort of will for Cenric not to turn and walk to his farmhouse and demand that Isolde at least come and hear Titus out, but his daughter knew her father well and had forced him to swear an oath on the memory of her mother that he would not do any such thing.

Instead, while he did not want to crush the young man's hopes, he also knew he owed him the truth; nevertheless, he began by equivocating, "I don't know the future, Titus. And," he did offer a slight smile, "women are as much of a mystery to me as they clearly are to you. But," the smile vanished, "if I had to guess, I don't think so. You hurt her, boy," he finished quietly, and while he felt certain calling Titus a boy would engender at the very least a harsh reply, Titus' lack of reaction in some ways was even worse...and it was telling.

"Will you at least tell her that I'm sorry, Cenric?" Titus was determined to maintain his composure, but he felt the tears beginning to push against the back of his eyes, so he did not wait for an answer, yanking Thunor's head around in a manner that he never would have done otherwise, going immediately to a trot, leaving Cenric to call out to his retreating back, "I will, Titus!"

It was, Cenric thought unhappily as he walked to the farmhouse, a truly sad situation. Isolde was waiting for him, her arms crossed and chin lifted in a manner that Cenric had learned from her childhood, the sign that she was determined to stand her ground on a particular subject. She's expecting me to try and change her mind, he realized. Which, he admitted to himself, he had been prepared to do, but he knew that look and what it meant.

Consequently, all he said was, "Titus said he was sorry."

This earned him a contemptuous snort from his daughter, and she scoffed, "He's sorry that he got caught rutting with that...*cow*. That's what he's sorry about."

That, Cenric thought ruefully, was certainly part of it, but he did feel compelled to say, "I think it's more than that, daughter."

For the briefest instant, perhaps for the span of a heartbeat, Cenric saw the expression on his daughter's face change, the flicker of doubt that actually got him to move out of the doorway in the event she went rushing out of the house. But then the moment was over, signaled by a curt shake of her head, then in a pointed albeit silent message, turning her back to return to the table to resume laying out the bowls for the evening meal. Cenric and Isolde never spoke of that moment again.

This marked a period of three months where Titus never set foot in Wiltun, choosing instead to devote all of his time and energy in his duties helping Lord Otha with the Thegn's main source of income, horse breeding, although he tried to spend almost as much time training the skills that he not only viewed as the most important for a Saxon man, but as absolutely vital to furthering his larger ambitions. The main problem he encountered very quickly was running out of willing sparring partners among Lord Otha's other warriors who shared the Thegn's hall. Even the strongest of Otha's men, Hrothgar, began making excuses when Titus sought him out after the younger man's daily chores were done.

"The lad's forgotten the difference between sparring and fucking fighting," Hrothgar complained to Willmar, Aelfwine, and Ealdwolf, his three closest friends among Otha's men at arms one evening when they had actually gone into Wiltun to The Boar's Head to discuss the matter without fearing that Titus overheard them, taking advantage of the Berserker's refusal to come into the town.

The other three men nodded their agreement, each of them having arrived at the same conclusion, and having the bruises to show for it.

"It's because of Isolde," Willmar offered, earning him a derisive snort from Hrothgar.

"Oh, do you think so?" Hrothgar shot back, adding what for him was a gentle shove that almost knocked Willmar from his spot on the bench. "I *know* why," he continued. "The question is, what do we do about it?"

There was a brief silence, which was broken by Aelfwine.

"Hope that those pig fucking Danes get as tired of this peace as we are," he said gloomily, missing the others exchanging amused glances, each of them knowing to one degree or another that, despite his truculent words, Aelfwine was not the most enthusiastic warrior of Otha's men.

He certainly was no coward, and he was a competent swordsman, but one of the things that his comrades all knew was that, when it came time to form a shield wall, Aelfwine would be perfectly content to assign himself to a spot in the second rank, bolstering a bolder comrade.

"If it hasn't happened by now, it's not likely to," Willmar pointed out, "so stop wasting your breath."

"Should we speak to Lord Otha?" Ealdwolf spoke for the first time, but while this was not met with the same kind of reaction as with Aelfwine, the response was still a unanimous shaking of heads.

"No, we need to handle this ourselves," Willmar said, which prompted Ealdwolf to turn to demand from the others, "Did anyone speak to Uhtric?"

"He's the first one I went to," Hrothgar assured Ealdwolf. In a hint of what to expect, Hrothgar leaned over and spat on the rush-covered floor, ignoring the squawk of protest from the tavernkeeper to say, "I'll let you guess what he had to say about it."

"Then that means we need to speak to Lord Otha!" Ealdwolf argued, but this time when he met the same resistance, he was prepared, firing back, "Then let it be on your heads if Titus hurts one of us. Or," he finished in a quieter, but more intense tone, "worse."

None of the others argued, but neither did they go to Lord Otha; it would be a decision that would bring further recriminations and turmoil in the relatively near future.

If there was one benefit to Titus' refusal to go into Wiltun and his comrades' reluctance to train with him, Titus had little more to do than concentrate on his duties, and even though Otha had long suspected that the youth had a latent talent working with not just horses but animals of all sorts, watching what was an astonishingly rapid development in a short period of time confirmed that suspicion. It was more than just a matter of technical skill, Otha observed; Titus had an innate gift whereby he seemed to form a bond with each of the horses under his care, and while he would never have uttered it to anyone else, it was to Wulfgifu that he expressed his thoughts.

"The lad has a sensitive streak in him," he told his wife one night as they lay in bed, just before they both drifted off in what had become almost a ritual of their marriage, one that, although they never said as much to each other, they both treasured. "Which," he admitted, "I never would have guessed once I saw him fight."

"You're good with horses," Wulfgifu assured him, misunderstanding her husband's motivation for speaking.

Her words earned her an impatient shake of his head, although his tone did not match it.

"It's more than that, Wulfie." He used his pet name for her, knowing that it pleased her that he did. "It's like Titus understands how they *feel*, and not just because of how they're behaving. Oh," he waved a hand, "anyone who's dealt with horses enough knows that when the tail moves back and forth, or its ears go back, something bad is likely to happen. But Titus seems to know *why* they're behaving that way." Now that he was engaged in the subject, Otha rolled over, ignoring his wife's sigh at this sign that their conversation was likely to last longer than she would have liked. "Why, two days ago, I was sure that Spadehead was going to challenge the Bay for the mares, and so did Leofsige, but before any of us could do anything, Titus hopped into the enclosure. Even," Otha's voice

18

hardened, "after I told him not to. But Spadehead was already blowing and had bared his teeth, and that bastard is probably the meanest horse I've ever been around."

Despite herself, Wulfgifu was interested; Otha had not mentioned this the night before, and while she would never admit it, she enjoyed hearing her husband telling stories about the horses, if only because it was one of those times when he came alive, reminding her that he truly loved working with the animals.

But he stopped, saying nothing more, and it was not until it was too late that she realized he had been teasing her, knowing that she was now invested in the story, but in the moment, she cried, "Well? Are you going to tell me what happened or just lie there like a lump?"

"Ah, so you *are* interested?" he teased, earning a slap on the arm, but he continued readily enough, "It turned out that Spadehead had just been bitten by a horsefly, but on his opposite flank and we couldn't see it. That cursed fly drew blood, and we had to make a mud poultice for it."

"Maybe Titus saw the fly buzzing around," Wulfgifu suggested, but Otha shook his head.

"He was farther away from Spadehead than we were," Otha replied. "But when he looked at how the beast was behaving, he somehow just knew that Spadehead wasn't going after the Bay, that there was something else bothering him."

"I don't know why you keep that animal around," Wulfgifu sniffed, missing Otha rolling his eyes because of the darkness.

This was neither the first nor would it be the last time they would have this conversation, but what compounded matters for Otha when it came to explaining why he kept this unruly, foul-tempered animal, whose name derived from the fact that, when looking at him straight on, his head *did* resemble a spade, the Thegn could never seem to find the right words. Whereas, for example, the fact that large bay stallion was only referred to its color was a tacit sign that Otha had designs to sell the animal to an Ealdorman or high-ranking Thegn like Lord Eadwig, and these men always preferred to confer a name themselves. Spadehead would never be sold, if only because by this point, the amount of money spent in feed and care had already exceeded any amount that Otha could hope to get for him, but in the back of his mind, Otha had also begun entertaining the idea of using Spadehead as his own war mount. It was not that Tiw, the mount he had ridden into battle for more than five years now was inadequate to the task, and before Spadehead, Otha had been completely satisfied with the animal, a chestnut who stood seventeen hands and never shirked or balked when Otha guided him towards the fighting. What was missing in Tiw, however, was a ferocity that Spadehead had in abundance; Tiw might not shy from battle, but Spadehead reveled in it, which was attested to by the scars that covered the animal's neck and shoulders.

Knowing that an answer was expected, all Otha offered was a yawn, followed by, "I like having him around."

Wulfgifu's response was seemingly unrelated, but Otha knew better, so that when his wife said, "I worry about him, Otha," he knew about whom she was referring, and it was not the horse.

His initial instinct was to reassure her, but when Otha opened his mouth, what came out was a sigh, followed by, "So do I, Wulfie. So do I."

"Mind you, I don't blame Isolde," she added, and he heard the slight stiffening in her voice, but Otha knew why; even after more than a decade, the anger and pain stemming from Otha's own indiscretion that had occurred early in their marriage was still there, and he had resigned himself to the idea that it always would be; more importantly, he had learned his lesson and now his whoring was only done when he was far enough away from Wiltun that no prying eyes and gossiping mouths were about. "She has every right to feel the way she feels," Wulfgifu went on, and Otha, wisely in his opinion, did not reply, but nodded with enough vigor that she could see him do so despite the darkness. He was completely unprepared, however, for her to add with what, to his ears anyway, sounded like tangible satisfaction, "But from what I hear, she won't be grieving much longer if Hereweald has anything to do with it."

At first, Otha was confused.

"Hereweald? The smith? But he's already married! To," he thought for a moment, but could not think of the name, "what's

20

her name?"

"Astridr," Wulfgifu provided, laughing as she did so, "but that's not who I meant, silly man. The son! That's who I'm talking about!"

This brought Otha bolt upright, and he stared down at his wife in obvious dismay and, Wulfgifu noticed with some unease, a fair amount of alarm.

"What are you trying to say?" he gasped. "That Hereweald's pup is going to ask Isolde to marry him?"

"That's the rumor in the market," his wife answered cautiously, but she was beginning to understand Otha's concern, which prompted her to ask with a touch of fear, "You don't think Titus will try something, do you? He won't try to hurt Hereweald?"

"Wife," Otha answered grimly, "if Titus decides to go after Hereweald, he won't *try* to hurt the lad." He hesitated, but then decided he was unwilling to go into any real detail, saying only, "You've never seen what Titus can do when he's angry; I have."

Like all women, especially when it came to this part of the world of men, Wulfgifu was intensely curious, and she longed to ask Otha to be more forthcoming and explain this cryptic comment, but she also knew that it was a forlorn hope. Instead, she said, "I'll offer prayers that Titus keeps his head and doesn't do something that will only make things worse for him."

"Not just him," Otha reminded her grimly. "He's my sworn man, remember. And," he sighed, "Lord Eadwig isn't the most forgiving man in the world." Understanding how his words would be interpreted, he added quickly, "Although God knows that in his own way he's fond of Titus, and he owes him for saving Eadward's life."

And, with that, there was nothing more to be said or done that night, but while they both tried, sleep was long in coming.

Later, the only thing that was commonly agreed upon among the people of Wiltun was that it was inevitable that, sooner or later, Titus the Berserker would learn that, not only was Cenric's warning about Isolde's future warranted, but events had transpired since then that would bring home that reality in a way that was impossible for him to ignore. Indeed, what was almost as common was the shared surprise that it took as long as it had before he did, and it was the building tension arising from his visits that the townspeople would remember for some time to come. When Titus finally came to Wiltun for the first time almost three months to the day from his last visit that resulted in his losing Isolde, crisis was averted thanks to Leofflaed sending Uhtric to Cenric's farm ahead of Titus to warn Isolde that she needed to forego what had become a habit of hers that had been noticed by the more sharp-eyed townspeople of visiting the smithy to share the noon meal with young Hereweald, the result being that Titus was blissfully unaware of anything on that first visit. Additionally and at the same time, it had been Hrothgar's task, assigned to him by Otha, to rush to The Boar's Head, where the warrior issued a warning to the townsmen who were regular customers about what would happen to any of them who thought it might provide some entertainment to inform Titus that Isolde had found comfort in the arms of the smith's son. The Thegn's choice of Hrothgar was no accident, because he was still widely regarded as the strongest man, not just in Otha's service, but in the Wiltun area by those who had never witnessed the sparring and wrestling at Otha's holding; the fact that this was no longer the case was something with which Hrothgar still struggled.

What was surprising, not just to Hrothgar but, frankly, to Otha and his men, was that Titus had proven to be sensitive to the blow to the older man's pride and had never done or said anything that indicated the young warrior reveled in his new status as strongest warrior in the shire. It also helped that Titus still sought Hrothgar out for advice and pointers on ways in which he could better exploit the advantage of being so much stronger than almost all of his opponents, which helped soften the blow to Hrothgar's pride. Consequently, when Titus returned to Otha's that after that first visit, he was still happily ignorant of the burgeoning relationship between Isolde and Hereweald, and he would remain so after his second, third, and fourth visits. While most of the people who were aware of this admittedly small but compelling drama were relieved that there was no trouble, this was by no means a unanimous feeling. And, as often happens in the aftermath of dramatic events, it became accepted wisdom that of *course* it would be because of the enmity Hrodulf held towards Titus, an enmity about which Titus had been completely unaware of until what would be their first and final confrontation at The Boar's Head.

For those townspeople whose sense of humor ran to the mordant, there was extra scorn for Hrodulf, even after what happened to him, because of his spectacular misjudgment, not just in choosing to taunt the Berserker, but because his hatred towards the young warrior was based in his mistaken belief of Aslaug's version of events. In her telling, what Titus had done was rape; the fact that Aslaug's father had done nothing about it she ascribed to his lack of paternal feelings and sense of duty of defending his daughter's honor, and her mother's indifference she ascribed to jealousy of her daughter's beauty. It was no secret that Hrodulf longed for Aslaug to be his and his alone, nor was it a secret to anyone but Hrodulf that his fellow Saxons viewed him as just barely above being the town idiot, that title being claimed by the halfwit son of one of the town's two tanners, Eardwulf, the son bearing the same name. Indeed, the only person in Wiltun who did not know that Aslaug had no intention of binding herself to him was Hrodulf, and this was certainly not the impression she had given him once it became clear that her plot to ensnare Titus had failed.

"I'd never marry a man with no ambition," she had informed Hrodulf, who had naturally come running to answer her summons to meet her in Eastmund's barn. "You understand that, don't you, Hrodulf?"

He assured her that he did, but he was finding it hard to concentrate because, for the first time, Aslaug had not knocked his hand away when it reached for her breast, although she barely seemed to notice. Perhaps if he had not been distracted, he would have noticed the frown on her face, recognizing it as the expression she wore when she was busy calculating something. It was accepted that Aslaug was at least as shrewd as her mother, who was known to be the mind behind her father's cloth business, although this did not matter to Hrodulf in the slightest.

Quelling the urge to slap his hand away, Aslaug dropped her voice to a husky level that experience had taught her made her target more pliant; provided, of course, that her target had a cock, and she went on by challenging, "How do you plan to show me you're a man with ambition, Hrodulf? What did you have in mind?"

"What?" Hrodulf frowned, and as was a habit of his when he was confused, began blinking rapidly, because the truth was that he had only heard the last question. "In mind for what, Aslaug?"

"To show me you're worth my time, you fool!" she snapped but recognized her error immediately. Like most men of Hrodulf's limited capacity, being reminded of that limitation, especially by a woman, was counterproductive, so, without any noticeable hesitation, she grabbed Hrodulf's hand, which he had instinctively pulled away at her ill-tempered words, and placed it back on her breast as she practically purred, "I apologize, my love. I did not mean to be so harsh. It's just that while I *want* us to be together, you can't expect me to choose a man just because they're handsome and strong, can you?"

Never in his life had anyone, even his mother, who had died when he was twelve, called Hrodulf handsome, but, until the arrival of the Berserker, Hrodulf had been considered to be at least the third or perhaps even the second strongest man in the shire behind Hrothgar, although Hrodulf was not a warrior. His father was a *ceorl* who had a holding of three hides a few miles from Wiltun, but Hrodulf had had the further misfortune of not being the eldest son, and after a falling out with his father, now eked out a living hiring himself out as a laborer to his neighbors when he was not needed on his father's farm.

Even under the best of circumstances, Hrodulf did not think quickly, and it took him a span of heartbeats to get to the heart of her question, which he answered cautiously, "No, I suppose not."

"So," she said patiently, "it's only fair that I have some sort of idea what your plans for the future are. That," Aslaug smiled up at him, "is the kind of thing husbands share with their wives."

To his credit, Hrodulf somehow understood what was expected of him, because rather than inform her of a plan that, just a matter of heartbeats earlier, had not even been a consideration, he asked her, "What do you think, Aslaug? What do you want me to do to prove I'm worthy of you?"

In her mind, Aslaug was certain she heard the sound of the trap snapping shut, but she was too cunning to spring it on Hrodulf immediately, so she pretended to think about it, knowing that timing was going to be crucial.

"It doesn't have to be anything that would take a long time to do," she spoke slowly, knowing that she needed to convince Hrodulf that she was thinking as she spoke, "like paying off your debt." As she expected, mention of the debt made him flush, which he had incurred because of a drunken brawl that Ealdorman Eadwig had ruled was his fault, when he had gouged out one eye of another *ceorl* named Wynnstan. It had been something of a minor miracle that, although he had had the right to demand the full amount of the *wergild* judgment for the loss of an eye the year before when the Ealdorman made his ruling, the *ceorl* had needed help in the fields with the harvest more than he needed the shillings, and Hrodulf had agreed to offer his help for two seasons, but harvest was still several months away. Taking a deep breath, Aslaug continued in the same slow manner, "Maybe some sort of a...demonstration of how much you care about me." She was pretending to be staring off in the distance, but she was studying him intently out of the corner of her eye, and when she saw him begin to nod, she decided this was the time to add an emotional element, in the form of a sudden bursting into tears that she made sure he saw begin before burying her face in her hands, whereupon she began sobbing so vigorously that her entire upper body shook. It was badly overdone, and either a more experienced or clever man, or any woman, would have instantly recognized this and responded with a roll of the eyes, but it had the desired effect on Hrodulf.

"Aslaug, what is it?" he cried out, having instantly, if temporarily, forgotten her breasts.

"He humiliated me, Hrodulf! He dishonored me!" Aslaug managed between sobs, peering through her fingers as she did so. While Hrodulf certainly looked upset, she did not see the anger there, and her own ire was unfeigned as she said accusingly, "And nobody cares! My father is a *coward*!"

Somehow, she managed to find enough saliva to spit on the stable floor to emphasize her words. "He's terrified of Titus! So is every...so-called *man* in Wiltun!"

"I'm not!" Hrodulf declared. "I'm not scared of him! I'm not scared of anyone!"

It took some effort on her part, but Aslaug managed to keep the satisfaction from her voice, although she did not try to hide the challenge in her tone as she replied, "Those are words, Hrodulf. It's deeds that matter."

Suddenly, there was a part of Hrodulf's mind that grasped that this was not at all what he had intended, but he was a young man, strong, and certain that he was in love, and it was that part of him that elbowed its way to the front of his mind, and he heard himself say, "I'll prove it, Aslaug, I swear on the Rood! The next time I see him..."

"He's here in Wiltun now," she replied, and now she was calm and completely in control of her emotions. In fact, if Hrodulf had retained his presence of mind, he might have become suspicion at the look of what could only have been described as happiness as she informed him, "I saw him go into The Boar's Head just before I came here."

It had taken some time for Titus to talk himself into entering The Boar's Head, but he had turned down Willmar and the others' invitations to join them on his previous forays into the town, and he was beginning to worry that this might be the real cause behind their reluctance to spar with him. The result was that, after pacing back and forth outside the entrance for a few moments, he finally entered the place, unsure about what kind of reception he would receive and hoping that it would be warm, or at least cordial. His first instinct was that he had made a terrible mistake because, on his approach to the table where Aelfwine, Willmar, and Ealdwolf were seated, none of them even glanced in his direction, seemingly too busy engaged in bickering about something.

Then, still not looking up at him, Willmar grunted, "Took you long enough. I thought you forgot where the place is." Before Titus could respond, Ealdwolf called out to Wigmund, the owner of the alehouse, "Bring us a new pitcher and a cup,

Wigmund!" For the first time, Ealdwolf grinned, and it was shared by the others. "I know it's been a while, but I'll wager you remember how much the Berserker here can drink."

"How can I forget?" Wigmund grumbled. "I lost a shilling!"

He had lost it to Willmar, but the warrior was completely unrepentant, saying only, "I warned you. You can't say I didn't."

By the time Wigmund returned to the table, Titus' concerns about any awkwardness had been assuaged, and he found himself laughing more than he had in the previous months. It did not completely dispel what he would have described as a leaden ball that seemed to have taken up permanent residence deep within his gut, but he was finding it impossible to keep from laughing at the jests from his comrades. Oh, it had been awkward at first; despite his distraction, Titus recognized how careful Willmar and the others were being to avoid anything that might arouse his temper, and he felt a stab of satisfaction at what he took as a sign of respect. That it was likely to be just as much because of the bruises they feared at his hands in the sparring ring as it was because of their regard for his feelings made it just a bit sweeter. Of course, the ale helped as well, and as the day passed into the evening, the four of them were joined by others whose daily routine found them retiring to one of the three alehouses, the third having opened just a couple months earlier during Titus' self-imposed exile. Two men at arms who served Ceadda, one of Lord Eadwig's Thegns and who were friendly with Otha's men, Wigmund and Aedelstan arrived, and while it was a bit more raucous than usual, it was nothing out of the ordinary. Nor was it unusual that, as the alehouse became more crowded, those already involved in their revels were not paying attention to the new arrivals unless they joined a particular table, so neither Titus nor his comrades noticed when a lone figure arrived, stepping to one side of the doorway as he surveyed the now-crowded alehouse.

Titus was not drunk, yet, but he would have acknowledged he was on his way, while by prearrangement, Willmar had deliberately limited his intake of ale because he would be Titus' escort back to Otha's estate. All in all, from Willmar's and the others' perspectives, things were going well; Titus was not his old self, but he was certainly closer to it than he had been in months, and it was good to see him laughing. Willmar was thinking that very thing when his eye was drawn by someone moving in their direction, and it was from a habit formed of a lifetime that he was sitting facing the door, yet when he glanced up and saw who it was, he gave the man barely a passing thought. What's his name? Willmar tried to remember, but he could only come up with the fact that he was the second or third son of a *ceorl* who had gotten into some sort of trouble during a brawl, and that he was considered to be one of the strongest men in Wiltun and the surrounding area, and that he was something of an idiot. He did notice that the man looked nervous, but that only became noteworthy later, and Willmar spent a fair amount of time in the aftermath wondering if he had paid closer attention whether it would have made a difference.

Hrodulf was not the only nervous person in Wiltun that evening, but for Isolde, the reason for her state of nerves was decidedly different. She and her father Cenric had been invited to dine with Hereweald and his family, but while she had been relentless in her questioning of Hereweald the son, he had refused to divulge his father's intentions, and as far as Isolde was concerned, had been maddeningly smug about it. Her father had not been much better, insisting that he had no idea what the smith intended to discuss, but she did know he was speaking the truth when he assured her that if the smith intended to discuss a marriage, by custom, neither Isolde nor Hereweald the Younger would have been present, and although it was not always enforced for the males, she had never heard of a case where the female was present. Nevertheless, she was nervous, and she could tell her father was at the very least intensely interested, and not in the food. They took the cart, leaving the boys behind, and they did not speak much as they reached Wiltun, unaware that Titus was actually a matter of a couple streets away. Like Willmar and a number of others with some sort of stake in what would be taking place shortly, afterward, Isolde would wonder if she had known, whether or not she would have made some sort of excuse that kept her and her father on their farm. As one might expect, she was wearing her best linen shift, dyed green, while Cenric was wearing the tunic he wore to Mass and had endured Isolde's attempts to comb his hair and beard, but although he grumbled, it had been good-natured.

The door was answered by the female Danish slave that, if one listened to them, some of the more sharp-tongued women of Wiltun insisted was due to the smith's wife's pretensions and need to impress the other women of the merchant class, and Isolde surprised herself by wondering if being married to Hereweald meant that she would have a slave of her own; the fact that she also felt a stab of excitement at the thought made her feel slightly ashamed. Consequently, she immediately shoved the thought away as unworthy, her effort to do so aided by the appearance of Hereweald, not the father but the son, and the man she had decided that, if he did ask for her hand as she expected, she would say yes. What she did not say, to anyone, not even to Cyneburga, was that while she liked Hereweald a great deal, she had never experienced the same sensations that she felt whenever Titus had been in her presence. Even as she stood there in the large main room, watching Hereweald enter, she realized that she missed the sudden racing of her heart, the flush to her face...and to the other parts of her body that she experienced whenever Titus just smiled at her. There was a moment of awkwardness, both young people acutely aware that, while the actual formal proposal of marriage might not be up for discussion on this evening, the topic itself would inevitably be introduced, so that neither of them were sure of the appropriate form of greeting each other.

Fortunately, they were saved by the senior Hereweald, who entered the house from the smithy, greeting Cenric in a booming voice as he extended a hand. "*Wes hal,* Cenric! And," he turned and made what might have been a bow, "to you, fair Isolde! It's always a sight for these old eyes of mine to see such a beauty as you!"

"Thank you for your invitation, Hereweald," Cenric replied, as courtesy required, although he was sincere.

Hereweald's wife Astridr appeared then, and although she was as polite as always to Isolde, privately, Isolde tended to agree with the women of the town about her pretensions, and she gave Isolde the strong sense that Astridr thought her son could do better for a wife. Despite her belief, Isolde could not fault how Hereweald's wife greeted Cenric, who was becoming more at ease, and when Hereweald suggested that a pot of ale was just the thing as they waited for the meal to be prepared, Cenric's enthusiasm was unfeigned, and it ignited a flare of concern in Isolde, acutely aware of her father's love for ale.

"Isolde, why don't you come and help us?"

Correctly interpreting this as a command, Isolde followed the woman she supposed would be her future mother-in-law out of the main room, silently envious that there was actually a separate room for the preparation of the family meals. What it meant was that she did not hear the commotion outside in the street, just the reaction of the two Herewealds and her father as, for some reason, they suddenly began talking all at once, loudly enough that it alerted Astridr and Isolde something unusual was happening, the pair exchanging an alarmed glance, although Isolde let the older woman lead the way into the main room. What greeted the women was the elder Hereweald standing in the open doorway, peering out into the darkness, and Isolde heard a man's voice, but while he was shouting, she could not make out his words, just that there was something potentially alarming taking place somewhere.

It was the expression on her father's face that gave her the first pang of disquiet; when he suddenly broke eye contact and looked away, that uneasiness increased, but it was left to the younger Hereweald to tell her, with an expression that communicated even more than the words themselves, "It's the Berserker. He just killed a man at The Boar's Head."

It had happened with an astonishing and bewildering rapidity, not just to Titus but to every man who could have conceivably done something to intervene. Working in Titus' favor was that there was no doubt as to who was the aggressor, and in fact, mainly because of Titus' confusion, he had been surprisingly docile in the beginning, at least when compared to his reputation. This docility was due to the profound state of shock he experienced when Hrodulf, who he only knew by sight and name, had uttered something in what seemed to Titus to be

30

an afterthought but was actually Hrodulf's last, desperate attempt to provoke the young warrior, and only after hurling a number of other insults. Sitting next to Willmar but in fact facing in the opposite direction as he listened to Wigmund, seated at the next table, talking about a boar hunt he had participated in with Lord Ceadda a few days earlier, from Titus' perspective, Hrodulf seemed to have materialized out of thin air to stand on the opposite side of the table directly across from him.

Pointing a shaking finger at Titus, the laborer shouted over the low roar of men on their way to becoming drunk, "You dishonored Aslaug, daughter of Wulfnod, Berserker! You..." he hesitated, and in the back of his mind, he did wonder if this was going too far, but then he remembered the look on Aslaug's face, "...promised to marry her, then *raped* her when she said no!"

The sudden silence was something that the onlookers would remember, but nobody was more shocked than Titus, who had turned back to face Hrodulf and could only manage to protest mildly, "That's not true. I didn't rape anyone, especially Aslaug." At this point, he was still too surprised to feel angry, but he did feel a rush of heat to his face as he remembered what *had* taken place in Eastmund's barn.

This clearly enraged Hrodulf, which was made clear why when he bellowed, "You *lie*, you...you...*bastard*! She would *never* lay with you, you turd-eating *dog*!"

Matters between the two were made infinitely more complicated by the reaction of what had to be at least a dozen men inside the alehouse, all of whom began guffawing at Hrodulf's declaration of Aslaug's chastity. It was a lacerating kind of laughter, but more than that, it was informative, although of the pair of men at odds, only one of them was surprised, because in the intervening months, Titus had learned more about Aslaug than he ever cared to know. By rights, Hrodulf should have turned his rage on the laughing men, but he did retain enough presence of mind to remember who he was there to punish at Aslaug's command. The problem was that his foe did not seem inclined to take the bait; if anything, he seemed almost determined to avoid a physical confrontation, so that it was with a growing sense of desperation that Hrodulf increased the stakes...and sealed his fate in the process.

"Isn't it bad enough that you drove Isolde into the arms of Hereweald and they're getting married? Now you want to ruin Aslaug's life, when all she wanted to do was be a friend in your time of need?"

Titus heard but did not really register Willmar's sudden hiss of indrawn breath, and he also missed the looks of alarm that his friends on either side of him exchanged, only barely managing a strangled cry. "You *lie*! Isolde isn't marrying anyone!"

"Oh?" Hrodulf shot back, and for the first time since walking in, he felt as if he had recovered the initiative. "I just saw her and her father at Hereweald the smith's door on my way here! And everyone in town knows that they've been seeing each other!"

Now Titus, remembering he was with friends, and to Willmar's horror, turned to him first, demanding, "Is this true, Willmar?"

"Is what true?" Willmar replied, hating himself for his weakness, but Titus was neither fooled nor was he willing to indulge the older warrior's attempt to dissemble.

"Do. Not. Lie. To. Me." Titus bit the words off, then repeated with a menace that was no less palpable because he did not raise his voice. "Is it true?"

"Are they betrothed?" Willmar began, then instantly realizing how this might be taken, rushed on, shaking his head adamantly, "I haven't heard a word about anything like that, I swear it!" He hesitated, then admitted, "But I know that they have been...seen together." He swallowed what he was certain was a lump the size of his fist before continuing, "And I did hear that Hereweald had invited Cenric and Isolde to dine with them."

Everything that happened after this occurred with a rapidity that, even if Willmar and the other men had been prepared, it was unlikely they could have stopped him. In fact, Willmar did try, grabbing Titus' arm when his friend suddenly stood up; he did not remember anything after that, at least until he was slapped awake by Ealdwolf, having been knocked

32

unconscious from a single blow, just before Titus, using the bench as a platform, leapt across the table, his feet clearing Aelfwine and Aedelstan, both of whom were sitting on the opposite side with their backs to the door. Hrodulf never stood a chance, although he did manage one wild swing that struck Titus just above his eye, but Titus did not even flinch, nor did it slow him in any perceptible manner as he slammed bodily into the laborer with such force that both of his feet left the wooden floor as he staggered backward. However, somehow he did not lose his feet, but with what any experienced warrior knew was unusual, the fact that Hrodulf remained upright actually was what sealed his fate, as he was essentially unable to fall backward because of the upper bodies of the two men seated at the table nearer to the door that prevented him from doing so, although most observers also agreed that the end was probably inevitable, given the level of ferocity that the Berserker displayed.

It was something of a small mercy that Hrodulf was essentially unconscious, despite remaining upright, after Titus' first blow that struck him on the point of his chin. Perhaps if Titus had been in possession of his senses and not overcome with that fury that he had experienced only a handful of times in his life to this point, including during the ambush where he earned his nickname, knocking Hrodulf senseless would have been enough, but despite his outward denial of Hrodulf's claim about Isolde and Hereweald, Titus absolutely believed that the laborer was speaking truthfully. Isolde was marrying another man, he knew it in his soul, which in turn meant that all of the pent-up emotions he had been struggling with for more than three months came bursting out from behind the barrier he had tried to create inside himself. While it was true that Titus was not aiming his blows, as Lord Otha, Uhtric, and the other men sworn to the Thegn had seen firsthand, when it came to combat, Titus exhibited an almost preternatural gift for inflicting damage on an enemy. The result with Hrodulf was that, despite the laborer weaving back and forth and his eyes rolling back in his head, Titus' next blow unerringly struck the laborer directly on the bony protuberance that protects a man's windpipe, although this was not his intended target. He was just blindly lashing out, his only goal to inflict as much pain as he was feeling in that moment. Regardless of the fact that he was unaware of the sound, almost every other man in the alehouse heard what, even to hardened warriors like Willmar, was a sickening crunching sound as the cartilage tube that supplied the air to a human's lungs just...collapsed.

Even then, Hrodulf did not drop to the rush-covered wooden floor, which meant that he was struck at least four or five more times by Titus, who had not heard the telltale sound of a mortal blow because he was snarling unintelligibly, his entire being consumed with nothing more than the idea of destroying this man who, with a few ill-chosen words put into his mouth by a scheming woman, was now his enemy, and all enemies were to be destroyed. Seeing that Hrodulf was finished, and with Willmar still lying on the floor out cold, it was left up to Ealdwolf and Aelfwine, with help from Wigmund, to attempt the unenviable task of pulling Titus off of the laborer. Fortunately, in a small mercy and to the relief of the three warriors, Hrodulf finally collapsed onto the floor in the space between the benches, lying face up and with his body twitching with ever-growing violence as his lungs vainly struggled to draw in air through his shattered windpipe. It was grotesque to watch, and more than one man went pale as they watched in silence, meaning that they could all hear Hrodulf's last, hopeless struggle to remain in the land of the living. Ealdwolf had hold of one of Titus' arms, while Aelfwine the other, but Titus did not put up a struggle, it quickly becoming clear that the battle madness, if not completely gone, had at least subsided enough so that, like the others, he was staring down at Hrodulf as the dying man's face turned purple and his tongue began to protrude, and his eyes opening wider than one would think possible. Finally, he arched his back, gave one last spasm, then his body went limp. Later, men who had witnessed violent death before all commented about how the only thing missing was the last, rattling breath, which they unanimously and correctly attributed to the circumstances of his death.

It was Titus who broke the silence and created another crisis, when he suddenly muttered, "I'm going to talk to Isolde."

Not surprisingly, this was met with alarm by Titus' friends, although there were other men who began to whisper to each other excitedly about the prospect of seeing even more carnage, some of them even moving in the direction of the door, ready to follow the young warrior to wherever he was heading.

When it had become clear that Titus was done with Hrodulf, Ealdwolf turned his attention to Willmar, who was now sitting up and shaking his head groggily in response to Eadwolf's slaps across the face, but this brought him around.

"Titus," Ealdwolf spoke cautiously, not wanting to arouse whatever it was inside the young warrior that enabled him to do what he had just done to Hrodulf with such devastating ferocity and ease. "I don't think that's a good idea."

He was shocked when Titus readily admitted, "No, it's probably not. But," for the first time, he looked away from Hrodulf, who had just suffered the final indignity of his bowels releasing, filling the air with the stench, and he regarded Ealdwolf with a level look, "I'm going anyway." He paused, then asked quietly, "Are you going to try and stop me, Ealdwolf?"

"No," the older warrior answered immediately, but Titus turned his attention to Willmar next, who had regained enough of his senses that he obviously recalled what had taken place because he was glaring up at Titus from his sitting position on the floor, although he was blinking rapidly as he did so in an unconscious attempt to gather his wits.

"I'm sorry, Willmar," Titus mumbled. "You didn't deserve that."

"Did he?" Titus stiffened at Willmar's challenge, but before he could say anything, Willmar pressed, "You know that this is that bitch Aslaug's doing, don't you? That she put him up to this?"

Despite the fact that it was true that Titus had begun to grasp that this was likely, neither was he willing to acknowledge it. Consequently, he shot back, "Then more fool him for believing her!"

Before this could escalate, Titus, without glancing down again, stepped over Hrodulf's corpse and exited the alehouse, but this time, he did not relish the manner in which the men in his path scrambled out of the way. Immediately after Titus exited the alehouse, Willmar climbed unsteadily to his feet, but when he made as if to follow, he was stopped by Aelfwine.

"Someone needs to go with him," Willmar argued. "He's likely in enough trouble as it is." This caused him to look about for Wigmund, spotting the owner speaking urgently to one of his slaves, and while he guessed what Wigmund was doing, he nevertheless asked, "Are you sending him to Lord Otha?"

When Wigmund nodded, only then was Willmar satisfied, but when he headed for the door, he saw it closing and just glimpsed Aelfwine's back, forcing him to hurry to catch up. It was not until he got outside that he saw by the light of the hanging lamp outside the alehouse that Aelfwine and Ealdwolf had been joined by Ceadda's men, and while they did not run, they moved quickly down the muddy street, trying not to worry that Titus was nowhere to be seen and that Hrodulf had been right about where Isolde could be found.

It was actually young Hereweald who correctly guessed that Titus would show up, while Isolde insisted that this was ridiculous.

"There's no way he even knows we're here," she had argued. When Hereweald was unmoved, she added, "Besides, you don't even know what the argument was about."

She had said this while the older Hereweald and Cenric had gone out to find out more about what had happened, leaving Isolde to fend for herself while trying to ignore the disapproving glare from Astridr, who was making it clear, at least to Isolde, who she blamed for this. Hereweald's response was nonverbal in nature—just a long, level look before he offered a slight shrug—but before Isolde could say anything, there was a knocking at the door. It was not all that loud, nor insistent, but the three people understood that it was not likely to be the smith returning to his own home or Isolde's father for that matter; however, when Astridr began moving to the door, she was stopped by her son, who gave her a firm shake of the head while he walked to the door himself.

"Hereweald!" Isolde whispered, her tone urgent, and she heard the fear in her voice as she said, "No, don't! I'll answer it!"

"Absolutely not!" Hereweald replied in well above a whisper, but before he could react, she had gotten past him, dodging his outstretched hand and reaching the door.

Before she could change her mind, she jerked it open, and while she was expecting him, it took a physical effort on her part not to gasp aloud. In fact, from Titus' perspective, her face could have been carved from stone, and she saw the sudden unease, recognizing the expression of uncertainty on his face as well.

This did not stop him from blurting, "Is it true?"

"Is what true?" she asked coldly, but before he could repeat himself, there was a sound of onrushing footsteps coming from out of the darkness, which caused Titus to spin about, dropping into a slight crouch as he did so, although he did not make any other overt reaction as the elder Hereweald and her father materialized from the darkness, nor did Titus seem surprised to see Cenric.

She was relieved to see that Titus was not armed, but that feeling lasted only long enough for her to catch the glint of reflected light created by an object held in the smith's hand, then a heartbeat later recognizing that it was a hammer used by smiths throughout Saxon lands, with a long enough handle that it could double as a weapon, which was clearly the use the smith was intending by the way he was holding it. Giving barely a glance at Hereweald, Isolde turned and stared at her father, trying to communicate to Cenric what a monstrously bad idea it was for the smith to think that he would do anything other than enrage Titus, but all she got from her father was a helpless shrug, it being impossible in the moment for him to assure her that he had tried to dissuade the smith from thinking that a hammer would provide any kind of protection from Titus the Berserker. While it was true that the elder Hereweald had been part of the *fyrd* raised by Lord Eadwig like his son, it had not been to fight but for his skills in repairing weapons and armor, so while the smith had heard about Titus' exploits, he had not seen any of them almost four years earlier. Cenric had, but more than that, he had experienced Titus' raw power back when he was fourteen and completely untrained; he was eighteen now and had devoted himself to pursuing a warrior's life to a degree that was remarkable even among other Saxon warriors. More than anyone else present, even including Titus himself, Cenric knew that the likelihood that at least one of the Herewealds, and probably both of them ending up seriously injured, and that was if they were fortunate, was close to a certainty, yet he had no idea how he could stop it. Never in his wildest dreams did he imagine that not only would it be Isolde who neutralized the threat posed by Titus' question, but how she would do it, in the form of a simple, one-word answer.

"Yes," Isolde said quietly. When Titus gave no sign that he heard, or understood, she added, "Yes, it's true, Titus." Father and daughter never spoke of it, but it was hearing her own voice that gave Isolde the courage to say, "I plan on wedding Hereweald." Suddenly, she realized something, and she glanced over her shoulder to look at the younger smith and added shyly, "If, that is, he will have me."

Hereweald did not hesitate, assuring her in a hoarse voice that communicated the depth of his feeling, "I will. I swear it, Isolde!"

Later, what Cenric remembered the most was the look on Titus' face, and so did Isolde. Obviously, she had never been stabbed in her vitals before, but she could not imagine it being much more painful than what she felt as she studied the face of the man she had been certain she would spend the rest of her life with until a few short months ago. As horrible as it was seeing the expression on Titus' face, it was the awful silence that seemed to stretch on into the night that threatened Isolde's resolve, and she was just opening her mouth when the smith finally did something foolish by taking a step towards Titus, although it was his lifting of the hammer and brandishing it in a threatening manner that precipitated what came next. Personally, Cenric did not think that Hereweald was actually intending to do anything more than shake the hammer at Titus, but he could not argue that it was entirely possible that he was wrong. It was just that, while he was not close friends with the smith, he had never seen the elder Hereweald do anything as foolhardy as what he was doing now. And, as Cenric could have warned Hereweald, Titus the Berserker still moved more quickly than any man his size Cenric had ever seen, meaning that it would have been hard for his eye to track even if it had been broad daylight, and impossible to stop. Along with lifting the hammer, Hereweald had taken a step closer to Titus, closing the distance, which Titus crossed in two steps that, while he did not appear to hurry, still happened quickly enough that Hereweald could only register surprise as Titus first slapped the smith with an open hand, which he cupped slightly and aimed for the man's ear. It was an alehouse brawlers' trick that Cenric had seen before, and he had been told by a man who had absorbed such a blow that his ear had rung for a week later, but more importantly in the moment, it was extremely disorienting, and the pain of it wrenched a sharp cry from Hereweald and enabled Titus to use his left hand to slap the hammer from the smith's hand with a contemptuous ease, sending it spinning into the darkness. The smith's son did not hesitate to respond, but once again, Titus was quicker, pivoting to turn and face young Hereweald's charge, stopping him in his tracks with nothing more than a look.

"If you take another step, I'll kill you, Hereweald."

Anyone with eyes could see that Hereweald still wanted to lunge, but it was Isolde, who, thinking quickly, spoke up.

"Is it true that you killed someone at The Boar's Head?"

There was a challenge in her tone, as if she was daring him to deny it, but it served her purpose because Titus turned his attention to her, while young Hereweald was obviously as interested in the answer. Astridr took the opportunity provided by the momentary distraction to go rushing to her husband's side, the smith having dropped to his knees as he shook his head, clutching his ringing ear with one hand.

Seemingly ignoring this, Titus took a long time, but finally answered Isolde in a toneless voice, "Yes."

"Who was it?" Isolde asked.

"Hrodulf," Titus replied, finding that he was unable to meet her eyes.

It was young Hereweald who made the connection first.

"Aslaug," he whispered. "This is Aslaug's doing."

Despite keeping his voice low, Titus heard Hereweald and momentarily forgot his enmity towards the smith's son to exclaim, "She told Hrodulf that I raped her!" As soon as the words were out of his mouth, Titus also realized that he had broached, however inadvertently, the event that had led to this moment, and despite the darkness, he saw the pain flash across Isolde's features. Despite this, he felt compelled to cry, "You know that I didn't rape Aslaug, Isolde..." His voice dropped to a whisper, yet they could all hear the pleading note. "...don't you? You know I wouldn't...do that?"

There was a part of Isolde who wanted to remain silent, to punish Titus with that silence, but the pain she was experiencing now was not assuaged but was exacerbated by the anguished expression on Titus' face.

"I know you didn't," she finally spoke, and Titus' shoulders slumped as he broke his gaze from her to stare at the ground in front of him.

He was still staring at the ground when he spoke, addressing young Hereweald.

"Treat her well, Hereweald, because if you don't..." He looked up then, and the gleaming from the unshed tears in his eyes did nothing to disguise the awful promise in his words. "...I'll kill you, and it won't be quick like it was with Hrodulf."

Then, moving once more with a lithe speed, Titus the Berserker vanished into the darkness. The smith, with his wife's help, had climbed to his feet, and while it was not a stagger, he was clearly weaving a bit as he walked over to where his hammer was lying in the dirt, leaving the other three standing motionless.

It was left to Astridr to break the silence, and while they never spoke of it, Isolde would always view this as the closest the older woman would ever come to an apology when she said grimly, "I believe that Aslaug's father needs to know what his daughter has done. Will you come with me?"

"Absolutely," Isolde answered without hesitation.

"We better go along," the elder Hereweald said to Cenric, who agreed.

By the time they actually reached the home of Wulfnod, a fair number of the citizens of Wiltun, having been alerted to what had taken place at The Boar's Head, then learning that Aslaug had been involved in some way, were gathered in the market square; all they needed was a leader to focus their ire, and Astridr provided it. Aslaug was driven from Wiltun that very night, allowed to take only the clothes on her back, and a small purse that her mother had managed to pass to her; she was never seen in Wiltun again.

"He was provoked, Lord," Otha informed Ealdorman Eadwig when the lord summoned him to his estate just outside of Wiltun the next day.

"Yes," Eadwig nodded, "Eadward was in Wiltun last night, and he told me he heard as much himself." Otha, standing in front of Eadwig as he sat in the high-backed carved wooden chair where he liked to sit when discussing official matters, began to relax. Then, however, Eadwig growled, "But this isn't the first time we've had to discuss the Berserker and his...troubles in the town."

This was certainly true, but while Titus had badly beaten four different men, and had administered a beating to the same man twice, this one had been one of Lord Ceadda's men, who Ceadda had been forced to admit had been talking for weeks before their first altercation his desire to show everyone that Titus was nothing but an overgrown boy who had just been luckier than he had been skilled in combat, and he would prove it. Their first confrontation had resulted in a black eye for Titus, but Wulfred, Ceadda's man, had a broken nose, two black eyes, and several missing teeth. This kind of thrashing had been enough to dissuade the other three men who had challenged him for a second chance, but Wulfred was also renowned for his stubbornness, and the second beating had been more severe, to the point where Wulfred's days as a *seaxe*-wielding warrior came to an end because his sword arm had been so badly broken from Titus stomping it that he could not perform most of the thrusts. That time, Titus had escaped punishment because of Wulfred's behavior, and while the circumstances were similar with Hrodulf being the aggressor, neither could Otha really fault his lord's concern.

Nevertheless, Otha still felt compelled to point out, "Wulfnod's daughter has vanished, so she won't be making any more trouble, at least."

"That's well and good," Eadwig said sourly, "but that

doesn't change the fact that I've been informed that the dead man's father will be at the next hundred court to demand the *wergild*."

This caught Otha by surprise, though he realized he had no idea why it did, but then something that someone had mentioned in passing came back to him.

"But I thought that Hrodulf was indentured to..." He searched his memory but could not recall the name. "...another *ceorl* for at least another season for his own debt!"

"He was." Eadwig sighed, then gave Otha a sour smile. "To Wynnstan, whose eye Hrodulf gouged out, and I ruled in Wynnstan's favor because Hrodulf was drunk, and according to witnesses, started it. Oh," he waved a dismissive hand, "I'll make sure that Hrodulf's father pays off his son's debt before he gets a shilling for Hrodulf."

While this sounded straightforward, Otha was troubled by something, but he knew that he had to tread carefully; as good a relationship as the Thegn had with Eadwig, whose star had been on the rise ever since four years earlier when he had disobeyed the former Ealdorman Wulfhere and answered King Alfred's call instead of hewing to the Dane Guthrum as Wulfhere had ordered his Thegn, Eadwig could still be stiff and touchy about any perceived challenge to his status and authority.

Consequently, he asked cautiously, "Does that mean you've already made your decision concerning Titus, Lord?"

Eadwig did not explode, nor did he even get irritated; if anything, Otha thought, he looks a bit ashamed, which the Ealdorman explained, at least partially, "There are...factors at play right now, Otha, that make it a bit more complicated than it might seem." The nobleman stopped then, looking down at the rush-covered floor before he continued, "Our King has become...troubled by what he sees as the unruly behavior of our warriors, Otha. And, he has expressed that he wants to see some steps taken by his Ealdormen. And," he added pointedly, "his Thegns, to get the men back in hand and under a firmer hand." Offering a helpless shrug, Eadwig finished, "And what the King desires, it's our duty to provide."

A thought came to Otha, a horrifying one that caused him

to gasp aloud, "You don't plan on *executing* Titus, do you, my Lord?"

To Otha's intense relief, Eadwig looked up at him in startlement, his eyes going wide.

"By Christ, no, Otha! The lad's not in danger of losing his life; just money!"

While this was reassuring on its face, Otha also experienced a stab of bitter amusement at the Ealdorman's blithe attitude, that Titus would have two hundred shillings, which was actually ten pounds and was the *wergild* price for a low-ranking *ceorl* just lying around in his coin purse. Otha was certainly wealthy by the standards of his time, but there was always a scarcity of hard cash in their world, and while Titus was not profligate in his spending, and he had been rewarded, not just by Otha but by Eadwig, if Eadwig found that Titus was liable for the full amount, he would be forced to hand over almost every item of value in his possession, perhaps even the arm rings that he had been awarded by both Otha and Ealdorman Eadwig himself, which would be as shaming as it was costly. The Thegn also knew that it was extremely unlikely that Lord Eadwig would do this, not only because it had been established that Hrodulf was the aggressor and had already been fined for his role in the blinding of Wynnstan, but Otha knew that, while he had not spoken of it in some time, the Ealdorman still felt obligated to the young warrior for saving young Lord Eadward's life during the ambush before the Battle of Ethantun. However, hearing that King Alfred was displeased with the actions of the men like Titus also meant that the Ealdorman was not going to be willing to risk upsetting Alfred, no matter how he felt about Titus. And, as Otha knew, Titus was far from alone in having problems adjusting to a more peaceful time; it was something that many young warriors went through, and Otha had been no exception.

While he had been born a Thegn, Otha's father had shown little interest in improving his family's fortunes, seemingly content to scrape by and live a life that was barely distinguishable from those of the *ceorls* who provided his support. Father and son never spoke of it, but Otha had long believed that his father felt some guilt about the Saxon system of patronage that meant that farmers paid part of their hard-earned income, although it was rarely in hard cash, to men like Otha's father, all because a Thegn possessed weapons, armor, and the skill to use them, ostensibly to protect those *ceorls* from enemies of one sort or another. However, while it was rarely spoken of, the reality was that a Thegn could use his iron and skill at killing against a *ceorl,* or group of *ceorls* who refused to pay what was deemed by the King and his nobility to be their due. It was, Otha had long believed, just the way things were, and naturally, Thegns owed more than just their swords and spears to their Ealdorman, they owed payment as well, although this was almost always cash, either in the form of coinage or more commonly, pieces of silver that usually had once been part of something decorative, earning the term hacksilver. And, of course, the Ealdormen ultimately paid the King for the privilege of ruling over one of the shires that comprised Wessex, albeit through the shire Reeve, who was also appointed by the King and, much to the irritation of more than one Ealdorman, technically outranked them in royal matters since the Reeve spoke on the King's behalf. Unlike his father, Otha had no such misgivings, and he had been assiduous; some of his *ceorls* would have said ruthless, although only when out of his hearing, in accruing more wealth. At first, this had only been for himself back when he was young and before he had married Wulfgifu, and he had struggled with what men like him viewed as a nasty outbreak of peace in much the same way Titus and the other younger warriors were at this moment. Regardless of his sympathy, there was no question that Otha would support whatever it was that Lord Eadwig deemed suitable for Titus, and he could only hope that the lad would accept whatever it was without making things worse for himself by fighting it. Which, Otha thought worriedly, was a concern.

"Where is he now?" Eadwig asked, intruding on Otha's own ruminations.

"At my estate, Lord," Otha assured him. "I told him that he's not to leave, and Hrothgar is keeping an eye on him. Although," he hurried to add, "I know he won't disobey me."

Eadwig only nodded at this, then made a gesture that Otha knew was his signal that the matter was concluded, but just as

Otha was about to exit the hall, the Ealdorman called to him.

"Don't tell the lad this, but he doesn't have cause to worry," Eadwig said, just loudly enough for Otha to hear. "I think that spending the next few days stewing about what might happen to him will be punishment enough, don't you?"

Even if Otha had not agreed, he would not have said as much, but he did, and he assured Eadwig of this, and he left the Ealdorman's estate astride Tiw in a much better frame of mind. That lad, he thought with amusement, has Christ and all of His Saints looking out for him; in the near future, in fact, a bit more than a week later, this would be confirmed in a manner that seemed beyond all doubt.

Chapter Two

It began with an urgent summons from Eadwig, ordering Otha, who still held the position of Eadwig's senior Thegn, Ceadda, and Aelfnod to his estate a week after Titus' killing of Hrodulf. On their arrival, they found Eadwig pacing back and forth, while Eadward, who was now sixteen, and much to his father's delight, had finally experienced a growth spurt so that he was now at least two inches taller than his father, sitting carelessly in his chair placed next to his father's. He had also filled out, his shoulders broadened, and most importantly, he was no longer the clumsy boy who was likely to trip over his own feet, and while he was no longer his primary tutor, sharing that role with Titus, Otha was almost as pleased at Eadward's progress as his father. Although he would never say as much, the Thegn gave a great deal of the credit for Eadward's development, especially over the last year, to Titus. Not surprisingly, despite the social gulf between them, the pair had a bond, first formed when a stableboy had stood over the corpse of Eadward's horse Thunor, protecting the lordling he barely knew who was trapped underneath. The fact that they were the youngest members of Eadwig's *fyrd* had also played a role, yet to Otha's surprise, while Eadward's attachment and adulation of the older youth was understandable, what had become clear was that Titus viewed himself as something of an older brother to Eadward. And, Otha also acknowledged, Titus had done him a favor by volunteering to relieve Otha of one of his three days a week where he traveled to Eadwig's estate to tutor Eadward. Now, while it was clear that something important was taking place, to Otha's eyes, the Ealdorman was not displaying the same air of suppressed excitement and concern as he had when Alfred had summoned the *fyrd* four years earlier. In a more tangible sign that this was not quite as urgent, the Ealdorman was content to wait until cups of ale were brought, although he did not stop his pacing.

Finally, he stopped to face his Thegns to announce, "A

force of Danish ships have arrived on the coast near Hrofoscester (Rochester), and the townspeople have sent a messenger to the King asking for help." He paused, knowing there would be a reaction from the three Thegns, and Otha noticed that, if anything, young Eadward looked smug. Probably because he already knows what's coming, he thought. Continuing, Eadwig said, "The King has decided that he will answer this threat himself, and he's ordered a force be raised."

Although Otha noticed the wording, so did Ceadda, who beat him to asking, "You said he's 'raising a force'. Does that mean he's calling the *fyrd*?"

"No." Eadwig shook his head. "He's charged me with supplying twenty-five men, along with calling on the other Ealdormen, but he only wants experienced warriors. And," he added meaningfully, "he wants as many men who know how to swim as he can get, and who have served aboard a warship before."

The fact that all eyes went to Otha did not surprise him, and he could not help feeling a bit smug in the moment, considering how much mocking he had taken, not just from his fellow Thegns but even from Lord Eadwig on occasion about what they considered to be a peculiar obsession, his insistence that every man in his service learn how to swim, at least to a degree where they were not immediately condemned to drown in water over their head. Somewhat oddly, none of them had bothered to ask Otha why he had developed this habit, which stemmed from a childhood incident when a young Otha had almost drowned when he had ventured too far out into the river near his home. He had been saved by one of his father's slaves, a Northman who, being a member of a seafaring people, knew how to swim, and had taught the young Saxon noble. To Otha, it was a sensible precaution to take, and he actually enjoyed swimming, although he did not do it as often as he would have liked.

"If the King is making that a requirement," Aelfnod spoke up, "that must mean he plans on going to sea and not trying to trap these Danes ashore."

"How many Danes, Lord? Do you know?" Ceadda asked.

"The people report seeing at least eight ships, perhaps as

many as a dozen," Eadwig answered, then added dismissively, "but you know how common folk exaggerate, so I won't be surprised if it's half that number."

This, Otha knew, was certainly true, but he pointed out, "Even just four ships would mean around two hundred warriors, so let's pray that they *are* exaggerating." Before the Ealdorman could comment, he asked, "When are we to be ready? And where are we supposed to meet with the King and the rest of his forces?"

"You leave in four days," Eadwig replied.

Otha noticed it immediately, but so did Ceadda, who asked carefully, "Will you not be leading us, Lord?"

Eadwig did not hesitate in answering, "No, the King has ordered that I stay behind." He had looked at Ceadda, but then he turned to Otha as he added meaningfully, "The King has commanded that all of the Ealdormen conduct their business as scheduled, and as you all know, it's time to hold a hundred court." Otha felt his stomach clench, but then before the Thegn could respond, Eadwig added with a feigned casualness, "Of course, if some of the parties that are to stand before me aren't there because they have legitimate business elsewhere..." his beard partially obscured his mouth twitching, but Otha saw it, "...especially if it's at the express command of the King, then that can't be helped, and the other party will just have to accept that."

Otha knew to hide his pleasure, but he did offer his Lord a slight nod of thanks, which Eadwig ignored.

"Since you're not going to lead us, who are you placing in command?" Ceadda asked, and while his tone was respectful, the other men, especially Otha, knew there was a challenge there, one that had been building for the last couple of years as Ceadda became less circumspect about expressing his belief that he should be Eadwig's senior Thegn and his *de facto* second in command, at least until Eadward got old and experienced enough to assume that role.

And, to his credit, Eadwig did not hesitate in responding, but in the span of time it took him to utter the name, Otha, Ceadda, and even Aelfnod, who had never once expressed a desire for the position, were as flabbergasted, and were united

48

in their response.

"Eadward is going in my stead, and he will be in command."

"*What?* My Lord, are you serious?"

The only reason that it was Ceadda who almost shouted this was only because he beat Otha to it, but within the span of a dozen heartbeats, Otha was offering a silent prayer of thanks for it. For his part, Eadwig did not match his Thegn in volume, but as they all knew, the Ealdorman was at his most dangerous to subordinates when he spoke quietly, and one did not need to know him to hear the icy anger in his voice when he replied, "Do I seem as if I'm jesting, Ceadda? Do you see me smiling? And," now he raised his voice, not much, but enough, "are you challenging my authority?"

Ceadda, who was of a swarthy complexion that was accentuated by black hair and mustache, visibly blanched, his face turning a deathly pale, but it was the way that he stammered that was most telling.

"N-no, my Lord, not at all, I swear it on the Cross! I...I was just surprised, my Lord, that's all!"

Eadwig did not reply, choosing instead to regard Ceadda with a long, cold stare for several heartbeats before, in a clear signal, turned away from the Thegn to demand from Otha, "And you, Otha? Do you have anything to say about my decision?"

Otha had used his reprieve wisely, choosing to listen to the exchange between his Ealdorman and his fellow Thegn to study young Eadward, who looked as if he wanted to be anywhere other than where he was. He doesn't want this any more than we do, he realized, which was what enabled Otha to reply, "No, my Lord. It's your decision to make, and I trust your judgment."

Taking advantage of being out of the range of Eadwig's vision, Ceadda gave Otha a glare, which was ignored, and Eadwig did stare at Otha for an extra span of time before, apparently satisfied, said, "Go make your preparations, and I want the list of men each of you will be taking no later than tomorrow morning. As far as how many of your men you supply, work it out among yourselves. All I care about is that you provide twenty-four men, including yourselves. Which," he finished with heavy humor, "would seem to be easy to divide between the three of you." Turning to Eadward, he ordered, "I'm putting you in charge of gathering the necessary supplies for the march to join the King. Once with him, the King will be responsible for your feeding and supply."

"Yes, Father," Eadward answered, then licked his lips, which Otha had learned meant that the youngster was about to broach a subject that was potentially contentious or liable to rouse his father's ire. "I would like to say something about your decision to put me in command if I could..."

"Not now," Eadwig cut him off. "We'll discuss this in private. They," he waved a hand at his three senior Thegns, "have much to do."

Understanding this was all the dismissal they would get, Otha wasted no time in exiting the hall, pointedly ignoring Ceadda's attempt to get his attention. Lord Eadwig was right; there was much to do, but that had nothing to do with his refusal to spend any time with the other Thegn, and in the back of his mind, Otha understood that this was a problem that he had been ignoring for too long. Now he could only hope that Ceadda did not use the absence of the Ealdorman to try and convince Eadward to usurp Otha's status. He was not worried about once they joined with the rest of the force King Alfred would be commanding, but their march to join him could last just a day, or several, depending on where they were meeting. That, however, was a problem for later, and he spent the ride going down the list of men he would be taking with him.

Not surprisingly, Titus was in a state of anxiety as he waited for Lord Otha to return from Ealdorman Eadwig's estate, and he tried to absorb himself in his chores, understanding that, now that a week had passed since his killing of Hrodulf, there was no reason to expect that Lord Eadwig would delay his decision any further. Today, he was helping Leofsige perform the monthly examination of the hooves of the breeding stock, and prior to the night before, Leofsige had finally acceded to Titus' pleas to let him try shoeing one of the animals, it being inevitable that in the preceding month a shoe had loosened or needed to be replaced, and he had been excited at the prospect. Now, when the older man had reminded him that this was the day for it, he had tried to sound enthused, but he could see that Leofsige had not been fooled. Leofsige had not been at The Boar's Head the week before, although he had certainly heard about it from Willmar, Ealdwolf, and Aelfwine, and he was sympathetic, even offering Titus an awkward pat on the shoulder.

"From what I heard, you're not at fault, and this is just something that Lord Eadwig has to do with the hundred court to appear to be fair," he had said.

While this caused Titus to wonder if Leofsige's words had been given to him by someone, perhaps Willmar, since this was exactly what Willmar had said to him when Titus arrived from where he now lived with Uhtric and Leofflaed, it was still nice to hear, and he certainly hoped this was the case. What bothered him most was a feeling that he could not shake, that both he and Hrodulf were victims of Aslaug, a belief that, as time passed and was reinforced by his friends, became an article of faith. It would not be for another four days after Hrodulf's death that he learned that Aslaug had vanished, which he immediately realized was a blessing, because he knew himself well enough to understand that if he had seen her again, it was a distinct possibility that he would have beaten her to death just as he had Hrodulf. As far as the laborer's killing was concerned, he heard what he had done from Ealdwolf and Aelfwine on their ride back to Otha's; Willmar was still too angry to speak to him at that point, although by the time Titus arrived from Uhtric's just after dawn the next day, he was sufficiently mollified by Titus' repeated apology on the way home and a night's sleep to add his version of what he had seen, which was essentially the same. Despite the fact that it was not the first time, Titus had no real memory of any of his exploits; by his count, this was the fourth such time he had been unaware of anything other than a terrible, ferocious rage that seemed to wipe his memory clean, rendering him insensible until he was standing there, or as at the ambush, on his knees, covered in blood that, to this point, had never been his own, and bewildered about what had just taken place. Of the night before, his last memories had been of Willmar grabbing his arm, and to his shame, he did remember striking his friend, launching himself across the table, then Hrodulf landing the one blow that had opened up a small cut above Titus' left eye that he did not notice until the next morning. Everything after that was gone until he was standing over Hrodulf in his death throes, his foe's face turning purple, although it was the way in which his tongue seemed to swell as it protruded from his mouth, while his eyes bulged out to a point that Titus expected them to pop out of his skull that made him shudder to think about. How Hrodulf had gotten like that, however? Titus had no idea, and even after the others explained it to him, he found it hard to believe, although he also understood they had no reason to lie to him. Now Hrodulf was dead, and it was because he had believed Aslaug's lies. This was the thought that kept intruding into Titus' mind, making it difficult to concentrate on something that, as Leofsige had reminded him more than once, he had been pestering Leofsige to do.

Finally, in exasperation, Leofsige dismissed Titus, telling him to occupy himself, and it did not surprise anyone that Titus immediately headed to the part of the yard that Otha and his men used as their training ground, where there were several stout wooden poles in the ground, each of them scarred and gouged from the thousands of strikes from swords and spears. It was one of the few places where Titus, called the Berserker, felt truly comfortable with himself, savoring the feeling of security that he experienced whenever he held his sword, which he kept sheathed when he was training, both to protect the blade and because he found that the extra weight made the blade, a Danish sword that he had taken from the warrior he had slain in single combat and not the more common *seaxe* favored by his fellow Saxons, feel noticeably lighter when he used it unsheathed. He would never know that he was using the same method as the huge Roman for whom he was named, although in his case, the Romans used a wooden sword whose edges were lined with lead, and the handle was filled with the metal to make it even heavier, for the very same reason. Very quickly, as he worked up a sweat and his body began to respond to the rhythms of thrust and recovery, he forgot his troubles, and he became so absorbed in what he was doing that he did not even notice Lord Otha's arrival until the Thegn was dismounting in the yard. Stopping his exercises, Titus stood uncertainly, watching as

Otha strode in his direction, his features, which were always hard to decipher, seemed to be set in an even harder plane than normal, and all of the assurances that Willmar and the others had offered Titus fled from his mind. He looks, Titus decided with an almost overwhelming dread, as if he got some bad news from Lord Eadwig.

"I thought you were supposed to be helping Leofsige," Otha broke the silence abruptly.

"I was, Lord," Titus admitted, not sure how to put his dismissal. "I think Leofsige..."

He got no farther, because Otha muttered, almost as if to himself, "Never mind, it doesn't matter anyway."

He crossed over to the side of the barn where an iron bell was hanging from an eave, picked up the piece of iron attached by a thong, and began striking it in a rhythm that was three strikes, a pause, then three strikes, but at a measured pace that, as Titus learned very early on, was the signal that the Thegn was sounding an assembly that, while important, was not an emergency. Once they were all assembled from their various responsibilities on Otha's estate, there were twelve men, although one of them, Osric, who had lost his right arm at Ethantun, was no longer marching with his comrades, though he performed a variety of jobs and was still fully accepted by the others. Of course, Osric was not the only man of Otha's who had been grievously injured four years earlier, but Uhtric had compensated for the loss of his eye to the point that there was no discernible reduction in his abilities, although he had been forced to make some changes in his style. The most notable was how he now seemed to almost be looking off to his left, even when he was facing his opponent squarely, to compensate for his narrower field of vision. Over the intervening four years, two more men had entered Otha's service, including Snorri who, despite the Danish name, had a Saxon father but Danish mother. Snorri liked to boast of his prowess, and he *was* very fast, and somewhat unusually for a Saxon favoring an axe, but Titus knew that he was not alone in viewing the newer man with quiet skepticism, although he was fair enough with himself to acknowledge that it was very likely that this was due to the fact that they had not faced battle together. The other new man had been with Otha for less than a year, and his acceptance into Otha's service had made Titus the second-youngest man. Wilwulf was his name, and he was Otha's nephew, the oldest son of his sister, his father a *ceorl* with a ten-hide holding in Hamtunscir who had finally given up on the idea of his son following in his footsteps, the youth having long before been seduced by the idea of being a warrior like his uncle. Wilwulf was eager and willing to learn, yet as much as Titus tried, he could not warm to him, seeing him as a callow boy despite the fact that he was only a year older. Deep within himself, Titus understood why he had this reserve, but it was something that he would never share, particularly with Otha, because Titus was certain that Wilwulf's only chance of making old bones was to return to his father's farm. He was not alone in this belief, but as Willmar, Leofsige, and even Uhtric had learned to their detriment, when it came to Wilwulf, Otha had a blind spot where his nephew was concerned.

"Not everyone is like you, boy," he had roared at Titus one day when, after a sparring session where Wilwulf repeated the same mistake that he had been making for weeks, Titus had worked up the courage to do what his comrades had done and failed at by approaching Otha. "Not everyone is born to this! Tell me who works harder than Wilwulf among the lot of you! Eh? Who?"

Now it was certainly the truth that Wilwulf was a hard worker, but it took most of Titus' willpower not to retort that Otha was looking at the one man who did, correctly deducing the folly of that. Despite the circumstances, this was something that, while it worried Titus, had faded into the background of concerns, especially that day, and it was a mark of Titus' view of himself that, as he waited for the others to assemble, he convinced himself that whatever it was that Otha was about to announce had to do with him. Not, he would have argued, without a certain amount of logic; Otha had been to see Ealdorman Eadwig about Titus, after all, and now here he was calling an assembly of all of the men in his service.

As was his habit, Otha did not use unnecessary words, announcing, "Danes have been raiding the coast around Hrofescester, and the King is raising a force to stop them. He's charged Ealdorman Eadwig with supplying twenty-five men between the three of us, including myself, Lord Eadward, Lords Ceadda and Aelfnod, and we have three days to prepare; we leave on the fourth day." Like Eadwig had, he paused to let his men react to that, and presumably, those who could perform the mental calculation, determine that this meant that at least seven of them would be going with Otha, and he was quietly amused to see them working this out, signaled by them suddenly giving each other sidelong glances as they tried to determine which of them would be going. Realizing something, he resumed, "There's one thing you all should know, and that is that the King not only wants experienced warriors, he wants as many men who know how to swim as possible."

This elicited another reaction as the import of this hit his men, but he ignored it, and he was not surprised that it was Uhtric who said, "That can only mean one thing. The King is taking us to sea to fight."

Suddenly, the eagerness and excitement that had been on display at the prospect of relieving the monotony vanished, reminding Otha that, while he had required these men to learn how to swim, it did not mean that they enjoyed it to the same level that he did, and as far as their antipathy towards going to sea, Otha shared the Saxon abhorrence for nautical matters.

More to forestall any potential unpleasantness, Otha said, "As of right now, I want each of you," remembering Osric, the Thegn shot him an apologetic glance, which the one-armed man acknowledged with a curt nod, "who are able, to consider yourselves as going as of this moment. Once I hear from Ceadda and Aelfnod how many men they can supply, I'll let you know how many of you are going. Until then, you need to inspect your weapons, armor, and shields, and let me know what needs to be done. Only," he finished with a warning, "once you're done with your normal tasks."

As he expected, there was some grumbling at this, mainly at the thought that there would be no trip into Wiltun this night, which he ignored. To his chagrin, he was also reminded that he had forgotten the other purpose of his trip to Lord Eadwig's estate when he heard a cough, and he turned to see Titus standing there, forcing Otha to stifle his groan, which was aimed at himself for forgetting.

"Lord, when you said that we need to prepare as if we're going, did you mean me as well?"

Despite himself, Otha could not resist the urge for a bit of fun, only regarding Titus with a raised eyebrow for a handful of heartbeats before he gave Titus an elaborate shrug before saying, "Well, if you prefer to stay here to stand before Lord Eadwig at the hundred court and have him pass judgment on Hrodulf's father's claim for *wergild*, that's very commendable. Now," he allowed, "if it was me, I'm not sure I would be that noble, but I'm sure that Lord Eadwig will take your sense of honor into account."

"No!" Titus exclaimed, holding both hands out. "I don't, Lord! I mean, I know it would be the right thing to do, but I wasn't suggesting that I was..."

Otha, feeling a bit ashamed, cut him off, "Titus, you're going, no matter how many men I end up taking." Thinking that he owed the youth this much, and that Lord Eadwig would forgive him, Otha added, "And that's not my decision, Titus, that's Lord Eadwig's. He told me as much this morning. And," his features hardened, "if Hrodulf's father has a problem with that, he can take it up with the King, because that's who you're going to be serving."

And, just that quickly, Titus experienced yet another change in his fortune.

As Otha expected, given the King's requirement for men who could swim, there was not an even division between Eadwig's senior Thegns, and he ended up providing nine men, but it was his choice of his nephew that created what, from Titus' perspective, was the closest thing to an outright revolt among Otha's men as he had ever witnessed during his time.

Leofsige had been elected as the spokesman, but he had been joined by Hrothgar, Willmar, Uhtric, and much to Titus' discomfort, while helping his pride, Leofsige had asked him to be present as well, explaining, "You're just a year older than he is, and you've done more work with him than the rest of us, so you need to be there."

They were not in the hall; at Leofsige's request, they had

actually all mounted and ridden to the far side of Otha's estate. While none of them thought that Wilwulf should accompany them, neither did they have any desire to humiliate the youth, if only because of Otha's obvious feelings about him, but it was not just that; Wilwulf was a very likable young man, and it was this that caused Titus some guilt where he was concerned.

Otha listened, but while Titus watched, he could see the Thegn's lips thinning down, which was always a sign that he was struggling to control his temper, and when Leofsige paused for breath, Otha asked coldly, "Are you through?"

To Titus' discomfort, rather than answer Otha, Leofsige turned to him.

"What say you, Titus? You've worked with Wilwulf more than the rest of us. And," he added, superfluously in Titus' estimation, "you're closest to him in age. Do you think he should be with us?"

Any feeling of being flattered that he had been brought along was swept away by the cold glare from Lord Otha, and he desperately wanted to be anywhere else, but he still felt compelled to be honest.

"Perhaps if it was in a few months, my Lord," Titus began carefully, "then Wilwulf would be a good addition, but he is too green right now."

"So says the boy who showed up not knowing what end of the *seaxe* to hold," Otha retorted, cutting Titus off.

Titus felt his face begin to burn, but he was determined to maintain his composure, and he replied calmly, "Which is why you had me working in the stables with Dudda, Lord. And," he added quietly, "you were right to do so."

"Oh," Otha sneered, "I'm so pleased that my decision then meets with your approval. But," he jabbed a finger at Titus, "you were also only fourteen!"

It was Uhtric, who had been opposed to dragging Titus into this in the first place, who took pity on his brother-in-law by breaking in, "He was also bigger and stronger then than Wilwulf is now, but that's not why we're concerned, Lord. And," he did maintain the same kind of quiet tone Titus had adopted, because he knew his words were likely to further arouse their Thegn's ire, "I think you know that. But I agree with the others, and that's why I'm here. Wilwulf isn't ready, my Lord, but it also means that we're leaving behind someone with more experience."

Uhtric stopped then, but when Hrothgar, who was sitting next to Leofsige opened his mouth to offer his own opinion, he was stopped by a hand on his arm from Leofsige, who had divined that this was fruitless, which was confirmed when Otha said flatly, "Wilwulf is going, and that's the last we speak of it."

Then he turned Tiw, and without another word, went cantering back to the buildings of the estate, leaving the others to commiserate.

"At least we tried," Uhtric sighed.

"And if anything happens to that boy, do you think Lord Otha is going to remember that?" Leofsige asked bitterly.

They let Otha get a lead of a few hundred paces before they followed behind, none of them willing to run the risk of overtaking their Lord.

The next days passed in a blur for Otha's men, and Titus was no exception to this, although it was not nearly as frenzied as the days after the King called the *fyrd* before Ethantun. Over the intervening time, Titus had, through a combination of purchase and trade, expanded his collection of weapons and protective equipment so that it now bore little resemblance to the motley assortment that, he was now ashamed to admit, had been a source of extreme pride. The first thing he replaced was the shield that he had been given by Aedelstan using some of the precious silver pennies he had been allowed to keep, having it made, but what he had not counted on was how much he would grow, and now, while the shield was in perfect condition, having never even been used in battle, it looked absurdly small in Titus' hand. It was not just a matter of appearance, however; the fact was that it did not protect enough of his body, but while it was something he had intended to correct, he had never gotten around to it. Now, because of the urgency, he was in a substantially weakened bargaining position, yet his parsimony, coupled with his innate stubbornness meant that he actually considered not correcting the matter. It was Leofflaed of all people who got through to him, albeit by losing her temper.

"If you're going to needlessly risk your life to save less than a shilling, that's one thing, but you need to remember *him*," she had thrust a dramatic finger at Wiglaf, who at that moment was more interested in chewing on a piece of honeycomb, with most of the contents ending up smeared on his face, "and how he'll feel when his Uncle Titus doesn't come home!"

This had the desired effect, and Titus was given leave to go into Wiltun to speak to a woodworker there who, while it was not his main business, had learned the arcane skill of making what was considered to be the best, made of multiple layers of strips of wood, each layer in an alternating pattern and affixed with glue made from boiling the bones of either cows or horses, although the specifics not only differed from one craftsman who used glue, but they carefully guarded their particular formulation, each of them believing their concoction was superior. Because of his size, Titus required a shield that was more than three feet in diameter, but thanks to his strength, he also was able to accommodate a shield that was thicker than what other men could handle because of the weight. However, when he related this to the craftsman, a wizened man who looked even older than his mid-forties named Burgred, Titus got nothing more than a disbelieving laugh, although Burgred did not address the reason for this directly.

Instead, he asked, "When did you say you needed this shield?"

"We leave in three days," Titus replied, although it was now actually four, but he was not comfortable cutting it that finely.

"Berserker," Burgred might have thought Titus was a fool, but he certainly was not, and he had immediately realized how his initial reaction could be viewed by this huge warrior, so he spoke respectfully, and almost gently, "that kind of shield takes more than a month to construct."

"A *month*!" Titus exclaimed in dismay, but while he was angry, it was at himself, the thought that crossed his mind was that now he would have to listen to his sister recount all the times she had nagged him about his procrastination. Aloud, he asked without much hope, "Is there anything you can do to help me?"

"You're going to meet the King, yes? To drive away those Danish dogs?" Titus nodded, and the craftsman thought for a moment, then said, "While I don't have anything already made that would be the size you require, I can make a riveted shield using solid pieces of alder that will be the thickness you want. Now," he raised a hand in caution, "I'm not going to pretend that it will be a match to the kind that you're asking for over time, but it will do the job well enough. Provided," he offered his version of a smile, displaying a mouth that was more gums than teeth, "you lot don't take too long to send those heathens to Hell."

"Lord Otha said that we should be done by early autumn," Titus answered, guessing that this was really what Burgred was after, some sort of information that he could brag about at his favorite alehouse. Dreading the answer, Titus asked, "How much will this cost, and when can I pick it up?"

Answering the second question first, Burgred replied, "You said you need it in three days, so be back here at dusk on the third day and it will be ready. Unpainted, of course, and you'll have to nail the boss to it yourself," he warned, which Titus had expected, and had been one of the reasons he had dissembled about their real departure date. Burgred hesitated then, rubbing his chin as if he was thinking about it, but this was a common merchant's trick that did not fool Titus in the slightest, and he braced himself. Finally, Burgred said, "As far as the cost, I think eight pennies is fair."

To Titus, this was anything *but* fair, and he was actually opening his mouth to refuse what he considered to be nothing short of outright robbery, when, from the back of his mind, something that Uhtric had once said to him pushed its way to the forefront.

"The cost of anything should be measured by how much you need it," he had counseled Titus, when, in a similar moment, Titus had been certain that he was being charged too much for something.

That time, it had been a new tunic, after Uhtric, at Leofflaed's quiet insistence, had bluntly told his brother-in-law that the one he was wearing, and the only one he owned at the time, stank to a point that it could not be ignored, or endured, even after it was washed. And, as Titus knew was inarguable, a shield that kept him alive was essentially priceless. Regardless of this reality, while he agreed to the terms, it was done curtly, and he very grudgingly reached into his purse and withdrew a piece of hacksilver that was roughly the same weight as the four pennies, half of the total cost as custom called for, slightly surprised when Burgred weighed it in his palm for perhaps a heartbeat before accepting it. The next item he did not even try to find in Wiltun, and while he had only been given leave to come into the town, he did not think that it would get him in trouble because he knew exactly where to go. Mounting Thunor, he still moved at a rapid trot, heading to the estate of Thegn Ceadda, where he knew that one of Ceadda's men was selling his spare *seaxe*. While he had been intending to get a new shield for some time, his decision to add a *seaxe* to his arsenal was more recent, although he had started training with it occasionally more than a year earlier. He still favored his double-edged Danish sword that was almost a foot longer and was heavier, but he had learned there were times when the shorter *seaxe* was a more effective weapon, and while he had no practical experience in seaborne combat, of Otha's men Ealdwolf and Aelfwine had fought aboard ship; Snorri also claimed to have done so as well, but Titus did not place much weight on his claim. Of the two men he trusted, both of them declared that, given the cramped conditions aboard any kind of seagoing vessel, whether it be a Danish or Northman longship, or the slightly wider Saxon style, a *seaxe* was the superior weapon, but to Titus, it was Ealdwolf's insistence on this that had the most impact, because Ealdwolf was the best of Otha's warrior with a spear, and if he was willing to forego using it in favor of a *seaxe*, that was all Titus needed.

Unfortunately for Titus' purse, a *seaxe* of a decent quality was more expensive than a shield, but he also knew that this *seaxe* met his standard because Uhtric had taken him to examine it just a couple months earlier when his brother-in-law was considering buying it for himself. Seeing it for himself had been one thing, but it had been who was selling it that meant as much to Titus as seeing the weapon with his own eyes, because it had been Aedelstan. While he also hoped that their relationship, which had begun the day of the ambush, when Titus' actions had not only saved Eadward, but Aedelstan, who had given him the spear that was still in his possession, along with his first shield, although this he had replaced very quickly, as a token of thanks, would come into play, Titus was not counting on it. The scene at Lord Ceadda's was almost identical to what he had left at Otha's, and it took him a bit of time to find Aedelstan, then he had to wait until the other warrior was through with his task of scraping several hides. To his pleased surprise, it became clear that Aedelstan did take their prior relationship into account, charging Titus substantially less than he might have expected if he had sold it to a stranger.

He learned why when Aedelstan admitted, "I was wondering if you'd be coming. We're going to need good men for this."

Titus was flattered, but there was something in Aedelstan's demeanor that struck him as odd.

"Have you ever fought on ship?"

He got the answer even before Aedelstan answered by the manner in which the warrior, who was ten years older, shuddered.

"Yes," Aedelstan answered, then added vehemently, "and I've prayed every day since I never had to do it again!"

While neither Ealdwolf or Aelfwine had spoken in glowing terms about shipborne fighting, they had not expressed anything close to what he was seeing from Aedelstan, and he asked cautiously, "What makes it so bad?"

The look Aedelstan offered him indicated to Titus that the other man thought Titus had lost his senses, and his tone made it clear he thought the answer was obvious. "Why, because you're just as likely to drown as you are to get stabbed, that's what makes it so bad!"

"You don't know how to swim?" Titus asked in surprise, then hurriedly explained, "Lord Otha told us that the King has ordered that every man be able to swim, that's all."

This made Aedelstan laugh, but it was both bitter and mocking, "Yes, yes, Lord Ceadda told us the same thing. And yes, I know how to swim. But," suddenly, Aedelstan turned slightly so that he could poke Titus in the chest with a finger, something that the younger man normally despised, but he was sufficiently unsettled at Aedelstan's behavior not to notice...much, "swimming in a river or a lake is *nothing* like swimming in the sea." He paused, then in a quieter tone, he said, "I was on a ship named *Widow-Maker*, and we were doing the same thing that the King wants us to do here, run some raiders down, although these were Northmen. Well," he gave a bitter chuckle, "we caught them, but it was a trap. I don't even know where their other ships came from, but it was where one moment we were grappling with one ship, and we outnumbered their crew two to one, then we were surrounded by three other ships. One of them sheared our oars off on one side while most of us were aboard the first Norse ship, and they just fed men onto that ship from the opposite side so that we couldn't use our numbers to at least take some of those heathens prisoners to bargain with."

He paused long enough for Titus to ask, "Was this with Lord Ceadda?"

"No, this was Thegn Oeric. I served him before I joined Lord Ceadda." Continuing, Aedelstan said, "They had us surrounded, and they launched fire arrows at us. And," he shrugged, "it didn't take long before there was fire burning in too many places for us to stop it. We were in sight of land, and the sun was going down, so some of us decided that we'd rather risk drowning than burning to death."

He stopped again, and after a long span, Titus asked, "How many of you made it to shore?"

"Just me," Aedelstan answered, then explained, "and only because I found one of the broken oars and used it to stay afloat." He shuddered, then just above a whisper and without looking at Titus, "Sometimes I can still hear the others screaming. Some men waited until they caught on fire before they threw themselves into the water, but it was very choppy, so unless they had some way to stay afloat like I did, they went under really quickly."

Titus asked no more questions, and with their business done, he said awkwardly, "I'm sure we'll see each other on the march."

Later, he blamed his distraction caused by Aedelstan's story on making him forget that he had decided to bypass Wiltun on the way back, telling himself that he had been fortunate that on his trip to Burgred's he had not run into Isolde, or even worse, Hereweald. Naturally, this meant that he would run into them both, and in such a way that he could not have turned about or ducked down a side street. He spotted her first as she emerged from around a corner just a block ahead, but while he saw her immediately, her attention was straight ahead of her as she began crossing the muddy street that Titus was traveling down on Thunor. Since she was alone, or so Titus thought in the moment, he nudged Thunor to move a little more quickly, intent on talking to her at least once more before he left. It was less than a heartbeat after this that, from around the opposite corner, Hereweald came striding into view, and Titus realized they had seen each other and were walking towards each other, and in the manner of young lovers everywhere, were oblivious to anyone else's presence. That, at least, was how it began, but in a natural reflex, Hereweald glanced, first to his right in the opposite direction, then to his left, checking for any oncoming travelers. It was something that everyone did without thinking, dating back to when one or both of their parents warned them of the danger of stepping into the path of oncoming traffic, even other pedestrians; or, men on horseback, and indeed, the young smith's head was already turning back towards Isolde, and Titus clearly saw the broad smile on his face. That smile vanished as Hereweald's mind caught up to what his eyes had seen, immediately turning into a scowl. And, of course, Isolde, seeing Hereweald's reaction, turned her head to follow his gaze; Hereweald's reaction was not unexpected, but watching Isolde go deathly pale made Titus feel as if he had been stabbed in his vitals. It also put him in what he considered an untenable position, as part of him screamed that he should turn Thunor about, and he was actually listening to that voice when Thunor took the matter out of his hands, literally, when he either saw, or more likely, recognized Isolde by her scent. Yanking the reins out of Titus' hands, the horse quickened his pace, blowing through his huge nostrils, his ears pricked forward in the sign anyone familiar with horses recognized, and without any hesitation, he unerringly thrust his big nose into her midsection at the spot where she normally hid the treat she fed Titus' horse during happier times. Despite the tension of the moment, she laughed with delight, and while it was painful for Titus, he experienced a deep sense of satisfaction at the sight of Hereweald's face.

"I can see someone didn't forget where to look," she said, still laughing, but then she seemed to remember the circumstances, acutely aware that the passersby were beginning to pay attention. More to change the subject than for any other reason, which Hereweald later refused to believe, she asked Titus, "I suppose that you're going to join the King?"

"I am." Titus nodded, then looked pointedly down at Hereweald. With justifiable pride, and a fair amount of scorn in his voice, he added, "The King only wants his best men, and Lord Otha told me that Ealdorman Eadwig asked for me by name. But," he sneered, "you don't have to worry, Hereweald. The men who are staying behind will keep you safe."

Hereweald flushed, and he was clearly angry, actually taking a step closer, but Isolde reached out and grabbed a sleeve of his tunic, which seemed to snap him out of his rage because, in an equally calculated insult, he stepped backward to stand next to Isolde, then put one arm around her shoulder, but it was what he said next that tilted the field back to the young smith's favor.

"Well," Hereweald said coolly, "*if* you come back, you can congratulate us because we're getting married soon."

"Soon?" Titus asked suspiciously, but he addressed Isolde, demanding, "How soon?"

Cenric's daughter did not seem able to look up at Titus, so it looked as if she was speaking to the mud in front of her as she answered quietly, "Within a month, maybe two."

As surreptitiously as he could, Titus shifted his grip from the reins to his saddle because he suddenly felt as if the world around was reeling, yet he did his best to maintain what to his ears sounded a neutral tone. "Yes, well, I'm afraid I must get back to Lord Otha's. There's still much to do."

Ignoring Hereweald's smirk, Titus spun Thunor about, which meant that he missed Isolde wiping it off her betrothed's face with a few well-chosen words.

Calling out, and more loudly than necessary, Isolde told Titus, "I'll say a prayer every day for your safe return, Titus of Cissanbyrig!"

It had been a running joke between them, that she was the only person who refused to call him Berserker, and while this as much as the words themselves made him smile, the tears that threatened to push past his eyes were not as sweet.

For Alfred, King of Wessex, the previous four years had proven to be as challenging as the time when he had been in open conflict with the Northern invaders; it was just that the challenges were different, although he often thought, with rueful amusement, that he would have never believed that ruling during a time of peace could be as challenging as war. In fact, in some ways, it was more difficult, because when the Saxons were fighting for their existence, things were much more straightforward; there was an enemy to defeat, on the battlefield and in the most elemental manner possible. Certainly it was true that there was a great deal of diplomacy involved in managing his Ealdormen, keeping egos in check and each of these men, all of whom were ambitious in their own right, as close to happy as it was possible for them to be, but that cause was aided in the form of a common enemy. Now that Guthrum had been subdued, and the Danes had been substantially reduced, both by force of Saxon arms and by the nature of the Danes themselves, many of whom had sailed to other lands, like Frankia, the challenges were quite different in nature.

Alfred was well aware that many of his Ealdormen believed that he was overreacting with this expedition against these Danes, but while he would never admit it, as with everything he did, Alfred had a much larger ambition than just subduing a group of Danish ships marauding along his coast. Something that his noblemen had learned about their King, who by temperament and inclination would have been happier to be a scholar, was the fact that they seldom understood until later that there was almost always a bigger design. This situation was no exception, for there was one thing that Alfred, King of Wessex, understood, that the real source of Northmen's power and what made them an existential threat was their longships, and the mobility that it gave them. It was an article of faith among those people who fought against the predations of these wild savages from the frozen lands to the North, that one would have just as much success in trying to tie a knot in a column of smoke as pinning the Northmen down in one place if they did not desire it to be so. Their ability to appear, and to disappear, without any warning and with no seeming way to stop them was one thing that made them so feared, and Alfred had reached a seemingly simple conclusion; the only way to stop them was to beat them with their own tactics.

Consequently, it was Alfred's ambition, one that was still secret at this point in the Year of our Lord 882, to command a Saxon navy that would be the match of anything the Northmen could put to sea. And, to that end, he first had to prove that they could be beaten, not on land, which he had already decisively proved at Ethantun, but on their own favored terrain of the sea. This was why Alfred was personally leading this expedition, and it was also why, under the guise of conducting business as normal, he had ordered that all of his Ealdormen remain in their domains and handle their business accordingly. This was not true with all of his senior nobility; he had actually thought about having Lord Eadwig at his side, but almost as soon as the thought came to him, he dismissed it, knowing the kind of jealousy it would arouse among the others. At his palace in Wintanceaster, he received reports from the east in Cent, where Wiglaf, who had been serving as the commander of his scouting arm, which had grown in size to number almost a hundred men, and most importantly, a fleet of small boats, manned by men who made their living fishing...and doing other things up and down the coast, sent regular reports. This was why Alfred had a certain level of confidence about not only where the Danes were located, but most importantly that, contrary to the reports that he had not only allowed to circulate but had actually spread with the help of some silver, the actual number of Danish ships was eight, or more, and not the four that he was having his men report. It was something that did bother the pious King; it ran against his grain to lie about anything, but he understood that, in order to achieve his larger goals, his subjects had to believe that there were not four hundred or more bloodthirsty Danes on the loose, but half of that number. Because of the circumstances, Alfred had taken on the mundane but important job of coordinating the preparation for this campaign that he hoped would not take long. In fact, if all went as he hoped, the actual campaign would not take as long as the preparation, and as closely as he guarded the secret of the Danes' real numbers, the fact that it would be at the very least a month, and more likely six weeks, before the man who would be his second in command deemed the Saxon force would be ready was something that only he, and that second knew.

As controversial as this would be, more than that, the identity of the man he had selected as his fleet commander would have caused Alfred unimaginable trouble and strife from his Ealdormen if they had been present. The fact that the man was a Dane, Knut Knutson, although he was more commonly known as Knut One-Eye in recognition of the disfiguring wound that he refused to hide with a patch so that there was a puckering, scarred hole where his right eye should have been, was not ideal for Alfred from a political perspective. Regardless of this, Alfred did not consider anyone else, understanding that, while there were Saxons who were competent seamen, when it came to maneuvering and fighting from a ship, only a Northman could hope to defeat one of his own. There were currently only two other Saxon lords who knew Knut's role and identity, his chief councilors Lord Mucel and Lord Eardwulf, both of whom had served the House of Wessex, beginning as a companion of Alfred's father, King Æthelwulf, then all three of Alfred's brothers for their varying reigns, although it had been Æthelred, who Alfred had succeeded, who had trusted them the most, and it was a judgment that, at least to a degree, Alfred had shared. Mucel was too cautious, even for Alfred's tastes, but he was also in his early sixties now, and it was relatively rare for a man, even of noble birth, to live to this advanced an age, while Eardwulf, slightly younger, was more aggressive, which made the pair balance each other out. However, while Alfred had not had an individual in mind, it had been Mucel who broached the idea that his King needed a seafaring Northman in a high position, subordinate only to Alfred.

"There is a Danish proverb that says that a man without a falcon must use an owl to do his hunting," Mucel, who had a habit of using witticisms and sayings, the more arcane the better, to help make his point, had begun. This was something that was usually lost on Alfred, whose mind did not run along these lines, and he had only offered Mucel a blank stare, forcing the nobleman to explain, "We Saxons are without a falcon in the sense that we do not have anyone who is as skilled at seaborne warfare as Danes or Northmen, perhaps with the exception of Ealdorman Sigeræd of Cent, but can he be trusted?"

Even before Mucel was finished, Alfred saw the sense in what the old nobleman was saying, especially about the question of the Centish Ealdorman's reliability, and he signaled his acceptance by musing aloud, "I'll send a message to Aethelstan to see what he suggests."

Mucel had learned very early on after the Treaty of Wedmore not to react when his King referred to the Dane by the Saxon name Guthrum had selected as part of his adoption by Alfred, but he shared the skepticism of the majority of Saxons of all classes that Guthrum's embrace of Christianity was sincere. Like many of his noblemen, however, Mucel had learned that Alfred was especially touchy about the matter, so his only reaction was a nod of his head, while he kept his face expressionless. As he left Alfred's presence, he also was forced to acknowledge that, so far, Guthrum had adhered to the terms of the treaty, and while it was grudging, Mucel acknowledged to himself that perhaps he had been wrong about the Dane, because four years of peace, or what passed for it during these times, was not an insignificant achievement.

With Wiltun being west of Wintanceaster, it made sense for Otha and the rest of the men provided by Ealdorman Eadwig to join the King there and accompany him to the coast, although the actual destination kept changing on a daily basis. And, just as had occurred four years earlier, Eadwig held a feast for the departing men, albeit a smaller affair for only the men and their families. This suited Titus perfectly, since it meant that he would not have to see Isolde and Hereweald again, as he was still smarting from the meeting in Wiltun, so much so that he had actually been compelled to talk to someone about it. Most people within his circle would have chosen Uhtric, because they had grown even closer over the previous four years, which was natural given that the one-eyed warrior was now his brother-in-law, but most people would have been wrong, because it was to Leofflaed that he had turned. Indeed, the only person who was not surprised was Uhtric himself, because he had seen how close his friend was to Leofflaed, going back to before they had known each other, when Titus was an overgrown child trying to understand why his father Leofric hated him with such vehemence. Titus had gone to Leofflaed about what had happened in Wiltun somewhat reluctantly, expecting to hear another lecture about how it was nothing that he did not deserve, but she was sympathetic, and while she tried to be optimistic, she was also honest.

"I don't know if you'll ever truly get over her, Titus," she had said quietly. "I think that perhaps the best that you can hope for is that you just learn to live with it, like a wound that old warriors talk about and how it bothers them on cold days."

It was not exactly what he wanted to hear, but it was still better than nothing, and while he had resolved not to drink much ale at the feast, it was due more to the fact that he had been drinking too much and did not want to spend at least the first half of their day-long ride to Wintanceaster with a sour stomach and pounding head. He had prevailed on Uhtric to retrieve the shield from Burgred in Wiltun, and once his final tasks given to him by Otha were done, he spent his time working with the shield, attaching the boss and shaving down the handle to conform to the contours of his hand, then performing the exercises out in the training yard to get a sense of how it handled compared to his old shield. To his delight, and a fair amount of surprise, while it was thicker and larger and was clearly heavier, it did not seem to be when he moved it about. At first, he suspected that Burgred had chosen a lighter wood than he had said he would use, but he quickly dismissed that, able to see as much because it was unpainted. Once he determined that he would not have to spend much time learning how to wield it effectively, he painted the shield in the colors of Thegn Otha's house, although he had to content himself with one coat, and it would have to be put on one of the carts to completely dry. The feast started earlier than normal, with barely sixty guests, but there was also a subdued mood among the people, and Titus was certain that he knew why. Now that he lived with Uhtric and Leofflaed at their small holding almost exactly halfway between Otha's and Wiltun but still within the land Otha had been given by Lord Eadwig, and while he did not like the thought of eavesdropping, in a two-room house, it was impossible not to hear their whispered conversations late at night, and the last night he had spent with them had been no exception, having decided that he would stay in Otha's hall as they made ready.

"I worry about you being at sea, that's all."

As was his habit, Uhtric usually tried to make a joke of it.

"Oh? And what about a Dane poking me with his sword? That doesn't worry you?"

Titus was certain that one of the things that Uhtric loved about his sister was that she was his match when it came to wit, and it took an effort on Titus' part not to burst out laughing when she shot back, though in a whisper, "Then you'd know how I felt being poked with your...sword...all the time! Every time I turn around, you're trying to...poke me!"

Uhtric had no need to muffle his amusement, and he roared with laughter, which prompted Leofflaed to call an apology to her brother; Titus pretended that his brother-in-law's laughter had been what woke him, but despite this humorous moment, he knew this was a real cause of concern, and not just for the families and loved ones. As the day for departure approached, what lay ahead became the overwhelming topic of conversation, not the prospect of battle against the Danes but where the fighting would take place. Since Ethantun, the Saxons who had faced the Danes no longer viewed them with the same kind of dread that had been the prevalent attitude before that victory, when they had seen the previously feared Danes and Northmen fleeing the field for their lives. Now the prospect of being out to sea, and more troubling to every one of them, out of sight of land, was what occupied their time, to the point that, while separately, both Ealdwolf and Aelfwine had gone to Otha to complain that that their duties were being interfered with because they were spending so much time answering queries from the comrades who were going with them. But all that was over now; it was the night before the departure, and Titus was doing as he had promised himself, limiting his intake of ale while trying not to think about the last departure feast he had attended, back when he had been a stableboy and had spotted what he was certain was the most beautiful girl in the world not far away from his spot at the very back of the hall, the girl sitting next to a *ceorl* he actually knew and was the first man he had met on his arrival in Wiltun, and who, along with his friend Heard, had administered a beating to the fourteen year-old at Lord Otha's order. It was later that night of the first feast that he learned that Cenric had been this girl's father, but on this night, he thanked God and all His Saints that neither the *ceorl* nor his daughter were present. And, he thought with some satisfaction, this time, he was not sitting at the rear of the hall, but was with Otha, at the Thegn*'s* table nearest to the Ealdorman's, which also put him close to Eadward, who was seated at Eadwig's right hand, the rightful place for a nobleman's heir.

Titus had not had much time to speak to Eadward, who, next to Uhtric, was Titus' closest friend, despite their social gulf, but he knew that his friend was worried about his father's decision to name Eadward as the nominal commander of the group that would be representing the Ealdorman. As had happened at the first feast, there were rituals to be observed, as the three senior Thegns swore to their Ealdorman before God that they, and their men, would acquit themselves in a manner that brought only honor to their lord, and while it was unspoken but was implicitly understood, their own names. Unlike most of his comrades, Titus did not pay close attention to the politics of Alfred's court; for men like Willmar, and to a lesser extent Leofsige, both of whom Titus knew held ambitions of their own that extended beyond serving their Thegn, their interest in the goings-on in Wintanceaster was never-ending. However, he *was* interested in why, from his viewpoint and that of the other men ultimately sworn to Ealdorman Eadwig, the King was obviously so reluctant to give their Lord what they all considered to be his due, which in their collective view was to confirm him as Ealdorman of the entire shire of Wiltscir since Lord Eadwig had been acting as Ealdorman, but had yet to receive the royal charter for the shire. To Titus, and to those comrades to whom he had spoken to about the matter, it was not just straightforward; it was a matter of simple justice. When Alfred, hiding in the swamps of Athelney after he had been forced to flee from Cippanhamm, had called the *fyrd*, Wulfhere, at the time the rightful Ealdorman of Wiltscir and by Saxon law Titus' Ealdorman and through Owin, the Thegn of Titus' home village of Cissanbyrig, had chosen to side with the Dane Guthrum.

Wulfhere's decision to ignore their King was why young Titus had walked all the way from his father's farm to Wiltun, because Lord Eadwig, who was only the Lord of Wiltun at the time, had defied Wulfhere and been loyal to his King, despite the fact that Alfred was confined to a pestilential marsh and significantly outnumbered, with only a veritable handful of loyal adherents. It had been, every member of every class had acknowledged, a brave and noble thing for Eadwig to do; he was defying his Ealdorman, even if it was for his King, but while nobody would admit as much, most men had not given Alfred much of a chance to defeat the mighty Danes, even those men like Lord Mucel who had remained loyal. And, as was now known across the island, in the far north and even across the sea to Irland, Alfred had won a resounding victory, one in which Eadwig had played a minor but pivotal role. Consequently, to not just his men, but to those around him, it made sense that Eadwig be rewarded by being named Ealdorman of the entire shire, and not just Wiltun and the surrounding area. In fact, there was some disagreement about whether Eadwig should be considered an Ealdorman at all; granted, he was more than a Thegn by any practical measurement, but for reasons that could only be speculated about, the King had seemed content to leave things as they were. Nevertheless, the evening progressed in a traditional manner, although when it came time to end the feast, the only ones who were roaring drunk were the men like Osric who would be remaining behind, but when Titus, astride Thunor, began taking the fork that would take him along with the rest of Otha's party back to the Thegn's hall, while Uhtric and Leofflaed headed in the opposite direction to their home, it was Leofflaed who stopped him.

"You should come with us," she said casually.

"Why?" Titus asked in surprise, and she replied tartly, as if the answer was obvious, "Why, to see your nephew, of course!"

"But I'll see Wiglaf in the morning!" Titus protested; he had convinced himself that a good night's sleep was the best thing for him, and he did treasure his slumber.

It was actually Uhtric who spoke, saying apologetically, "I promised him that we'd bring you with us tonight."

"And you know how he is when he doesn't get what he wants," Leofflaed pointed out, and her tone was all she needed for Titus to understand the unspoken part there, that his nephew was simply behaving in the same manner as her brother had when he was Wiglaf's age. "Do you really want to subject me to that?"

The truth was that he was tempted to risk his sister's wrath; now that the idea had been planted in his mind, he *really* wanted to sleep.

What came out of his mouth was a grumbled, "No, I suppose not. Besides," he knew he sounded petulant, but he did not care all that much, "you'd never let me forget it anyway."

Consequently, the remaining ride was mostly silent, although neither Uhtric nor Leofflaed seemed to mind all that much, and because of the darkness, Titus missed the several conspiratorial glances the couple exchanged, although he did catch Uhtric grinning for no apparent reason. He was about to comment on it, but it occurred to him that it was probably because of what the couple planned to be doing in the immediate future, and he was in no mood to hear about it. Titus had not lain with a woman since Aslaug, and it was beginning to wear on him, although he had a vaguely formed plan to correct that, maybe as soon as Wintanceaster, depending on how long they were going to be there. It was only as they rode into the yard that something else occurred to Titus; he would have to get up even earlier than planned to ride back to Otha's to pick up the gear that he would be carrying on his person, although his pack was already loaded in the lone wagon that would accompany the party, along with the two carts. This soured his mood even more, but he was completely unprepared for what was coming when, after Uhtric dismounted, then helped Leofflaed down from her mare, his brother-in-law abruptly thrust the reins of their two animals at Titus.

More out of a reflex action than anything, Titus accepted them, but then Uhtric said, "Will you stable the horses, Titus?"

"Why? Where's Gunni?"

Gunni was the eleven-year-old Norse slave that had been a gift to Uhtric on his name day from both Leofflaed and Titus, and one of his duties, aside from chopping wood, was tending the animals.

"He's watching Wiglaf, of course!" Leofflaed replied, making it sound as if it was an absurd question.

"Well, have him come do it," Titus shot back, his bewilderment rapidly turning to irritation, something that the couple had known would be a possibility even under the best of circumstances.

"He's...busy right now," Leofflaed said, and Uhtric had to hide a wince at how lame this sounded, nor was he surprised that Titus was completely unimpressed.

"Nothing he's doing is that important, so call him so that I can kiss my nephew good night then get to sleep. Since," he glowered at his sister, "I have to get up earlier to go back to Lord Otha's!"

"Titus," Uhtric's tone was almost gentle, "please, would you just trust me? Take the horses into the barn. I swear that you won't regret it."

While he was still irritated, Titus was now curious enough that he did not argue any longer, leading the animals into the barn, although he was grumbling as he did it. He peered into the darkness but saw nothing that offered any indication of something out of the ordinary, and while he heard straw rustling, he assumed that it was either the milk cow, oxen, or one of the pigs or their packhorse. Very quickly, he became absorbed in the task of unsaddling the horses, doing it by feel because of the utter darkness, not that it impeded or slowed him down in any way. Of all the places where fire was forbidden, a stable was at the top of the list, and especially during the winter months when daylight was in such short supply, anyone who worked in one learned to do it in the dark. Aside from the soft crunching sound of one of the horses he had just unsaddled munching on some hay, it had fallen silent, so Titus was completely unprepared for the relative quiet to be shattered; that it was a voice, and a feminine one at that did not lessen his shock.

"Titus?"

He heard his sharp cry of surprise, but while it would have embarrassed him normally, during the eyeblink of time it took for him to spin about in the direction of the voice, his mind identified it. Regardless of his recognition, watching Isolde materializing out of the gloom wrenched a gasp from his lips.

"W-what are you doing here?" Suddenly, another thought occurred to him, and he scowled as he swiveled his head, searching the barn as he demanded, "Where is he? Is Hereweald here?"

"He doesn't know I'm here," Isolde replied softly, but while she had walked closely enough for Titus to just make out her features, she got no closer.

It's as if, he thought suddenly, she's waiting for me to do something.

Instead of moving, he asked bluntly, "Why are you here?"

"I...I don't know, really," she answered haltingly. "It's just that, when I woke up this morning, all I could think of was that you were leaving...and I may never see you again."

A part of Titus wanted to desperately say something else, but what came out of his mouth was a cold, "And? You'll be married *when* I come back!"

This served to rouse Isolde's temper, and she snapped, "And why am I marrying another man, Titus? Because," she was the one who moved then, taking a step to stand in front of Titus then poking him in the chest with her pointing finger, "you chose to lay with Aslaug! So don't you try and blame me for this!" Before he could respond, she dropped her voice to mutter, "I knew this was a mistake."

She stepped away from him, then began to move past Titus; his anger and his hurt were swept away by a torrent of what was close to panic at the thought that she was walking out of this barn, and as confident as he was in his abilities as a warrior, he also knew that it was a distinct possibility that she was right, that he would never see her again, so he reached out and grabbed her arm.

"Wait." He tried to make it a command, but feeling her pull her arm from his grasp, he was forced to plead, "Don't go! Please?"

She obeyed, turning slowly back to face him; neither of them uttered an intelligible word for the next several hours.

While it was from a different cause than a hangover, Titus' mind was in some ways even more occupied the next day by the events of the night before than if he had been absorbed in physical misery. He was also feeling the effects of not getting any sleep, although he had no regrets about that. What troubled him was what the night before had meant, although Isolde had been very clear, and had been so before they made love for the first time.

"This will never happen again," she had said, and in a tone that he recognized as the one Isolde used when her mind was made up. "And we will never speak of it when we see each other again."

As Titus thought about it the next day, despite the nature of their conversation and its seriousness, he still grinned to himself as he had the night before.

"Wait," he had held up a hand, "I thought you said you might not be seeing me again. So, which is it?"

Because of the darkness, it was the memory of the sound of her laughing that made Titus grin the next day, which Uhtric, who was riding next to him noticed, but guessing correctly that it had to do with the night before, looked away without comment, a smile of his own on his face.

It had been so...natural, Titus thought as they rode, but while it was *almost* as if nothing unpleasant had happened, there was something there that told him that things had indeed changed between them, and he was certain Isolde felt the same way. Titus also learned that Uhtric and Leofflaed had not only known about Isolde's plan to visit beforehand, his sister had had

Uhtric move the milk cow out of its stall, then spread fresh sweet hay, which was covered with blankets. They had begun kissing while they were still standing, but Isolde, who knew about the stall, led Titus there, and they lay down, helping each other pull their clothes off.

Titus knew that he should not bring it up, but he could not help himself from asking, "Have you and Hereweald made love yet?"

He had his arms around her when he asked, and she felt her stiffen, but after a heartbeat of silence, he felt her relax and she admitted, "No. But," she sounded almost defiant, "we've done...other things."

Relieved and amused in almost equal measure, Titus echoed her teasingly, "'Other things'? What other things? Not...*that* thing?"

As he expected, he did not need to elaborate, while Isolde was relieved that it was dark so that he could not see her blushing furiously as she agreed, "No, not...*that*." She hesitated, then added shyly, "That was only for you."

As Titus got older, and more experienced, he would learn that, contrary to what most men claimed, when it came to oral sex, their steadfast insistence that they were only the recipients and never the givers of oral pleasure was one of the biggest lies they told each other, but at this moment, he was still of an age that he accepted this. With Isolde, it was the opposite, at least in the sense that women were not shy about disabusing the younger members of their gender what big, fat liars men were when it came to that act, but it was something she never intended to share with Titus, or Hereweald for that matter. Yes, she was marrying the young smith, and she would be faithful, but she had already accepted that their union would never have the same passion, the same depth of feeling, or the sense of wanton abandonment that she felt whenever she was with Titus, but neither could she bring herself to forgive him for his betrayal. Maybe, she would think, if it had been anyone but Aslaug, she could have, but it had not been, and now here she was, in a barn, giving this man she knew she would love until her last breath the one gift that she could offer him that demonstrated the depth of her love, even as she was determined that this would be the last time. Like every person of both genders of her class, Isolde was uneducated, and everything she knew about the nature of sin and redemption came from the priests; in her case, it was from Father Cerdic, who was as illiterate as she was but had the advantage of having memorized the Mass and the catechism, at least to a reasonable degree of accuracy. Despite her lack of education, Isolde was intelligent; as Cenric liked to say, she had a quick mind, she did not miss anything, and she did not suffer fools, so despite what Father Cerdic said, she refused to believe that what she felt for Titus, and the fact she was willing to make love to him on this night, was wrong in any sense of the word, and that God would forgive the both of them. They made love four times that night, dozing in between, both of them treasuring the sensation of closeness as much as the actual carnal acts. For Isolde, it was savoring the feeling of safety she experienced nestled in the crook of Titus' huge arm, with her head resting on his massive chest, and while she did feel a pang of guilt, it was actually from the sense of satisfaction that she got as she silently compared Hereweald's physique with Titus'. Hereweald was certainly muscular; being a smith required a level of strength over that of the average *ceorl*, but Titus was, and always had been since she first laid eyes on him, in a class unto himself. It was more than just his sheer mass, she knew, although she could not place her finger on exactly what it was. Perhaps it was how he moved, with a lithe grace that bespoke an ability that, in their society, was valued far more than the skill with a hammer and forge. Whatever it was, it seemed to emanate from him, even as he lay there in almost total darkness, in a light doze.

Titus' thoughts, such as they were, ran along similar lines, if for different but related reasons; the idea that what he was doing with Isolde was wrong did not even occur to him, but he was as certain as she was about him that she was a singular being, one that he would never encounter again, and while he hid it, he was filled with sadness. Oh, a part of him hoped that Isolde would roll over, tell him that she had forgiven him, and that she would break off her marriage to Hereweald and wait for him to return, then they would be wed, just as he had always believed they would, almost from the first night he had seen her in Lord Eadwig's hall. He also knew that it was too late, that Leofflaed had been right; he had hurt Isolde in a way that could not be repaired, and even if she convinced herself that she had forgiven Titus, the hurt would always be there, just under the surface. Worst of all, he knew that there would be moments where he would see it in her eyes; it was the thought of this that fueled his understanding that they would never be together after this night. Shortly before dawn, he rose, explaining that he had to return to Otha's to prepare for their departure, and they shared one last kiss before he mounted Thunor. It took a massive effort on his part not to look back over his shoulder as he rode away.

It had been three years since Titus had been to Wintanceaster, but he had heard of the changes the King had ordered made; seeing them, however, was something else entirely. The fact that they were still more than two miles away when the newly constructed higher, stouter walls were visible told Titus more about the scale of Alfred's ambitions than anything else.

"He learned his lesson," was Uhtric's comment.

"I heard that he's planning on fortifying every town," Willmar remarked. "A ditch and wall for every one of them."

Titus listened, and while he had no reason to doubt Willmar, he found it hard to believe that this was true. Certainly, Wiltun was large enough to deserve that level of protection, and either on his own, or perhaps at King Alfred's order, Lord Eadwig had ordered a wall constructed around the town two years before, but he could not imagine the same for Cissanbyrig. He had not been back since he had retrieved Leofflaed and Eadgyd and burned down his father's miserable shack in the process, but he could not fathom the village of his birth being considered important enough to warrant the kind of effort it would require to construct anything like this level of fortification. As always happened, and despite his best efforts to avoid it, thinking of Cissanbyrig inevitably led to thoughts of his father Leofric, although there had been no word about his whereabouts for more than a year, when he had been spotted in Cippanhamm by Uhtric, who had been in the town delivering a horse to a local merchant. Leofric and Uhtric had seen each other simultaneously, and Uhtric had related how Leofric's reaction was to turn and flee, ducking down an alley and vanishing.

"The thing is," Uhtric had related with a laugh, "I didn't have any intention of speaking to him, let alone chase him."

"He's a coward and a thief," Titus had replied sourly. "That's what they do."

Uhtric knew it was a sensitive subject, but he still felt compelled to comment, "Better that it was me who saw him than you, eh?"

Titus' response was just a grim nod, but he had struggled with that question for the previous four years. After all, he had sworn an oath, in front of witnesses, that if they crossed paths again, Titus would kill Leofric, but while he knew that his sisters not only did not fault him for making such a bloodcurdling promise against their father, and in fact would not have judged him at fault if he did, it still bothered Titus. What he had never shared, not even with Isolde, was that what worried him was his complete lack of feeling whenever he thought about the prospect of plunging his blade into his father's body and ending Leofric's life. To Titus, it was straightforward; a son killing his father was not a natural thing, so that son should feel *something* at the prospect, some sort of remorse or regret, but that simply was not the case for Titus. In fact, his concern about this lack of feeling in himself was based in nothing but practical considerations, especially since his killing of Hrodulf; he could not expect to be allowed to go around killing other men with impunity, even if he did have some pretext for doing so, and he worried that, without any deep-seated sense of remorse about what the Church taught was one of the most serious mortal sins, just the practical issues would not be enough to stop him. However, that was also a problem for tomorrow, and it might not ever come up, he told himself, although he did not really believe it.

Eadward was as preoccupied as Titus, albeit for entirely different reasons, and he had wasted most of the day's ride putting off the conversation that he had resolved to have with

Otha, but it was the sight of the walls of Wintanceaster that prompted him to draw up and wait for the Thegn to reach him. For his part, Otha did not seem surprised, either at how Eadward had spent the ride avoiding him or his sudden appearance now that their journey was almost completed.

"My father said that we're to go directly to the King's palace," Eadward said without preamble, but all he got from Otha was a nod, igniting a stab of irritation in the young nobleman, having forgotten that Otha had been present when his father had given Eadward the order. That irritation was complicated by Eadward's other problem when dealing with Otha, that he viewed the Thegn in some ways as even more of a father figure than his true sire, understandable since Otha had been his primary tutor in arms, and by extension, what it meant to be a warrior.

He cleared his throat once, then another time, until it was Otha who lost patience, snapping, "What is it, Lord? Come on, spit it out!"

How, Eadward thought ruefully, can he make "Lord" sound like an insult?

Aloud, he said with as much authority as he could muster, "When we meet the King, I'm to be the one who speaks for us, as the representative of my father the Ealdorman."

"Yes," Otha answered dryly, "I am aware of that. Your father made it very clear."

"I...I just wanted to make sure that you remembered," Eadward stammered, almost wincing at how he knew this sounded.

"I know that I'm old, my Lord," Otha replied with a biting sarcasm, "but my mind hasn't completely deserted me."

"Oh, I didn't mean to imply that it had," Eadward protested, only realizing after he said it that Otha had been having some fun at his expense. With a growing sense of desperation, he blurted out, "Otha, if I'm being honest, I'm not any happier with my father than you are."

This caught Otha completely by surprise, although he hid it well, only regarding Eadward with a raised eyebrow, knowing the young man well and how, if he kept his mouth shut, Eadward would blurt out the cause for his own discontent soon enough. He was rewarded when, exhaling a long breath before doing so, Eadward continued, "I may be young, and in some ways I might be foolish, but I'm not a fool, Otha. I have no business making any decisions that might endanger the men." He had been looking straight ahead over the ears of his horse, a roan stallion that was the original Thunor's replacement, named Liegitu (Lightning), but he turned to look directly at Otha as he finished quietly, "But at the same time, I *am* the Ealdorman's son and heir, so I have a proposal."

This deepened Otha's surprise, and he asked cautiously, "And what is that?"

"That whenever possible, we'll consult beforehand about what I might be expected to decide in my capacity, and all I'll be doing is relaying your orders."

This not only mollified Otha, it impressed and relieved him in equal measure because, unknown to the young lordling, Otha had been happy to be left alone by Eadward during their ride as he wrestled with exactly how to say essentially the same thing while making it sound like a suggestion.

"That," he answered gravely, "is a very wise decision, Lord Eadward." However, while this was a sound solution as far as it went, Otha had given it as much thought as Eadward, and he pointed out, "But we won't always be in a situation where we can discuss matters beforehand."

"I've thought of that," Eadward answered quickly, and proved that he had by saying, "but that's going to be in battle, and despite our different...stations," was the word he settled on rather than "rank", "...you are far more experienced than I am. In fact," he added, congratulating himself for this act of diplomacy, "I daresay there's only a handful of men more experienced in war than you are, so it would only be natural that I defer to you."

With every word Eadward spoke, Otha was more impressed, and while it was politic to say so, it was not in the Thegn's nature to speak just to hear his own voice, or to curry favor, which Eadward knew, making this a moment he would long remember.

"You've got an old head on those young shoulders," Otha said the words lightly. Then he added an assurance that was a major cause of Eadward's hesitance, "And this will be something your father never needs to know."

He did try, but Eadward was unsuccessful in hiding his relief, slumping a bit in the saddle, and more to change the subject, he asked abruptly, "How's Titus?"

While he had expected the subject of Titus to come up at some point and had given it a fair amount of thought, Otha still took a moment to consider the question carefully before replying, "I'd be more worried about him if we were still back in Wiltun, Lord. As long as Isolde and that smith's son are there, I'm not sure how long he would have lasted without killing him. Now," he shrugged, "he's got other men to kill, and that may be just what he needs right now."

It was not only an astute observation, Eadward reflected, but it aligned with his own thoughts exactly. For a brief instant, Eadward actually thought about the poor Danes who were destined to cross Titus' path, but he felt not a flicker of pity for any of them. The dogs were marauding in Saxon lands, and they would pay for that, and Eadward could not think of anyone he would rather have near him in a fight than his friend, especially at sea.

In the intervening days since Alfred had summoned the warriors that he would use to drive off the Danes, Wiglaf had been sending reports back, and with this information, the King believed he was beginning to determine a pattern in the Danish predations. More importantly, he was growing more certain that, at most, there were no more than eight or perhaps nine Danish longboats, which did not suit his purposes at all, and only Wiglaf, who was literate and used a special code devised by Alfred, along with Lord Mucel, Lord Eardwulf, and Alfred's personal chaplain Father Aethelred knew the truth. Alfred was often accused of being parsimonious, an accusation that he would have denied, although he would admit to being careful with money, but while he bridled at doing so, he had been liberal in spreading silver around to perpetuate the idea that there were only four Danish longboats, or perhaps six but no more. However, this also created another dilemma, because if that was true, then it meant that he had to raise a force that would at the very least match the Danes in numbers or it would arouse suspicions. Helping his cause was that only part of his force was meeting in Wintanceaster, while the men sworn to the noblemen of Sussex and Cent were going to meet him downriver at Hamtun (Southampton). He had given all of the Ealdormen the number of men he expected from each of them, and five days to prepare. Because of the distance between Wiltun and Wintanceaster, he knew that the contingent of men sent by Lord Eadwig would be the first to arrive from the shires to the west, while those men sent by Ealdorman Odda would not arrive for another two days. The Thegn sent by Cuthred of Hampscir, Bede, was already present in Wintanceaster, with thirty men, while the men from Cent and Sussex coming to Hamtun would be coming by sea from the east. This was the topic of the meeting that Alfred was holding with Knut One-Eye, attended by Alfred's council and Ealdorman Cuthred, along with the two Danes Knut had named as his second and third in command, and at his own stubborn insistence, Cyneweard, the commander of Alfred's personal bodyguard, who would be providing the rest of the fighting men of Wessex.

Alfred was not afraid of Knut, not because of any belief that his skill at fighting would protect him, but because there would be no profit in his death for Knut, who would be cut down immediately, and Danes were not known for self-sacrifice for political ends. Also, it had been four years since the Treaty, and the Dane formerly known as Guthrum had proven to be reliable in upholding his part of it, at least for the most part. Most importantly, the Danes had retreated north and east of the borderline that had been agreed upon along Watling Street, and aside from an occasional raid emanating from the region that was now called the Danelaw, mostly into Mercia, things had been peaceful. This was why, consequently, when Guthrum; even Alfred still privately thought of him as Guthrum and not by his adoptive name of Aethelstan, had sent a messenger swearing that these Danish marauders were not from the Danelaw, but from across the sea in Frankia, where a portion of The Great Heathen Army had now settled as they ravaged those lands, he was inclined to believe him. When Alfred had sent his urgent request to Guthrum for assistance, he had sent Lord

Eardwulf to deliver the message personally, and his councilor had stressed that providing that assistance would help assuage Alfred's suspicions that these raiders were operating with Guthrum's knowledge, if not his blessing, which Eardwulf had put diplomatically, of course. There had actually been two requests by the Saxon king; the first being sending at least ten Danes who were experienced seamen and fighters, and the second that at least half of them spoke English. Knut One-Eye did speak the Saxon tongue...after a fashion, and at this moment, he was explaining his idea to Alfred.

"When will men arrive?" he asked, and Alfred, through fits and starts, explained that his entire force would not be arriving all at once, but that he expected at least twenty-five men from Wiltun at literally any moment, but it was unlikely that more would be arriving that day.

While Alfred had never explained the relationships and roles of the other Saxons present, the Dane had turned and addressed Ealdorman Cuthred.

"Your men already here, yes?"

Cuthred's features darkened, clearly not liking the peremptory tone of the Dane, but he was wise enough to not make an issue of it, although he matched Knut, answering curtly, "I'm providing our Lord King with thirty men."

"That will be enough," Knut said with satisfaction.

"Enough for what?"

"To provide one crew to leave now to go to Hamtun," he explained. "They will make ships waiting there ready to sail."

Cuthred was the one who responded with obvious surprise, exclaiming, "I thought their crews would already have been hard at work with that!"

Since his attention was on the Dane, the Ealdorman missed the glance that Alfred exchanged with Mucel and Eardwulf, although it was unlikely that he would have interpreted their meaning. And, Alfred had every intention of explaining to the Ealdorman why they had done so, but this was when there was a rapping on the door to the King's council chambers, which Cyneweard hurried to answer.

Returning quickly, he announced, "Lord Eadward of Wiltun and Thegn Otha have arrived, Lord King, and are awaiting your pleasure."

This, Alfred thought, complicates things, but he did not hesitate to have them ushered in, deciding in the moment that he might as well handle what was likely to be unhappy news all at once. While he had no need to do so, Alfred rose from his throne; the truth was that he hated sitting in the thing because it was uncomfortable, but he also understood what was expected of him, especially when dealing with men like this Knut.

Accepting the two Saxons' bow with a nod of his head, Alfred said with only partially feigned joviality, and with honesty, "Eadward, I swear that you've grown since Yule!"

As he expected, this made the young man blush with pleasure, who replied, "My mother said the same thing, Lord King. But," he added ruefully, "she was complaining because I've already outgrown the tunic she made for me."

Alfred laughed, but he was already turning to Otha, whose expression, he saw, might have been a match for the Dane who was standing there, studying the pair of Saxons. Neither of these men want to be anywhere near this place, Alfred thought with amusement, while aloud he welcomed Otha, unknowingly echoing something Eadward had said not long before.

"Otha, I can think of few men I would rather have at my side than you for what lies ahead."

"Thank you, Lord King," Otha bowed again, but while Alfred was not overly familiar with the Thegn, despite his impassive expression, Alfred was certain that the warrior was pleased at the compliment. Which, he thought, is good, because his pleasure is not going to last long.

Alfred, now at the age of thirty-four and having been King of Wessex for more than a decade, had learned how, with even the slightest modulation of his voice, he could send a message to those under his rule, and he employed this technique now, asking out of seeming curiosity, "And, is the Berserker marching with you?"

He watched Otha and Eadward exchange a glance, but Otha offered the younger nobleman a barely perceptible nod, and it was he who answered, "Yes, Lord King. Titus is with us."

"Good," Alfred nodded, but he hardened his voice, not much but enough to be noticeable. "If he's going to wantonly kill men, I would rather it was not one of my subjects."

Otha knew that the wise course was to simply keep his mouth shut, but he heard himself protesting, "While he did kill the man Hrodulf, Lord King, it wasn't without provocation."

"Provocation?" Alfred asked, raising an eyebrow. "What kind of provocation?"

"He was accused of raping a local girl, Lord King," Eadward interjected quietly. "But it was not true."

What neither of them knew was that Alfred was aware of the circumstances of what had taken place in Wiltun; he had even been told the girl's name, although he could not remember it at the moment, but he feigned surprise.

"Oh? So he didn't touch this maiden?"

As he expected, this made the pair begin shifting uncomfortably, although it was Otha who acknowledged, "No, Lord King. They...lay together."

"Out of wedlock?" Alfred demanded coldly. "Are you saying Titus lay with this...person before they enjoyed the sacrament of marriage as required by Holy Church for man and woman to lay together?"

Why, Otha thought miserably, did I open my mouth? Once they left the palace, Eadward would demand to know the same thing, but in the moment, neither of them possessed the words that would extricate either of them from this predicament, and they both knew it.

Finally, it was Eadward, understanding that just standing there mutely would not suffice, who conceded, "No, Lord King. They were not married."

"Where is the woman now?" Alfred demanded, and this time, he was asking sincerely.

While he had neither the time nor the interest in keeping track of every wanton slut who thought they could trap a man by opening their legs, he nevertheless did not like the thought that a woman like that was out and about, wandering Wessex and seeking to ensnare another man. And, he admitted silently, and as he had observed firsthand when he met the fourteen-year-old Titus of Cissanbyrig then heard about his exploits, there was something about the youngster, over and above his size and strength, that marked him as a man of exceptional abilities, provided, of course, he survived, and at this moment, that was questionable given Alfred's admittedly little interaction with the large, young Saxon. Whether or not it would be because he fell in battle, or his fortune finally ran out and he killed the wrong man in a drunken brawl in an alehouse over a woman, only God knew.

"She fled Wiltun, Lord King," Eadward answered honestly. "And we have not seen her since."

"Well," Alfred decided he had spent enough time on this subject, "if I have the time, I will be having a conversation with young Titus the Berserker about his behavior." Looking directly at Otha, he said quietly, "Make sure you tell him that."

Otha assured him that he would, and Alfred then moved on to the next subject, the one that he had secretly been putting off with his query about Titus, although as he expected, it was Ealdorman Cuthred who had the strongest reaction, requiring Alfred to finally assert his authority as King before Cuthred subsided. Neither Eadward nor Otha were any happier, Alfred could plainly see, but they were content to keep their mouths shut and let their social superior bear the brunt of their King's displeasure.

Chapter Three

"When should we tell them?" Eadward asked Otha, and it took an effort for Otha not to groan aloud, mainly because he had been certain that the younger man would ask him, but Otha still dreaded the question.

The fact that Otha did not have a ready answer did not help matters.

More thinking aloud than providing an answer, Otha responded, "We're to be down at the docks at first light. Maybe we should tell them then and let them enjoy their night in Wintanceaster."

"But if we don't tell them beforehand, we're going to have to explain why we're not letting them get drunk and go whoring," Eadward objected, and while this made Otha curse, it was because Eadward was right.

Regardless, he was still not willing to capitulate, pointing out, "But if we tell them right away, then we're going to have to listen to them all night. And no," he acknowledged, "they won't be drunk...but they will be angry, and they'll let us know about it."

Eadward did not reply; there was, he thought miserably, no good answer. Since they had not known any details of where the men were going to be housed, or for how long, for that matter, they had left them at the western gate, which was now in sight, their men dismounted and standing in a huddled mass around the wagon and carts. He was about to suggest that they stop and duck down a side street to discuss the matter further when he saw Willmar suddenly turn in their direction. Even worse, he clearly saw the pair because he raised a hand in a signal that he had seen him.

"Fuck us all," Otha muttered.

To Eadward, this made his decision for him and he braced himself, but when they reached the others, he found himself calling out, "I know a good alehouse and inn not far from here, and that's where we're going next! The first round is on me!"

Ignoring Otha's glare, Eadward led the way to the Hart and Hound, which had the distinction of being the favored establishment by young Eadward, mainly because it was the only one he knew, and he knew it through his father. The fact that it was also a brothel and was the one both father and son frequented whenever they traveled to Wintanceaster, which was about four times a year, made it a very popular choice, at least at first.

"You said you're buying the first round," Otha muttered to Eadward as they led the boisterous men deeper into the city. "How many rounds do you plan on letting them drink?"

Eadward shrugged, clearly not having considered it, then offered, "Two? Or three?"

"And when are you going to tell them?" Otha demanded, earning him a startled glance from Eadward.

Before he answered, Eadward glanced over his shoulder, but saw that their men were too occupied in boasting to each other about how much drinking and whoring they would be doing to pay attention.

"What do you mean, when am *I* going to tell them? I thought we would both tell them."

This earned him a laugh and a shake of the head from Otha.

"Your father was very clear, Lord. You're in command, and it's the commander's duty to keep his men informed."

It was what Eadward had expected to hear, but he still made a face, then in a tacit acceptance, asked, "Which do you think I should tell them first?"

Now Otha faltered a step, just a matter of a dozen paces from the entrance to the Hart and Hound, the grin vanishing from his face, turning into a grimace as he thought about it.

It was, he realized, a good and not unimportant question; and, Otha thought sourly, there was no good answer, which was why he said with a shrug, "Flip a coin, Lord. That's what I do for important decisions when you're fucked no matter what you decide."

Eadward did not find any humor in the thought, but he also realized this was likely what he would do. Then they were at the door, which he pulled open, and, with a smile as false as that of the proprietor who had been alerted to the arrival of a large party of armed warriors, waved the men inside, exchanging banter with each of them, most of them joking about how thirsty they were. There was only one exception, and while Titus returned his friend's grin, he did not say anything, and Eadward gave Uhtric, who was just behind Titus, an inquiring look, but the one-eyed warrior could only offer a shrug. The owner, long experienced in dealing with rowdy warriors, led Eadward and his men to a separate room that was almost as large as the main one that he reserved for the highborn and men for whom violence was not just a profession but their preferred method of handling potential disputes. Very quickly, cups of ale were brought, and Eadward told himself that he would let them down this one before he broached the two pieces of information that they had learned from their King. Since each table only seated four men, and like warriors of all nations, Eadward's men congregated with those they felt closest to, it meant that Titus, Uhtric, Aelfwine, and Hrothgar were seated at one table, although as the night progressed, there would be some movement as men circulated around the tables.

Waiting until Aelfwine and Hrothgar became absorbed in their own conversation, a long-running debate on the merits of one of the whores back in Wiltun, Uhtric said lightly, "You didn't talk much on the ride." With a grin, he added, "I'll wager I know why."

Titus gave his friend a wan smile, then understanding some sort of response was expected, he replied half-jokingly, "I suppose I'm still a bit tired."

"I can imagine." Uhtric laughed. He was torn, extremely curious about Titus' night because, while he had no intention of telling his friend, he *had* made a wager, but with Leofflaed.

"After a night with Titus, Isolde is going to change her mind," he had assured his wife confidently. "She's going to forgive him, and when we get back, they'll marry."

"Oh? And what makes you say that?" Leofflaed challenged, although she suspected she knew.

Her guess was confirmed by Uhtric's broad grin as he replied, "It may have been a while, but you've seen him naked! There's no way that Hereweald's...hammer...is that mighty!"

He had roared with laughter at his own wit, and even

Leofflaed giggled, but she shot back, "You men think that the only thing that matters is the size of your...*hammer*," she scoffed, "but the way you swing it is just as important." They shared the laugh, but then she sobered a bit to warn Uhtric, "And I'm not so sure that just a night with Titus will be enough to mend what he broke, no matter how mighty his hammer."

"I'll wager you a new piece of jewelry that I'm right," Uhtric had replied.

"And what would I have to give up?" Leofflaed asked, clearly suspicious, but Uhtric just laughed again.

"Nothing that you aren't already going to give me when I come home."

Now, sitting in the alehouse, Uhtric was eager to hear if his judgment was going to be confirmed and he would win what was the most important thing, the right to crow to his wife that he had been right for once.

"So?" he pressed. "Did you do *any* talking?"

"Some," Titus admitted, but this time, his grin was a bit broader. "Not much, but some."

"And?"

Titus sighed, realizing now what Uhtric was really asking, and while it caused another stab of pain, he answered honestly, "And she's still marrying Hereweald."

"*What*?" Uhtric exclaimed, much louder than he intended, with heads turning in their direction, and this and Titus' glare caused him to lower his voice to ask, "But...why?"

It was Titus who looked a bit uncomfortable now, which was explained by his admission. "I didn't ask." Before Uhtric could say anything, he added in a tone that his friend interpreted immediately, "That's all I'm going to talk about it...ever, Uhtric."

Trying to hide his disappointment lest Titus start to ask some questions of his own, Uhtric nodded. Fortunately, he was saved by Lord Eadward, who had finally decided it was time to break the news. That was, at least, his intention; by the time he was through, all his men knew was that their night was going to be cut short early because they would be leaving for Hamtun at first light, although he did not say why. It did put a damper on the evening, but when the young nobleman was pressed for more information, he made his excuses, disappearing to procure rooms for the night for the men, leaving Otha to glare at him, but the Thegn had refused to divulge anything to Ceadda or Aelfnod, so he was not about to say anything to the rest of them. There was a great deal of grumbling, but it did not amount to anything, and of all of them, Titus was thankful for the chance to get some sleep at last.

The first indication to the men that there were things they had not been told was that, along with Cuthred's men, there was a party of a dozen Northmen waiting at the southern gate, all of them astride the small ponies that they favored, yet despite their best attempts, Lord Eadward still refused to offer any explanation. Otha's men could tell by their Thegn's behavior that he knew at least part of the story, while Ceadda and Aelfnod looked as angry and bewildered as they felt. It was Titus who had the idea of enlisting Hakon, the Danish slave who had driven the wagon and who, somewhat unusually, Titus considered a friend because of the bond they had formed during the Ethantun campaign, to ferret out the truth.

"You can at least find out if they're Danes or Norsemen," Titus had said. With a grin, he added, "Especially now that you look more like a Saxon than a Dane."

Hakon had returned the smile, readily admitting, "That is all Enflaed's doing." The smile faded, and he glanced over to where Eadward was standing, speaking to the Thegn who served Ealdorman Cuthred and was commanding the Hampshire contingent, and there was no mistaking the anxiety in Hakon's voice. "Will you make certain that Lord Eadward knows that I'm doing what you asked me to?"

"I will," Titus assured the Dane. "Don't worry about him."

Satisfied, Hakon promised, "I will think of something to get close to them...Titus."

It had been a chore to get Hakon to stop calling Titus "Master," but Titus had also accepted that Hakon would only do so when they were out of earshot of other Saxons because of an incident a year after Ethantun when a visiting nobleman had taken offense at the Dane's familiarity with the young Saxon warrior. Despite the fact that Hakon had been addressing Titus and not the nobleman had made no difference, while Ealdorman Eadwig, who had invited the man to Wiltun with an eye towards forging an alliance, had proven deaf to Titus' pleas, having Hakon flogged, although without the scourge. Unfortunately, Eadward had not been much better; it had taken Titus administering Eadward a thrashing, albeit under the guise of a sparring session, to convince him to treat Hakon at least a modicum better than his father did. As far as why Titus felt this connection to the Danish slave, he honestly could not have articulated, although he came close when Isolde had questioned him on why he had been willing to risk his friendship with Eadward who was, by any measure, a better and more important friend to have than a Dane who had been born a slave, owned by his own people. Certainly, their time when Titus had been the stableboy, assisting the grotesquely fat Dudda up until his slaughter at the ambush on the way to Egbert's Stone, and Hakon had been such a help played a role, but it was more than that. Hakon and his circumstances had opened Titus' eyes to what was in reality a far more complicated dynamic than he had believed when he was nothing more than the son of a one-hide *ceorl* in Cissanbyrig. Everything had been simpler then; the Danes, and their Norse cousins, were bloodthirsty pagan marauders who drank the blood of babies, raped nuns, and were the despoilers of all good things in this world. The fact that Ealdorman Eadwig had acquired Hakon, not through battle, but as a far more mundane transaction, with Eadwig selling cattle and receiving Hakon and a couple of other Danish slaves in trade, had shaken Titus to his core, it never even crossing his mind as a possibility that two sworn foes like the Saxons and Northmen could conduct routine business.

Their conversation was interrupted by Eadward, who shouted the command to mount their horses, while Hakon hurried to their wagon, joining the pair of wagons belonging to Ealdorman Cuthred's men, prompting a spirited disagreement between Eadward and the Thegn, who Titus had heard called Bede, about who would lead the column out of Wintanceaster. The quarrel was settled when one of the Northmen, a one-eyed brute who was not Titus' size but was close, kicked his absurdly small pony and, followed by his countrymen, led the way out of the gate. Normally, neither Titus nor any of his comrades would have appreciated this effrontery, but this time was different, and they shared grins as they kicked their own mounts to follow Eadward and Bede, who almost went to a gallop in order to catch up, looking to Titus quite ridiculous in the process. Riding in a column four men wide, Titus was more talkative than he had been the day before, but he was still preoccupied, although this time it was because of the composition of their party. He was not alone in sensing that the inclusion of these Northmen strangers was significant, but nobody among their party could offer a possible reason for their presence that was not immediately hooted down by the others. It did help pass the miles, and it was at their first rest stop that the mystery was solved, which in turn unleashed a crisis still several miles north of Hamtun. Titus had to concentrate on not watching Hakon, who had climbed down from the wagon and taken a meandering route to the stream where the Northmen were standing in a small cluster, watering their ponies, but he could not stop himself from surreptitiously glancing over at the slave.

"Are you listening?" Uhtric demanded, and Titus was forced to admit that he was not, but before his friend could repeat himself, Hakon detached himself from the group and made a beeline directly for Titus.

There was no mistaking the suppressed excitement, but Titus knew Hakon well enough to see there was also concern in the slave's expression. What happened next was Titus' fault, because rather than think to take a step away from Uhtric, Titus beckoned to Hakon to come directly to him.

"Those men are Danes," Hakon began breathlessly, and then, without thinking about the larger implications, blurted out, "and they will each be the master of one of the ships that we sail in, along with another Dane at the steering oar."

This was met by a thunderstruck silence, finally broken by Willmar, who, without thinking, practically shouted, "Those pagan dogs think that they're going to command *me*?"

Otha, standing a few paces away, heard Willmar, and was the first to realize that someone had discovered the thing that Eadward had avoided bringing up the night before.

Consequently, and without thinking, he bellowed, "Shut

your mouth, Willmar, or by the Cross, you'll be sorry!"

But it was too late; Eadward had been speaking to Bede, and in fact they had been discussing the subject when the young nobleman heard the uproar, spinning about to see almost every one of his warriors striding towards him.

Instantly understanding, Eadward barely had time to groan aloud when Willmar, speaking with the bare minimum of courtesy expected of social inferiors, demanded, "Is it true, Lord? We're going to be under the command of these Godless savages?"

Eadward's first instinct was to prevaricate slightly.

"Not when we're actually fighting," he replied, but he immediately saw that this counted for nothing, which Hrothgar confirmed by asking indignantly, "So if we need to piss, we have to ask their permission?"

Eadward had to fight the urge to snap that this was ridiculous; first, Hrothgar was probably the dimmest man in Otha's service, but one of Ceadda's men, Leofsige, who somewhat oddly was actually Aelfnod's cousin, interjected with a more cogent question.

"And how much time will we be spending actually fighting, Lord Eadward?"

He would have preferred to treat this challenge as a rhetorical one, but Eadward saw that the men surrounding him were expecting him to answer, which he did, reluctantly admitting, "Not much, Leofsige." Then he had an idea, and while it was not in his nature to do so, he hardened his voice in what he hoped was a credible approximation of his father's, turning the tables on not just Leofsige but all of them. "But this is what our Lord King Alfred has ordered, Leofsige. Are you suggesting that you know better than our King? Or," he added warningly, "are you suggesting that you have no intention of obeying these men that our King has placed in command...in *nautical* matters?"

It worked better than he had dared dream; within a span of a half-dozen heartbeats, the crisis was over, every warrior gathered around him suddenly more interested in staring down at their feet, avoiding his gaze, but while he was tempted to press his advantage by demanding that they answer, he decided this was enough of a victory.

"We've been stopped long enough," he said instead, then ordered crisply, "Back on your horses, quickly now."

They obeyed, some of them looking a bit ashamed, others sullen, but the important thing was they did as he ordered. Suddenly, he remembered that there was another thing that they had not mentioned, but just as he opened his mouth to call them back, Otha appeared at his side.

"You handled that well, Lord," he murmured as they both watched the men swinging into their saddles, although Otha glanced over at the Danes, who had been watching the proceedings with what appeared to him to be equal parts interest and amusement, and he worried that one of his warriors would see them and take offense.

His attention was diverted by Eadward's sigh, followed by, "Yes, but they only know about being under the heathens' command aboard ship, not the other thing. So we might as well get this over with."

Alarmed, Otha reached out and grasped Eadward by the arm, lowering his voice and saying urgently, "Lord, I don't think that's a good idea."

"Why?" Eadward asked, surprised and, frankly, a bit irritated. "You were angry with me for not telling them last night, but now you're saying I shouldn't tell them everything?"

"Considering how they took being under the Danes' command," Otha countered, "I think telling them the rest of it right now might be more trouble than it's worth. Let's let them cool down the rest of the way. They'll be finding out the rest soon enough."

Eadward had opened his mouth to argue, but he snapped it shut, realizing that Otha was right.

He grinned and asked teasingly, "So you're saying I did the right thing by not telling them last night?"

"No," Otha answered immediately, but while he was not smiling, Eadward saw the humorous gleam in the Thegn's eye. "I'm just saying it wasn't wrong."

They were still laughing as they swung into their saddles, and the column resumed heading for Hamtun.

Unlike Wintanceaster and its small and, frankly, ramshackle dock, Hamtun's location at the mouth of the protected bay called the Solent, made it one of the most important hubs for fishing and seaborne trade in southwestern Wessex. The protection was created by the Isle of Wihtwara (Wight) which, prior to the Treaty, had served as a haven for the invading Northmen, but was now considered firmly under the control of Wessex, and was part of Cuthred's domain of Hampscir. This did not mean there were no Northmen left; in fact, there was a small fishing settlement about a mile inland from the northern coast of the Isle, on the one river, called the Medina by the locals, the name dating back to the days of the Romans, and most of the inhabitants were Danes. For reasons that could only be guessed at, Alfred had chosen to turn a blind eye to their presence, and the truth was that they were eking out a subsistence living, taking up land that none of the Saxons particularly coveted. The major benefit provided by the Isle was sheltering the bay created by the Rivers Test and Itchen, the latter of which led directly to Wintanceaster, and as the men of Alfred's naval force would learn, it was why Hamtun had been chosen as the base of operations.

"Your men are not sailors," Knut One-Eye had said to Alfred bluntly. "If I take them to open sea immediately, they will die."

Despite expecting something like this, Alfred did not like hearing it put so baldly, but he had curtly agreed to what Knut had proposed because, ultimately, he knew that Knut was right. The Saxons were, at the most, coastal sailors, and what they did by ship was almost exclusively fishing and hauling cargo; they did not go raiding, and they certainly had not done much fighting at sea. When their ancestors had crossed the sea between Saxony and this island, they had quickly abandoned their seaborne roving and concentrated on wresting the land of the island from the Briton tribes. This was why the arriving Northmen had proven such a challenge, because the Saxons were ill-equipped and unprepared to face, let alone defeat a highly mobile foe who could appear suddenly, vanish, then reappear dozens and even a hundred miles away. It was something that Alfred was determined to correct, and this incursion by these Danish ships had provided his first opportunity to take the initial step to correct what he considered to be the largest strategic deficiency facing him in his larger goal of a united England. The resistance he faced from his own noblemen when it came to the idea of creating a Saxon navy was due more to inertia, parsimony, and relative indifference, particularly for the Ealdormen and senior Thegns whose holdings were inland and were now, thanks to the Treaty, relatively safe from the predations of the seaborne Northmen.

When it came to his dream of a united Saxon kingdom, where all men were ruled by one set of laws, spoke the same tongue, used the same currency, and was universally Christian, matters were much more complex. When men had spent their entire lives thinking of themselves as Mercian, Centish, and Northumbrian even before Saxon, this was difficult enough, but then there were the enmities and grudges between petty lords that went back for multiple generations, where ancient grievances were nursed, despite the fact that, when pressed, none of the men involved could recall the actual events that led to the dispute. Overlaying all of this was the one thing that none of his noblemen ever said within his hearing, the question asking *why* it should be Alfred to be the man to unite England instead of one of them? Alfred knew all of this, both because he understood how the men of his class thought, and because he had spies in the halls of every Ealdorman and highly ranked Thegn in his domain. At this particular moment, however, what mattered was these Danish marauders, and he had begun the Saxon response by sending Bede and the stripling Eadward with Knut One-Eye to Hamtun.

There were still several hours of daylight left when Titus and his comrades arrived in Hamtun, which meant there was enough time for the second of the surprises that were waiting for them to be sprung. Nobody in the party was surprised when they followed Eadward, or if they were one of the men from Hampscir, followed Bede, through the northern gates, then through the town, to the dockyards, which were understandably much larger than the one in Wintanceaster. Nor were any of the men surprised to see ships moored to the docks waiting for them.

Of Otha's men, it was actually Uhtric who was the first to ask, "Where are the crews?" With a laugh, he asked, "Or are they still in the city debauching and whoring and didn't know to expect us?"

Eadward and Otha exchanged a glance, but to Eadward's surprise, it was actually Otha who beat him to it.

"No, they're not whoring," he replied, then rather than prolong matters, he informed them, "because *you're* going to be the crew."

Later, when things had calmed down, Eadward had been adamant that Otha's advice earlier had been sound.

"If we had told them that immediately after they learned that those Danish pagans were going to be in command, I don't think we would have made it another mile."

The only consolation for Eadward was that, if anything, the Hampscir men had taken this news even worse, and it had actually taken Bede threatening to execute the more recalcitrant of his warriors before they subsided enough that it appeared that, while extremely unhappy about it, they accepted their collective fate.

Nevertheless, this did not mean that their indignation at the idea that they would be consigned to pulling an oar was eased in the slightest, and it was Hrothgar who essentially summed up the collective feeling of the Wiltun contingent when he complained, "I'm a Saxon, not a Northmen dog! Saxon warriors don't pull an oar! That's for fishermen and slaves, not free men!"

He had bellowed this, but it was the fact that he had turned to look directly at Knut One-Eye as he did that created the first tense moment between the two parties, but while he did not comment on it, Titus had been impressed by the Dane's response.

Without flinching, and without any obvious anger, Knut had replied coolly, albeit in his broken English, "No Dane who pulls an oar is a slave, Saxon, and your King is wise enough to ask for our help because he knows this is true, and we have carved a piece of land out of your island because of this."

From Titus' perspective, it was probably a good thing that

Hrothgar did not have a clever bone in his body, because he had no idea how to counter Knut's reply, and in fact looked to Uhtric, who was accepted to be the cleverest of Otha's men, for help; all he got in response was a helpless shrug.

Finally, all Hrothgar could manage was to bluster, "Well, I don't like it!"

This did not quell further disturbances, but it did help to blunt the protests of the Saxons; it would have taken a very bold man to continue their importuning, because they all knew that King Alfred was going to be joining them, and none of them wanted him to learn they had been one of those complaining. It was purely by happenstance that Titus, standing on the outer fringe of his comrades surrounding Eadward, happened to notice that Knut and his Danes, who were standing in a knot several paces away and next to one of the ships tied to the dock, were clearly almost as upset as the Saxons, although it was impossible for him to tell why, even if he had been close enough to hear their muttered conversation. However, they would soon learn the cause of the Danes' dismay, thanks to Otha's quick thinking and his brief conversation with Snorri the night before, who he had chosen for no other reason than this.

"I want you to listen in on what those Danish bastards are talking about whenever possible," the Thegn had instructed the warrior. "But do *not* give yourself away, do you understand?"

Naturally, Snorri had obeyed; after all, he had been the one who informed Otha when he came into the Thegn's service that he had learned the Danish tongue from his mother, although he readily admitted, "I understand it better than I speak it."

This was why, at the first opportunity, which came sooner than expected when, without saying a word to either Eadward or Bede, Knut led his men away from the docks, leaving the Saxons to stand there, most of them open-mouthed and all of them mystified.

"What is that about?" Otha asked Eadward, but before the young lord could respond that he did not know, it was Snorri who interjected.

"They're unhappy, Lord Eadward," Snorri informed him.

"That's clear," Eadward replied with some asperity. "But what about?"

102

"They're not happy with the ships King Alfred is providing," Snorri explained, prompting them to all turn and examine the half-dozen ships, bobbing in a slow rhythm to the incoming tide.

"They look sound to me," Eadward said, trying to sound confident, but it was Otha who voiced his own thought. "If the Danes are complaining about those ships, they must have a reason for it."

This prompted Eadward to ask Snorri, "Did you hear why they're upset?"

"No, Lord." Snorri shook his head. "I just caught the very end of what they were saying before they left."

While they were all uninformed, and some might have argued the point, it was actually a good thing that none of the Saxons were aware of Knut's concern in the moment, given their own discontent.

"The Saxon expects us to catch other Danes with *these*...?" The man who spoke this, Einarr Thorsten, used a Danish term that was untranslatable into the Saxon tongue that essentially meant a floating piece of shit. Knut hissed a warning to Einarr to keep his voice down, but his second in command scoffed, "These farmers don't understand anything we say, especially when we're talking about ships. If," Einarr spat on the ground, then used his head to indicate the Saxon vessels, "you want to call those ships."

Knut did not necessarily disagree with Einarr; he had been explicit in ordering his men to gauge the Saxons' reaction whenever they were in earshot and instructed them to use provocative language that he was certain would arouse a reaction from their ostensible allies if they understood what was being said. They had done so during their march, yet not once had any Saxon betrayed any sign that they understood that the Danes were calling their mothers whores and the various other insults they conjured up. As far as Einarr's sentiment, he wholeheartedly agreed, and he was as distressed as the other Danes at what now had gone from a moderately challenging task in turning a mob of landmen who were more at home behind a plow than an oar into competent crews into something infinitely more difficult. Even if, he thought glumly, every one of those Saxons was as large and strong as the youngster he knew, with a mixture of amusement and anger, was called the Berserker, they would not be able to generate the kind of speed it would take to catch a Danish ship. In simple terms, what they were looking at was more suitable to hauling cargo, or fishing, than a warship.

"What are you going to do, Knut?" Einarr asked, but at that moment, Knut had no idea.

It was Oddbjorn the Bald, his third in command, who asked, "When does the Saxon king arrive?"

"He's supposed to be here tomorrow, or the next day at the latest," Knut replied, although he was only partially paying attention.

"Perhaps the other ships that are joining us are better than these?" Dagfinn Grimmarson queried; he was the youngest of the group, and his hopeful note was a sign of not just his youth, but was part of his personality, which was in direct opposition to his older brother Sigmund, which was why neither Knut nor the others were surprised when it was Sigmund who said scornfully, "Don't be a fool, little brother! That," he pointed at one of the ships in an almost accusing manner, "is probably the best ship these *burlofotr* have!"

This epithet was one of the most common used by men of the North, both Danes and Norsemen, although it was not reserved exclusively for Saxons, but for any foreigners who were not seafaring people. It meant "clumsy foot," which registered the disdain they had for these men who, if Knut was any judge, would be stumbling all over themselves aboard ship. How long it would take to turn these men into crews that would not be more of a threat to themselves, and to Knut and his men, as to the Danes who were *Viking* up and down the southern coast was what concerned him. Oh, they might be good warriors, Knut allowed, though only in private and to his men; he was a relatively recent convert to this viewpoint, after Ethantun and the decisive victory by Alfred and these men, but fighting on land was an entirely different matter than fighting on a pitching, rolling longship. And now that he had seen what he had to work with, both in the form of these ships and with the men he had been observing during their admittedly short time together, Knut One-Eye was not in an optimistic frame of mind.

"Let's go get something to drink," he said abruptly. "I need to think."

His men obeyed eagerly, but as they headed back into the town away from the docks, they were stopped by Eadward and Bede, but while the youngster was the higher ranking of the pair, he was clearly content to let the older man speak for them.

"Where are you going?" Bede demanded, earning an indrawn hiss from the men of Knut's who understood the Saxon tongue, but Knut did not share their indignation, instead answering mildly, "We're going to find an inn, and a place that serves something besides your horse-piss ale."

Bede, misunderstanding, nodded and said, "We'll go with you."

"Why?" Knut countered, the eyebrow above his missing eye raised in surprise.

"We need rooms as well, Knut."

This came from Eadward, but neither Saxon were prepared for the Dane to shake his head, then jerk a thumb back over his shoulder. "You and your men will be staying on the ships. You need to get accustomed to living onboard."

"On whose authority?" Bede did not actually shout, but it was close.

Knut smiled thinly, relishing this moment, having already recognized that this Saxon Thegn was going to be a problem; the pup Eadward did not concern him in the slightest.

"By the command of King Alfred," Knut replied. Sensing that more was needed, he shrugged and added casually, "He asked me what should be done to help get you prepared for what is coming, and I told him that you needed to become accustomed to living aboard ship, even when it's docked."

He did not wait for either of them to reply; watching them stand there openmouthed in shock was ample reward.

Alfred did arrive the next day, but while he had braced himself for the anger from his Saxons at the indignity of being forced to live aboard the ships, he was completely unprepared when Knut One-Eye, after a barely acceptable obeisance, said flatly, "I cannot do what you are asking, Lord King."

Alfred's feet had barely touched the ground from dismounting, and frankly, he was tired and filthy, a condition that the fastidious king despised; the fact that it reminded him of his period of humiliation, hiding in the swamps of Athelney from Guthrum was something that he only shared with his wife Ealswith, who had shared the ordeal with him.

This was what prompted him to snap, "What do you mean, you 'cannot do what I am asking'?" Even as he tried to mimic the Dane's accent, he was ashamed of himself, but while Knut flushed, clearly understanding the jibe, he maintained what was, for him, a respectful tone, but on the spur of the instant, instead of offering an explanation, he asked, "Have you seen the ships you have given me, Lord King?"

Alfred became wary, acknowledging cautiously, "No, but I was assured that they were seaworthy and in excellent condition. Is this not the case?"

Now it was Knut's turn to be uncomfortable, because he was forced to admit, "No, Lord King. They are seaworthy. But," he shook his head, "that is not the problem."

"Then what *is* the problem?" Alfred demanded, but before Knut could answer, the King realized this was a waste of time, and with a sigh, he turned and swung back up into the saddle as he said shortly, "Show me, Knut."

Hiding his relief, Knut turned and, since he did not have his pony nearby, began moving at a brisk trot towards the docks, forcing Alfred to kick his mount to catch up. He probably did that on purpose, he thought sourly; he likes the idea of a Saxon king chasing him through the streets like an urchin.

When they arrived at the docks, it took Alfred a moment to take in the scene. The ships were still moored to the docks, bobbing in the tidal swell, but now there was a row of makeshift shelters that, from what he could determine, were made with men's cloaks, but while it made it difficult, he could see the men underneath the cover lounging on the benches that, while he was inexperienced in nautical matters like the rest of his countrymen, he knew served as makeshift bunks, although it meant that men were either consigned to lying on their backs with their lower legs hanging over the edge, or curled up into a tight ball on their sides. Along with his personal fastidiousness, Alfred despised sloth, one of the seven deadly sins, and the sight of men lounging about during the daylight hour mortally offended him, which did not help his temper.

"Why are these men just...just...*lying about*?" Alfred did not shout this, but despite their scant acquaintance, Knut still felt a stab of concern, hearing the anger there and aware that, Saxon or not, Alfred was a powerful man.

"I have not given them orders yet, Lord King, other than to assign them to a ship." he answered, then added hurriedly, "Because these ships are not acceptable."

"But you just said they were seaworthy," Alfred protested, but before Knut could answer, he held up a hand to stop him so that he could dismount and walk to stand in front of Knut, facing the Dane, who, while a large man, was still forced to tilt his head slightly to look the Saxon king in the eye, Alfred being nearly as tall as Titus. In a reasonable tone, Alfred said, "Explain to me what your concerns are."

Understanding that it had been wrong to expect Alfred to see the problem just by pointing at it, Knut had to think for a moment before he could explain.

"These ships are at least a pace wider across the beam than the ships we will be chasing, Lord King," Knut began. "And they have a deeper draft than a Danish ship. That means that they will be slower, even before you man them with a crew." He waited for a moment, then seeing Alfred's head beginning to nod, it encouraged him to continue, "The ships we will be chasing are narrower in the beam and with a shallower draft, which makes them move faster through the water, and they are longer, so they have at least two more oars per side."

"Which means," Alfred said tonelessly and as if to himself, "they will be able to outrun us. And," he continued, his mouth turning down into a frown as he began to more fully appreciate the problem, "a narrower ship cuts through the water more cleanly."

Knut tried to hide his relief that the Saxon had grasped this without further explanation, but while he considered making the other point, that a narrower ship was also more maneuverable, he decided against it, settling for saying, "Yes, Lord King, that is exactly what it means."

There was a silence between them, while the Saxons aboard the ships had begun to rouse themselves as the word that their King had arrived spread from one ship to the next, with Alfred spending that time staring in obvious disapproval.

Finally, Alfred broke the silence, saying flatly, "Obviously, this is, as you say, a problem. But," he turned to give Knut a hard look, "I do not believe that it is an insurmountable one. There are more ships coming from Lord Odda from Devonscir, although I do not know how many yet, and Lord Sigeræd is coming from Cent, and he promised five ships. The Centishmen are more skilled in nautical affairs than we in Wessex are, so it is possible that their ships will be a match. And," he added, "Sigeræd may come across these heathen bandits and dispatch them himself." Knut did not know Alfred well, but he was certain that the King was speaking more from hope than conviction, and considering how he had raised his voice, assumed that the words were for his men and not out of any real belief this was the case. This seemed to be confirmed when, lowering his voice so that only Knut could hear, Alfred continued, "In the event that this is not what happens, we need to come up with a strategy that will allow us to accomplish our goal, and I will be counting on you and your men to aid me in this new plan, in accordance with the agreement made with Lord Aethelstan. Is that understood?"

Knut did not answer immediately because he was now struggling to contain his temper; it was bad enough that this Saxon dog insisted on calling Knut's king by that abominable name, but Guthrum was the *King* of what the Saxons now called the Danelaw, not just a lord. He also could see in Alfred's eyes that the Saxon was aware of what he was doing, and there was a silent battle of wills over the course of a few heartbeats as both men stared at each other.

Finally, Knut managed, albeit through clenched teeth, "Yes...Lord King." In something of an insult, Knut turned away from Alfred, but under the guise of seeming to examine the ships, and he was sourly amused to see that all of the Saxons aboard were now standing and wearing expressions that looked very much like boys who had been caught stealing honey cakes. His back was still turned when he said, "The first thing we will need to do is to take them out into the Solent and see just how much work needs to be done with them."

Alfred expected this, but it was Knut who was surprised when Alfred replied, "Can we begin today?"

"Today?" Knut was startled, and he turned to look over his shoulder at the Saxon, half-expecting that Alfred was jesting, though he did not seem to be the type. He got his answer in the steady gaze from the King, which prompted him to glance up at the sun. "I suppose it is possible," he began doubtfully, "though not for long. It will take at least an hour to get the ships that we have already crewed ready. But," he pointed to the men who had come with Alfred, "we will need to assign the men who came with you to fill out the rest of the crew of the ship manned by these men from Wiltun. The men sent by Lord Cuthred will be enough for the second ship, although they will still be short four oarsmen."

This did not please Alfred, but he did not argue, instantly understanding that this was at least partially his fault for sending the men to Hamtun in a piecemeal fashion.

"Very well," he said abruptly. "We'll only go out with these two ships, and I'll have men of my guard serve as crew. I will leave Lord Mucel here to supervise our part. Who is your second in command?"

"Lord Einarr, Lord King." Knut pointed to him, while Einarr shifted uncomfortably. Anticipating the question, Knut assured Alfred, "He speaks your tongue as I do, Lord King."

The truth was that Alfred had privately carped to Mucel about how Knut was barely understandable, but the King held his tongue about the likelihood of Einarr being similarly impaired, only nodding instead.

"Good," he said briskly. "Let's get started, shall we?"

This was when Knut realized something, and he blurted out, "Surely you do not intend to come with us, Lord King?"

"How else am I going to know how much work they'll need?" Alfred was no less surprised than Knut at the idea that he would not be coming, not that the Dane could argue even if he did not see the logic.

Knut made what was as much of a bow as he was willing to offer before turning his attention to the waiting Saxons; it was the last moment of inactivity that these men would be experiencing for some time to come.

By the time a week had passed, Titus was certain of a few things. One was that he had never been as exhausted, or as sore, at the end of every day as during this period when he was sitting on a bench pulling an oar, and that soreness was not restricted to his upper body. The second was that his comrades had absolutely no sympathy for his plight, and by the end of the second day, they had banded together to inform him that if he opened his mouth to voice his complaints again, he would be summarily pitched overboard at the first opportunity.

"You're bigger and stronger than all of us," Uhtric had snapped during the evening meal when Titus had begun to grumble about the soreness of his arms, back, and ass. "Do you hear us whining about it?"

Fighting the urge to assure Uhtric that, in fact, he had heard his brother-in-law and every other one of his comrades express how the hours they had spent rowing up and down the Solent had left them aching and exhausted, Titus had bowed his head, concentrated on his bowl, and kept his mouth shut. The truth was that, while he was sore, he secretly relished the work that stressed different muscles than his normal activities, even with the aching. He also had to learn to refrain from his natural proclivity to demonstrate how much stronger he was than his comrades, the need for which was expressed to him in the form of the one-eyed Dane bashing him across the back with a rod that he carried with him and used liberally on all of them. Not surprisingly, this was not just painful, it enraged Titus, but the presence of their King, standing at the rear next to the Dane manning the steering oar, watching impassively meant that the young warrior kept his seat, though he did glare up at Knut, who was completely unimpressed.

"You are big, you are strong...and you like showing that off, *boy,*" Knut sneered, fixing Titus with a cold stare from his single eye. In a fractionally milder tone, he said, "But that is not what is required when a man is at the oar." Using the stick, he indicated Hrothgar, who manned the oar on the opposite side, his presence across from Titus no accident, then the others. "He must match his crewmates, or it will require the steersman to constantly fight the steering oar to keep this ship running straight and true." He raised his voice then, addressing all of them, "You must stop thinking like *burlofotr*!" Raising his free hand, he held it up with the fingers splayed out. "You are not this..." He curled the fingers together to form a fist. "...You are *this*! Not a group of men anymore! You are a *crew*!" He paused, trying to think of an appropriate analogy, and he was slightly inspired to add, "Think of this as a shield wall at sea. You must rely on each other to do their part, and in the same way that you must do your part."

It would not be the last time Knut used his rod on Titus, but it would be the one he would remember most vividly, nor did Knut spare its use on the other men, especially the first day when, if Knut was to be believed, they did not do a single thing to the Dane's satisfaction. Perhaps the only blessing from Titus' perspective was that, of the half of his comrades who were struck with seasickness, he seemed immune, while his afflicted comrades learned very quickly how to retch without breaking the rhythm that was called out by the young Dane named Dagfinn manning the steering oar. Anything that threatened to disrupt the steady rhythm of the oars dipping, stroking, then rising out of the water brought retribution, in the form of Knut, who moved about the ship with an astonishing speed, slashing down with his rod just as he had with Titus. The fact that they spent barely three hours on the water that first day before returning to the docks in Hamtun was only recognized as a blessing in hindsight the next day, when they left the harbor just as the sun was peeking over the horizon and did not return until the bottom of the orb was touching the western lands, in a pattern that would repeat itself for the foreseeable future, the only difference being that King Alfred spent that day on the other ship. While he did not feel that way, Titus was fortunate in that, because of his size, he was given a spot on the centerboard to sleep, unaware that it was the wider design of the Saxon ships that allowed for the wide plank that allowed for this comfort and was missing in Northmen's ships. It also meant that he was constantly disturbed because Knut set a watch, despite the fact that they were moored at a dock in a Saxon town, requiring a man to walk from bow to stern, back and forth all night. The only thing that was not done aboard ship was cooking, and they were informed that the standard practice if they remained at sea overnight would be to consume cold rations.

In a signal to his men, the King did not avail himself of one of the inns that lined the street just a short distance from the docks, instead having his tent erected on a patch of cleared ground next to the southern wall. What this meant in a practical sense was that Alfred was an almost constant presence, insisting on going out into the Solent, although he chose a different ship every day, as did Knut. Once more men arrived to man other ships, Knut was needed elsewhere, and Einarr Thorsten was named the master of Eadward's ship, and it did not take long for the Saxons to detest him as thoroughly as they had Knut after the first day, a feeling that was clearly returned by Einarr, who, like Knut, carried a length of ash that was a cut-down spear shaft, which he used just as liberally as Knut. The only men he did not strike were Eadward and his Thegns, who were also exempt from pulling an oar, as were the other Thegns on the other ships, and for the most part, they were ignored by Einarr, who devoted himself to snarling curses when one of the Wiltun men and the men of Alfred's guard who had been added to fill out the crew lost their grip on an oar, or thrust their oar into the water at either too deep or too shallow an angle, disrupting the rhythm. Not surprisingly, it was Uhtric who noticed something first.

"Why haven't we used our sail once?" he muttered during one of the brief respites where they were allowed to drift. "What's it even there for if we never use it?"

This was on the third, or perhaps it was the fourth day, which meant that they had learned that, if they saw Einarr approaching and raising his staff to strike one of them, warning their comrade would earn them a swipe of their own, and his blow caught Uhtric across the shoulders, knocking him sideways and almost off his bench; fortunately, he managed to catch himself so that he did not fall down into the bottom of the ship, which was filled with at least a foot of what was a foul-smelling combination of spray, piss, and the puke from the men whose stomachs still had not become accustomed to the rolling and pitching.

"We will use a sail only when *I* say we are ready," Einarr bellowed, shifting his gaze to each man in Uhtric's part of the ship, the challenge unmistakable. "And you *skreyja vitskertr* are nowhere near ready! A crew of Danish *children* would put you to shame right now, so do not ask about a sail again!"

He spun about and stalked back to the stern, with Uhtric soothing his pride by spitting at Einarr's retreating back, while Aelfwine asked Snorri, "He used a new word this time." As Snorri had informed them, "*skreyja*" meant incompetent. "What's a..." he cocked his head, trying to remember, "...a *vitskertr?*"

Snorri answered readily enough, though he looked a bit uncomfortable; if his answer angered Aelfwine, it would not have been the first time one of the others took it out on him. "It means halfwit."

"He's not wrong," Uhtric said ruefully, shrugging his shoulders in an attempt to ease the pain from the blow. "If I had known just how fucking miserable we'd be, I would have figured out a way to stay home."

Alfred was not much happier, albeit for different, more pressing reasons. None of the four ships that Odda brought with him were acceptable to Knut and his Danes, and in fact were considered to be in even worse condition than the Hamtun vessels, which Knut had made clear in a manner that Odda found offensive, to the point that Alfred had been forced to intervene when the Ealdorman had leapt to his feet and appeared intent on assaulting the one-eyed Northman. Fortunately, the altercation had been inside the royal tent, but the leather walls did not block the sound of bellowing voices, and naturally, Odda had enormous sympathy from the men, all of whom hated their temporary masters with a passion. There had been slightly better news when Sigeræd had arrived, because two of his ships met with Knut's approval; when he learned that it was because they were actually captured Danish ships, he was not quite as happy, though he did his best to hide it. However, to Alfred's surprise, and Sigeræd's consternation, after spending a day with the Centish crews, the Dane had flatly declared that only one of this group was acceptable to man one of the Danish ships.

"Who would you suggest crew the other one?" Alfred had asked.

To Alfred's surprise, Knut had answered without hesitation, "The men of Einarr's ship." Seeing the Saxon's reaction and ignoring the Thegns representing Ealdorman Odda and Sigeræd's spluttered exclamations at what they saw as an insult, Knut said with a shrug, "They are the best of what you have given us, Lord King. They learn quickly for *burlo*..." He caught himself; while he was fairly certain none of those present knew the meaning of the term, he also knew underestimating a man like Alfred was a foolish risk, and Knut was no fool, so he amended it to, "...men who are inexperienced at sea."

While he said nothing more, Alfred was certain there was something more there, but rather than press the issue, he asked, "So you intend to give..." he looked over to Ealdorman Sigeræd of Cent, who, in a display of independence, had chosen to come himself instead of obeying Alfred's order to remain within his shire, with an inquiring expression, and the Ealdorman understood, supplying the name of the ship, "the *Sea Viper* to Einarr and his crew. When," he asked pointedly, "do you intend to begin training them in how to fight from shipboard?"

Knut considered for a moment, then said, "They will have to become accustomed to a lighter, faster ship. It will be in a week."

"You have four days," Alfred replied quietly, but when Knut opened his mouth to protest, the King held up a hand, and his voice, while not getting louder, hardened in a perceptible and unmistakable manner. "Four days, Knut. Then you will begin to teach my warriors how to fight from a ship."

Knut did not respond immediately, then after a heartbeat's pause, signaled his acceptance with a bow that, while only fractionally so, was deeper than any he had offered the Saxon king.

Sigeræd waited until the Dane had left the tent before

turning to address Alfred, but his King had anticipated and was prepared for this, so that while his tone was almost apologetic, his words were as unyielding as they had been with Knut. "Lord Sigeræd, while I understand why you are unhappy, I have been informed that the raiders landed at Lyminster yesterday. They were driven off, but not after several buildings were burned, a dozen men were butchered, and ten women were taken." Leaning forward, his voice throbbed with an intensity that was impossible for any of the observers to mistake, "My people are suffering, Lord. And every time these heathens land on our soil, every time they kill my subjects, and take my women and despoil them, it is an *insult*. Not," he shook his head, "just to me, but to you, to every lord whose sacred and solemn duty is to safeguard those of whom God has placed in our protection. We must respond, and we cannot afford to waste any more time, Lord."

Sigeræd was not assuaged...but he was no more of a fool than Knut, and knowing that the only right answer was to respond with as much humility as he could manage without being patently false, he inclined his head as he replied, "Yes, Lord King. I understand, and of course *Sea Viper* is yours to do with as you deem best."

Satisfied that he had made his point with the Ealdorman of Cent, for the first time, Alfred turned to address another of the men present, who had done his best to appear as if he was just part of the furniture.

"Young Lord Eadward," Alfred said gravely, "I have but one question for you."

"Yes, Lord King?" Eadward managed, hoping that neither Alfred, nor the others, heard the quaver in his voice.

"Are your men up to this task?" Alfred asked. "Can I count on them to be the tip of my spear?"

It was a moment that the lordling would remember, but more importantly, it would be one his King would recall, because rather than respond with the kind of boastful confidence that is the province of the young, instead Eadward took a moment to actually consider the question. What came to his mind was not the recollection of a moment, or some advice his father had offered, but the mental image of one of the

115

warriors who was completely oblivious to what was taking place in the King's tent. As long as Titus is with us, Eadward thought, I'll charge the Gates of Hell.

Still, he did not mention his friend's name, nor even refer to his existence as the reason for his answer, but he said with a quiet confidence, "Yes, Lord King. You can count on the men of Wiltun. We won't let you down."

It was something that they would never speak about later, and Eadward mistakenly believed that the slight smile that his King offered was solely because of his words, and not the fact that, like young Eadward, the Saxon King's mind had gone to the huge young warrior, and it was for the second time that Alfred was struck by the thought, if I had God's favor and one hundred men like Titus the Berserker, there is little doubt that I could drive these Northmen from our lands. Hard on the heels of that thought was another, less pleasant one as Alfred recalled one reason why Titus was with Eadward and Otha, and he realized that he had intended to address this with the young warrior, but it had slipped his mind.

The first day crewing the Danish ship was almost as bad as their first day on the water, the crew quickly learning that with a narrower beam and shallower draft, sudden changes in direction could create instability, which Hrothgar learned in an unforgettable way when he fell overboard, although he managed to catch his oar and hold on long enough to be hauled back aboard by Einarr, with the help of Ceadda's man Wigmund, who manned the oar immediately behind Hrothgar. The second day was better, and the men actually began to enjoy the more responsive nature and greater speed of the Danish ship, and while neither Einarr nor Knut were happy about it, at dawn of the fifth day, the crew began what they had either been eagerly anticipating, like Titus, or resigned to, like most of his comrades, learning how to fight aboard ship. However, when they were finished with their morning routine, instead of rowing out into the Solent, Einarr summarily ordered them off the ship, then led them outside the southern wall to an area that, to the eyes of the Saxons, contained nothing more than an assortment of unfamiliar wooden constructions. They were too small to be considered structures, but too large to be some form of device, although it was Otha who came closest to guessing their purpose.

"Maybe they're going to use whatever these are to train us," he commented, but when Uhtric asked how, Otha glared at him and snapped, "How should I know?"

To the surprise of his comrades, it was Hrothgar who pointed to something that would turn out to be important.

"The frames aren't anchored to the ground," he said. "I wonder if that's so they can move it about for whatever they have in mind."

Hrothgar would be proven correct, though not in the manner in which he thought, which they learned very quickly, when Einarr pointed at Titus first.

"Come here, boy," he ordered, but he was disappointed when Titus showed no irritation at the Dane's slur about his youth, and realizing that the Saxon had become accustomed to it, he silently resolved to find something else; if things went as he intended, that would be happening in the span of a few heartbeats. "Hop up on that." Einarr pointed to the horizontal length of wood that, now they had gotten close and had a moment to examine it, they could see was about three inches wide and stood about waist high, supported by the vertical legs of the frame.

Also, as Hrothgar had been the first to notice, the frame holding the horizontal pieces, which was about ten feet long, was not anchored to the ground, but just before he hopped up the three feet to stand on the horizontal piece, Titus also noticed that the bottom of the frame to which the vertical legs were attached was slightly curved. Correctly guessing that this meant that the horizontal piece would rock slightly when his weight landed on it, Titus compensated so that he landed on the smooth wood without pitching off headfirst when the frame rocked in the direction of his motion, and he gave Einarr a triumphant grin, which earned him a glare from the Dane that was completely counterfeit. The fact was that Einarr had seen Titus looking down at the frame and recognized that the Saxon had guessed the frame would move when he landed on the beam, so he was not surprised to see Titus land cleanly. Let's see if you're ready for this, *bacraut* (asshole), he thought, but without giving himself away, Einarr pointed to the second frame, identical to the first, but about five feet away.

"Now hop from this one to that one," Einarr commanded, but Titus did not immediately obey, choosing instead to examine the frame, looking for some sort of hidden trick and seeing that it was identical in construction to the one upon which he was standing.

This would be the critical moment for what Einarr intended, but while Titus did glance over at Dagfinn, who was standing nearest to the second frame but at least a couple of paces away, and holding a staff with a piece of curved iron on one end that was used to snare loose lines, the young warrior was clearly not suspicious of the young Dane, because he turned away, took a breath, then leapt across the space. Titus knew that the second frame would rock at an even greater degree because of his momentum in the opposite direction as he was traveling like the first one in response to his weight landing on it, but he was confident that in the instant when his feet touched the beam, he would feel the degree with which it would move and be able to compensate enough to keep his footing. What he was completely unprepared for was how Dagfinn, in one smooth movement, dropped the staff from vertical to the horizontal, and using the iron end, pushed, hard, against the second frame, but towards Titus, just as Einarr had instructed him to do. What it meant was that Titus overshot the beam with his leading foot, and amid a chorus of gasps and sympathetic groans, smashed into the horizontal beam in a straddling posture, almost as if he was leaping astride Thunor and landing in the saddle, except that there was no saddle, only hard wood, for which Titus was completely unprepared, but he was only astride the beam for perhaps a heartbeat before toppling to the ground, both hands clutching his groin, his eyes closed but without enough wind to do more than offer a breathy moan. Perhaps if Einarr had not looked so smugly triumphant as he stood there, hands on hips looking down at Titus, Otha would have restrained himself, but it was doubtful, and while he never said it aloud, even Dagfinn thought that what Einarr had done deserved retribution. He knew that, while his master did not like his Saxon crew overmuch, he harbored a real hostility for the largest, strongest, and the youngest of Lord Eadward's Wiltun men save for Wilwulf, and of the men of Alfred's bodyguard who had been added to complete a crew of forty. It had been from his older brother that Dagfinn had learned that Einarr had once aspired to become a member of what, to the Danes and their cousin Northmen, was a secretive sect whose rituals and ordeals were a topic of much speculation but little hard information because of the oath of secrecy those men took. What *was* known was that part of their ordeals was to survive a Northern winter with only a cloak made of the skin, or skins, of one of the two spirit animals sacred to the Berserkers, a bear or wolf...and an ax.

"Einarr did not last a month before he came back," Sigmund had told Dagfinn with a broad grin that made his older brother look like a snarling wolf himself because of the jagged stumps of his upper and lower teeth in between his canines. "So when he hears that Saxon being called the title he could not earn?"

He did not finish, for there was no need, and besides, in the moment, why Einarr despised Titus did not matter; what did was Otha, moving at close to a sprint, went charging at Einarr, although he slid to a stop a matter of a few inches from the Dane, who, while not flinching, did look a bit wary. From where Dagfinn was standing, it was equally likely that, while Otha had been the first to close with Einarr, he had been followed by the men that Dagfinn had determined were loyal to this Thegn and not Ceadda or Aelfnod, and Einarr was as concerned with them as he was with the Saxon Thegn.

"Why did you do that, you *oskilgetinn*?" Otha snarled, eliciting a gasp from Einarr, which, in Dagfinn's opinion, was as much from surprise at the Saxon using the Northman word for bastard as anger at the slur itself, and it was the first time any of the Saxons had given any indication that they knew their tongue, which made Dagfinn shift uncomfortably as he tried to think of all the times he had used that term when discussing the crew, realizing it was too many to count.

Einarr's voice was unusually calm, which was an even stronger indication that he was at the very least aware that he and Dagfinn were heavily outnumbered, replying to Otha's demand, "To teach him."

"Teach him what?" Otha snapped. "That his balls are vulnerable and shouldn't be crushed?" Before Einarr could respond, Otha jabbed a finger in Einarr's face. "And don't think that I haven't noticed that you've ridden Titus harder than any other member of this crew!"

As Otha continued, it was clear to Dagfinn that the Saxon was growing angrier, but he was as unprepared as Einarr clearly was when, without any warning, Otha struck Einarr with a powerful punch, sending the Dane reeling backward, but while he tried to stay on his feet, he could not keep his balance and landed on his ass, then sat there shaking his head trying to clear it as Otha closed the distance, clearly intent on hitting the Dane at least once more.

"What is the meaning of this?"

The words were not shouted, but they did not need to be, because everyone present either saw the man speaking them, or if they were standing in a position where their backs were turned, they recognized the voice as belonging to their King. As angry as Otha was, he nevertheless stopped in his tracks, then he had to turn to face Alfred, who was sitting astride his horse, with Knut and Lords Mucel and Eardwulf flanking him.

While Otha did not kneel, he did bow his head, but the anger was still clear in his voice as, without looking over at him, the Thegn indicated Titus, who was now at least sitting up, with a gesture, as Uhtric knelt next to him while Otha explained, "Lord King, Einarr needlessly injured Titus by having Dagfinn move this..." Suddenly, Otha looked embarrassed, which he explained, "...whatever they call this contrivance, when Titus was in midair and couldn't do anything about it."

For the first time, Alfred seemed to notice Titus, who was now being helped to his feet by Uhtric, which was made more difficult because Titus was still clutching his balls with both hands, causing Alfred to visibly redden.

He did ask, "Are you seriously injured, young Titus?"

From Dagfinn's perspective, it was clear that what Titus *wanted* to say was quite different from his mumbled, "N-no, Lord King. I'll be fine once I catch my breath."

Alfred did not look convinced, but he turned to Einarr and

demanded, "Is what Lord Otha says true, Einarr? Did you instruct your steersman to move this while Titus was in midair?"

"I did, Lord King," Einarr answered.

"To what purpose? And," for the first time, Alfred looked at the frames, "what are these things?" Before Einarr could reply, Alfred nodded, deducing, "These are designed to rock back and forth, are they not? To mimic the motion of a ship?"

"Yes, Lord King," Knut stopped Einarr from answering with a hand. "They are being taught how to leap from the side of their ship across to the ship they are attacking. And," he added meaningfully, "it is more common than not that either the ship they are leaping from or the one they are boarding will roll or dip in an unexpected manner."

This, every man present understood, was true, but every one of them who had witnessed what happened with Titus also knew this was not why Einarr had done it, but what mattered was that this seemed to satisfy Alfred. The King was not fooled, however; while he did not know the details, he sensed that there was more to this incident, but he would also remain silent in his opinion that it was not necessarily a bad thing for young Titus to undergo. Yes, he had earned his reputation, and yes, Alfred sensed that there were hidden depths to this young warrior that went beyond the obvious physical advantages given to him by his size, strength, and the simmering rage that had earned him the title Berserker among his fellow Saxons, a title that Alfred refused to use because of its heathen origin. Still, in Alfred's opinion, Titus needed a bit more humility, and perhaps Einarr had given him a dose. It was his thoughts running along this line that prompted him to nudge his horse to approach Titus, who was on his feet now, but when the youth saw his King approaching and made to drop to his knees, Alfred waved at him to remain standing, not entirely unsympathetic to Titus' plight.

"We have not had a chance to speak, Titus of Cissanbyrig," Alfred began, adopting a tone that warned Titus this would not be a lighthearted moment, which was confirmed when he continued icily, "Not since you slew one of my subjects."

As Alfred intended, this caught Titus completely by

surprise; oh, he had been warned by both Lord Eadward and Lord Otha that Alfred had been unhappy with what had happened with Hrodulf, but never in his wildest dreams had he thought that the King himself would broach the subject, and in such a blunt manner.

"I...I...I was defending myself, Lord King," Titus protested, but this did not impress Alfred, who retorted, "Surely a warrior of your prowess and strength should be able to defend himself from a *ceorl* without killing him."

To his credit, Titus immediately understood that further protest would not be wise, so he bowed his head and said with as much humility as he could manage without sounding completely false to his own ears, "Yes, Lord King. You're right. I should have controlled myself."

In truth, Alfred was slightly torn, realizing that a part of him had hoped that this youngster would try and argue that what he had done was within the law, which was true enough, but he was also impressed that Titus had clearly recognized the futility of arguing a point of law with a king.

"Do you remember what I told you the first time we met?" Alfred demanded elliptically but said nothing more.

Titus froze, though his mind raced as he tried to recall the moment, and for the span of a heartbeat, nothing came to him, then without consciously realizing it had, he blurted, "Yes, Lord King. You told me that I needed to pray regularly, and that I should only ask God what I can do to serve Him better, and to forgive me of my sins."

This earned him an approving nod from Alfred, but while he still sounded reproving, it was with an audibly gentler tone that he asked, "And what do you think our Lord and Savior would say about your actions with the man you killed, Titus?"

"That I had sinned," Titus admitted honestly.

"And did you ask our Lord for His blessed forgiveness after your deed, Titus?"

"Oh yes, Lord King." Titus nodded emphatically, lying through his teeth; the truth was that it had never occurred to him that he even needed to do so. Hrodulf had started the fight, and Titus had finished it, but he added piously, "I do so every day."

Alfred nodded again.

"As you should. You must learn to show mercy, Titus. Not," he added, suddenly recalling why they were there, "to our enemies, like these Danes marauding our lands as they rape and pillage. Those savages deserve to die." His voice had hardened again, although he did think to add, "But not," he turned and indicated Einarr, who, if anything, looked bemused, "these men who my adopted son Aethelstan has sent to help us repel these invaders. These Danes are not just on our side, Titus, they are on the side of our Lord and Savior. Even if," suddenly, Alfred turned and fixed Einarr with a hard stare, "they have given you cause to want to take vengeance." With this, he nudged his horse and walked it to Einarr, stopping so that he could look down at the Dane and fix him with a cold stare. "And you will not harm my men again for no reason. Is that clear?"

"Yes, Lord King," Einarr assured him.

Satisfied, Alfred said, "Then continue with the training. I will expect a full report at the end of the day."

Waiting for Alfred and his party to disappear back into the town, Titus limped past Einarr to rejoin the others.

"This isn't over," he said quietly, but while Einarr said nothing, he sneered at the young Saxon, then spat on the ground after he walked past.

But Dagfinn, who knew Einarr better, could see that the Dane was worried; as he should be, Dagfinn thought. Despite his youth, Titus the Saxon was not a man Dagfinn wanted to anger like Einarr had.

While Titus was excused from further training that day, he refused to take advantage, insisting that he was fine, and there were no more repeats of any trickery. Indeed, Einarr was scrupulous about warning the crew about when he would have Dagfinn use the staff on one of the frames, and his explanation made sense.

"While I will always try to position our ship so that the bow is heading into the swell, as will our foes, that will not always be possible, so we may be turned athwart when the command to board is sounded. You must learn to anticipate how the ship will behave when it is rolling. This way," he finished with a shrug, "at least you will not drown if you miss."

"But your balls may look like apples," Uhtric muttered, nudging his brother-in-law, "eh, Titus?"

Titus was not surprised that the rest of the crew thought this was a fine jest, roaring with laughter, while Titus glared at Uhtric, muttering a promise that he would find a way to even the score, which did not cow Uhtric in the slightest. The morning of the first day was spent with the men performing their leaps as individuals, and Titus took comfort that he was not the only one to misjudge their jump, although none of his comrades suffered as spectacularly as he had since Einarr announced beforehand that Dagfinn would be rocking the second frame. He also added a wrinkle as they learned what the iron hook was for, when instead of pushing the frame towards the frame from which they were leaping, he sometimes used the hook to yank the second frame in the opposite direction, mimicking the rolling of a ship away from the first one. Naturally, it did not take long for the spirit of competition to take hold, as comrades wagered each other on whether or not they would manage to successfully make the jump onto the beam that represented the side of the target ship. If they were wrong, and went crashing to the ground, their defeat was met by raucous laughter and cries of triumph by the men who had bet against the leaper, and it was in this manner the first part of the day passed quickly. Once every man had successfully negotiated the leap once, Einarr increased the difficulty by standing by the first frame, but instead of using a pole, he used his bulk to rock it back and forth to compensate for the weight of the crewman standing on it.

Not surprisingly, the failure rate went up once both frames were moving, which meant that before long, almost every man had failed to negotiate the problem at least once, some multiple times. By the time they stopped for the midday meal, there was only one warrior who had not lost his footing once; the fact that he was the oldest and was the senior Thegn was not lost on any of them. Of the others, only Titus had only fallen once, which not surprisingly, was ascribed to the fact that his balls could not have possibly taken another bashing like that and for no other reason, while Titus stoutly insisted that his bruised testicles had nothing to do with it. While he pretended to be fine, after the midday break, Titus was regretting not taking advantage of the offered respite, and he realized that sitting down had been a mistake, forced to stifle a sharp cry of pain as he climbed to his feet. When Uhtric urged him to go to Otha, insisting that their Thegn would not begrudge him foregoing the second part of the day, it was his pride that took control, while the rational part of his mind screamed at himself to do what Uhtric suggested. Instead, as if they had a mind of their own, his feet followed his comrades back to the frames, where they resumed their training, but this time not as individuals. Starting in pairs, they learned the different challenges that came when it was more than just one of them, while the rate of failure increased sharply. Indeed, not one pair managed to make their jump where both men landed successfully the first, or the second time through, but in something of a surprise, when the grumbling inevitably began, it was actually young Lord Eadward, who had participated just like the rest of the crew, who beat Otha, or the other two Thegns, for that matter, in chastising the men.

"We're not leaving here until every pair of us has managed to do this right at least three times," he snapped, and it was his rare show of anger that had more of an impact on his men than the words themselves. "I don't care if we're doing it in the dark. I won't allow us to fail at this." In a slightly more reasonable tone, he added, "Besides, remember that the King wants a report at the end of the day, and I doubt that he'll let us continue our training until we can complete every task that Einarr sets for us until we get this right."

This was enough to mute the grumbling, and spurred the men to increase their efforts, yet it was still dusk before each pair had met Lord Eadward's requirement, and on their return inside the walls, Titus took some consolation in that he was not the only one hobbling, although he was the only one whose infirmity came from his groin. He was surprised by Dagfinn, who, under the guise of dropping something, had stopped to wait for Titus, then fallen in step with him, though he did not say anything at first, while Titus, unsure of the Dane's purpose, just gave him a sidelong glance but remained silent.

Finally, Dagfinn blurted, "I am sorry that I played a part in...in...your injury."

This caused Titus to look over now with a startled expression; while he was uncertain about what Dagfinn might say, an apology was the last thing he had expected, which prompted him to ask, in mild astonishment, "Why?" Before Dagfinn could reply, Titus went on, "You were just doing what Lord Einarr told you to do. I don't blame you for that."

Dagfinn looked relieved, but then, after a quick glance at the other men around them, he lowered his voice so that only Titus could hear. "You need to be careful when we go out onto the water. I do not think Lord Einarr is going to be satisfied with what happened to you today."

"But why?" Titus asked in equal parts anger and bafflement. "I haven't done anything to him for him to hate me...yet," he finished grimly.

Dagfinn briefly considered telling the Saxon what he had learned from Sigmund, then decided that it would probably make things more complicated, and he did not know how the Saxon warrior felt about his cognomen, because he had observed that, when one of Titus' comrades had called him "Berserker," the young warrior had seemed uncomfortable with it.

Instead, he only offered a shrug, answering vaguely, "That I do not know. I just know that, if I were you, I would keep my eye on Lord Einarr."

Titus nodded thoughtfully, then said, "Thank you, Dagfinn, and I'll heed your warning." They were almost to the gate, but just before they reentered the town, Titus asked without forewarning, "Is there anything you'd suggest that might help me prepare for whatever Einarr has in mind?"

As it turned out, Dagfinn did, and he did not hesitate to share it, and they parted at the *Sea Viper*, with Dagfinn heading to the inn with the rest of the Danes, while Titus and his comrades were resigned to another night bobbing about in the water and sleeping in the bottom of the ship in between the wooden benches. Of all the adjustments that were required by the Wiltun men, the transition to the narrower Danish ship had proven to be hardest on Titus, since there was no centerboard, and he was far too large to use his bench, but he did not complain.

As usually happened in war, especially where the Northmen were concerned, Alfred's plans to train his landbound warriors in the arcane art of fighting from ship called for a month of preparation; Knut had pressed for two, but in the end, three weeks to the day after the arrival of the Wiltun men and their comrades in Hamtun, a messenger astride a lathered horse came pounding up to the King's tent. As it happened, or as Alfred's chaplain, Father Aethelred, made sure to spread about, in a clear sign of God's favor, the King had decided to forego going out into the Solent to observe the progress of his scratch navy, and was with his councilors Mucel, Eardwulf, and Sigeræd, along with Knut, to receive the report that would alter Alfred's plans.

"Lord King! A messenger from Lord Wiglaf is here with urgent news!" Cyneweard, Alfred's chief bodyguard who happened to be on duty called out from his post outside the tent.

Cutting Mucel off in midsentence, Alfred bade the man to enter, the courier spattered with mud and clearly almost as exhausted as his mount, who Alfred could see through the open flaps of the tent, telling the King that the courier had not spared his horse getting here, a potent indication that it was an urgent matter.

Stopping him from dropping to his knees and going through the ritual of obeisance that would waste time, Alfred asked only, "What news?"

"Lord Wiglaf sent me report that the Dane *Vikings* split their fleet, and two ships sailed up the Ouse!"

"They raided Læwe (Lewes)?" Mucel gasped in disbelief. "With *two* ships?"

"No, my Lord." The messenger shook his head. "They didn't even attempt it. They sailed upriver, although the defenders at Læwe said they managed to inflict serious damage on one of their ships."

While Alfred understood Mucel's concern, Læwe was one of the most important towns in Wessex and was subsequently one of the most heavily fortified in the kingdom because of its vulnerability being located on a navigable river. In fact, along with his aspirations to create a navy that could defeat the

Northmen, even more ambitious was Alfred's determination to fortify every town of a certain size in his kingdom along the lines of Wintanceaster and Læwe. Consequently, he had almost immediately dismissed the idea that two ships, with perhaps one hundred Danish warriors at most, would be able to penetrate the defenses of the town, and he gestured at the messenger to continue.

"They attacked Hamsey," the courier informed the King and his councilors, his voice grim, and there was something in his expression that suggested to Alfred that either the man had seen the results himself, or perhaps he knew someone from the village, most of which was situated on an island in the middle of the Ouse, although as it had grown, there were a cluster of habitations on the western bank, the two clusters serviced by a flat raft that served as a ferry powered by a single man with a pole.

"When was this?" Alfred asked.

"Late yesterday, Lord King," the messenger answered, prompting a disappointed sigh from Eardwulf, who commented, "Then they've undoubtedly sailed back downriver by now. There's nothing further upriver that would be worth their efforts."

"But they haven't, my Lord," the messenger replied. "Gone downriver, I mean. They're still at Hamsey. Or," he added quickly, "some of them are."

Alfred had been seated on his camp stool, and this got him to his feet to ask sharply, "What does that mean?"

"It means that while half of them are still at Hamsey, the other half left the village at dawn, and most of them are on foot. The bast...the Danes at Hamsey are working on the ship that was damaged by the men of Læwe."

"West?" Mucel frowned, trying to think what lay west of Læwe, but it was the cleric Aethelred, who had crept into a corner of the tent, eager to hear the news, who was the first to think of a possibility.

"Could they be intending to raid Steyning, Lord King?"

This startled Alfred, but he was doubtful at first, shaking his head as he said, "Steyning is almost twenty miles from Hamsey."

"It's also where your father, Lord King Aethelwulf, is buried, in the church built by the blessed Saint Cuthman," Aethelred replied.

"But not anymore," Alfred countered, although he was beginning to shift from one foot to another, the sign to those that knew him well that he was actually thinking about this as a possibility. "I moved my father's bones last year."

"In secret, Lord King," Mucel interjected. "Which means it is unlikely they know."

This was true, and aside from the theoretical presence of his father's remains, Steyning and the Church of Saint Cuthman was not a wealthy one, but while it made sense on one level, Alfred was still doubtful. However, Aethelred had introduced something that, very quickly, made him stop moving, his eyes narrowing as his mind raced.

"They're heading to the monastery at Stanmer."

As soon as the words were out, the others, save for Knut, realized their King was right, and they all began talking at once, while Alfred saw that, if they had just been a bit more patient, they would have known this already, and he raised his hand for silence to ask of the messenger, "Was this part of your message...?"

"Adalwolf, Lord King," the messenger replied, interpreting the slight lifting in tone and feeling the glow of pride that his King now knew his name. "And yes, Lord Wiglaf said that I needed to be sure I told you that he was certain they were heading to Stanmer, though he has sent men to the monastery to check."

Turning to Knut, Alfred asked, "How soon can we be ready to sail?"

"Sail?" Knut repeated, in a state close to shock, but he considered for a moment, then asked, "How far is this Ouse River?"

"About sixty-five miles overland," Alfred answered.

"It will take two days to be ready to sail," Knut answered, although he was not all that surprised when Alfred answered, "We're sailing immediately. But," he held up a hand, "not with every ship."

"How many are you thinking?" Knut asked cautiously.

"Two," Alfred replied, and now it was Mucel and Eardwulf's turn to object, but the King was not through. "To begin with. Our two Danish ships I want leaving as quickly as possible, definitely before dawn. Then," he paused to think, "the rest of Lord Sigeræd's ships will follow later tomorrow."

"You plan on attacking this Hamsey with just two ships?" Knut asked skeptically.

"No." Alfred shook his head. "They are *not* going to attack Hamsey."

Then he talked for the next few minutes, and by the time he was through, while Knut was not openly agreeing, he was nodding thoughtfully.

Finally, he allowed, "That could work."

Chapter Four

Like his comrades, Titus was looking forward to returning to Hamtun, downing a tankard of ale and devouring as much food as he could manage without raising the ire of the rest of the crew, which was a daily battle. The presence of the King waiting on the docks was not particularly noteworthy; while Alfred usually went out to sea with them, on the largest of the Saxon ships that was now his official flagship that he had named the *Redeemer*, it was not a daily occurrence, and those days like this one where he stayed ashore, he could be counted on to be waiting for a report from the ship masters on the day's training. As usual, Einarr's vessel and the other Danish ship led the procession that now numbered ten ships that would be the main force charged with locating the Danish raiders, taking advantage of their superior speed. And, as usually happened, the two crews were fiercely competitive with each other, but in this, the Centish crew of Lord Sigeræd, commanded by Thegn Beorhtweald while the ship was commanded by Sigmund Grimmarson, Dagfinn's older brother, showed the value of experience. To date, Titus' ship had not managed to beat the Centishmen's vessel to the agreed-on finish line, the southern bank of the Itchen River, which jutted out slightly and allowed them enough room to slow to approach the docks safely.

This day, however, the *Sea Viper* had a slight lead over the Centishmen, and for once, Einarr's hostility towards Titus was nowhere in evidence as the Dane strode up the center of the ship to stand over Titus and roar, "Use those muscles, boy! Today is our day! You are our strongest oarsman, so now is the time to prove it to those Centish ass-lickers!"

Einarr's attempt to motivate Titus almost rebounded, simply because Titus was so shocked that the Dane was not cursing him but the Cents, and not using a Danish curse to do it, but he managed to maintain his rhythm and intensified his effort, while Otha, Eadward, Ceadda, and Aelfnod all added their voices, roaring their encouragement to the entire crew. Not only Titus responded, but every man at the oars put all of their energy into the effort, even those men like Snorri and Willmar, both of whom ranked second only to Titus in feeling the taste of Einarr's rod across their back for holding back on their strokes. The distance from the docks to the river mouth was almost a quarter-mile, and naturally, the oarsmen could not see them since they were facing the opposite direction, so it was left to Eadward, who, shading his eyes, recognized the tall figure of their King.

Almost as importantly, he also recognized one of the men standing next to him, and he turned from the spot at the bow that he shared with Otha and the other Thegns to shout excitedly, "The King is there, but so is Lord Sigeræd! Let's show him what we Wiltun men are about!"

As rapidly as both ships were moving, the spray soaked every man, but they did not care, and the two were barely fifteen paces apart from oar tip to oar tip, which meant that they could hear Beorhtweald shouting the same kind of encouragement, as Sigmund bellowed out the count, while the second Dane, slightly older than Dagfinn, manned the steering oar. It was exhilarating, yet as fast as they were moving, as Titus was approaching utter exhaustion, to his fuddled mind, he became convinced that some magical force was at work that was conspiring against his ship. Yes, they were moving, but nobody in a position to know was shouting that they had reached the finish line, so clearly, some unseen power was moving the river mouth. Maybe, he thought dimly as his body responded on its own, the hour upon hour of repetition built up over the previous three weeks paying their dividends now, it's the same fairies who moved those huge stones at the place called Stonehenge some thirty miles to the north were making mischief here. This was what was in his mind when, from the bow, Eadward and the others erupted in cheers, joined by Einarr and Dagfinn at the stern, and only then did Titus and the others learn that they had, in fact, defeated the Centishmen for the first time. Afterward, it was decided that it was probably a good thing that the Wiltun men were too breathless and exhausted to revel in their victory, or it would have likely devolved into a physical confrontation once they were moored. As it was, their momentum allowed them to slide upriver, with Dagfinn the only one doing any work, guiding the ship towards its mooring berth, the rest of the crew slumped over their oars, panting to regain their collective breath.

"The King doesn't seem to be that interested in our victory," Otha observed quietly, prompting Eadward to turn his attention ahead from where he and Ceadda had been gloating about what they would be saying to Beorhtweald that evening when they went into the town, the noblemen of the fleet exempt from the restriction on going into Hamtun.

"No, he doesn't," Eadward agreed, though he was not all that alarmed, but then he glanced over at Ealdorman Sigeræd, who looked quite agitated. It *could* have been because of their victory over his men, yet Eadward did not think so, but it was when he saw Father Aethelred, who truly looked so distraught, he appeared to be on the verge of tears that it stirred in him a deep unease. "I think," he said slowly, and pitching his voice low so that the pair of oarsmen who manned the first set of oars, Ceadda's man Leofsige on the port side, and one of Aelfnod's men, Beornræd, on the starboard side, "our training might be over."

Otha looked at him with surprise mixed with respect, because this had been the thought that began running through his mind now that he had examined the waiting noblemen more closely. Then, as he had been taught to do by Einarr, Otha bent over and snatched up the coiled cable tucked next to the prow, minus the pagan figurehead, then hopped up onto the side, paused for a brief moment as the ship slid closer to the dock, then leapt across the expanse of water to land on the wooden dock. Dropping a loop onto the piling, he snugged the cable by pulling on the free end, drawing the ship towards the dock, while Dagfinn did the same at the stern, pulling the ship alongside the dock. In another change of routine, Alfred did not wait for Eadward and his Thegns to come to greet their King to give their report of the day's training, which would be followed by Einarr, who normally flatly disagreed with the Saxons' assessment of the crew's performance. Instead, the King strode down the dock, offering his nobles an impatient wave when they began the formalities of greeting him.

"We have no time to waste," Alfred said peremptorily. "Wiglaf has just sent news that the Danes have divided their forces, and two ships attacked Hamsey."

To his embarrassment, Eadward did not immediately recall the village, glancing over at Otha, but it was Ceadda who whispered, "It's a village three miles upriver from Læwe, Lord," which jogged his memory of the place.

Ignoring this slight interruption, Alfred continued, "While we do not know with any certainty why, it's possible that the reason they further divided their forces from two crews to one is because there are reports that the men in Læwe managed to damage one of the Danish ships as they passed the town. What we *do* know is that while one crew is still at Hamsey, the other has marched west, mostly on foot, though some are mounted on stolen horses."

"West?" Aelfnod spoke up, but before Alfred could say anything, the Thegn gasped, "They're going to Stanmer, aren't they, my Lord King?"

Alfred was surprised, but he did not hesitate to answer, "That's what we believe, Aelfnod. But," he asked curiously, "how did you conclude it was Stanmer so quickly? It could have been Steyning."

"Steyning is closer to the Arun than the Ouse for one thing, Lord King," Aelfnod answered without hesitation. Shaking his head, he continued, "But that's not why I thought of it. My youngest brother is a monk there, and he's told me of its wealth."

"What do you think they're talking about?" Titus asked Uhtric as they finished their tasks that secured the *Sea Viper* for the evening.

Uhtric studied the group for a moment, then admitted, "I don't know, but it doesn't look like it's anything good."

Depending on the personality of the individuals, the fact that they did not have to wait long was either a good thing or a bad one; for Titus, he was just happy to get the news before they had settled down for the coming night. His reasoning was, if rest and sleep were going to be in short supply, better to know sooner rather than later. However, when Eadward, Otha, and the other Thegns strode back to the ship, their expressions identically grim, Titus noticed that, for some reason, Lord Aelfnod was paler than the others, and he wondered why. Not that he had any time to dwell on it, and to the surprise of all of them, it was actually Lord Eadward who spoke, not Otha, as was normal.

"The King has been informed that two of the Danish ships sailed up the Ouse, but instead of trying to attack Læwe, they raided the village of Hamsey, then the crew of one ship left Hamsey and is heading west, towards the monastery at Stanmer. The King has ordered us, along with the Centishmen, to leave immediately to intercept them. We will row up the Ouse with Lord Beorhtweald's ship, but our task is to debark and march to Stanmer to stop the Danish crew, hopefully before they can finish sacking the monastery. The *Dragon's Fang* will anchor downriver from Læwe, in a position to block those Danes in Hamsey if they try to flee downriver."

It was then that Otha spoke up, anticipating the question before it was asked, "We're going to catch these Danish bastards on land, before they get back from Stanmer. But only if," he finished harshly, "you lads get your thumbs out and are ready to sail by midnight."

That was the last moment of relative inactivity, as Einarr reasserted control in his role as master and began roaring orders that sent the crew scrambling, each of them given a specific task.

There was enough time for Hrothgar to grumble, "Why did we just spend three weeks on this cursed ship, puking our guts out if we're going to kill them on land like normal men?"

"Would you rather face them on the water with all of three weeks of practice?" Uhtric countered, winking at Titus.

"Well, no," Hrothgar admitted, but the second largest Saxon of the Wiltun men was not one to surrender a complaint easily. "I'm just saying that it doesn't seem...right that we just wasted our time."

Before Uhtric could have more fun, Einarr snarled, "If you have the breath to chatter, you are not working hard enough. Now," he pointed, "get those barrels filled! Your tongues are going to be hanging out from thirst soon enough. We have a long distance to travel and no time to do it!"

Titus desperately wanted to know if they would have time to eat, but he thought better of it, offering up a prayer to God that He would hear his stomach's plea, then thought with a mixture of guilt and amusement, recalling his conversation with Alfred, I don't think the King would be happy to know that when I pray, it's usually about food...and other things I hunger for, but I *know* he wouldn't appreciate that.

It was in fact two hours before midnight that the two captured Danish ships slipped away from the docks, heading for the Solent, leaving the rest of the crews of Alfred's ragtag collection of ships working to depart as soon as they were able. The King did not think the other vessels would be needed, or even have an opportunity to engage with the pair of Danish ships, but he decided that it would be good practice for the moment when the opportunity to intercept the enemy presented itself. Just before they departed, Titus' prayer on behalf of his stomach was at least partially answered, when Otha disappeared briefly, returning with two large sacks containing loaves of bread and some cheeses; naturally, it was not enough for Titus, but it was better than nothing. The mood among the crewmen was pensive, although it was partially because they had only sailed at night once before, and even Einarr was more subdued than his normal self. It was now early May, so the darkness was relative, and he was familiar with the part of the Solent they would be rowing through before they were safely away from the shoreline, and they were also aided by a three-quarter moon, but there was a reason even experienced sailors preferred to only sail in the daylight hours. There was an added blessing, at least as far as the crew was concerned, in the form of a freshening and stiff breeze from the west that enabled the sail to be unfurled, and after a shouted discussion with Sigmund over on Beorhtweald's ship, it was decided that once they were safely away from the coast that they would allow the men to rest for a bit and move by sail alone. It was also tacitly understood that, if Alfred had chosen to accompany them, this would not have been the case, but when Lords Mucel and Eardwulf, and Ealdorman Sigeræd had prevailed on him to remain in Hamtun to wait for his flagship to be made ready, he had reluctantly agreed, to the intense relief of both crews. When they were informed that they would not be required to row, the men let out a low cheer, choosing to forego the muttered complaints that had become a nightly routine about the discomfort of sleeping aboard ship, thankful that they would be getting some rest. This was how it started, at least, but as they quickly learned, sleeping on a bench or in the bottom when the ship was moored at the dock compared to being under sail on the open water were two different things, and the cloaks they wrapped themselves in quickly became soaked from the spray created by the brisk movement of the ship. Some of the men chose to lower themselves down into the bottom, curling up in between the benches, but as they quickly discovered and Titus had already learned, while it protected them from the spray coming from over the sides, that moisture collected at the lowest point, and they found themselves lying in a puddle of water, forcing them to use the leather buckets that were kept for the purpose of bailing, or in the case of some of them, return to their bench, accepting the spray as the lesser of the two evils.

Uhtric, who had chosen to move before quickly returning to his bench, summed it up by muttering, "Now we know why those Danes and Northmen are such hard bastards. They spend weeks like this when they're coming from the North."

This summarized Titus' own feelings perfectly, and not for the first time, he was struck by how often he and his brother-in-law and best friend's thoughts so often ran along identical lines, not that it helped alleviate the misery of the moment. Nevertheless, Titus jerked in surprise when Einarr bellowed the order to rise and make ready at the oars, and he realized that he must have dozed off, although it was still dark, but when he looked to his right, because of the moonlight, he could barely make out the dark bulk of land off to port, his next, natural thought wondering where they were.

Like his comrades, he pissed over the side, and was sitting down on his bench when he just made out that the dark shape moving up from the rear deck was Dagfinn, and he asked the steersman, "Where are we, Dagfinn? Do you know?"

"Of course," Dagfinn replied in what was for him a sharp

tone, nettled that Titus might actually think that the man responsible for guiding the ship was not aware of their location. "Now that we are under oar, we are about three hours from the mouth of the Ouse."

Before Titus could respond, Einarr shouted something in Danish to Dagfinn, who replied in kind, then resumed moving forward, where Eadward and his Thegns had passed the night in comfort, relatively speaking. While Titus waited for the order to begin rowing, he strained his ears, although he did not turn on the bench to face the bow, but the cracking sound created by the sail made it impossible to hear, but when Dagfinn returned to the stern, Eadward was with him.

"Did you get any sleep?" Eadward asked Titus as he passed by, and while Titus was tempted to make the lordling feel guilty by lying, he admitted, "Some, Lord. I'm more hungry than tired."

As he expected, this made Eadward laugh, the young noble quipping, "So it's a normal day, eh?"

"A normal day, Lord," Titus agreed, though he only grinned because, truth be told, he *was* perpetually hungry.

A few heartbeats later, Dagfinn called out the order alerting the crew, then began the count, and within a few strokes, the ship was moving at a more rapid clip, and Titus momentarily forgot that he was hungry as his stomach began to react to the fact that, with every stroke, they were drawing closer to a fight.

"It's a risk, Lord." Eadward nodded, knowing that Otha was right, but he also wanted to hear the Thegn's reasoning about Eadward's proposal aloud, so he said nothing, just regarded Otha with a raised eyebrow, which Otha interpreted correctly. Holding out a finger, he began, "Yes, landing west of the Ouse so that we can march due north to Stanmer instead of marching from Læwe will save us time. And," he nodded at Aelfnod, "Lord Aelfnod has visited his brother at the monastery several times, and they went for ride to the south in this direction. It's hilly, but he said there's a beach that's a bit more than three miles from Stanmer where we can put in that's directly south of the monastery. That," Otha warned, "is the good news." Waiting for Eadward to indicate he should continue, when the lordling nodded, he continued, "But that means the *Viper* will be vulnerable, unless we leave enough men behind to protect it."

Eadward turned to Einarr, asking him, "How many men would you leave behind, Lord Einarr? If you were conducting a raid like this?"

Einarr considered, then answered, "At least eight, Lord. But ten would be better."

"That would cut our force to thirty-four men," Eadward mused, accepting the larger figure. Returning his attention back to Otha, he asked, "But how likely is it that the ship still at Hamsey will sail down the Ouse, get past Beorhtweald, then head west? Especially alone?"

It was, Otha thought, a good question, but he realized that he had not made himself clear.

"I'm not talking about the Danes we know are at Hamsey, Lord. There are still at least six ships we don't know the location of, and probably more. For all we know, the larger group may be on their way to join these two. And," he glanced over at Einarr, because it had been the Dane who had put the idea in his head, "I think it's not only possible but likely that these raiders have been joined by others from Frankia. It's been six weeks since we learned of the first raid. That's more than enough time for more of these bastards to show up."

Eadward considered this, then set it aside for the moment to ask Einarr, "Are you familiar with this beach that Aelfnod knows about?"

He was slightly surprised when the Dane nodded, although Einarr did demur slightly.

"If it is the one that I am thinking about, then yes, Lord, but I do not know about anything further inland."

For a brief moment, Eadward felt the urge to question Einarr about why a Dane who had been their enemy just a matter of four years before would know about the coastline and possible landing spots in southern Wessex, but he quickly suppressed it.

Instead, he asked, "Assuming that it is the same spot, how long before we get there?"

This, Einarr was prepared for, replying immediately, "If the crew puts their back into it, we will reach the spot about an hour before dawn, perhaps even earlier if they pull like Loki is chasing them."

"And Stanmer is only three miles from the coast, so if we hurry, we can hit those heathens before the sun is fully up," Eadward mused, ignoring the reference to the Northmen god of mischief and mayhem. "Which will help alleviate having less men."

This was the sign that the young lord had made his decision to leave some men with *Sea Viper*, and it helped that Otha, as well as Ceadda and Aelfnod agreed that it was the right decision, but when Eadward turned suddenly to move to the port side, lifting his hands and cupping them around his mouth, Otha barely got there in time, and while he knew that it was technically a breach of protocol to grab a man of higher rank, he was not worried given their relationship, but he did not intend to speak so sharply.

"What are you doing, Lord Eadward?" he demanded, and Eadward replied in surprise and a bit of anger, "We need to let Beorhtweald know that we aren't going with them to the Ouse." He hesitated then before he added, "Don't we?"

"We could," Otha seemingly agreed, but he pointed towards the other ship, "but what do you think his reaction would be? Yes, you're the son of Ealdorman Eadwig, and he's only a Thegn, but you've already seen he thinks he's in command. What if he forbids us to do that?"

As Otha intended, this made Eadward bristle, and he snapped, "He can 'forbid' us all he wants!" But then he subsided and agreed, "But yes, you're right, Otha. Better to just avoid any possible trouble." Addressing the others, Eadward sounded older than his years as he imbued his voice with a confidence that he did not really feel. "We're going to put ashore south of Stanmer, then we're going to catch those savages before the sun comes up."

The nerves of the moment turned out to be a blessing for the crew of the *Sea Viper*, because by rights, they should have needed time to recover once they rowed up onto the beach, which was unusually composed of a sand that reflected the moonlight quite well, making it much easier to see from the water. There was a moment of excitement because, since the Centishmen's ship was on their port side, it required Einarr to give the command to lift oars for a few beats to slow the *Viper* down before giving the order to resume rowing while Dagfinn pushed the steering oar over, the ship heeling hard to port to cut through the wake of the other ship. Even over the sound of surf and wind, they could hear the alarmed shouts of Beorhtweald, and Sigmund, but obeying Eadward's directive, they were ignored. The Centish ship slowed dramatically, and for a span of a hundred heartbeats, it appeared as if Sigeræd's Thegn would give the order to pursue the *Viper*, but then they vanished in the darkness behind them, with Beorhtweald's voice thinning out as he shouted what, to Titus' ears, seemed to be imprecations and threats. This was followed by a brief argument about which ten men would stay behind, and Titus was not alone in noticing that, while most of the crew argued against being left behind, there were a couple of exceptions among the Wiltun men, and one of them was Snorri, but in his case, Otha did not hesitate.

"No, we need you with us because you speak these dogs' tongue," the Thegn said in a tone that, while Snorri had only been with Otha a relatively short time, at least knew meant he would brook no argument, so he did not try, contenting himself to give Otha's back a sullen glare as he walked away.

Titus was surprised when he heard Einarr inform Eadward that he would be going with them, leaving Dagfinn behind in command, and he caught the surprise in Eadward's voice, although he did not argue with the Dane. Once the ship was beached, the men began the process of turning from a crew into a war party, each of them withdrawing items from their packs and donning their armor, while unfastening their shields from the sides of the ship. For Titus, it also meant reminding himself not to put on the leather vest with the iron rings that he had learned was the best choice for shipboard combat, which had been the advice Dagfinn had offered when he warned Titus that Einarr had more humiliation in mind when they moved from the wooden frames outside Hamtun to out on the water.

"He's going to make sure he dunks you, and if you're wearing your mail, you're going to sink to the bottom," Dagfinn had informed him.

"You mean he wants to *drown* me?" Titus had gasped, but Dagfinn shook his head.

"No, when we begin training on the ship, we'll be in shallow enough water that anyone who goes in won't drown. If," he had added ominously, "whoever it is does not panic. All you will have to do is stand up...as long as the bottom is not too muddy. But if you are wearing your mail, you will sink like a stone, no matter how strong you are."

As several of Titus' comrades had learned, Dagfinn was right; even strong swimmers like Aelfwine had plummeted to the bottom of the Itchen, although they were quickly fished out. Titus had not, thanks to the leather vest, and he had worn it exclusively whenever armor was called for over the previous week, but he caught himself when he reached for it, reminding himself that they would be on land. Assembling on the beach, there were thirty-five warriors, including Eadward, the Wiltun Thegns, and Einarr, and they immediately began marching north, while of the Wiltun men, Wilwulf, Theobald, Odda, and Deorwine stayed behind with six men from Alfred's guard. The men who had manned the oars were all tired from their exertions, though the tension of the moment helped most of them ignore the fatigue as they made their way through the darkness, aided somewhat by the moonlight and able to see the bulk of a hill looming above them. Like most of his comrades, Titus was wearing a sword on his left hip, the Danish sword he had won as spoils from the Dane he had slain in single combat on the day of the Battle of Ethantun, while carrying his new shield, and his helmet was strapped to his chest. However, in another difference from his comrades, he did not carry a spear, choosing instead a Danish-style ax hanging from his belt on the right side. The party moved in a loose formation, with Aelfnod's man Beornræd, Ceadda's man Aedelstan, and Willmar acting as the advance guard some two hundred paces ahead of the main body. There was no talking; even if they had not been tired from their exertions, the prospect of what lay ahead would have quelled any desire for talk, so the only sounds were footfalls and the light panting as the men negotiated the undulating terrain. They had gone perhaps a mile when Titus noticed what he at first thought was a figment of his imagination, a faint glow to the north, but he learned he was not alone in seeing it.

"It looks like something's on fire," Uhtric, who, as was normal, was next to Titus, muttered.

Titus said nothing, but he instinctively looked over to Lord Aelfnod, having heard that the Thegn had a brother who was a monk at the monastery, wondering what was going through the Thegn's mind. While he had seen the Danes in battle, Titus had only heard stories about the kind of rapine and plunder that made the men of the North so feared and hated when they went *viking*, and while he would never say it aloud, he always felt a shiver of dread running up his spine whenever he heard them. Without a word being said, the men of Wiltun picked up their pace, the predominant sound becoming the panting as they negotiated the hilly terrain until they reached a point where a low ridge was the last obstacle between them and the monastery. Reaching the base, Otha, to whom Eadward had silently ceded authority, called a brief halt to enable the warriors to catch their breath, choosing to do it where they were still out of sight.

"Once we get to the top of that," Otha indicated the crest of the ridge, "we'll have a better idea of what to expect, but we're not going to waste time. All of you can see what's happening there."

This was nothing more than the truth; the sullen glow that Uhtric had noticed had become an intense orange glow, shimmering and dancing against the night sky in a manner that needed no explanation, even to those like Titus who had never personally witnessed structures on fire in the night. The ascent to the top of the ridge was not excessively steep, but it seemed to take far more time than necessary to Titus. Once they reached the top, Otha had no need to call a halt, the men involuntarily stopping to stare down in horror at the sight of the blazing buildings that had once been a prosperous monastery. The blaze was not restricted to the buildings of the religious order itself, but the cluster of structures that was, in effect, a village that housed all of the lay people who supported the monastery. In terms of population, there were perhaps three hundred souls at Stanmer, and every single one of them was in mortal peril, if they had not already been put to the sword.

The sight was more than enough incentive, but Otha drew, then thrust his own sword into the air, the flames glinting off the iron of his blade as he roared, "Men of Wiltun! Follow me!"

In strict terms, it was probably a bit too far to launch an all-out charge at the run, but in the moment, it did not matter to the men of Wiltun, who, to the man, bellowed their own promise as they followed the Thegn in a headlong charge down the slope. As usually happened, Titus' longer legs showed their advantage once the Saxons had covered a hundred paces, so that he was leading the way down the hill, his shield held out from his body so that it did not hinder his progress. Many of his comrades were not far behind him, but as he careened downhill, Titus unconsciously unleashed the characteristic that had earned him the title of Berserker, a boiling, uncontrollable rage, and it almost immediately became stoked by the sight of what was clearly a woman, outlined against the flames, running in their direction, though not because she had spotted Titus and his comrades, instead looking over her shoulder at the two Danes who were in pursuit.

"Woman! Run to us and don't look back! It will slow you down!"

Titus recognized Ceadda's voice, but his attention was on the pair of Danes who had just spotted the onrushing Saxons, both of them skidding to a halt then, without any hesitation, turning about and resuming their sprint, but in the opposite direction. One of them was faster than his companion, and Titus closed the distance rapidly on the laggard who, like the Dane a few paces ahead of him, was shouting the alarm to their comrades scattered about the cluster of buildings that surrounded the monastery. He saw a handful of figures standing around another group of people kneeling on the ground, and while part of him noticed that the standing men were now rushing in his direction, he had a more urgent priority. Realizing, with some chagrin, that he had not drawn his sword yet, he extended his shield arm fully and out from his shoulder, then swung it, aiming the edge of it for his quarry as he brought it across and in front of his torso, striking the Dane's left shoulder. Even without his full strength behind it, the blow was enough to send his foe reeling to the right, not enough to knock him from his feet, but enough to make him stagger and for Titus to dispatch him, but only by reaching down and drawing the ax stuck in his belt. He did so in one motion, withdrawing, raising, then bringing the ax down as the Dane, almost as if by design, exposed his neck to the blow as he reeled, while Titus' aim was true, slicing through the thick muscles and bone, nearly but not quite decapitating the Dane. His momentum helped him yank the ax free, which was a good thing, because the Danes who had been guarding their prisoners were rushing at him, focusing on him because, as usual, he had outstripped his comrades and was several paces ahead of them.

The night air was pierced with a combination of shrill screams of the women who were suffering from their misfortune of being in the wrong place at the wrong time in their supporting the monastery and the bellows of both Saxons and Danes as they rushed at each other. Barely registering his first kill, Titus' attention was already riveted on a Dane with a beard that hung below the middle of his chest and, thanks to the lurid flames, looked like copper fire, although it was a sword that might have been the twin of the one suspended in its scabbard at his left hip that had Titus' attention. The weapon was raised above his foe's head, prepared for an overhand blow that, if it landed, would split Titus' helmet, while he held his ax, dripping blood from its first victim, up and away from his body, the head tilted outward. With a bellow that needed no translation, the Dane brought his sword down in a powerful yet obvious blow, clearly intending to force Titus to respond by bringing his shield up. Instead of relying on his shield, Titus instinctively swung his ax across his body, the head of his weapon striking the shaft of the Dane's sword, creating a small shower of sparks and making his entire arm go numb while knocking his enemy's sword aside but putting his own weapon out of position for a counterstroke. For the second time, Titus used his primary defensive weapon, essentially repeating the same maneuver of swinging the shield across his body. This time, however, instead of using the edge of his shield to inflict damage, he twisted his wrist and aimed the cone-shaped boss that came to a point for the Dane's face. Unable to bring his own shield across his body in time, the point of the iron boss punched into the man's cheekbone, and Titus felt as well as heard the crunching sound of collapsing bone, followed immediately by a muffled, gurgling scream from the Dane who went reeling off to Titus' right, the man dropping both weapon and shield to clutch his ruined face with both hands.

Then, there was a shattering collision as Titus' comrades reached him just as the other onrushing Danes arrived, the previous sounds a whisper compared to the roars, curses, and screams of the combatants finally closing with each other, the sharp cracking of wooden shields crashing into each other, and punctuated by the clanging of metal striking metal coming less than an eyeblink later. While he would have preferred to draw his sword, Titus was not given the opportunity, immediately engaged with another Dane, although this man used an ax like he did, but without a shield. In the span of the perhaps three heartbeats he had, Titus sized his opponent up, recognizing that this Dane was even younger than he was, with a sparse, patchy beard and a boiled leather vest that was missing several iron rings. It was the wild, poorly aimed swing of his ax that was most instructive, and with a contemptuous grin, Titus knocked his foe's blow aside, once again using his wrist to twist the shield slightly outward, a trick Uhtric had taught him that helped prevent edged weapons from embedding themselves in the wood. Although, he thought with a detachment that was a result in the lack of skill of his foe, it might have been better if he had allowed the ax blade to remain lodged in the shield, knowing that his strength would enable him to yank the youngster about and into a posture that would enable him to dispatch him. Still, the power he used to knock the youngster's ax away caused the Dane to lurch a step to his right, and in a common mistake for novices, his shield dropped slightly in an unconscious reaction to being knocked off balance. Titus did not hesitate, but in mid-stroke, he once again twisted his wrist so that, instead of the ax blade cutting into the young Dane's unprotected skull, it was the flat side that crashed against his head. It would have still been a killing blow, but Titus also altered the amount of force he was exerting in mid-swing so that, while the youth dropped down to the ground as if his bones had suddenly vanished from his body, he would wake up to face whatever fate Lord Eadward deemed appropriate. It would not be until after the fight when, like warriors everywhere, Titus relived what took place in his mind, and he realized that he had had it in the back of his mind that having a Dane still alive to question might be a good thing. This marked the first time where he had been in battle where he thought in what could be called strategic terms, albeit in a rudimentary form, but it was an important step in his development that he would come to appreciate in the future. In the moment, however, he gave his fallen opponent barely a glance as he scanned the area in front of him for another threat.

Seeing that the Danes who had been guarding the prisoners were now all engaged with his comrades, fighting in a ragged line, but beyond them, Titus saw what he quickly counted as a dozen more Danes rushing in their direction. Glancing about him, to his dismay, he saw that when these warriors arrived, they would be outnumbered, and he saw that the only Saxons at this spot were Otha's men because for whatever reason, Ceadda and Aelfnod had taken their men and the men of Alfred's guard somewhere else. Along with Titus, only Lord Eadward, Hrothgar, and Ealdwolf were not currently occupied, but they seemed unaware of the impending threat heading their direction, or so Titus thought, and he was about to shout a warning when, for reasons that Titus could not immediately identify, all of the onrushing Danes suddenly changed direction, led by a man about Titus' size and with the same muscular build, wielding a double-bladed ax and a large round shield, who bellowed what was clearly an order, changing his direction of movement so that he was now running perpendicularly to their original orientation, now heading to Titus' right. He did not have to wait long to learn why; from in between the main monastery building, which was burning but not fully involved, and a long, low building that served as the living quarters for the monks, Ceadda and Aelfnod came rushing into view, leading the rest of the *Sea Viper*'s crew, and he spotted Einarr with them.

"Titus! Go with them! They're trying to escape and get back to Hamsey!"

Obeying Otha without hesitation, Titus broke into a run, hearing the Thegn shout for Hrothgar and Ealdwolf to follow him, but he did not slow to wait for his comrades. There was a large circle of light created by the fires started by the Danes, and Titus knew the immediate goal of their foes would be to escape that circle. The Saxon cause was aided by the fact that the buildings at the eastern edge of the cluster surrounding the monastery had been fired first as the Danes swept in from the direction of Hamsey and were now fully involved, but Titus saw with dismay that the large Dane and those immediately behind him were rapidly closing on the farthest edge of light and were the most likely to escape. Even as this realization hit him, Ceadda, Aelfnod, and the warriors immediately behind him reached the slowest of the fleeing Danes, two of whom skidded to a stop to turn and face their pursuers, presumably to buy their fleeing comrades time to escape. One of Ceadda's men, Wigmund, tried to slow down, but his momentum was too great, essentially running right into the spear thrust out by one of the Danes, eliciting a bellow of pain and rage from the Saxon, telling Titus that the blow was not immediately mortal. Ceadda, taking advantage of the Dane's focus on Wigmund, struck his own blow, thrusting his *seaxe* into the enemy's chest, and even from the distance he was, Titus clearly heard the gurgling quality of the man's moan that indicated at least one lung had been punctured. Taking this as the sign that matters were in hand with these stragglers, Titus veered slightly but enough to avoid being engaged, setting his sights on the leader of this fleeing group. Just as Titus neared the edge of the light, he risked a glance over his shoulder and was relieved to see that Hrothgar and Ealdwolf chose to follow him instead of staying with Ceadda and Aelfnod, but he also saw a third figure, slightly behind the pair. Is that Lord Eadward? he wondered, but he could afford no more than the heartbeat's worth of time he had taken looking over his shoulder before he returned his attention to the situation ahead of him. Just before the last of what he had counted as four Danes following the large warrior most closely vanished into the gloom, the rearmost Dane glanced over his shoulder, wrenching a curse from Titus' lips. He had hoped to use the darkness to his advantage and close the distance without being spotted, but this pagan bastard had ruined it.

Turning his head slightly, Titus yelled over his shoulder, "They know we're chasing them! Hrothgar, Ealdwolf, follow me! We'll run them down!"

He had drawn his sword after shoving the ax back into his belt, but the exertion and the radiant heat from the burning buildings had made him sweat profusely, and he desperately wanted to wipe his hands while the sweat was running from his hair down into his eyes, blurring his vision at the worst possible moment. Nevertheless, he did not slow his pace, once again relying on his longer legs, but while his ultimate goal was the large Dane, one of the four men behind him glanced over his shoulder again, and despite now being outside the circle of light, there was no way for the Northman to miss Titus, outlined by the flames and just a matter of ten paces behind him. For the span of a few normal heartbeats, the Dane desperately tried to increase his pace, and even over the sound of his own harsh breathing, Titus could hear the Dane panting. The Dane abruptly slowed then, trying to spin about to face Titus while still in motion. Perhaps if it had not been dark, he might have succeeded, but ultimately what mattered was that his feet got tangled with each other, and his momentum made him reel backward then land heavily on his back, dropping both his ax and shield when he hit the ground. Barely slowing, Titus bent over and thrust down with his sword, but because of the darkness and his own speed, he missed the Dane's throat, the point instead punching into the mail vest protecting the man's left upper chest, and as sometimes happened, the metal of Titus' sword was caught by the iron rings of mail. The effect was that, instead of recovering the blade smoothly, Titus' arm was jerked backwards as his momentum carried him past the Dane, who was screaming in agony, and he almost lost his grip on his sword. For a brief instant, he thought of relinquishing it and returning to the ax, but while he had become more adept with the weapon favored by the Northmen, his instinct told him that when he faced his true quarry, he would be better served using the weapon with which he was most comfortable. Consequently, he slowed long enough to wrench the blade free, jerking another roar of pain from the prone Dane, who remained on the ground, writhing in an agony that was destined to last only long enough for Ealdwolf, a few paces behind Titus, to dispatch him. Titus heard the last shriek, but it barely registered, his senses now fully engaged in keeping his quarry in sight.

Even outside the light from the fires, Titus was aided by both the three-quarter moon, and the fact that they were crossing the open ground of a pasture, used by the sheep that were tended by the monks that provided the brothers with cheese, wool, and meat, so he could still make out the fleeing men, albeit as little more than dark shapes, while Titus' quarry was distinguishable only because it was larger. He was certain he was closing on him, but not quickly enough, and only gradually did Titus recognize the meaning of what appeared to be just a darker line several feet higher. Those are trees, he thought with a stab of worry. Once they make it into those woods, even with Ealdwolf, Hrothgar, and perhaps Eadward with him, the Danes would still have an advantage and might turn and fight. Yes, it was likely that they would be more concerned with making their escape to Hamsey, but it was not a certainty, and he actually found himself faltering in his pace for perhaps two or three heartbeats. However, while he was older, and somewhat wiser, he was still not far removed from the fourteen year-old who had endured the lacerating scorn and hatred from his own father Leofric, so his hesitation did not last long, and he resumed his pace and covered the last fifty paces to the first line of trees. At first, it was not that difficult, because the underbrush had been cleared away, though this did not last long, and he felt as much as saw the first of the small bushes and shrubs that lashed against his lower body, but he was also now less than five paces behind one of the Danes. Not the large warrior, although Titus caught glimpses of his target, thanks to glints of moonlight off the warrior's helmet, and with a burst of speed, he closed the distance to the nearest Dane, who, unlike his comrade, had neither looked back nor tried to turn to face Titus. It meant that he was completely unprepared for the thrust from Titus that punctured his back, slicing through the boiled leather vest the Dane was wearing and, as Titus intended, piercing the man's heart, who did not have the time or the breath to cry out, just collapsing after a couple more paces. This time, Titus' blade withdrew cleanly, and he was able to continue his pursuit, but he was worried that he would still have to confront at least one or two more Danes before facing the foe he wanted. However, there was a sudden shout off to his left, and while the words were unintelligible, he recognized Hrothgar's voice, followed instantly by a combination of sounds that included the ringing of metal against metal. Less than a full heartbeat later, something similar took place, this time slightly behind him and to his right.

"Titus! Go get that big bastard! We're fine!"

Needing no more encouragement, Titus continued pushing through the undergrowth, leaving the sounds of the struggles behind him, and it took a few heartbeats before he was far enough from the noise to realize something, and the recognition of this change brought him to a stop. There was no longer sound of a fleeing man ahead of him, no crashing through the brush, nothing to indicate where the big Dane was, and how far ahead he still was. Stifling a curse, Titus came to a stop, his hearing impaired by the sound of his own breathing, but he did take the time to quickly wipe his hands on the lower edge of his tunic before taking a cautious step forward. Using a trick that Lord Otha had taught him, he held his mouth open, which helped hearing, but it seemed to work only at night for reasons not even Otha knew, then moved his head from side to side, straining to hear something, anything that would help him locate his foe. Yes, it was possible that the Dane was moving stealthily away, leaving Titus behind, but for reasons he would not have been able to articulate, he was certain that the warrior was here, nearby, and probably doing the same thing he was doing. Taking another step, he began to move a bit more quickly, but still pausing after every couple of paces, only vaguely aware that the noise behind him had subsided, and not because of the growing distance. He could only hope that it was because either Hrothgar, Ealdwolf, or perhaps Eadward had prevailed, but there was no way he was turning back, although when he thought of Eadward, he was tempted to do so. This was his mistake, letting his mind wander, even the slightest bit, but as King Alfred would have surely insisted, God saw fit to make the Dane step on a large branch as he came rushing at Titus, making a loud snapping noise that warned Titus, giving him just enough time to turn to face the Dane, who, with a roar, launched himself at the young Saxon before he could get his shield up and in front of him.

The collision was terrific, catching Titus flat-footed, and he felt himself falling backward, while at the same time, a hand that he felt certain was made of iron clamped around his throat. Before his mind had time to adjust to the sudden attack, his back slammed into the ground, the impact made even more severe by the Dane's weight on top of him, the air leaving his lungs through his nose since his windpipe was blocked by the Dane's grip in an explosive snort. Somehow, he managed to retain his grip on both shield and sword, but he let go of the shield to grasp his foe's right wrist, with the intention of wrenching the Dane's grip from his throat. It was like grabbing a thick oak branch, hard and unyielding, and even with his own prodigious strength, to Titus' frustration and growing sense of panic, he could not budge the man's hand at all. Despite the darkness, he could see the Dane's face clearly enough just above him, the bearded mouth twisted into a snarl and he felt the spray of the man's saliva, and the man's eyes were alight with the kind of savage joy that Titus himself had experienced at the thought of slaying an enemy. With a growing desperation, Titus brought his sword up, though rather than try to maneuver it so the point was oriented toward the Dane so that he could stab with it, he swung the pommel of the blade, aiming for the Dane's head, but even with the roaring sound in his ears, he heard the cracking sound of the pommel striking wood, telling him that his foe had maintained his grip on his own shield and, most importantly, kept it in position to protect him from just such an attack.

"You're useless and *pathetic*, boy! You're not worth a jar of tanner's piss! You should have died the same time as your mother and saved me all the trouble and grief you caused me, but you're about to die now, and that suits me!"

It was as if, somehow, Leofric had been magically transported to stand next to the struggling pair, so clearly did

Titus hear, and recognize, his father's voice, the contempt and hatred that was a daily feature of life with his father dripping from every word. Even now, four years since he had last seen Leofric, and sworn to kill him the next time they met, Titus' sire had been an almost constant presence in Titus' inner life, lurking in the recesses of the young man's mind, something that he never spoke of but could not hide from his sisters, and once Leofflaed had described what Titus had gone through at the hands of his father to Uhtric, his brother-in-law. What mattered in this moment was that there was a darkness ringing his field of vision, a black fog that was moving towards the center, where he saw the snarling face of the man who was about to kill him, and the contemptuous words of his father in his ears.

Whereas before, fragments of what took place would come back to Titus, like they had with Hrodulf, and the Dane whose armor he now wore and whose sword he carried, although there would always be gaps, this time was different, not only because the missing time never came back, but what was missing was how he extricated himself from what seemed to be an impossible predicament. No matter how hard he tried to recall, in his memory, it was just that one moment he was futilely trying to break the iron grip of the Dane straddling him, and the next he was climbing to his feet, his throat feeling as if someone had poured hot coals down it, while the Dane was a dark shape on his hands and knees, shaking his head as he tried to clear it. The other important difference was that, while his shield was still on the ground, Titus was holding his sword, whereas he caught the dull glint of the Dane's double-headed ax on the ground, and while it was within his foe's reach, it was between him and Titus, meaning that the warrior was now faced with a choice; he could get to his feet, or he could snatch up the ax, but he could not do both, and it was obvious by the manner in which he reacted that he understood this. For his part, Titus did not hesitate, much, just long enough to suck in a deep breath; ironically, the pain from the air flowing down his damaged windpipe did more to clear his head than the air itself, but then he was moving, his sword held out from his side, low and parallel to the ground. Understanding he had no chance to grab his own weapon, the Dane instead did something completely unexpected, rolling on the ground away from Titus, but as Titus quickly determined, it was a shrewd maneuver by an experienced foe because it bought the Dane just enough time to scramble to his feet. Reaching behind him, the Dane drew a long dagger, almost as long as a *seaxe*, but nowhere near the length of Titus' sword, and the Saxon felt a surge of confidence, although it was also tempered with a healthy slice of caution, reminded of his enemy's strength by the throbbing of his throat.

"I am going to kill you, Saxon," the Dane spoke in heavily accented but understandable English. "I am going to gut you! I will gouge your eyes out and fuck the empty holes with my prick! I am..."

"Going to talk me to death?"

This, at least, was what Titus intended to say, but not only was it indistinguishable to a frog croaking to Titus' ears, it hurt too much to finish, so instead, he lunged before he was finished. He had to take a larger step than he would have liked, robbing him as it did of having his legs under him, but he *really* wanted to kill this Danish bastard, so even after what had just happened, he took the risk. Launching his thrust, he felt the tip bury itself in the Dane's left arm, and while it was gratifying to hear the man roar with pain, he knew that it was not particularly damaging. It did prompt the Dane to retaliate with a slicing blow of his own, to which Titus responded instinctively, just barely managing to parry it with a sweeping move across his body, the small shower of sparks providing an eyeblink of faint illumination. Because the blade was now positioned across his body at waist level, Titus executed a backhand slash, something he did not normally favor, and it was the Dane's turn to block his opponent's attack, but while he managed to do so, Titus' heavier sword, along with his own strength, showed its advantage, knocking the dagger all the way across the Dane's body and out of position, either for his own offensive counter, or another defensive tactic. Once again, instead of using the point, Titus punched at the Dane with the pommel of his sword, but this time without a shield and with his dagger out of position, Titus landed a solid blow against the Dane's cheek, and he felt the bone give way with a crunch, the sensation transferred up through the pommel to accompany the sound and sending the Dane staggering. To his credit, while he let out a groan, it was not a full scream one would anticipate from such a damaging blow, but more importantly, the Dane not only did not drop his dagger to clutch his face as Titus expected, in fact he lashed out with it, which Titus walked right into as he pressed his advantage.

In another sign that Alfred and the more pious of his comrades would have insisted was a sign that God was watching out for Titus, either because of the pain, the darkness, or perhaps because Alfred and the others were right, the Dane misjudged, not by much, but enough so that, instead of the point of his dagger punching through Titus' mail into his body just under his sternum as he aimed, it struck at an angle in a glancing blow that sliced along Titus' left side. Later, Titus would discover several broken and missing links, the edge of the blade cutting through his padded undertunic, tunic and skin, wrenching a gasp of pain from his lips, but it also gave him another opportunity for an eyeblink's worth of time, and he did not hesitate. Nor did he repeat his attack with the opposite end of his sword, instead using the point and, in a final and fatal irony, launched a sweeping underhand thrust targeting the same spot the Dane had aimed for less than a heartbeat earlier, except that Titus' aim was true, and with his feet under him and using all of his strength, he drove his sword into the Dane's body, transfixing him and only stopping when the handguard struck the Dane's armor with enough of an impact that it would have knocked the wind out of the man if it had been a punch. They were standing face to face, and Titus was blasted with the breath of his dying foe, yet despite the darkness, he could see the white of the Dane's eyes as they went wide from the shock of the mortal blow. He knew that he should twist the blade, yet for some reason, he did not, instead letting the Dane fall backward and off the blade, watching as the warrior collapsed onto his back, his face up to the night sky.

To his surprise, Titus realized that he was no longer angry, but even more unsettling was that he was not nearly as satisfied as he thought he would be, and he seemed to be frozen in place, staring dumbly down at the Dane, whose mouth was working as the blood pouring from his mouth shone black in the filtered moonlight. He did observe that the Dane's right hand seemed to be reaching for something, his arm moving with an increasing and growingly frantic energy, and Titus' initial thought was a regret that he had not finished the Dane off, until the answer came to him. He's trying to find his weapon, Titus realized, and immediately understanding why, he turned, scanned the ground, and saw the ax a couple paces away. Before he could talk himself out of it, he retrieved the ax then, after making sure that the dagger was out of the Dane's reach as well, he dropped it, not directly into the Dane's hand, but a few inches from it, and the dying man managed to grab the handle before closing his eyes. For a moment, Titus thought the Dane had succumbed from the wound inflicted by Titus' sword, which was still in his hand, but then his eyes opened again, and he turned his head slowly as if he was searching for something else, then he saw Titus standing over him.

"What...what...is your name?" He whispered this, creating a spray of blood as he formed the words. "So that I may tell my gods when I reach Val...Valhalla who slew me."

He briefly considered refusing to answer, suspicious even now that this Dane had some final trick planned, perhaps some sort of curse against his name, but he heard himself answer, "Titus. Titus of Cissanbyrig."

For a heartbeat, he thought about adding his "Berserker" title, then decided against it, but as he quickly learned, there was no need.

"Titus?" The Dane frowned, but before he could say anything else, he began gagging, and turning his head, expelled a huge gout of blood, while his breathing now had a wheezing quality that told Titus he was within a matter of heartbeats from death, but then he surprised Titus by saying, "That is not a common name with you Saxons, is it?"

"No," Titus admitted.

"We have heard of a Titus who you Saxons call a Berserker who is said to be a great warrior," the Dane said, and Titus heard the recognition in the man's voice, and the astonishment. "This is you?"

Not liking the man's tone, Titus only said tersely, "Yes.

I've been called that."

"How old are you?" the Dane asked with a disbelieving tone to Titus' ears, and before he could stop himself, Titus snarled, "Old enough to have killed you, Dane!"

The Dane hissed something that sounded like some sort of curse or epithet, then his body suddenly spasmed, and feeling a stab of shame, Titus blurted out impulsively, "What is your name, Dane? So that I can tell my comrades who I've slain?"

He could tell this pleased the Dane, but his strength was fading rapidly, his chest heaving as he struggled for his last breaths to answer, "My name is Sigurd Gunnarson, although I am more commonly known as Sigurd the Bold. I am," his face twisted, and while it could have been from the pain, Titus did not believe so, "I *was* the leader of this *viking*."

Part of Titus was not surprised; somehow, he had known this Dane was an important figure, even if he had not known the specifics, and it was this implicit knowledge that had made Titus pursue him, and he felt that he should acknowledge this somehow.

"Go be with your gods in Valhalla, Sigurd the Bold. And," he lowered his voice to a whisper because, behind him, he heard Eadward's voice calling his name, "tell them that Titus the Berserker will be sending more of your warriors to them."

Sigurd's last sound sounded like a strangled cough, but Titus was certain that it was a laugh. Then, he died, and Eadward found him still standing over another foe that he had vanquished.

"Titus! Titus! Where are you?"

Recognizing Eadward's voice, Titus felt a stab of relief, though he did not hesitate to call back, and he heard the noise of more than one man before he saw there were three dark shapes approaching. They reached him, and Titus saw that Eadward was holding his left arm awkwardly.

Trying to hide his concern, Titus asked what had happened, but it was Ealdwolf who beat Eadward to tell him, "He got stuck with a spear by one of those turd lickers." Then, when Eadward turned to glare at him, he added quickly, "But Lord Eadward made him pay for it right enough."

Titus was certain he knew what Eadward was up to when

the young lord changed the subject by pointing down at Titus' side and asked in an almost accusing voice, "But what about you? I can see blood shining in the light."

While Titus was aware of his side, this was the first time he actually looked down, and he was surprised, and discomfited, to see the blood that had oozed out through the rent in his mail shirt, which made it hurt more.

"It's nothing." More to change the subject, and to mollify Eadward, he asked, "Lord, should we strip the dead now?"

As he hoped, this distracted Eadward, but he only considered for a moment before he shook his head.

"We need to get back to the monastery," he decided, but then for the first time, he bent over to examine the dead Dane more closely, exclaiming softly, "By the Rood! He's got a lot of arm rings!" Counting quickly, he grinned up at Titus. "Eight! And at least two of them are gold!" Then, before anyone could comment, he ordered, "Take the rings, and we'll come back for the rest."

Without thinking, Titus bent down to comply, wrenching a gasp of pain from him, but when Ealdwolf made to help, he snarled a curse at his comrade, then quickly removed the eight rings, and he felt he could be forgiven for wondering if he would be given any of them since he had been the man to slay the Dane.

He surprised himself by saying as he straightened up, "His name was Sigurd Gunnarson, but he was known as Sigurd the Bold. And," he added with a pride he felt was perfectly justifiable, "he is...he *was*," he corrected himself, "the leader of this raid."

"Of course," Eadward said in mock disgust. "It would be Titus who kills an important man."

While it hurt, it also felt good to laugh because it meant he was alive, and Titus and his companions turned and headed back to the lurid orange glow of Stanmer as it burned.

For the most part, the fight was over, and the Wiltun men had managed to put out the fire in the monastery before the building was completely destroyed, although more than half of the other buildings, more than a dozen altogether, were either already completely destroyed or were too involved to save. In Eadward's absence, Otha had taken command, and they found him with Ceadda, standing next to a half-dozen kneeling men, and for reasons he could not express or really understand, Titus was relieved to see the young Dane he had spared among the prisoners.

Seeing Eadward approach, Otha deftly carried on the fiction that it was the young lord in command, saying more loudly than necessary, "My Lord, here are the prisoners you ordered us to capture so that we could gather more information!"

Eadward had done no such thing, and his initial instinct was to say as much, but Otha, knowing Eadward as he did and that he was honest almost to a fault, gave him a quick shake of the head that, thankfully, Eadward interpreted correctly.

"Excellent, Otha!" He tried to match Otha's tone, but he saw Titus' smirk at the fiction. Ignoring his friend, he continued, "How many of these savages did you slay?"

"Thirty-four, Lord," Otha answered immediately.

"And we ran five of them down ourselves," Eadward said, then after a brief hesitation that only Titus noticed, added, "and Titus slew their leader."

"How do you know?" Otha asked, not in a challenging manner, clearly curious.

Instead of answering, Eadward turned to Titus, nodding at him to explain, and he replied, "He told me before he died." Then, without thinking much of it, he added, "He said his name was Sigurd Gunnarson, but he's known as Sigurd the Bold."

None of them had noticed that Einarr had joined them, but he announced his presence with a hiss of indrawn breath that was unmistakable, and as one, the Saxons turned to stare at him, but Otha forgot to let Eadward speak, because he was the one who observed, "That name obviously means something to you, Lord Einarr."

For the first time in Titus' memory, by the light of the flames of the buildings that could not be saved, he could see that Einarr looked acutely uncomfortable, although the Dane clearly understood that he would have to say something, and he gave a reluctant nod and answered, "I know him."

This time, it was Eadward who noticed the wording, and while he was normally intimidated by the large Dane, this was nowhere in evidence as Eadward pounced. "You said you know him, not you know *of* him, which is different. How do you know him?" Before Einarr could respond, Otha, whose mind had immediately begun working, interjected, "Was he one of Guthrum's men? Is that bastard behind this?"

This angered Einarr, but he was still more uncomfortable than angry, actually taking a step back from the Saxons, who were beginning to crowd around him as Otha's words awoke their own suspicions that had been lying, if not dormant, then at least unspoken.

Regardless, while they were prepared for Einarr to swear, "No! He does not serve King Aethelstan! He was not at Ethantun; he was in Frankia at the time!" they were all shocked when Einarr said, "He is the son of my father's brother."

There was a stunned silence, but it was Hrothgar, whose mind was not the swiftest under the best circumstances, who verbalized the connection that his comrades had made within a heartbeat. "That means you're cousins!"

Despite the tension, this elicited some chuckles, and Einarr answered with heavy humor, "Yes, Hrothgar, even with Danes, it means he is my cousin."

For Titus, it was a stunning revelation, and he could have been forgiven that the first thing that came to his mind was the conflict between the two; and now, he thought dismally, I just killed his cousin. Truly, Einarr had been startled, yet he did not seem overly upset, but immediately on the heels of that thought another one came to Titus; he's also standing here, outnumbered, so he could be acting, and even now he's plotting his revenge.

As much to change the subject than for any thought of concern, he asked, "What about Lord Aelfnod's brother? Did he survive?"

Otha shook his head, saying sadly, "No, they killed all but two of the monks, but we showed up before they could finish the last two off. And," he sighed, "unfortunately, Aelfnod's brother wasn't one of them. He's with him now, saying goodbye and preparing him for burial."

"So," Eadward mused, "we've accounted for forty-five of these heathen savages, which means there should only be four or five unaccounted for."

"No, my Lord," Otha sighed. Indicating the six kneeling Danes, he explained, "According to these bastards, there were at least sixty of these vermin who came to Stanmer. Some of the men with the other ship insisted on coming with them. And," he added grimly, "we learned that there *are* nine ships, and they're expecting more to join them from Frankia."

"Christ's blood!" Eadward exclaimed, prompting an amused glance from some of the other men, knowing that the young lord would never have uttered such a blasphemous curse anywhere in his lord father's hearing. Eadward had known the true number of ships from the King, who had sworn him to secrecy, so instead, he focused on the other bit of news the prisoners had offered. "So that means there's more than a dozen men somewhere around here free? That many Danes running loose in the countryside around here can cause all manner of damage!"

"Did you see any others running back towards Hamsey?" Otha asked, but the four men all shook their heads. "Then my guess is that they either ran north or to the west to get away from us before they turn back east to get to Hamsey."

"And how many men did we lose, Otha?"

"None of mine, Lord," Otha assured him, and Titus was not alone in showing his relief, but he felt a little guilty when Otha continued, naming Aelfnod's man, "Beorn ræd is dead, my Lord. And Sigeweard took a serious wound to the thigh, so he'll need help getting back to the ship, although he insists he's able to row, and Wigmund ran himself onto a spear, but managed to twist aside so he has a nasty gash on his side that will need to be stitched. And Wulfnod had his cheek laid bare to the bone. But," Otha grinned, "as I told him, it's actually an improvement. Of Alfred's men, we lost one of them, Dunstan, while Godric sustained a wound to the side. If it does not corrupt," Otha shrugged, "he should be fine, though I do not know if he can row."

The first men Otha mentioned were sworn to Ceadda, while neither Eadward nor Titus were inclined to mention their own wounds, the former having it bound by Ealdwolf with a strip of cloth for a bandage as they returned to the monastery, while Titus covered his own wound by not raising his left arm and holding his shield against his side, which was easy to do given how much it hurt when he did, although he also knew he was simply postponing the inevitable chastisement from Uhtric who, Titus knew, would immediately assume that his brother-in-law had been reckless.

"We did well," Eadward said with what he felt was justifiable pride, but Otha shook his head, and his tone brooked no argument as he said flatly, "We did well because we were fortunate, Lord. We caught them by surprise, and after they'd already gotten into the wine and ale. We can't afford to let this go to the men's heads, my Lord, because this isn't over." Eadward did not reply verbally, though he did give a curt nod. Glancing in the direction of Hamsey, Otha saw that the horizon was now a deep pink, the sun's rim just visible above the trees; daylight was almost upon them, and he was about to issue the order, but he caught himself, and addressed Eadward, "Lord, what are your orders? Should we head back to the ship now? Or do you want us to help the survivors?"

Contrary to Otha's fear, Eadward did not hesitate, saying, "No, we can't afford to stay. We need to get back to the ship so that we can help Beorhtweald's men like the original plan called for, and we don't have time for these people. It is," he added hastily, "a tragedy, but it can't be helped."

This was exactly what Otha would have ordered, but there was another surprise coming for the Thegn.

Pointing to the prisoners, he asked Eadward, "And, what about them, Lord?"

"Kill them," Eadward answered, again without any sign of indecision. "They chose to go *viking* in our lands. This is the price they pay."

He had turned away when Otha cleared his throat, but rather than speak aloud, he walked to Eadward to whisper something, and when he was finished, Eadward looked a bit abashed.

"Yes, I should have thought of that," he muttered, then more loudly, he said, "Lord Otha, please go find Lord Aelfnod.

I think this is one task he would be happy to carry out on his own."

It was not much, they all knew, but perhaps it would give Aelfnod some satisfaction. Titus considered intervening on behalf of the young Dane he had spared but discarded the idea almost as quickly as it had come, telling himself that this was his way of offering Lord Aelfnod some solace of his own. While the prisoners were being dispatched, Eadward led Titus, Ealdwolf, and Hrothgar back to the scene of the fight, able to move quickly because it was now almost daylight. While none of them said as much, they all had expected some of their comrades, once they had heard there was the chance of more plunder from dead Danes, to go skulking off under the cover of darkness, but to their collective relief, the bodies were undisturbed, and not dead long enough to begin to stiffen or stink...much, although the stench was from released bowels. Now that they had light, Titus was surprised to see that Sigurd had had red, flaming hair, with only a few streaks of gray in his beard, and if it had not been for those streaks, he would not have looked much older than Titus, more like Uhtric's age. And, as Titus had seen, and learned the hard way, the dead man had been as muscular as Titus himself. As he stood there staring down at the corpse, Titus felt what, for him, was a disturbing sense of melancholy, not the elation that he had always felt after vanquishing an enemy before this. Knowing they had to get back, Eadward made his decisions quickly, giving Titus the double-bladed ax, three of the eight arm rings, although only one of them was gold and inscribed with what he would learn were called runes, and almost as importantly to Titus, the boots that he had been eyeing now that he had had the opportunity to examine them in the daylight, mainly because they were the right size for his feet. It was a never-ending struggle for the young Saxon, who was still growing, and it seemed as if barely more than a month or two passed before his toes started pressing against the front of whatever pair he was wearing. The shields were discarded, none of them willing to carry them back to the ship when they were not an improvement over what was available to them, while all but Sigurd had been wearing boiled leather vests, and Eadward took the mail vest, though not to keep for himself but to award to one of the Wiltun men who did not have one as a reward. They were carrying a fair amount of money, in the form of coins, some of them Frankian, and hacksilver, but also English shillings, and this was the only thing that Eadward claimed, not for himself but for his father, and while none of them liked it, they also knew this was the way that things were done in their world. By the time they returned, Aelfnod had taken his revenge, the bodies of the six prisoners, all with their throats cut, sprawled in the dirt, but they could all see that the Thegn was far from satisfied, though none of them commented on his red, swollen eyes.

They moved as quickly as they could back to the coast, each of them carrying their spoils, but Titus made sure to stay behind Einarr. He was not *really* worried that the Dane would try to stab him in the back, not now anyway, but he wanted a chance to observe the man without being noticed. This, at least, was his plan, but as usual, Uhtric noticed almost immediately, and he sidled up next to Titus as they strode up one of the hills between what had just a day before been a thriving, prosperous monastery and where Dagfinn and the rest of the crew was waiting with the ship.

"I don't think it's possible to kill a man by glaring at his back, but if it is, you'll be the first," he commented, causing Titus to yelp in surprise, having been so focused on the Dane he had not noticed his brother-in-law's appearance.

Despite his embarrassment, Titus was not swayed, retorting, "You heard him. Sigurd the Bold was his *cousin!*"

"Yes," Uhtric acknowledged, "I did hear him, and yes, they were cousins. But," he shrugged, "that may not mean anything. Take my cousin Oswald. We grew up together...and I wouldn't piss on him if he was on fire!"

Between the imagery and the cheerful tone Uhtric used, Titus could not suppress a laugh, but while he was somewhat mollified, it was not completely, and he lowered his voice to ask, "What if he's not like you with Oswald? What if they were close?"

Uhtric had not really thought his ploy would work, and he also acknowledged to himself that it was a valid concern given how Einarr had treated Titus, who had informed him what Dagfinn had finally divulged to him about why Einarr resented the young Saxon so deeply.

"Do you trust me, Titus?" He asked quietly.

Startled, Titus blurted out, "Of *course* I trust you!"

"I'll be watching your back just like I always have," Uhtric assured him. "But," he allowed, "judging from what I've seen, I don't think Einarr and this Sigurd were all that close."

"I hope not," Titus mumbled, unhappy at even this admission of what he saw as weakness.

Just as their conversation finished, they topped the ridge and got their first glimpse of the water, glinting in the early morning sun, although the beach was still shielded from view by another, slightly lower ridge, meaning that the *Viper* was not in sight. Nothing was said about it, but there was a palpable tension that ran through the men that was only resolved when, once they summited the last hill, they saw it pulled up on the beach, the most potent sign that there had been no trouble. They had commandeered two horses, one for the body of Beornræd, while Sigeweard clung grimly to his own mount, the bandage on his leg already soaked red from the blood from the wound to his thigh. Once aboard, Beornraed and the other bodies were wrapped in their cloaks, but true to his word, Sigeweard limped to his bench, sat down, and slid his oar out. Since Dagfinn was the only man trained to the oar to take Beornraed's place, he was pressed into service to make for even numbers, though they were now one pair of oars short, while Einarr took over the steering oar, and the *Sea Viper* was shoved out into the water. The men who had participated in the march to Stanmer were all exhausted, but they did not complain...much.

Just as they were reaching the mouth of the Ouse, from the bow, Ceadda, who had taken on the role of lookout, pointed ahead and slightly to port, suddenly shouting, "I see a sail!"

Without Einarr ordering it, Dagfinn immediately shipped his oar, and with an ease and speed that spoke of long practice, shinnied up their own mast to get a better look, meaning that the man of Alfred's guard opposite him, Aedelwine, was given a respite. It was something that every Saxon crewmember both envied and had tried themselves, including Titus, who had attempted it twice, failing both times in embarrassing fashion, much to the delight of his comrades, who, as they loved to remind him after his failure, were heartily sick at Titus being better at everything than they were. Einarr bellowed at them to keep their rhythm, but all eyes forward of the mast were on Dagfinn as he peered ahead, shielding his own eyes from the morning sun. While it was in his own tongue, they all understood that the first words out of Dagfinn's mouth was a curse, and he twisted about to shout down to Einarr, but this time, most of them did not understand him. Snorri, however, did, and he let out a gasp that needed no translation that it was not good news.

Twisting about, Snorri called out to Eadward and the Thegn in the bow, "Lords! That sail doesn't belong to the *Dragon's Fang*! It's a Danish sail, but it's not heading towards us; it's sailing west! Dagfinn thinks it's the ship that was at Hamsey and that it's headed to join the other Danish ships!"

Not surprisingly, this got the four noblemen moving at what passed for a sprint aboard a bucking, rolling ship, and they quickly gathered around Einarr at the steering oar.

"Is that right, Einarr?" Eadward demanded. "That's not Lord Beorhtweald's ship? It's a Danish sail?"

"Yes, Lord," Einarr answered grimly.

Turning to Otha, Eadward said, "That means one of two things. Either that ship at Hamsey got past Beorhtweald and his men. Or," his voice turned grim, "we've found one of the other Danish ships that have been missing. What do you think Otha?"

The Thegn did not hesitate.

"I'm willing to wager a hundred shillings that it's not one of the other Danish ships, because it's going the wrong direction for one thing, and it seems unlikely that it would be by itself. No," he shook his head, his voice every bit as grim as Eadward's, "that's the ship that was at Hamsey. So they either gave Beorhtweald and his Centishmen the slip or..." He did not finish, for there was no need.

This was what Eadward had surmised, and he nodded in a signal that this was the case, then he ventured half-heartedly, "Maybe we should chase them down before they have the chance to rejoin the other ships." Before any of the Thegns could object, he went on, "But no, we need to go find out what happened and see if those Centishmen need help. Besides, the men are already tired from all that they've done."

With that settled, the orders were given, and once they reached the mouth, Einarr steered the *Viper* upriver.

The good news was that the Danish ship at Hamsey had not escaped by somehow defeating Beorhtweald and his men, although in the immediate aftermath, the Centishmen might have argued the point about how good a thing it was given what they had to endure from the Wiltun men.

"They got past Beorhtweald and his bunch in the darkness," Otha had informed the Wiltun men after he, Eadward, and Einarr had taken the small dinghy and rowed over to the *Dragon's Fang* to find out what had happened. "They just drifted downriver and used the darkness to hide them, and those Centish bast...men didn't have any idea."

This was met with an almost equal mixture of outrage and glee by the Wiltun men, each of them relishing the idea of all the fun they would be having at the Centishmen's expense for the foreseeable future, and it was Hrothgar who summed up the sentiment.

"Those bastards," he had no compunction in using the epithet, "have been lording it over us for being 'landsmen,' while they're supposed to be the only sailors worth a jar of piss. Now look at them!"

This was met with exclamations of agreement, along with other choice words, and Otha knew that it was nothing more than the truth; Beorhtweald and every one of his men had been insufferable in their arrogance about their supposed prowess when it came to nautical matters, yet whoever it was that commanded that longship had made them look foolish. Nevertheless, he knew very well that he, Ceadda, and Aelfnod would have to work hard to keep the gloating by their men to a minimum on those occasions when they were back together at Hamtun.

To that end, he reminded them, "What matters is that we get back in pursuit of those heathens."

It was now midafternoon, and the next decision was

whether they wait at Hamsey, which was now a village in name only, or row back downriver in anticipation of meeting with the King and the rest of the Saxon fleet. There was some discussion about spending that time helping the villagers begin the process of rebuilding, starting with dragging away the debris, in the form of charred and still smoldering timbers and helping to bury the dead, which Beorhtweald favored.

"He's just trying to postpone his meeting with the King and having to explain how that ship got away," Eadward murmured to Otha. More loudly, he said with the kind of tone that he thought his father would have used, "We're not going to spend any more time here. We came to Hamsey to stop the Danes...*all* of them. We," he gave Beorhtweald a level look, "didn't do that, so we need to keep the pressure up. Besides, the people in Læwe can help them."

For a moment, it appeared as if Beorhtweald was going to argue the point, but what he could *not* argue was that Eadward, as the son of an Ealdorman, outranked a Thegn, even if he was from a different shire; it was probably the presence of Otha, standing just behind the young lord, that had more do with his acquiescence than any intimidation he felt from Eadward.

"We'll be ready to depart shortly...Lord," Beorhtweald muttered before turning away to return to his ship, pointedly ignoring the Wiltun men, who, to a man, had chosen to be in a position where they could witness the Centish Thegn's humiliation.

However, never in their wildest dreams could they have imagined what was about to happen. It began with an alarmed shout, alerting everyone within earshot, "Ships approaching!"

The call came from further downriver, and a slight bend obscured the approaching ships from view, sending the men into a frenzy of preparation in anticipation that the fleeing Danish ship was returning with reinforcements. Their activity was short-lived, because the first ship that rounded the bend was unmistakable, both because of the vessel itself and because of the man standing in the bow.

"It's King Alfred and the *Redeemer*!"

None of the warriors hid their relief that they would not be going into battle again, but for Titus, that feeling was even stronger because his side was throbbing from the exertion of rowing, and the bleeding had not stopped because of the constant motion. It was the feeling of lightheadedness that concerned him the most, and taking advantage of the excitement of the King arriving along with the rest of the Saxon fleet, he unbuckled his belt, then stripped off his armor, or at least, this was his intent. The pain when he began to shrug the mail shirt off was so intense that he became dizzy, and he dropped back onto his bench, looking about him to see if his discomfort had been noticed. Happily for him, everyone else's attention was on Alfred's flagship as it approached the muddy beach, and when it became clear that the King intended to put ashore, men from both ships dragged the small fishing vessels and rafts used by the villagers out of the way. Using the distraction provided by the King's arrival, Titus gingerly worked the mail shirt up and over his shoulders and head, dropping it at his feet, then braced himself for what he had to do next, pulling off the padded undertunic, which, like his regular tunic, was now stiff from dried blood and, most problematically, was stuck to his side. Meanwhile, Alfred, barely waiting for the prow of his ship to slide up onto the mud beach, hopped down and strode to where Eadward and the Wiltun Thegns and Beorhtweald and the Centish counterparts to Otha, Ceadda and Aelfnod were standing, waiting for their monarch. If Titus had not been occupied with other matters, he would have noticed, and taken great pleasure in the differing expressions between the Wiltun nobles and the Centishmen, particularly their ranking Thegn, who, to Titus' eyes, seemed to be considering turning and fleeing in the opposite direction from their approaching King. Despite his own predicament, and the pain it was causing him, since Titus could hear the conversation from where he sat, he actually welcomed the diversion, mainly because it gave him an excuse to stall the inevitable.

"Lord King," Beorhtweald began, "whilst we were unable to save Hamsey, as you can see, we *did* manage to save the monastery at Stanmer, and we exacted a terrible punishment on the heathens, slaughtering the entire crew of one of their ships!"

It was such an astonishingly brazen thing to say that it

almost worked, if only because Eadward and his Thegns were so incredulous that they could only stand there, open-mouthed and speechless, but as Titus had once been told by Otha, King Alfred missed next to nothing, and it was their expressions that warned him that there was more to the Centish Thegn's report than was obvious from his words. Rather than address this directly, Alfred actually turned and made a show of examining the muddy beach, pointing to what had been Sigurd the Bold's ship.

"I see one captured vessel," he said in what was a conversational tone for him, "and I assume the crew of that one is those you say were slaughtered." He paused for a heartbeat or two, then asked suddenly, "And who was mostly responsible for slaying those Danes, Lord Beorhtweald?"

As willing as the Centish Thegn may have been to obfuscate, an outright lie was too far for him, if only because of the glare from the Wiltun men, but it was still in a grudging tone that he indicated them with a nod as he acknowledged, "That was done by Lord Eadward and his men, Lord King."

It was the truth, but it was also the bare minimum, yet in a demonstration of what Otha had once warned Titus about, Alfred's mind had already seized on something that Beorhtweald had mentioned in his attempt to accentuate the positive outcome.

"You said something about Stanmer being saved," the King pointed out, clearly puzzled. "But that's several miles to the west. What does Stanmer have to do with what happened here at Hamsey?"

To his credit, the Centish Thegn recognized that he had unwittingly given Alfred an opening, and understood that trying to prevaricate would end badly for him, yet he still hesitated before, taking a deep breath, he admitted, "As you obviously can see, Lord King, the other Danish ship managed to escape. Although," he added earnestly, "we did arrive in time to stop the entire village from being destroyed and every man slaughtered!"

Alfred did survey the village, noting that the reason there were no fires blazing was because the huts of the villagers had already been consumed by the flames, and as usually happened, the villagers had saved themselves by fleeing their island village to hide in the forest in between Hamsey and Stanmer.

Turning back to Beorhtweald, he asked coolly, "And what happened to the second Danish ship, Lord Beorhtweald?"

Even from where he was seated, Titus could see the Thegn flush deeply, and he replied, "They managed to evade us, Lord King. Under," he added hastily, "the cover of darkness, of course!" He actually looked over at the Wiltun men as he added in a challenging tone, "Why, I doubt that anyone could have seen them slip past us, Lord King! They," he lowered his voice to a conspiratorial level, "clearly had the help of some of their sorcerers to aid them in the endeavor, Lord King! You know how these Danes are!"

Although it was certainly true that Alfred believed as an article of faith that the Danes relied on all manner of otherworldly tricks, including the casting of spells by their men skilled in dark forms of sorcery, he did not think that this was why they had managed to slip away. However, he also understood that it was not politic for him to say as much here, so he managed a bland agreement. "Yes, no doubt that it was some sort of magic, Lord Beorhtweald."

Missing the irony in the King's tone, Beorhtweald nodded enthusiastically as he agreed, "You are very wise to have noticed, Lord King, truly!" Having escaped, or so he believed, Beorhtweald turned to the larger matter. "Did you manage to catch any other of those Danish bast...savages, Lord King?"

He was pleased that he had just managed to avoid the epithet, but his eyes were riveted on Alfred, and it was difficult for him to keep his composure as he stared up at the King, but neither he nor the other nobles, or any of the men within hearing were prepared for what Alfred had to tell them. In fact, from where Titus was watching, it appeared to him that Alfred was in a state of discomfiture very similar to what the Centish Thegn had displayed a moment earlier.

"No, Beorhtweald, we did not," Alfred answered, then hesitated for a heartbeat before he continued, "We did see the sail of what we believe to be the ship who escaped join with other ships to the east of the mouth of the river."

Misunderstanding the King's meaning, Beorhtweald

smiled and rubbed his hands together like a man about to tuck into a meal. "Then we can go in pursuit immediately and destroy these last three ships, Lord King! God be praised!"

It was actually Eadward who noticed something in Alfred's demeanor that caused him to ask cautiously, "Is there something else, Lord?"

"Yes, Eadward," Alfred nodded soberly, realizing that he had perpetrated this fiction that there were only four ships a bit too well. "It's not just three ships any longer, I'm afraid. It appears that the original raiders have been joined by more Danes."

Titus heard one of the nobles who was not aware of Alfred's fiction gasp, though he could not tell who it was, and Otha bit off a curse that the Thegn knew would have earned him a rebuke from the King.

"How many ships, Lord King?" Eadward asked quietly.

"We counted eight sails," Alfred answered, then held up a cautioning hand, "but it's entirely possible that there are more that were over the horizon when we turned upriver and lost sight of them."

Alfred had sailed on the *Redeemer* and six other ships, bringing the total up to nine, and if they had seen the entirety of the Danish raiding fleet, the Saxons would have a one-ship advantage now that the Danes had effectively abandoned the one damaged vessel at Hamsey, but their numerical advantage would be higher in another way. While the larger size and broader beam made the Saxon ships slower and less maneuverable, they did possess one advantage; they could carry more men. On the *Redeemer*, while it was manned by fifty men at the oars, there was also another forty men, all of them members of Alfred's personal bodyguard, commanded by Cyneweard, who, while it was not their primary duty, had spent time at the oars and could relieve the regular crew if it was required. The *Soul Stealer* was not as large as the *Redeemer*, but it had thirty warriors aside from the forty crewmen, and like their counterparts on the *Redeemer,* they had served a turn at the oars.

Turning to Eadward and his Thegns, Alfred questioned them about their actions at Stanmer, listening intently and only interrupting to ask a question, one of them causing Eadward some discomfort when he asked bluntly, "And who made the decision to beach the *Sea Viper*," a flash of what could have been distaste crossed the King's features, reminding them that he did not favor the traditional names for ships, preferring to name the vessels of what he viewed as his navy in the spirit in which he had named the *Redeemer*, in a display of piety, "and march overland instead of going with Lord Beorhtweald and the Centishmen and landing upriver as originally planned?"

Doing his utmost to sound confident in himself, Eadward answered firmly, "It was my decision, Lord King. But," he indicated Otha, Ceadda, and Aelfnod, "only after discussing it with my Thegns."

Alfred glanced at Otha, who gave a barely perceptible nod, prompting Alfred to say, "It was a very good decision, young Eadward, and it undoubtedly helped salvage something of the monastery, and save lives." The King turned to Aelfnod then, and although he sensed he knew the answer, he still asked, "And your brother, Aelfnod? Was he one of those your quick actions spared?"

"No, Lord King," Aelfnod replied, his voice hoarse, but otherwise, his inflection was flat and emotionless. "I am saddened to say that we were too late."

"That," Alfred said softly, but with real, unfeigned emotion, "is a tragedy, Aelfnod, and I am truly sorry for your loss. But he now sits at the right hand of our Lord and Savior, which is a suitable reward, is it not? Not," he added hastily, "that it makes your grief any less raw...or understandable. I will be sure and have Father Aethelred say a Mass for the repose of your brother's soul, who was doing God's work."

"Thank you, Lord King." For the first time, Aelfnod's composure began to crack, his gratitude making his voice throb with emotion. "I am most grateful, and I know that my parents will be as well."

Alfred nodded gravely, then Eadward, deciding that a change of subject was in order, broached the topic that he had been wrestling with from the moment it first came into his mind.

"There's something else I think you should know, Lord King," Eadward began, and while Alfred said nothing, he regarded the young lord with a raised eyebrow in a silent signal that he was listening, prompting Eadward to continue, "It concerns a piece of information that might be useful, and that's that these raiders now have a new leader."

"Oh?" Alfred asked clearly, and understandably surprised. "How do you know this?"

"Because Titus slew a Dane who was the leader of this raid. His name was Sigurd Gunnarson. But," he thought to add, "he was known to the Danes as Sigurd the Bold."

"Sigurd the Bold!" Alfred exclaimed, and by his reaction, the others could see that he was familiar with the name. "He was here and not in Frankia?" Before Eadward or the Thegns could react, the King suddenly frowned, and while he did not sound accusatory, it was obvious he was skeptical. "And, how do you know that this Dane was truly Sigurd?"

Rather than answer the monarch directly, Eadward turned his head and scanned the knots of men who were standing about working hard to pretend they were not trying to listen to the conversation. Spotting who he was looking for, Eadward summoned Einarr, and the Dane approached, squinting at the Saxons in obvious suspicion, although he did not hesitate to come to them.

"Did you go and look at the body like I asked?" Otha spoke for the first time. Obviously not needing to be specific about which body he was talking about, Einarr nodded but said nothing else, prompting Otha to snap, "And? Was he your cousin?"

This elicited a gasp from the normally unflappable Alfred, prompting the King to round on Einarr.

"Sigurd the Bold was your *cousin*?"

"Yes, Lord King," Einarr replied.

"And you didn't think to tell me this?" Alfred demanded, but this only got him a shrug from the Dane and a simple, "You did not ask, Lord King."

This, Alfred realized with some chagrin, was true, yet he was still sufficiently nettled to say curtly, "And you did not think this would be something I would have been interested in? That one of the most powerful noblemen among your people is your cousin?"

"Lord King, I had no idea that he was no longer in Frankia," Einarr protested, and there was a hint of anger in his tone. In a slightly softer voice, but laced with bitterness, he added, "The first I learned he was here was when I looked at his dead body not long ago."

It was not as much that Alfred was mollified as it was his recognition that there was nothing to be gained from chastising Einarr, but he did make a mental note to confront Knut about this, because he was certain that it was at least possible that Einarr had been aware of his cousin's whereabouts, not to mention that he needed to learn more about their relationship. Consequently, he pointedly turned away to look over at the *Sea Viper*, where Titus was seated, head bowed and clearly occupied with something around the area of his side.

Suddenly, he turned back to Eadward and asked sharply, "Was Titus wounded?"

"He said he has a minor cut on his side, Lord King," Eadward answered, feeling a stab of irritation that, despite the fact that his left forearm was now bound, the King had only given it a passing glance, and yet he seemed very concerned about Titus. "And," he hurried to add, "he manned his oar without any trouble."

It was actually the mention of Titus manning his oar that gave Alfred a pang of guilt that he had been about to order the crew of the *Sea Viper* to make ready to depart, because the Saxon King actually did have every intention of sailing downstream and out into the open sea in pursuit of the Danes. Yes, it was possible that there had been other Danish ships over the horizon, but for a reason he could not have articulated, he did not think this was the case. At the very least, he thought, we will be evenly matched in ships, or perhaps have a one-ship advantage, but with the extra men, he was certain that they had the advantage that could provide victory. It was thinking about the extra men that prompted Alfred to make a decision.

"We're going to pursue the Danes now," he announced, but then went on quickly because he saw not just Eadward but his Thegns opening their mouths, and he was sure he knew what their objection would be, "but your men have already done more than their share, and I know they are very tired. So I'm ordering the spare men from the *Soul Stealer* to man the oars while your men rest. By the time we run the Danes down, they should be fully recovered and ready to face what comes."

Not surprisingly, the Wiltun men thought this was a good idea, but Einarr was in the opposite camp, and he prevailed on Knut, who was the master of the *Redeemer*, to try and change Alfred's mind, though his attempt was half-hearted because he had gotten to know Alfred well enough to know when his mind was made up, and he also secretly agreed with the Saxon King's decision. What mattered was that, within an hour of his dropping onto the muddy beach of Hamsey, the Saxon ships pushed out into the Ouse and headed downstream.

Titus was relieved when the men from the *Soul Stealer* came aboard to take the oars, although it was cramped, and Einarr was anything but pleased at these men he considered interlopers suddenly on his ship. Titus' side ached abominably, but after what was an admittedly cursory examination, conducted while King Alfred was speaking with Eadward and the Wiltun Thegns, he had to grit his teeth when he first pulled his padded undertunic, then his normal tunic away from the wound to avoid crying out and drawing unwanted attention, he did not think it was serious. Grabbing a rag from his pack, he held it to his side to stop the bleeding, a common mistake made by inexperienced men, which he would be learning in a relatively short amount of time. He was encouraged that the bleeding stopped fairly quickly, but then he was confronted with what to do next, understanding that he should bandage the wound, using a roll of cloth that he did not possess, and he was unwilling to ask for help because it would draw attention to the fact that he was wounded, even if it was minor. His solution was to press the rag to his side, then instead of his mail shirt, he pulled out the boiled leather vest that had been his first set of armor because, now that he had grown, it had become tighter and the pressure it created actually lessened the ache. Alfred's presence had turned out to be a blessing, because even Uhtric, who could normally be counted on to hover about Titus—this, at least, was how Titus viewed it—was more interested in what was taking place with the monarch and not his brother-in-law.

Then the men from *Soul Stealer* arrived and clambered aboard, they were joined by his comrades, and there was a period of scuffling and bickering that was almost inevitable before Einarr bellowed at the new oarsmen to back the ship out into the river. Once the replacements settled into a rhythm that satisfied Einarr, Eadward ordered that the Wiltun men eat something before they curled up wherever they could find space to get some sleep, despite the fact that it was just noon. Naturally, nothing was cooked or heated, so the men were reduced to gnawing on cold pork or beef and eating bread that was already going moldy. Normally, this never bothered Titus, but when Uhtric thrust a hunk of salted pork at Titus and the younger man demurred, Uhtric stared at him in a combination of disbelief and concern.

"What's the matter with you?" he demanded. "Name the last time you turned down food!"

"Nothing," Titus replied. "I'm just not hungry."

For several heartbeats, Uhtric stared at Titus, but then he mumbled, "I suppose there's a first time for everything," then stuffed the hunk of pork he had offered in his own mouth.

This was odd enough, but Titus was unusually reticent, especially after a fight of some sort, yet when Uhtric pressed him for details of how he had slain Sigurd the Bold, all Titus could offer was an evasive shrug.

"I was just fortunate," was all he said, and this was so out of character for Titus that Uhtric became deeply concerned, and at the first opportunity, he slipped away and approached Otha.

"Have you noticed anything with Titus?" he asked the Thegn, but Otha shook his head, and he was actually somewhat irritated.

"What now?" he asked Uhtric. "Is he pouting because nobody has given him an arm ring for killing that Dane?"

"No, Lord," Uhtric answered, biting down his own retort. "I just offered him some food...and he turned it down."

He did not mention that Titus had in fact told him that he had been given three of Sigurd's arm rings by Lord Eadward, and Uhtric's comment did cause Otha to take Uhtric more seriously, yet at the same time, he had two dozen other men to worry about, and only later did he realize that he should have paid more attention.

"Did you ask him why?" he asked, and Uhtric shrugged.

"I did," he admitted, "but he said that he wasn't hungry."

"So maybe he's just not hungry."

"Lord," Uhtric asked quietly, "have you ever known a time when Titus wasn't hungry?"

This served to rouse the Thegn, although he was still more irritated than concerned, yet he did walk down the ship to where Titus was curling up, or trying to, at the feet of the man from the *Soul Stealer*, a bearded, heavyset warrior who Otha had seen about Hamtun but did not know, who had taken Titus' place at the oar.

"Boy," Otha said harshly, "Uhtric is worried about you. Should he be worried?"

Wrapped up in his cloak, despite the fact that the sun was shining and the weather was warm, Titus rolled over to look up at the Thegn, but when he saw Uhtric standing next to Otha, his glare was reserved for his brother-in-law.

"Lord?" He tried to sound confused. "What do you mean?"

"Uhtric told me that you wouldn't eat," Otha said. "And in the four years you've been in my service, I've never known you to say you weren't hungry. So," he glared down at Titus, "why aren't you hungry now?"

Titus did not answer immediately, acting as if he was actually thinking about it before, with a shrug, he answered, "I don't know, Lord. I'm just not hungry right now."

Otha turned to Uhtric to whisper, "Well? What do you think?"

"I don't know," Uhtric admitted. "But it's just...strange."

The fact was that Otha agreed with Uhtric, that it was strange, yet there was nothing overtly and obviously wrong with Titus, and he had other men to worry about.

"Well," he said so that only Uhtric could hear, "keep an eye on him, but I don't see what I can do."

And with that, he turned and returned to the bow as the *Sea Viper* beat east along with the rest of the Saxon fleet, searching for the original Danish raiding party and what all but a handful of men in the fleet believed were their newly arrived reinforcements.

Chapter Five

When Titus woke up, it was late afternoon, and the ship had begun to pitch and buck under him, the sign that the weather was changing. This was not why he woke up; it was because he was soaking wet, and his first confused thought was that he had somehow slept through a spell of rain, but when he opened his eyes, although it was cloudy, they were not rainclouds. It was when he sat up, or attempted to that gave him his first hint, and before he could stop himself, he let out a sharp cry of pain that in turn startled his replacement and caused him to falter in his rhythm. As they had long since learned, this resulted in a clash of oars with the man sitting in front of him, creating a cracking sound that would always summon Einarr and his rod for a thrashing. This time, however, the Dane just cursed and stayed at the stern with Dagfinn, who had returned to the steering oar, while Titus slumped back down to the deck, gasping from the pain in his side. When he had fallen asleep, it had been an ache, but now the pain was much worse, even more painful than the immediate moments after Sigurd the Bold had inflicted his wound, and he dreaded pulling off his leather armor.

It did not seem so in the moment, but Titus was fortunate that his shout woke Uhtric, who had picked a spot that put him close to Titus, because he did not hesitate, both to come to Titus' aid and also to remind his brother-in-law, "I *knew* there was something wrong with you."

He was tugging the leather vest as he spoke, which Titus could only answer with another groan, followed immediately by a gasp when Uhtric finally slid the vest over his head. The rag remained stuck to Titus' side, forcing Uhtric to make a choice about whether to carefully peel the cloth away or to yank it off, which would restart the bleeding. Since Uhtric was almost certain he knew what was happening, he chose the second alternative, bracing himself for Titus to curse him...at the least, yanking the rag from his side. Fortunately, Titus had seen what Uhtric was about to do and he had braced himself, yet he still let out a loud enough groan to earn him a couple of grumbled curses from Hrothgar and Aelfwine, who were nearest to him, although only Aelfwine actually raised his head for a moment before dropping back to sleep, but Uhtric barely noticed because of the sight before him.

"Who looked at this?" Uhtric demanded as he pointed down to Titus' side.

For his part, Titus was obviously reluctant about admitting, "I did." Then he glanced down and gasped in surprise. "But it didn't look like that!"

Uhtric was thankful that this had been caught in the early stages, but he was also angry at his friend and brother-in-law, and he showed it as he snapped, "That's because you didn't let someone who knows wounds look at it! There's something in there!"

Despite having surmised this as the likely cause a few heartbeats earlier, it still sent a shiver up Titus' spine that had nothing to do with his fever.

"What needs to happen now?" he asked, trying to sound as if he was only mildly interested, but Uhtric was not fooled.

"The wound has to be probed, and whatever is in there has to be fished out, Titus," Uhtric answered calmly.

It was this moment that the rain Titus thought had fallen when he was asleep actually began. If this was all it was, it would have been a nuisance, but even as Uhtric left Titus to inform Lord Otha that he would need the services of Theobald, the oldest of the men serving the Thegn, and the man considered to be the most skilled at tending battle wounds, the wind suddenly changed direction, strengthened considerably...and the rain really began. Not a slow, steady rain, but a gale that quickly grew in force, making the *Sea Viper* pitch and roll with a violence that made the timbers of the vessel shudder. Although this was not the first bout of heavy weather the crew had encountered during their short service, this quickly proved to be the most violent, and even worse, it did not appear that it was just a squall line passing through. Despite having become accustomed to the movement of the ship, when Uhtric made his way to where Theobald was resting near the bow, just in the few steps it took, he staggered when the ship pitched to port unexpectedly, and as Titus watched in horror, it appeared as if his friend would go overboard. Thankfully, the man at the oar nearest to him, one of the relief from *Corpse Stealer*, saw it happen and reached out with one hand to steady Uhtric while managing to keep his oar moving in rhythm, and Titus sagged in relief as Uhtric regained his footing. He roused Theobald, and the pair had equal trouble making it back to Titus, forced to grab at one of the lines that was strung down the center of the ship for such an emergency. It was, Einarr had told them with lacerating scorn, only there because they were *burlofotr*, clumsy Saxons who needed such things.

"You would never find such things on a Danish ship!" He had growled at the time, but the crew, especially the normal crew of the *Sea Viper*, all of them now roused because of the storm, were thankful for it, but none in that moment more than Uhtric and Theobald.

Crouching down beside Titus, they had to yell to be heard over the wind that was now roaring with a ferocity that only a handful of men aboard had experienced. Theobald was forced to cling to a strake with one hand while managing to examine Titus' wound, although because of the lashing rain that, from Titus' perspective, he practically had to thrust his nose up against his side, unaware that the older Saxon would have done the same if it had been calm to sniff it.

Straightening up, he shouted, "You're right, Uhtric! There's something in the wound!" With his free hand, he pointed to a spot on the otherwise straight red line along Titus' ribs that was visibly more inflamed and was already bulging slightly, although now that his bare skin was exposed to the storm, it was impossible to know if the wound was weeping pus in that spot. "It's probably a link from his mail!"

"Did you check your mail vest?" Uhtric asked and was not surprised when Titus shook his head.

"It was just a scratch!" he protested, matching their tone to be heard, amplifying what could only be described as the kind of protest one would hear from a teenager who has done something foolish. "There was no reason to check!"

Rather than reply, Uhtric simply pointed down to Titus' side, and his brother-in-law was wise enough to know not to argue.

"What do you need to do?" Uhtric asked in a lower tone, but Titus still heard him.

"We need to fish it out," Theobald answered, confirming Uhtric's suspicions, while Titus closed his eyes, dropping his head so his expression was unreadable.

"Can you do it now?" Uhtric pressed, though he was not altogether surprised at the look of horror cross Theobald's face at the idea.

"God's blood, Uhtric! Are you mad?"

"You've done it before!" Titus spoke up. "I saw you working after Ethantun on some of the wounds!"

"Does this look like Ethantun to you?" Theobald countered, completely unimpressed with Titus' argument.

At that moment, the *Viper* dipped into a trough, and for the span of what might have been a normal heartbeat, Titus felt his weight shifting and for an instant, he was certain that he was going to go hurtling down towards the prow, and either smash into it or, even worse, drop into the sea, just in front of the high bow of the ship. Too far away to grab the line, he snatched at the vertical piece of wood that supported the inboard end of the rowing bench, grasping the narrow edge with a desperate strength, feeling his fingernails beginning to tear out, but then, with an impact that sent a massive shudder through the ship that created an eerily human cry from the protesting timbers that made up the *Sea Viper*, the ship reached the bottom of the trough and began to climb up, as Einarr continued to bellow out the rhythm to the oarsmen, strangers on whose shoulders lay the entire fate of every soul aboard. Temporarily forgetting his worry about his wound, Titus admitted to himself that he had never been so frightened, and all of his comrades, the men he knew best, the Wiltun men who were now all awake and clinging to whatever provided the slightest handhold, looked the same way. When he turned to the bow, he saw that Lord Eadward, Otha, and the other Thegns were in essentially the same posture, clutching to the nearest piece of solid wood with all of their strength, and even with the obscured visibility from a slashing rain where the fat drops were almost horizontal, he could see that his Thegn's expression could have been switched with any of his men. If *he's* scared, Titus thought, then it must be bad. In a natural reaction, he turned to the stern and he saw Einarr, who, while he was holding on to the aft line running from the mainmast, did not appear to be in any distress, but it was when he said something to Dagfinn, who laughed, that, while it did not altogether disappear, did more to calm Titus' fear than anything else could have done.

Turning to Theobald, he asked, "What do we do?"

"Someone needs to ask Lord Eadward to order that Danish bastard to put into shore," Theobald answered immediately. "That's the only place where it would be safe to go hunting around in your side."

Uhtric had actually started to turn to go before Theobald was finished, obviously anticipating Theobald's requirement, but Titus shouted at him to stop.

"No! We're not going to do that!" Titus shouted, sounding angry because he was.

"This isn't the time for your pride, Titus," Uhtric shouted back, and it surprised Titus to hear Uhtric's own anger in his friend's voice, along with a fear that he somehow knew was not from the storm.

Normally, this would have roused his temper; four years earlier, being spoken to harshly by someone like Uhtric would have unleashed a number of feelings, mostly regret that he was the cause of their ire, and the anger would have gone inward...and outward. That, however, was four years earlier, but Titus nonetheless surprised himself by, instead of raising the volume of his voice, along with the aggression in his tone, he instead tried to sound calm and reasoning.

"It's not about my pride, Uhtric. Not," he added honestly, "all of it, at least." Pointing in the general direction of where he thought land was, he asked, "Where are we?"

"How should I know?" Uhtric retorted, then Titus saw the dawning of understanding in his friend's eyes, but Uhtric was not ready to concede. "Are you saying that you don't trust Lord Einarr to know where to put in along here? He's a Dane! He's one of Guthrum's men, and they've been sailing these waters for years now!"

"It's not just that," Titus countered, still maintaining what passed for a calm state under the conditions. "We're chasing those bastards, and the *Viper* and *Dragon's Fang* are the only two ships that are nimble enough to head them off and slow them down for Alfred and the rest of the ships. Are you willing to damage our chances of ending this?" He shook his head. "Because I'm not."

Turning back to Theobald, Titus said simply, "We have no choice, Theobald. And I trust you. Get whatever it is out of me and do it now."

For a long moment, Theobald did not reply, although it might have been because he was too busy clinging to the line as the ship essentially repeated its behavior of moments before, but like Titus, he was getting a sense there was a rhythm to a storm just like there was during calmer seas, it was just...faster, albeit with a few surprises thrown in, like the sudden roll to port that happened at that very moment.

"All right," he said at last. "I'll do my best not to kill you."

"If you do, I'll be sure and haunt you for the rest of your days," Titus replied, but it was with a grin that was only partially forced, and Theobald did his best to return it.

He reached into the satchel that he always wore slung over one shoulder with his free hand, and when he found what he was fumbling for and withdrew it, Titus experienced a momentary urge to tell Theobald he had changed his mind, but Uhtric had scrabbled over to his side, and the sensation of his brother-in-law's hand on his shoulder quelled it, although Titus did glance over to make sure that Uhtric was holding on to something solid with his other.

"Grab hold of something with both hands," Theobald ordered, then as Titus did so, Theobald clamped the metal probe between his teeth to withdraw a leather-wrapped wooden dowel and extend it to Titus, "and bite down on this."

The sensation of the dowel on his tongue, feeling the indentations from the teeth of how many men Titus did not want to know, almost made Titus gag from revulsion, but he managed to keep it down. However, Theobald did not make an immediate move, but Titus saw that he was watching the prow, and quickly discerned that Theobald was waiting for the next moment where, for the span of barely a couple of heartbeats, the ship stopped moving. The fact that it was as it was plunging down into a trough made Titus wonder if Theobald's admonition to hold on to something was because of that, or because of the excruciating pain that was coming. He got his answer less than two normal heartbeats later; fortunately, he was not conscious for anything after that.

When Titus awoke a second time, he was not as wet, and most importantly, he was not rolling about in the bottom of the ship...and it was close to sunset. There was enough light for him to see that above him were patches of blue sky among the clouds that, while gray, were not heavy with rain.

"I was wondering if I'd killed you."

Turning, he saw Theobald crouching next to him, but Uhtric was not within his range of vision, so he asked the older Saxon the most important question.

"Did you get it out?"

"I did." Theobald nodded, and Titus did not even try to hide his relief or show the stoicism that he normally believed a Saxon warrior should display at such moments.

He did close his eyes as he said with feeling, "Thank you, Theobald."

"If we'd been on land," Theobald laughed, "I could have found it with my eyes closed. But since we were bouncing about like a floating turd in a torrent, and pissing down like it was, it took a fair amount of time. Which," he hurried to add, "is what I want to tell you. I had to...cut a bit to get it out, so your side is going to be sorer than it normally would be. I wrapped it up tight, but as soon as we land, I'm going to have to put in a stitch or two."

It was probably inevitable that, as soon as the words were out, Titus involuntarily lifted his left arm, wrenching a gasp of pain from his lips, and he quickly dropped it back down.

"That's what you get for being a fool."

He clearly heard Uhtric, but it took Titus a moment to realize that his friend was back at his bench on the opposite side of the ship from Titus' normal spot, and it was then that Titus realized the Wiltun men were back at the oars. This prompted him to try and struggle to his feet, and his gasp became a yelp of agony at the movement, but more importantly, it summoned Otha, who was able to move down the center among the *Corpse Stealer* men who were now resting, with the exception of Titus' spot, although it was not the same man at the oar, the Thegn moving to block Titus' path.

"What do you think you're doing?" he demanded.

"It's our time to row, Lord," Titus protested weakly. "I just want to do my bit."

"You couldn't pull your own prick right now," Otha scoffed, pointing back down to what had become Titus' spot. "You were foolish once, *boy*, don't compound it."

It had been awhile since Otha had called him a "boy" with that tone, and while it made Titus bristle, he was also secretly thankful because he had realized as soon as he stood that he would have been unable to perform his duty at the oar, but when he turned to lower himself back down, he learned Otha was not through.

"Uhtric asked me to give you something," Otha said, but in what Titus took to be a small sign that he was making a concession for his condition, he crouched down so that Titus did not have to extend his arm to take what he held out to offer. At least, that was Titus' assumption, but as he quickly learned, it also placed the Thegn's face close to his as he dropped what he held in his hand into Titus' palm, which Titus could see out of the bottom of his vision was a single link of mail. Most of his attention, however, was fixed on Otha's face, and he could see real anger there, "The next time you put one of your comrades in the kind of danger Theobald was in trying to fix what you fucked up because of your pride, I'll gut you myself. Do you understand, Titus?"

"Yes, Lord," Titus replied immediately. "I've learned my lesson, I swear it!" he assured the Thegn, but if he was expecting immediate forgiveness and some gruff humor, which was what he usually got after a chastisement from Otha, this time, he was to be disappointed, another sign that he had truly roused his Lord's ire.

"I doubt it," Otha grunted as he stood, "but we'll see." Turning to go back to the prow, he did think to add, "Oh, and the Danish fleet gave us the slip in the storm. We're looking for a spot to pull ashore to camp and regroup."

He left Titus with Theobald, who looked embarrassed, but despite the pain it caused, and suppressing a grimace, Titus reached out and grasped Theobald's forearm, squeezing it as he said quietly, "Lord Otha is wrong, Theobald. I *have* learned my lesson, and I'm…sorry that I put you in danger."

He could see the older warrior appreciated the gesture, although he tried to shrug it off by saying, "Now I can brag about how I saved a man's life in a raging storm." Giving his hand an awkward pat, Theobald added, "And I know you have, boy. And it's all right. It's what we do for each other, eh?"

And with that, he went to his spot to relieve the *Corpse Stealer* man, who gave him the oar, and soon the ship was back to the kind of rhythm and feeling that could have made it just one of their normal training voyages, but things had changed for the crew of the *Sea Viper*. They had met the Danes, and yes, while it was on land, they had won an unquestionable victory, and victory was what mattered.

It proved hard to remember that fact over the ensuing week, a period during which, even with the combined fleet of Alfred's ships, they could not come to grips with the Danish raiders. Titus' spell off the oars only lasted two days, but it was mainly because Otha, and to a lesser degree, the rest of the Wiltun men had grown heartily sick of his constant importuning that he was fine. He was not, but he was also young, and by the end of that week, while he could still feel the pull in his side, Theobald had bound it tightly during the storm, then stitched it the first night ashore, it itched, and he was certain it was a sign that it was time for the stitches to come out. In the larger world outside of Titus' concerns, the Danes seemed to be tormenting them, allowing the Saxons to draw within sight, then always using the superior speed of their ships, which only the *Sea Viper* and *Dragon's Fang* could match, they would race out to sea. By staying within sight of the coast as they did, which Alfred ordered to prevent the Danish ships from landing, although it protected the settlements, churches, and monasteries along the southern coast, it also meant that every inlet, river mouth, and small anchorage had to be searched, because the Danes were also cunning masters at disguising their ships when they were beached, a skill gained from untold years of living by raiding other, more peaceful peoples, and Alfred could not discount the possibility that the eight sails on the horizon were no longer the only Danish ships about, especially after the storm. As far as he was concerned, it would be typical of Danish guile that they were using the number of ships they had assumed the Saxons had counted as bait, while another part of their fleet was skulking about, hoping that the Saxons would get frustrated and chase the Danes out far enough away from the coast to give them time to land, and more importantly, escape after pillaging another village or monastery.

As Alfred put it at a meeting of his commanders aboard the *Redeemer*, "We're only accomplishing part of our goal, my Lords. Yes, we're keeping the Northmen from landing and committing more depredations, but I am certain they are just waiting for us to give up and return to Hamtun." He addressed Knut One-Eye, "Would you agree, Knut?"

"Yes, Lord King," the Dane replied without hesitation. Then, with a shrug, he added offhandedly, "Our people do not hold Saxons in much regard when it comes to matters of the sea, and I am certain that whoever replaced Sigurd holds the same view. They will wait you out by staying far out to sea."

"Then why do we keep seeing their sails this close to land?" Cyneweard, the commander of Alfred's bodyguard and, probably understandably, one of the least trusting of these Danes who were supposedly aiding the Danish cause, his belligerent tone reflecting that distrust, asked, "If they're so far out to sea, how is it that we catch them this close to land? *Our* land?"

Knut's feelings for Cyneweard were no more of a secret than the Saxon's for Danes, and were fully reciprocated, but he replied coolly, "Because they are toying with you. They are hoping you make a mistake that they can pounce on."

In his own way, Alfred pounced, asking, "What kind of mistake are they waiting for?"

As his answer, Knut pointed to the two taken ships, *Sea Viper* and *Dragon's Fang*.

"Those are the only two ships that pose any kind of threat

to them," Knut replied. "And they would like to either destroy them. Or," he shrugged, "take them back."

"Yes," Alfred nodded, but he was smiling slightly, "I was wondering if they would take that as some sort of insult, that they could lose ships to..." he paused as if he was trying to think of the right word, although he knew it, "...what is it that you call us Saxons aboard ship? *Burlufotr?* Am I pronouncing that correctly, Knut?"

While it was certainly true that the Danes used any number of slurs in their own tongues, it was clear to Knut that the Saxon King knew the meaning of the word, even if the assembled Thegns whose men served as the crews of this hastily thrown together navy did not.

It was a noteworthy moment, because it was one of the only times Alfred had seen Knut who, while he still did not trust the man, had proven to know what he was about when it came to preparing men unaccustomed to manning an oar for days at a time so flustered as the Dane replied, "Yes, Lord King. That is how you pronounce it."

"What does it mean?" Cyneweard demanded, and now it was Alfred's turn to regret what was, when all was said and done, an indiscreet comment given the composition of the company.

"It does not matter, Cyneweard," Alfred said, and in a tone that told his longtime commander it was an order not to pursue the matter, but Alfred still hurried on nonetheless, "The question is, how can we turn this to our advantage? Because," he turned grim, "they are correct about one thing. I cannot afford to be away from Wintanceaster much longer. Being in Hamtun for such a prolonged period could not be helped, but I was at least in contact with couriers and could attend to some of the business at hand. So," he returned to the subject, "the obvious answer is to use those ships as bait. But to what end?"

"Go ahead," Otha whispered in Eadward's ear. "Tell him your idea."

"No!" Eadward whispered back, but louder. "I'm not going to do that! Are you mad? Me?"

To his embarrassment, Alfred did hear the exchange, or part of it, and he asked irritably, "You're not going to do what,

Eadward?"

"N-nothing, Lord King," Eadward stammered, then glared over his shoulder at Otha. "I...I just mentioned something to Otha, but it wasn't really a serious idea."

Seeing that Eadward did not have the courage, Otha spoke up, "The lad thought about the reason the Danes know that any ship like theirs coming from the west will be with you, Lord King." When Alfred nodded his understanding and taking it as tacit agreement, the Thegn went on, "So what Eadward thought was if we used the night with no moon that's coming up, and get *Sea Viper* and *Dragon's Fang* past them when they go back out to sea by staying closer to the coast than we normally do, then we come back from the *east*, they'd be more willing to let Danish ships approach."

"And then?" Alfred asked, noncommittally but clearly willing to let Otha to continue.

"Then," Otha answered forcefully, "we each attack a ship."

"But you'll be outnumbered," Cynewald, one of Ealdorman Aelfstan's Thegns, protested. "And as fast as those ships move, they'll have you surrounded quickly."

"Which means," Alfred spoke up, beating Otha to it, seeing it now, "they'll be in a small area and with their attention on the threat...from the east. Which means," he repeated, raising his voice so that all of his commanders could hear him clearly, "we must be nearby and ready to strike."

"They normally show themselves shortly before noon and the early afternoon," Cerdic, the Thegn sent by Odda of Devonscir, noted.

"Tomorrow night, there will be no moon," Alfred mused. "Therefore, this will be the day after tomorrow. We," he scanned the coastline although it was already dark, but he was stalling for time since he knew where they were, "are just west of Romney now." Remembering the presence of Beorhtweald, he asked hastily, "Do you agree, Lord Beorhtweald?"

This mollified the Centish Thegn, or at least seemed to as he agreed, "Yes, Lord King. The village," he turned and pointed in a northeasterly direction as the coast curved slightly north "is no more than fifteen miles away. But," Beorhtweald said with a degree of smug satisfaction, "there is no way just four Danish ships could take Romney, Lord King. Ealdorman Sigeræd has it well garrisoned."

"What about eight Danish ships, Lord?" Alfred asked quietly, then lied, "Or are you forgetting these raiders have been reinforced?"

"I haven't forgotten, Lord King," Beorhtweald's tone was respectful, but those who knew him heard the tight anger there, reminding all of them of the touchy pride of Centishmen. "But unless whoever commands them now is an utter fool, he can't commit all of his ships to attacking Romney, for the simple reason of our presence. They know we're here and nearby, and all we would have to do is block the river mouth."

This was true, certainly, and Alfred doubted that Sigurd's successor would be a fool...but they had called Sigurd "The Bold," and it was possible that whoever had replaced him was determined to make an even greater reputation. It was a problem that was secondary to the primary one of how to make Eadward's idea work, but it was potentially a more catastrophic one. Romney had grown over the previous two centuries from a nunnery into a prosperous village that had aspirations to become more than that, situated as it was at the estuary of the River Rother. Beorhtweald, however, was right; Sigurd may have been bold, but he had not been foolish enough to try and attack Romney, just like they did not try and attack Læwe with a quarter of their fleet. With four times that number, risking everything? he wondered. Would that be enough? He did not want to find out, which helped him cement his decision.

Addressing both Beorhtweald and Eadward, he asked, "Would I be correct in assuming that you kept the Danish sails?"

They both nodded, but then they exchanged a glance that caught Alfred's attention as, for probably the first time in their short association, Ealdorman Eadwig's son and the senior Thegn of Cent were of a like mind, which he found...bewildering. Not, however, for long, as it came to him.

"Also, as I recall, I ordered you to destroy those pagan idols the Danes use to decorate the prow and stern of their ships." He did not state it as a question, his voice stern and telling them he knew the answer.

For his part, Eadward was perfectly content to cede the field to Beorhtweald, who was anything but happy at the honor, but he did answer, "Er, yes, Lord King."

"But you didn't, did you? Either of you?" He wanted to make sure that Eadward knew he was included, turning to regard the young lord severely. "You kept them?"

"Yes, Lord King," they both said in a ragged unison, the older man mirroring Eadward now at staring down at his feet.

Alfred said nothing for a long moment, drawing it out before he said, "I suppose that both of you thought that they might be useful, in some sort of ruse. A ruse," he added dryly, "just like this one."

For the second occasion in a short time, the pair were enthusiastic partners in assuring him that they both, independently of course, had arrived at the same conclusion, but it was left to Eadward to remind Alfred, "We kept the sails in the event they would be useful for something like this, Lord King. So," he shrugged, "why not the heads?"

The lad, Alfred thought wryly, though his face did not give any of this away, has a quick mind, and he has you there. Still, he did not like being disobeyed, even if it was in hindsight a good thing that he was, but he was also fair, so he contented himself with pointedly changing the subject.

"We have to work out the details tomorrow as we sail," he said in a signal the meeting was over, "but I think that we have a way to pin these Danes down."

"We're going to be what?"

"Bait," Eadward repeated patiently to Hrothgar's question, although to be fair, he had not asked it the first time; that had been from Ceadda's man Aedelstan. "Tonight we're going to be rowing east."

"Is that why we're only under sail now? To let us rest?" Uhtric asked.

"That's part of the reason," Eadward agreed, reminded once again of how clever the one-eyed warrior was. Resuming, "Once we're well past Romney and it gets dark, we're going to change the sails and use the Danish ones. That's why we had you switch out the shields that wouldn't pass for Danish on the strakes when we landed, so this will help with the ruse."

It had been one of Alfred's demands, that not only would the sails be as uniform as possible in color, they would have a large black cross painted on it. He said it was to make the ships easier to identify, although most of the men who crewed the ships believed it had less to do with identification and more to do with their King's well-known piety, not that any of them would voice that opinion. At least not in Hamtun, since Alfred had brought a number of priests, who apparently had been given the task of patrolling the streets to keep the men of this tiny fleet from straying into alehouses and the brothels that inevitably came with them, and presumably listening for impious conversations. And, as they all knew equally well, their opinion did not matter, and ultimately, what sail they were under did not either, but what Eadward said next caused a bit more of a stir.

"And we're putting the heads back on the prow and stern to further the ruse."

"Ha!" Willibald, one of Aelfnod's men, jabbed his closest friend Odda in the ribs. "You owe me a shilling! I *told* you they didn't get rid of them!"

"What did King Alfred have to say about that?" Uhtric asked, because they had all been present when the King had seen that the crew of the *Sea Viper* had left the carved figureheads in place, the prow figure some sort of monster that could have been a dragon except with a more rounded head like a snake, but it was just the two carved wooden fangs in its open maw that had won the argument, and had been the inspiration for the new name. The piece on the stern was of the beast's tail, but it was forked like the representation of winged dragons they had seen, which had ignited the debate about the beast's origin in the first place.

Eadward's reply was rueful. "He was not pleased, but he also didn't chastise us...much, since they'll come in useful now."

There was a silence as the men absorbed this, but it was left to Wulfnod of Ceadda's band to ask nervously, "But if we're sailing with no moon, will we be able to see the coast?"

"No," Eadward answered, but indicated Einarr, with Dagfinn next to him, both standing with crossed arms at their normal station at the stern, "but Lord Einarr has assured me that he's sailed in conditions like this many times."

"Because he's a thieving pagan bastard," Theobald muttered, but quietly enough that, while Eadward and the Saxons around him could hear, the Danes presumably could not.

Ignoring what he had heard, Eadward continued, adding, "Besides, we're in Centish waters now, and Lord Beorhtweald and the *Dragon's Fang* will be leading the way, and he assures me they know these waters very well. As long as the Danes do what they've done every day so far, we're going to do the same thing, which means we should be around Romney when the sun sets, and as soon as it's dark and they go back out to sea, we'll begin. Until then, the fleet will stay under sail as long as we have a good following wind. So pray for that so that you can get some rest."

"Then what happens?"

"What do you think, you fool?" Otha snapped at Willmar, who had asked the question. "We're going to get close enough, then pick out two of the ships nearest to us, and we're going to go after them!"

"And," Eadward spoke up, seeing the looks of alarm, "that will be when Alfred and the rest of the fleet will arrive so that we can finish these heathen bastards once and for all." Seeing that he was not winning them over, despite feeling self-conscious about his youth, Eadward said earnestly, "Lads, this will work, and it's the only way that we can bring our superior numbers in men to bear. Or," he asked, "do you want to be rowing up and down this infernal coast until winter?"

"No!" The answer was as close to perfect unison as they would ever come to, and it was followed by a laugh by most, not all, but most of them, which Eadward took as a sign that he had made his point.

"I don't know about the rest of you," Titus spoke for the first time, "but I'm ready to get back to Hamtun so I can drink more than just one pot of ale." He paused, then with a grin, he added, "And there are...other attractions."

"You've got no chance with Aelflaed," Uhtric spoke up. "She's got her sights set on young Lord Eadward here! And he's much prettier than you!"

As Titus had hoped, this turned the attention away from the apprehension about what lay ahead, the crew not only laughing at the perceived rivalry between two of the three youngest members of the crew and immediately began wagering on the prospects for each. Not surprisingly, the consensus was that the heir to Ealdorman Eadwig had a distinct advantage, but Titus' reward was the nod of thanks his noble friend gave him. He had held a whispered conversation with the pair, asking for help if it appeared that the crew was dubious about what was, in effect, an order from the King, but because of their social hierarchy, had to come from Eadward and not Otha.

"I told Otha not to step in and take over," he had confessed to them, "but I still might need help."

"You have it," Titus had answered immediately, glad for once to not be a target of his Thegn's likely ire.

It was impossible aboard a ship, of course, but Titus had been trying to steer clear of Otha who, for the most part, made a point of ignoring him, the most potent sign that his anger had not subsided to a degree that made any contact a wise idea. Titus felt good about his small contribution, and he settled down next to his bench to try and get as much sleep as possible, lulled by the snapping sound of the sail and the hiss of the *Viper*'s bow cutting through the waves, without the slapping of the oars for once.

Aboard the *Redeemer,* Alfred stood at the stern with Knut and Cyneweard, and while he had long practice at hiding his thoughts, and his nerves, he could not help fretting about the plan. He was well aware there were flaws in it, but he also was acutely aware that, even after Ethantun, he was being carefully watched by the Danes for any sign of weakness. This was to be expected, but it was being watched by the high-ranking nobility of Wessex and, in some ways more importantly, those parts of England who still held aloof from Wessex that worried, and angered, him the most. Yes, much had been done, and Ethantun had been a massive step in the right direction of his larger ambition of creating one England, but he was acutely aware that he was not the only ambitious and powerful man on this island.

In some ways, it was the latter group that was most worrisome and dangerous, because in his belief, those men were more interested in power for its own sake than they were with using that power for a larger purpose, like creating one united country. None of this going through his mind could have been read on his features, and in fact, even as he was thinking about this, he was discussing with Cyneweard the idea of repainting the shields of his royal guard after this prolonged exposure to the sea air. If he lost the *Sea Viper* and *Dragon's Fang*, it would be a catastrophic blow, and not just from the loss of ships and men, but in the political consequences of failure. Of all the Ealdormen, he suspected Sigeræd harbored ambitions that extended beyond Cent, and losing his most senior Thegn and some of his most experienced warriors could be a pretext for refusing to cooperate in the future, and the fact that Alfred and his small fleet were in Centish waters protecting Romney would not factor in Sigeræd's decision, if Alfred was any judge. In the case of the crew of the *Sea Viper*, the oldest son and heir of a man who had proven to be a staunch and valuable ally was aboard that vessel; what would Eadward's loss do to Lord Eadwig? Would it shake his loyalty? Now that Alfred had his own son and heir, also named Eadward, though it was a common name, he could easily imagine how such a loss would sour the nobleman's view towards his King. They had briefly discussed keeping the extra men from *Corpse Stealer* aboard the *Viper*, but it was quickly dismissed because the extra weight would negate the speed they would need. In fact, they had lightened their load instead, offloading a couple barrels of water and foodstuffs to one of the larger ships, giving them enough for the day and no more, and now was the worst part, the waiting, and the hoping that came from the Danes repeating their same behavior of the previous days, for which Alfred had prayed at least a dozen times since rising before dawn. Keeping one eye on the sun as it climbed into the sky, Alfred changed the subject by addressing Knut.

"You believe that the men are sufficiently conditioned now for what's needed?"

Knut had answered this question the same the three previous times the King had asked it, so it took a massive amount of patience to repeat, "Yes, Lord King," and not remind him that he had already asked, but he did take a small revenge this time by adding, "They are not Danes, but," he shrugged, "for what is needed, they will do."

Cyneweard was long accustomed to his monarch's demand that anyone in his service not swear oaths or hurl epithets, so he contented himself with a low growl, earning him a glance of scornful amusement from the Dane, who stood a head taller than the bodyguard commander.

More to forestall yet another round of bickering that was becoming more pointed and heated every day at sea, Alfred asked a question that he had not thought to ask. "How will we know who the leader of this...*viking* is now that Sigurd the Bold is dead?"

Somewhat regretfully, they had been forced to leave the abandoned Danish ship behind because, as they discovered once the sun came up, the ship was seriously damaged, although Knut had dismissed the claim that it had been the garrison at Læwe who had caused the damage.

"They hit something submerged just under the water," Knut had judged without hesitation. Then, after scanning the riverbank, he added, "Probably a log since this is a mud-bottomed river." With a shrug, he finished, "It happens."

At least Beorhtweald's arrival had disrupted the Danish plans to repair it at the village by forcing the men left behind to flee in the second ship, and on the face of it, it seemed to have been a foolish decision by the dead Sigurd to take his crew roaming for more plunder. However, to Alfred, as soon as he learned more details, it represented something more than that; despite the victory at Ethantun, there were Danes out there who held his rule and his people with such disregard as a possible threat that he felt he had the time to travel the five miles to Stanmer, then return at his leisure, leaving a bit less than half of his men to repair the damage to the hull. It was, to Alfred anyway, a mortal insult, and it was typical Danish arrogance that would hopefully make tomorrow possible. Now came the hardest part, the waiting to see if they could finally close with these foes that had proven so elusive. *It is like*, he thought with bitter humor, *trying to tie a knot with a column of smoke*. To a mixture of relief and apprehension in roughly equal measure, the first Danish ship appeared, a bit later than the days before but not that much, and then all eight sails poked above the horizon, appearing to make a direct line for Romney, which Alfred naturally moved to intercept. And, as expected, while the Saxons were not quite at the estuary in time to block the Danes, who could have rowed up the less than half-mile to where the muddy beach and lone pier that served as the village's port, before the Saxons arrived, they did not attempt what would have been a foolish move, quickly turning to parallel the coast, but with the Saxons still far enough away that only the two Danish ships would have had a chance to catch a straggling ship. A straggler that would undoubtedly be acting on orders from whoever now commanded this raid to act as bait. Just as, Alfred thought with a certain grim amusement, we intend to do in a few hours. About an hour before sundown, the wind slackened enough that, from Knut, Alfred was informed that it was time for the entire fleet to row. Because of the varying speeds of the ships, vessels like the *Redeemer* had kept the men at the benches to add just enough extra speed to keep up with the smaller ships, particularly their two Danish craft. And, just as the sun's bottom touched the western horizon behind them, creating a long golden light across the shimmering waves, as they had before, the Danes turned south, away from the lure of plunder and to the greater security of the open sea.

Knut surprised him then by commenting, "Lord King, have you considered the possibility that these Danes are almost as desperate as you are to end this..." He searched for the word in English, but satisfied himself with gesturing in a way that Alfred could interpret.

"Dilemma, I believe is the correct word you were searching for, Knut," Alfred supplied, but he was intrigued. "But why do you say that? Your people spend many more days than this at sea, so surely they are better prepared for extended periods not being able to land."

Knut regarded him with a glint of sardonic humor in his eye, but he kept his tone respectful as he countered, "Lord King, if you think that no Danes from those ships have set foot on land for the past week, you would be...mistaken." Seeing Alfred's surprise, he explained, "They need water just as much as we do, and when we...I mean *they* are *viking*, they need to have as much room aboard their ships for plunder as possible, so they do not carry much extra rations, including water."

"So what are they doing?" Cyneweard demanded, although Alfred was just as interested to learn.

"They bring one of their ships a couple of miles from land, then take a small boat loaded with two men and as many barrels as the boat can handle, and land during the night to fill the barrels. Food," Knut went on, "is the problem, and I can promise you that there are men on those ships who have begun to grumble that this was not what they came along with Sigurd for, to row back and forth and play a merry game of chase. That," he finished, "will be a concern for whoever is now commanding this *viking*."

As soon as Knut said it, the King recognized this was undoubtedly happening, and he felt a stab of something that was hard for him to identify.

"So what are you suggesting?" Alfred asked. "That we continue this?"

To his surprise, Knut shook his head, "They have had some success already, Lord King, just not as much as they had hoped. But if you do not close with them and destroy them now...they will be back."

"Then why did you bring it up?" Cyneweard demanded angrily, but while Alfred was being worn down by the bristling hostility between the pair, it was a fair question, and he looked at Knut with a raised eyebrow in a silent command for an answer.

"Because desperate men fight harder," Knut replied quietly. "That is why I am telling you this. Lord Einarr says that the crew of the *Sea Viper* is good, and I have seen this myself, especially the young one that you Saxons like to call Berserker. But," he shook his head, "he is only one man. No," he did not point with his hand; he nodded with his head in the direction of the *Dragon's Fang*, perhaps two hundred paces ahead, "it is the Centishmen and their Thegn I am concerned do not have the stomach for a hard fight. And," he concluded quietly, "so is Sigmund," naming Dagfinn's brother who, over the

Centishmen's objections, had been placed aboard *Dragon's Fang* along with another Dane, Tjorborn Holgarson, who was the ostensible steersman, although he had not had much to do because Beorhtweald had insisted on one of his Centishmen serve that function once they entered Centish waters.

Since he did not know what else to say, Alfred replied with as much conviction as he could muster, "It is in God's hands, Knut. And it is our strength in our God that gave us victory at Ethantun, and it will give us victory here as well."

Alfred did not say it in an insulting matter, but as he knew that it would, it angered Knut to be reminded of the pivotal defeat that brought him to serve a Saxon king because his leader had not only been defeated, he had converted to Christianity. And, like most of Guthrum's followers, he had initially been convinced it had been done as a matter of political expediency brought on by what appeared to be a temporarily weakened position, but like he believed the Danes of this *viking* were experiencing, he was beginning to have his own doubts about his leader.

As soon as it was sufficiently dark, the crews of the two ships leaving the fleet behind lowered their Saxon sails, raised the Danish, and attached the figureheads before striking out east. And, as the darkness settled, it *was* dark, none of the Saxon members, not even the Centishmen, having sailed when there was no moon because of the danger. Even Einarr was uncharacteristically quiet, and while the pace was not fast, it was steady, and very shortly, the light of the campfires set by the men remaining behind became tiny pinpricks of yellow light, from which Titus found it difficult to look away. Then they were gone and there was nothing but the sounds of the oars sweeping through the water and the torpid flapping of the sail because the breeze was so light. There was no talking, but while early on they had been warned on the two night forays they had made out to the Solent and back, albeit when the moon was visible, about how much farther sound traveled over water, Titus was certain that it had nothing to do with that. When the sun came up, there would be a period where they could rest, then he assumed they would turn about and come back west, and then? Only God above knew what the day would bring. This was what occupied Titus' mind, and he felt confident that his comrades were thinking similar thoughts, but while he was learning these contemplations before a possible battle were natural and to be expected, most of them had a second worry, because this would be their first fight at sea, and he just hoped that what they had learned from the Danes was sound. He still did not trust Einarr, although since his slaying of Einarr's cousin, the Danish shipmaster had treated him with what could *almost* be considered a grudging respect, but Titus did trust Dagfinn, and had come to like the slightly older Dane immensely. He was far from alone, as all but the most fervent Dane-haters among the Saxons aboard the *Viper* felt the same way towards him, albeit to different degrees.

"He's not a bad sort...for a Dane," had been Hrothgar's judgment, and Titus had noted the heads moving up and murmurs of agreement, his among them.

Still, Titus and his Saxon comrades would have been lying if they said they had not wondered what the two Danes would do the moment battle came, although Einarr had answered that with his participation at Stanmer, and while Titus had quickly gone off in pursuit of what turned out to be Sigurd and some of his men, he had heard from Uhtric and the others that, while he was not in the middle of the fighting, Einarr had bloodied his ax, which, like most large Northmen, he favored, although he did carry a sword as well. Dagfinn did not seem like a killer to Titus; he was just too...*likable*, but as soon as the thought came to him, he immediately thought of his brother-in-law, who had a very similar disposition, and he had seen what Uhtric could do in battle. Whatever the answer, he hoped they would find out because, while the jest about Aelflaed had been preplanned, Titus was sincere in wanting to be back on land, but it was to go back to Wiltun, because he had decided something about Isolde. Although he hoped that he would be successful, he had also prepared himself for accepting that she and Hereweald were married by the time they got back as she had said, but if they were not for whatever reason, he would make one last, final plea, using the one and only weapon he had left: total, brutal honesty. He would confess it all, that it had been his pride, and yes, his arrogance and belief that Isolde should consider herself to be blessed by God to be his wife that had caused his refusal to not apologize and beg forgiveness immediately. And, that he had been foolish in not seeing Aslaug for what she was, and he hoped he never saw her again, because he had come to know himself well enough that the violence that was clearly stirring just beneath the surface of the face he showed the world might erupt. His night with Isolde had proven that she still had feelings for him, and he was determined that if those embers had not been extinguished in his absence, he would fan them back into existence. It was, he thought wryly, a strange thing for him to be thinking as the *Viper* glided through the night sea, the water blacker than any ink he had ever seen. Facing backward as he was, he had no idea if the *Dragon's Fang* was even visible, but this was one of those times he had to place his trust in Lord Einarr, Dagfinn, and Dagfinn's brother and the other Dane in the Centish vessel. In some ways, it was peaceful, and as he had discovered early on, he actually enjoyed pulling an oar, though more as a means to an end, because it worked muscles that he had not worked before and those muscles that he used for different purposes were worked in a different manner, and that made him stronger. It was not necessary for Einarr to bellow the stroke, speaking just above a conversational tone, nor was it a problem for Dagfinn when he spelled his fellow Dane. Stroke by stroke, they moved through the night, until Titus began to wonder just how far they intended to go.

"Are we going to row the whole night?" he muttered, thinking he was speaking too softly to be heard beyond the bench in front of him, where Willmar was pulling.

"If that's what it takes," Otha's voice sounded from just behind him, making him almost miss the recovery of his oar from the water because he jumped in surprise. "All you need to do is worry about your part, boy," Otha said coldly. "And if that's rowing until you drop dead, that's what you'll do. Remember," he reminded Titus mockingly, "you told me you'd changed."

"Yes, Lord."

Titus knew that was the one and only answer to offer, and

he did not utter another word.

As it turned out, they only rowed another hour, which they estimated to be past midnight before Einarr told them to ship their oars, and although he did not furl the sail, he did trim it so that the *Viper* was still moving east, just barely. Once the oars were shipped and the holes plugged, Titus was about to stand up, but Otha's words were still ringing in his ears, so his rear only got an inch off the wood before he sat back down, waiting to be told what to do next. Eadward and Otha walked down the center of the ship to talk with Einarr and Dagfinn, turning their backs to avoid being overheard, and they spoke in whispers.

"When do we turn about?" Eadward asked, surprised that Einarr was still moving east, but he soon learned why.

"Because the *Dragon's Fang* is leading us, and that is what they did." The Dane pointed, yet when Eadward turned and squinted, while he could just make out the shape of the ship that had hovered just fifty paces but slightly inland to the *Viper*, he could not make out their sail. "They know these waters, and they warned me that they would be doing this. We are making headway, but very slowly. Then we are going to come about in a wide turn that will place us a bit farther away from the coast so that we will be visible when the sun comes up behind us and make it look as if we have been sailing from the mouth of the Seine where the Northmen have taken control in Frankia. That is when we will drift for a bit because the Centishmen said that it will pull us farther away from the coast, which is good. These Frankia Danes will be suspicious," Einarr warned. "We are only two ships, and as you have seen, when we go *viking,* it is usually with more ships. Sigurd," it was the first time Einarr had mentioned his cousin's name since his initial admission of kinship, and they heard the pride there, "was called The Bold for a reason, taking just nine ships, so perhaps he angered the gods by being *too* bold. But," he returned to the subject, "there are also all manner of reasons that just a pair of ships show up. That storm we went through last week happens out in the open water between here and Frankia more often, so it is possible that those ships that showed up had more with them and there was a storm, they suffered damage and had to return to Frankia for repairs before they rejoined Sigurd. Perhaps," he added with what for him was humor, "we will see whether your one God is truly more powerful than ours and removed two ships from that Frankia fleet so they will be looking for them to show back up." It was not much of a jest, if it was one, but before either Eadward or Otha could respond, Einarr stiffened, pointed, and said, "They have begun the turn."

He turned and said something to Dagfinn in Danish, who grunted an acknowledgement and leaned against the steering oar. The Saxons felt the deck tilt slightly as the *Viper* began their wide, slow turn, but when Eadward was about to ask Einarr another question, the Dane held up a hand.

"Lord, I need to concentrate now and do not have time for more questions. There is nothing for you to do now, so you might as well try and get some sleep. We will wake you when it is time to prepare."

For a moment, Eadward considered making an issue of this discourtesy, but he was still intimidated by the Dane, and without a word, he spun and began heading for the prow, but Otha did not follow him, watching over his shoulder until the young lord disappeared in the gloom. By the time he was even with the mast, he could only make out something moving, and once he completely vanished in the gloom, Otha turned back to Einarr.

"Are you going to fuck us, Dane?" he asked quietly, but while this made Dagfinn hiss in surprise, Einarr seemed to have expected the question, which he had.

"Do you *want* me to fuck you, Saxon?"

"You'll call me Lord Otha," Otha growled. "Remember that I'm a nobleman of Wessex. And," he added savagely, "I've killed a *lot* of Danes, Lord Einarr. You would do well to remember that."

Einarr did not reply, not immediately, but there was a tone of respect in his voice, and he offered a partial explanation.

"You ask me if I will 'fuck' you...Lord Otha. Since your tongue is not my own, I am unclear on the meaning of some of your meanings of some words, but if you are asking whether we plan to *betray* you, no, we do not. We," he indicated Dagfinn, "and every one of the Danes who are part of this are sworn to

King Guthrum..."

"King Guthrum?" Otha asked in mock bewilderment. "I've never heard of a King Guthrum." Pausing just a fraction, he said, "Oh, you must mean King *Aethelstan*, who *our* King adopted as his own flesh and blood when he accepted the one true God."

The jibe struck home, although Otha had to take his satisfaction in the sound of Einarr's indrawn breath because he could not really make out the Dane's expression, but he could feel the rage radiating from the shipmaster.

"Whatever you wish to call him," Einarr's words had a sibilant quality that indicated he was clenching his teeth, "I have sworn my life to him, and these *oskilgetinn* and their *viking* threaten everything that my Lord King has worked hard to build for *his* Danes." He paused, and it was clear that he was regaining control of his temper, and his tone turned mocking, similar to Otha's as he added, "Besides, if you do not know that Danes have been killing other Danes long before we ever knew you Saxons existed, then you do not know much about us...Lord."

Both men had spoken their piece, and Otha turned and joined Eadward and the other two Thegns, and it was good that it was dark so that none of the others could see that both Otha and Einarr were grinning broadly.

The plan had been to rouse the men once the sun was above the horizon, but there was no need, for while the crews had rested, none had slept. Instead, they had huddled together with their closest comrades, some talking quietly, others not saying anything, all of them absorbed in their own thoughts about what was coming. For Titus, it meant sharpening his sword as he leaned against the side between his bench and Willmar's, while Uhtric sat across from him towards the center of the ship, using one of the remaining water barrels lashed to the deck to lean against, and Willmar sat on his bench, but facing forward. Hrothgar and Ealdwolf, who spent their leisure time together most often, were in similar postures on the opposite side of the ship, and as usual, it was Uhtric who was doing the talking.

"I wonder what Leofflaed is doing," he said, not addressing

it to anyone in particular, and Titus, accustomed to this, remained silent. "Probably trying to feed Wiglaf. That boy is *always* hungry!" He said this with a laugh, and this made Titus chuckle.

"So was I at his age," he replied, then as always, felt the wave of bitterness welling up, "but the difference is that Wiglaf didn't have a father like Leofric. We were *all* hungry, Uhtric, all three of us."

"I know," Uhtric replied, having heard this as many times as Titus had heard his pondering on the doings of his wife and child. "God has blessed me, there's no doubt." This caused Titus to lift his head from his work, and while he did not say anything, he raised an eyebrow and gestured with his head at Uhtric's eyepatch, but this did not dissuade Uhtric, and as he pointed to the patch, he shrugged. "This? This is a small sacrifice to make for all that I have now. And," his voice hardened, not much, but Titus knew him well and heard the iron in it, "that's why we need to stop these pagan bastards here and now. I swear, these Danes are like rats! You can kill them and kill them, but they just keep showing up!" This was said with such vehemence, and loudly enough to be heard that it caused Titus to involuntarily glance to the stern, but if Einarr and Dagfinn heard them, they did not indicate it. Seeing where Titus was looking, Uhtric said sheepishly, "I'm just sick of being on this boat, Titus. That's what it is more than anything else. We Saxons," he said loftily, "aren't meant to be men of the sea."

With that, Titus fervently agreed, and he said as much, then returned to his work, another silence descending before, at last, Einarr called out, "All right, that is enough time sitting on your asses! Back to the oars!" For one of the only times during their time aboard the *Viper*, the crew responded with a level of enthusiasm that caused the Danes to exchange an amused glance. Once the *Dragon's Fang* signaled their readiness, Einarr bellowed the now-familiar preparatory order that lifted the unshipped oars up, hovering above the water, waited a heartbeat, then called out, "Drop!" followed immediately by "Pull!"

With their sister ship, the *Sea Viper* began heading back west again, and while they were at least active, the men knew there would be a second period of waiting now, as all the men not rowing scanned the horizon for the first sighting of Danish ships to the south as they resumed their game with the Saxons of Alfred's fleet.

As Titus would learn, just as veterans of more than one campaign already had, the time an enemy is most likely to do what one does not expect is when a plan is being executed, and this day was no exception. For reasons that the Saxons would never learn, the new leader of this Danish *viking* had decided to row back to the coast shortly after dawn instead of waiting a few hours as he had done for several days previously, precisely for the reasons Einarr had explained to Alfred; it was not just the Saxons who were tiring of this. All Titus and his comrades of the two Danish ships knew was that they had been rowing barely an hour at a steady, controlled pace when Dagfinn, from his spot at the steering oar, said something in Danish, loudly enough to be heard by most of the crew, including Titus, and while he still did not understand enough of the tongue to know what he said, he heard the excitement and the tension in the tone.

They did not have to wait long, as Einarr shouted, "Lord Eadward! Sails!" He pointed off their port bow, which meant it was out of Titus' sight, one of the most frustrating aspects of life aboard ship for him. "And they are Danish!"

"All right, lads!" Otha bellowed. "Remember, we're Danes, not Saxons." He paused. "And when they find out we're not what they think we are, it will be too late for them!"

This elicited a ragged roar from the men, and Titus felt his heart begin to thud heavily against his chest bone at a speed not necessary for the pace they were keeping, while Einarr strode down the center of the ship to come to the bow.

Their eyes met, and Einarr said, "You will need to be a Berserker today, boy."

"Don't worry about me, Lord," Titus countered, the anger stirring, just as Einarr had intended. "You do your part, and we'll do ours."

"We will see," Einarr called over his shoulder, having already passed by.

Reaching the four Saxon nobles, he gave them a cursory inspection, although it was not the first time. Eadward looked ill at ease, which was to be expected, but it was not just from the impending action but from the fact that he was no longer wearing the armor of a young Saxon nobleman, and had put on the dead Sigurd's arm rings.

"It would be better if your hair was longer," Einarr commented, but before any of them could say anything, he added with a shrug, "but this will have to work."

As expected, the larger of the two groups of ships had spotted the pair at roughly the same time, and also as anticipated, two of the eight vessels suddenly veered in their direction. They were still a good way off, but now they were heading directly for each other, so the distance closed rapidly, which meant the tension increased with every stroke, which Dagfinn was now calling out, in Danish, although it did not matter to the crew at this point. They knew what was expected, and each man pulled, albeit with varying degrees of vigor and enthusiasm about what was coming. The only way they knew the moment was almost at hand was when Dagfinn suddenly altered the rhythm, slowing it, before calling out in English in a low tone the order to lift, then back oar a couple of strokes to kill their speed, then gave the order to furl the sail halfway down so that they could drift. On Titus's side, the port side, this was Aelfwine's duty, while on the opposite side it fell to the other experienced seaman among the Saxons, Ealdwolf, and they both drew their oars in, hopped off the bench, and quickly did as ordered. There was a brief silence as Titus sat, holding the oar above the water, noticing that his blade, dripping from the seawater a few inches above the waves, was not the only one quivering. *I wonder if they can see that from where they are,* he thought, but while he doubted it, he did offer up a quick prayer that his guess they could not was the correct one. Then Einarr cupped his hands around his mouth, and bellowed something, but there was no response for several heartbeats. The tension was almost unbearable, but it was not until a faint cry came that Titus realized he had been holding his breath, and this reply prompted a series of exchanges, all in Danish, although they could recognize names, like Sigurd Gunnarson...and Einarr

Thorsten. Why, Titus wondered, is he giving his real name? He quickly surmised why; after all, Einarr had been Sigurd's cousin. Was that what he was using to convince these suspicious raiders they were fellow Danes? Struck by another thought, Titus had to straighten up to peer across the ship to the starboard side, where the *Dragon's Fang* had been alongside them, but he immediately saw that they were now farther astern than he thought they should have been. What was that about? he wondered.

Before he could spend any more time thinking about it, after another exchange between Einarr and the other Dane, Otha relayed the order, "They said we can join them but must stay astern. Make ready."

Suddenly, Titus' mouth was so dry that he desperately wanted to dip into the barrel, tantalizingly close but effectively out of reach, but he had no chance to do anything about it because now, at a signal from Einarr, Dagfinn gave the order, again in Danish: "Drop!" then, "Pull!"

The ship began to move, and they were now within a matter of heartbeats of life, death, and for one young warrior aboard the *Sea Viper*, another chance to prove to his comrades, and to his people, that he was not the miserable failure his father Leofric was. And, as always, the mere thought of his father stirred the thing inside him that had proven to be so helpful and destructive in almost equal measure, giving him so much more than he ever thought possible, while robbing him of his heart's desire. Titus and the men of Wiltun were going into battle at sea at last.

On the *Redeemer* several miles west, Alfred was pacing, hands clasped in front of him, head bowed, the sign to his closest advisors like Lord Mucel and Father Aethelred that he was not just concerned, he was nervous, and it was something that he tried not to do in front of anyone but his most trusted advisers. Yet he could not help himself; despite making sure the fleet actually put out before the sun rose and they *were* slowly moving east, something did not feel right. Of all the things the Saxon King struggled with, it was these...feelings that he had missed something that were the most frustrating and terrifying.

To be fair, he did not get them often, but that was part of the problem, because the few times they *had* come in his life, every time he had ignored it, there had been a price, sometimes heavy. They were moving at the agreed-upon pace, the same they had maintained for six days, with the same result, so why did this day feel different? What was he missing? It was true they were doing things slightly differently, with *Corpse Stealer*, the second largest ship carrying the extra warriors immediately behind the *Redeemer*, and they were not as bunched together as normal; at Knut's suggestion, one of the Saxon ships, and the third fastest of his small fleet, was lagging behind, watching for a Danish attempt to sail north beyond the horizon to fall on Romney now that the Saxon fleet had passed it. However, it was Knut who had pointed out that this was unlikely.

"Yes, we Danes are comfortable out to sea, but we do not like moving at night under anything but sail if the wind is blowing in the right direction. They would have to do what the *Sea Viper* and *Dragon's Fang* is doing, and I do not believe this new leader will do that."

It made sense, but so did taking that precaution in the event Knut was wrong. That, however, was not the cause for this nagging worry for Alfred, it was something else. As he always did at such moments, he was offering a prayer to God, asking for His guidance, His wisdom, and His aid in helping His humble servant Alfred in what was, after all, a truly holy and just quest, making one nation, a Christian nation, where the old ways of pagan idolatry were put firmly in the past where they belonged. Suddenly, he stopped his pacing, standing still while staring, not ahead but astern, seemingly at nothing, while Knut gave Father Aethelred an inquiring glance.

"He does this sometimes," the priest whispered, "but I would be prepared for some orders. I believe he has come to some decision."

Father Aethelred was right, because within a couple of heartbeats after this, the King spun about and ordered Knut, "We are going to the oars now, Knut."

"Lord King?" Knut asked in surprise. "This early?"

"Yes," Alfred answered, without hesitation. "I believe the Danes are going to try and surprise us with something different, and if I am right, we will need to be ready to aid our two ships earlier than we anticipated."

This unleashed a mad scramble as the crew, having become accustomed to what was a leisurely beginning to the day, hurried to their assigned spots, while Ragnar Olafson, who served the same function as Dagfinn and Torbjorn, ran down the center of the ship and attached the red streamer, then ran it up to the top of the mast in the signal to the other ships of the fleet that orders were coming. Because they were so spread out, this engendered another delay as the process was repeated with the following ships, which Alfred bore with as much patience as he could muster. Finally, after what seemed to be an hour but was only a few moments, Knut bellowed the orders that increased the speed of the *Redeemer*. It was a fateful decision; indeed, as Father Aethelred spread the word of it, it was a *providential* decision whereby thanks to Almighty God, King Alfred discerned that the Danes were up to some sort of trick, enabling the Saxon fleet to arrive in time to spring the trap and rescue the *Sea Viper* and *Dragon's Fang*. It would come to be known as a resounding victory...for King Alfred.

From Titus' perspective, while they began slowly enough, events accelerated so rapidly that it was impossible to recall all but the most salient. Once permission was given for the two ships to join the raiders, the crews of the Saxon ships behaved as would be expected, rowing at a pace that allowed them to draw closer, but with the spacing customary for Danish ships sailing together.

"If we get within fifty paces before they realize we are not with them, we will be blessed by Thor," Einarr had told them, using the name of the pagan god as a deliberate provocation, but none of the Saxons took the bait, so he continued, "but I think it will be more likely about a hundred paces when they discover our ruse."

There was also some lateral maneuvering required, but in a way that did not arouse suspicion, so that the *Sea Viper* was in effect between the two ships, while the *Dragon's Fang* was to starboard, and would be on the opposite side of the second ship on the inland side, the plan being that, at their prearranged signal, they would immediately increase to ramming speed, then turn to port, using the high prow of the *Viper* to smash into the side of their target ship. The one advantage to performing this maneuver was that it was not uncommon, not just with the Danes, but with all seafaring nations, enabling the steersmen in the trailing ships to avoid collisions in the event something unforeseen with the leading ship occurred that caused it to suddenly lose speed. This, at least, worked perfectly, and then it was up to Einarr, and Sigmund on the *Dragon Fang* to gradually increase the rhythm, yet subtly enough that the acceleration was not immediately obvious. And, in this, Einarr showed his skill, because the only way Titus could tell that the pace was increasing was because he felt it in his arms, not much but just enough to be noticeable. He was also totally unaware that the *Dragon's Fang* was once again lagging behind, but it was noticed by Einarr, who alerted the three Saxon nobles who had been crouching below the side this entire time, leaving only young Eadward as the lone counterfeit Dane, who was still standing in the prow. The Thegns were the only men who could instantly be identified as such, but this was by design, because once aboard the other ship, it would be a maelstrom of chaos and confusion, making identification crucial. Titus, Willmar, Leofsige, and the three Thegns would be the first to make the leap that, hopefully, would be a short one, followed by Hrothgar and other men from the port side because, as they had learned, some the hard way, while the Danes treated a shipboard fight as if it was on land, it was a rocking, pitching patch of land, and maintaining equilibrium was absolutely crucial, and a sudden shift of weight from just one side of a ship could spell disaster. It began when there was a sharp call from behind Titus and over his right shoulder, where he judged their target to be, and while he did not hear alarm, he was certain he heard concern.

So did Einarr, who bellowed, *"Now!"*

This was the last really clear moment as the water on either side of the *Viper* looked as if it had suddenly been brought to a rolling boil, the spray flying as the twenty oars on each side slapped into the water.

"Pull! Pull, you bastards!" Titus recognized Otha's voice, who had finally stood up, while Aelfnod and Ceadda moved next to him but arraying towards the stern. He was wearing his Saxon helmet, disdaining the Norse style that had eye protection, and he had unfastened his cloak. "It's time to make these pagan, ass-licking, boy-fucking pieces of shit pay for coming to Saxon lands!"

Some of the men bellowed a promise to do just that, but Titus was not one of them; he preferred to save his breath for the task of the moment, putting every ounce of his prodigious strength into pulling his oar to his chest. The increase in speed was instantly noticeable, even more so because of the sleek lines of the Danish ship that, while he desperately wanted to get ashore, Titus had come to love as his own. He had learned to watch one of the Danes in the stern for any sign of what might be coming, seeing what direction they were looking at, what was occupying their attention, and he could see by Dagfinn's expression that they were gaining on their target. Then Einarr came sprinting down the center of the boat, displaying the kind of nimble feet that could only come from a lifetime spent aboard a cramped vessel like the *Viper*, rejoining his fellow Dane. Like his comrades, Titus did wonder what the Danes would do, and he seemingly got his answer when Einarr bent down, snatched up his helmet, strapped it on, and drew his ax, then sprinted back to the bow.

"Keep it up, lads! Keep it up!"

This was from Eadward, who had been expressly forbidden from leaving the ship, but then he suddenly darted down from the bow to grab at the center line, the most potent sign that a collision was imminent. No more than a half-heartbeat after he grasped the line, the *Viper* suddenly heeled over hard.

"Port side, ship oars!" This they had practiced over, and over, and over, so it was an automatic reaction, and it was followed immediately by Einarr bellowing, "*Brace!*"

Again in an automatic response drilled into him, Titus reached down and grabbed his bench with both hands and placed his feet against the back of Willmar's bench, one of the only men able to do so because of his height. His first thought was that the collision was not that bad, yet the shuddering that ran down the length of the ship, beginning at the bow, was also accompanied by a strange sound he had never heard, as if someone broke a stick over their knee but with a sodden quality to it, and he realized that they had accomplished their first goal in capturing a ship, snapping several of their oars. There was no mistaking what happened next, and even as prepared as he thought he was, he was flung backwards as the high prow of the *Viper* slammed into the side of the Danish ship. It was the second reaction of the *Viper* that caught him by surprise, because like a whipsaw, Titus' chest slammed into his knees with a force that it almost knocked the wind out of him as the prow of their ship did not penetrate the side but instead rode up it, so that now the snarling snake figurehead was pointing skyward, but he was fortunate. Because of his strength, he managed to keep his ass securely planted on the bench, but he saw farther astern one of Aelfnod's men perform a somersault, his legs flailing up in the air in an image that would stay with Titus. The noise was incredible, and unlike anything he had experienced; it was the sound and fury of the shield wall, but with the added elements of cracking timbers, snapping ropes that sent items that had been securely lashed down flying through the air, crashing against the side of the ship or smashing into men, at least judging from the shrill screams, all at once.

"Prepare to board!"

Since Titus had kept the Danish helmet he had taken as his first spoils, he did not have to worry about that because he was already wearing it, so he snatched a shield up off the strake, but just as he was reaching for the ax he had been carrying and had intended to use, he changed his mind, drawing his Danish sword instead, feeling a sense of comfort in his hand curling around the grip. This was the first moment he was able to see beyond his immediate world of the port side of the ship down to the stern, and when he looked to the prow, he saw that Otha was already leaping up onto the side, although like his Saxon helmet, he was holding a Saxon shield that, while circular, was larger and emblazoned with Lord Eadwig's rearing horse. He was holding his *seaxe*, compared to Titus' Danish sword that was almost a foot longer, and although his came to a sharp point and a double cutting edge, he was struck with an odd thought that, aboard ship, the *seaxe* would have been a better choice, which was why he had bought it in the first place, but his was in his pack, so that was all the thought he gave it as, in his desire to show what he was made of, he leapt up onto the side so that he could be second only to Otha, except that Lord Ceadda just beat him down by the stern. He did make a quick glance to his right just in time to see Einarr leap up on the opposite side of Otha, next to the snarling snake's head, and while the *Viper* had slid backwards a couple feet, their ship now seemed securely lodged on the Danish ship, with their prow about five feet from its own bow.

Otha clearly saw Einarr land on the side next to him, because the Dane's feet had barely touched the wood when the Saxon Thegn bellowed just one word, "*KILL!*"

No matter how hard he tried, Titus could never recall making the actual leap across and slightly down into the other ship, although he remembered it was less than three feet. It was probably because waiting for him was a wild-eyed Dane, with a helmet that had been knocked askew that made him look like a child wearing his father's helmet, one of those odd details that Titus would recall, although it was the ax that was raised above and pulled behind the Dane's head to which he paid the most attention. Perhaps if Titus had not been so heavy and so powerful, the Dane might have managed to hold his position, but it was not to be, as the young Saxon, with the shield pulled hard against his left shoulder, slammed into him, sending his foe reeling backward into another Dane. It provided enough room for Titus to drop down off the side, the first most important thing that had to be done to survive a shipboard battle according to Einarr, but he was more concerned with the spear thrust that came from his right, and it was done without thought and with nothing but pure reflex that Titus swept his sword up and out slightly and knocked the spearpoint up so that instead of punching through his side, it sliced into the air between his face and his shield. Then Willmar arrived, killing the spear-wielding Dane who should have been as worried about the threat to his front as to his right, and he paid for it with a crushing downward ax blow, and it would be the last time Titus faced anyone with a spear in this fight.

"The only time a spear is good for shipboard combat is as a defender to repel boarders," Einarr had assured them. "But once you get inside their point, it is useless."

Something slammed into Titus' shield, shoving it back towards his body, and he responded automatically, dropping his hips then twisting them to shove the attacker back, and he saw that it was the helmeted Dane, who made another swing with his ax, and it was then that Titus noticed the Dane had not snatched up a shield. Rather than tilt his shield to evenly spread the blow, he kept his shield vertical so that the bottom edge of the ax buried itself more deeply into the limewood. Using it as leverage, and with the strength of the oar-hardened muscles of his left arm, Titus pivoted his shield out from his body, not much but enough for him to snake his sword around the edge of his protection to bury the point in the Dane's gut, just below the ribs. They were looking each other in the eyes, and Titus saw the sudden expression of despair in the man's eyes, yet he experienced nothing but a cruel delight as he twisted the blade then ripped it across, feeling the spray of blood drenching his hand and arm, his mixed emotions at slaying Sigurd clearly gone. The Dane let go of the ax still in the shield, however, and Titus was faced with a choice, neither of them good. Having an ax embedded in the shield made it awkward to use, especially in this enclosed space, but the second most important thing that Einarr had stressed was the need to make room for his comrades by moving towards the center of the ship.

"If you are alone, I do not care how good a warrior you are, you will die," he had said flatly. "So instead of trying to win glory as a great warrior, shoving an *oskilgetinn* back out of the way will keep you alive."

He chose the latter, although he did not use his shield, instead launching a quick thrust over the top of his protection, aimed at a black-haired Dane, helmetless but with such a heavy beard that only his eyes were visible, or perhaps it was just because they were opened so widely. The blow did not land, which did not surprise him, but it caused the Dane to take a step backward, and Titus moved a step forward, or that was his intent, but his foot came down right onto the open belly wound of the dying Dane. What came from the Dane's lips was such a shrill scream of an agony that, no matter whether they were Dane or Saxon, they all shared the same, simultaneous thought:

none of them wanted to die that way. From a practical standpoint, Titus had another choice to make, and fighting the bile rising up in his throat, he did not hesitate, brutally shoving his foot down instead of lifting it and having one foot in the air for even an eyeblink, trying to pretend that it was not the dead man's spine that he was feeling under the sole of his boot. Rather than attack with his own ax, the black-haired Dane used his shield, but in a move of cunning, he swung his shield across his body, aiming at the handle of the ax embedded in Titus' own. If the ax had remained there, it would have certainly knocked the shield aside, and might have also knocked it from his hand, but once again, Titus was blessed, because the ax jerked from the shield and went spinning off to the side, and despite it jerking his arm aside, it was not out of position as much as the black-haired Dane's protection was across his body, and Titus did not hesitate, launching another thrust, but this one high up, punching through the thick black beard and into his foe's throat. Willmar reached his side, but while he didn't see it clearly, Titus sensed another Danish body land on the chest and head of the thankfully deceased dead man he was partially standing in, and there was a brief lull, at least in their part of the boat, though it only lasted perhaps a normal heartbeat. Lord Aelfnod was to his left, but his back was slightly turned as he furiously engaged a helmeted sword-wielding Dane, also in mail, marking him as a likely noble of some sort. This created a gap, but it was instantly filled by Uhtric, who grinned at Titus before using his *seaxe* to parry a thrust from a dagger; the fact that it was wielded by a shrieking woman, her golden hair tied back but flying out from behind her head as she threw herself at his brother-in-law was what shocked Titus. She would have been beautiful if her face had not been twisted into such a snarling grimace of hatred and fear, and the only reason she did not die immediately was because Uhtric seemed as surprised as he was.

"Kill the bitch!" Aelfnod, having just dispatched his opponent, had pivoted about, and even with all that was going on, Titus could see that his expression matched that of the Danish woman, but he knew there was a raging sorrow there as well.

His blade and Uhtric's struck the woman simultaneously, and there was a little more space to move in order to accomplish the third most important goal.

"You cut the ship in half," Einarr had instructed them. "From the mainmast. That way, your rear will be protected, and you just work to your end of the ship."

It was, Titus had thought at the time, simple, yet while he knew it would not seem that way when he was doing it, now, onboard, it seemed to be impossible. He felt more than saw Willmar shudder, turning just in time to see his comrade collapse backward, into the path of Ceadda's man Aedelstan, blood oozing from the hole in his leather vest, but it was the ashen expression that Titus recognized that told him that Willmar had been mortally wounded, his eyes already rolling back in his head. Willmar, who had been with him, and stood with him after his beating Hrodulf to death, even after Titus knocked him unconscious with a single blow, with his bad jokes, and his secret piety that he thought he hid from his comrades, knowing they would mock him for it, and now he was dead. And it was then that, as it had first happened to the huge Roman who shared his size, name and rage hundreds of years before, and had earned this Titus the title of Berserker, that *thing* that rested inside the men of the line of Titus Pullus roused itself.

"*Nooooooo!*"

Chapter Six

It was, once more, something that the men who saw it would never forget, but for his comrades, and his best friend, it would also be a tragic moment that they knew would stay with them the rest of their days, because they were certain that Titus of Cissanbyrig, the Berserker, who fully earned that title on the deck of a ship they never learned the name of, suffered the fate of so many young and prideful warriors. In the larger battle, Alfred's fleet had arrived and none too soon for the *Viper*, slaughtering the crews of six of the raiders and sinking five of the ships while sending two ships, including the one that had been the *Dragon Fang's* quarry, fleeing, whereupon Alfred and his victorious fleet had sailed to Romney, the nearest village, the number of their fleet grown by one in the form of the lone captured Danish vessel. That the destroyed ships were composed of the raiding force was proven by the recovery of some of the prisoners that had been taken to that point, more than two dozen, mostly women but four men and some children who had been facing a life of slavery, and one ironbound box containing plunder, although the rest was lost when five of the ships sank, including the ship the *Viper* had rammed, forcing the Wiltun men to scramble back aboard the *Viper*. Alfred's fleet had suffered one seriously damaged ship, as the *Redeemer* and *Soul Stealer*, the men manning the oars near exhaustion, and unfortunately, rendering them ineffective for the first part of the battle, arrived to find the *Sea Viper* surrounded by five Danish ships including, the Wiltun men would be quick to remind anyone who was willing to sit and listen, the second ship that had been the *Dragon Fang's* target.

"Those child-buggering Centishmen," Hrothgar had raged all the way back to Romney as they pulled at the oars. "I *knew* they couldn't be trusted! I swear, Thegn or not, if I ever see Beorhtweald again, I'll reach up his ass and pull his guts out with my bare hands! And," he declared, "I'm strong enough to do it!"

It was a sentiment that was shared by every man aboard, and they all knew the large Saxon, who, before the arrival of a fourteen-year-old from Cissanbyrig, had been the strongest man, not just of Otha's retainers, but of all of the Wiltun men, meant every word. Still, those within eyeline of Uhtric could not help glancing over at the one-eyed warrior, but he was staring straight ahead, pulling at his oar, having said no more than a dozen words since the fighting had ended when the *Redeemer* had arrived. The losses were grievous; for Otha's men, among the dead was Willmar, Aelfwine, but while nothing was said, it was the loss of the youngest of them in Wilwulf, who had had his skull split by an ax that made them worry for their Thegn, Lord Otha, who was overcome with grief, albeit briefly. Even so, it was the loss of the second youngest of the Wiltun men that was felt most keenly, and not just by Uhtric, but by all of them. Theobald had suffered a serious wound to his shoulder that, even if it did not corrupt and healed, had shattered the bone, and it was a practical certainty that he would never wield a weapon effectively again. Of Ceadda's men, Wulfnod took a sword thrust through his eye, the point exiting the back of his skull, but in one of those macabre twists, he was actually lying in the bottom of the *Viper*, still breathing, with his one good eye wide open and moving about, though not because he was tracking the movement near him, and Wigmund had died of an ax blow that almost severed his head. Like Otha's dead, they were wrapped in their cloaks, arranged along the centerline, but while the men sworn to Aelfnod had only sustained one death, although Odda was clinging to life and was not given much chance to survive through the night, that death was the Thegn himself. His death was shrouded in mystery; not the cause of it, which had been a sword thrust to his chest by what was likely the leader of this crew given that he was in mail like Aelfnod and had many arm rings, but how it had happened, because those who were the closest witnesses seemed to be split in opinion, and in the future, it would cause serious issues among the men sworn to Ealdorman Eadwig.

Of Alfred's men, Wulfsige and Eggbehrt were dead, and Godric would lose his left hand. Lord Eadward had obeyed Otha's injunction to remain in the ship, which proved to be fortuitous because of the Centishmen's failure to attack the second Danish ship, and he led the men who had yet to leap aboard the first Danish ship in the defense against their attack from the starboard side of the *Viper*. Although it was not serious, he did receive a slashing wound that laid open his cheek to the bone but, not surprisingly, next to Uhtric, he was the most affected by Titus' absence, which was intensified by the fact that he had actually seen what had happened from his spot in the bow of the *Viper*. The cause of Titus' death, and the fact that his body was not lying with their comrades in the center of the *Viper* was what was being discussed in one of the two alehouses in Romney that night. By Alfred's order, the alehouses of Romney, all two of them, had been closed to the townspeople and reserved for the men who had just destroyed the Danish raiders to a man. This was the official story, at least; four ships had been sunk, not five, with the sixth captured, their crews slaughtered to a man, prisoners and stolen plunder recovered, not all of the prisoners, but perhaps half of those taken, along with several Danish prisoners, although in reality, there were none. The moment the ships rowed up and either docked or beached themselves, Alfred had summoned the Thegns in command of his tiny navy, including Eadward, to a private meeting aboard the *Redeemer*, which had been emptied of its crew with the exception of the men of the royal bodyguard, who were stationed around the ship to ensure no inquisitive townspeople, or men from different ships who were curious to know what was going on got close enough. Otherwise, the rest of the warriors were given the freedom of the town, and the Wiltun men could be found in what was reputed to be the best of the two, with the most biddable whores, which Alfred pretended not to hear Cyneweard suggest to Otha as the best alternative.

"Your lads earned it, Lord," Cyneweard said, then waited for Otha to return to the *Viper* and give them the directions before escorting him back to where the King was waiting.

Now, by unspoken consent, the crew of the *Sea Viper* were all sitting in the corner of The Merry Widow together, with no interlopers from other ships eager to hear the details of the hardest fight of the day in exchange for a pot of ale allowed near, though they were all aware of the surreptitious stares of them seated a short distance away. There was certainly ale, a pot in front of each men, but it took a couple of them before it was Uhtric who addressed what would become the most contentious, but for him, the least painful topic.

"Lord Aelfnod," he said quietly, "let that Danish cunt kill him."

Nobody was surprised that this was met with disbelief, and it was Aelfnod's cousin Leofsige, although he served Lord Ceadda, who said defiantly, "That's nonsense! Aelfnod would never do that!" He looked to the other of Aelfnod's men who, as expected, were seated together at one end of the three tables that had been shoved together, but he noticed none of them would meet his eye, and he asked incredulously, "Are you seriously suggesting that my cousin let himself be slaughtered by a Dane? A *pagan*?"

Nobody spoke immediately, then Willibald cleared his throat before he said, "Well, it *is* true that he took the death of his brother hard."

"*Very* hard," Eoforwine, one of Aelfnod's longest serving warriors, said emphatically.

He was also glaring at Leofsige, and as the Wiltun men had learned over the intervening years, there was a fair amount of bad blood between some of Aelfnod's retainers about Leofsige's choosing to serve Lord Ceadda instead, especially with Eoforwine, and it was a subject that had been plowed more than a hundred-year-old field for those who were not involved in it, namely Otha's men.

"I know what I saw," Uhtric insisted quietly, and he looked up from his pot to look at Leofsige with his good eye, and his voice hardened, "and I'm not lying."

As the others expected, Leofsige was the one to break eye contact, and he mumbled in agreement, "Yes, I know he did." Sighing, he finished, "I had just hoped he'd get over it, that's all."

There was a moody silence, and Uhtric braced himself, knowing what was coming, although he did not know from whom it could come.

"The last time I saw him do something like that," Hrothgar

said, "I was sure I'd never see anything like it ever again."

All eyes went to Uhtric, and it was clear they were taking the cue from the most popular of their entire group, and the man closest to Titus, about whether to talk about what they had seen.

At first, it appeared as if Uhtric was not ready, but as he stared down into his pot, he said, "I'll never forget him running at those Danish bastards...with that bastard's guts wrapped around his ankle."

There was the briefest of pauses, then the entire table roared with laughter; it *had* been a singular sight, because in his rage, Titus either forgot or more likely did not care that he had stepped into the stomach cavity of what had been the first Dane he killed, but when he began his rush, a loop of the Dane's intestine had wrapped around his right ankle, and as he bashed into the Danes around the mainmast, the several feet that compose the human intestine had followed him, like a grotesque, bulging blue-green ribbon, dripping blood and offal. It was, they all knew, the kind of horrible thing that one had to laugh at, because what else could one do?

This broke the dam, and very quickly, those who had been in a position to see their young comrade in what they all were certain was his last battle began competing with each other.

"Has anyone ever seen a man slice through another man's thigh, all the way through with an ax?" Ealdwolf asked, then added, "With one hand? His *left* hand?"

It was an easy question for them all to answer, because none had ever seen anything like it. Clearly not even noticing the impediment of a man's guts wrapped around his ankle, while he had used his shield to batter down the first Dane he encountered, knocking the man, of a considerable size himself, off his feet that enabled him to kill him with a simple thrust to the chest, Titus had tossed the shield overboard to snatch his now-dead opponent's own weapon, a double-bladed ax with an unusually wide blade, even for a Danish ax. Almost as if he had planned it, and perhaps he had, Titus had first feinted a high, hard thrust with his sword that forced the next Dane to raise his shield, and in one smooth motion, swung the blade horizontally, across his body, slicing through the muscle and bone of the man's right thigh midway between knee and hip, severing it in one stroke. Adding to the spectacle, there was still enough power and momentum left for the blade to bury itself several inches deep into the inner part of the man's left thigh, the impact toppling the man to his left to leave, for the briefest of an eyeblink, the sight of nothing but a blood-soaked leg, briefly standing without its owner. There were more tales, of the same ax buried in the head of a helmeted Dane, and when Titus wrenched it loose, the man's face was split down to below the nose almost perfectly, as an eighteen year-old giant slashed and thrust and killed his way up the port side of the Danish ship, heading to the bow, leaving carnage behind him, but most importantly, a hole of space through which the *Viper* men poured, and at that moment, it seemed the battle was over. Then, the rest of the Danish ships arrived, and everything changed, the first to arrive sliding up the starboard side, and it was the turn of the Saxons to be surprised, but thanks to Eadward's quick thinking, he had organized the dozen men still on the *Viper* in a defense, just as the Danes began leaping to fill the space aboard the *Viper*, and even without the ability to build up speed, the impact of the two groups of men rushing at each other was terrific, and the ship began rocking violently from side to side as it became critically overloaded, the motion so violent that the prow of the *Viper* almost slid all the way off the first Danish ship. This was no shield wall, no skirmish, no ambush; this was butchery, where fury and rage were the most important ingredient, and nobody on either ship possessed more than Titus of Cissanbyrig, forever earning him the title Berserker.

"Why do you think Einarr jumped overboard?"

This did not completely silence the talking, but Wulfnod's question certainly subdued it, although it was Hrothgar who answered almost instantly, "Because he's a shit- eating, lying, thieving Danish bastard, that's why!"

"You weren't near that part of the ship, Hrothgar," Eoforwine said quietly. "I was, and it was right after Titus went over. And," he added quietly, "it was the same side of the ship."

"So?" Hrothgar's slowness was compounded by his extreme stubbornness once his mind grasped on to an idea or belief. "It doesn't mean anything!" Seeing the expressions of doubt around him, he chose to lift the pot to his lips and mutter,

"That's what I think anyway."

Before the conversation got any further, it was interrupted by the entrance of the Wiltun noblemen, bringing the men to their feet, but they were waved down by Lord Eadward, his cheek now stitched up and the blood cleaned away, not by Theobald, who was now resting in a barn that was serving as a makeshift hospital in the town, but by one of Aelfnod's men who had similar skills. Otha was visibly unmarked; he had several deep bruises along his torso and had been cut high on his left arm, but it was minor and had already been bound, the only sign of it the stain and slit in the cloth of his sleeve, while Ceadda was limping, but was otherwise unhurt. Ignoring the glances of the men from the other crews, they headed directly for the Wiltun men, who hastily found some stools for their leaders. Otha and Ceadda dropped down onto them, but Eadward stood for a moment, clearly intending to say something, though he seemed unsure how to begin.

He cleared his throat and began awkwardly, "I want to begin by saying that King Alfred sends his thanks to you for your courage, and for your actions this day, and while he is pleased with the outcome, he grieves at the losses we incurred."

"What's he going to do about the Centishmen?"

It was not asked loudly, but there was no missing the intensity in Uhtric's question, but before Eadward could speak, Otha interjected, his voice cold, "That's none of your business, Uhtric. It's not *anyone's* business but the King's!" He glared down the table, making eye contact with each of his sworn men first, but he did not stop with them, challenging every man seated and leaning against the two walls, the men of Alfred's guard already back with their own. In a softer tone, he addressed Uhtric. "I'm not saying it's not a good question, Uhtric. It is, but it's not our place."

For a heartbeat, Uhtric did not reply, then gave a curt nod, and Eadward took this as a sign to continue, although it would not get much better.

"He also wants us to know that we will be rewarded for our service, and that he is having a Mass said for our losses." They had debated the matter on the way from the *Redeemer*, but in an unusual moment, Otha had left it up to Eadward whether he brought it up. Eadward swallowed, and continued, "He mentioned Titus by name, and asked me if he had performed as he had at the ambush, and at Ethantun, and he was clearly aggrieved at the...news I had to give him. And," he swallowed, and they all saw the glint of tears, "he is personally lighting a candle in his private chapel in his memory."

It was, at least in their world, a supreme compliment, not just that a King would remember the name, but to ask after a lowly warrior of a Thegn would have been a moment each of them would have treasured for the rest of their days if it had been theirs Alfred had mentioned.

"Also," Eadward went on, "we're leaving for Hamtun as soon as it's safe to sail with our wounded, which means we'll be here for at least another day, probably more. And, while the King has graciously given us this night to grieve our losses, we're to return to the ship for the night...and we're to stay there for the duration."

He braced himself for the outpouring of protest, but in perhaps the most profound sign of how deeply affected the Wiltun men were, instead, it was Leofsige who broke the silence. "Lord Eadward, may I ask a question?"

"Of course, Leofsige," Eadward replied, his answer ready for what he was certain was coming, an explanation of why the King had given this order.

He was completely unprepared for Leofsige to ask, "You were at that end of the ship, Lord. What happened? Did Einarr abandon us and swim to that Danish ship? Or did he go in after Titus?"

How, he wondered, do I answer that? Because the truth was, he did not truly know the answer.

Ironically, while it might have been the blow to his helmeted head that almost killed him that knocked Titus from his fog of rage, it was equally impossible to discount the idea that it was the shock of the freezing water that did it, except for the fact that the first fragment of his memory was the sensation of falling and the sight of the prow of the *Viper* resting on the Danish ship, but from outside both ships that he recalled, and upside down. Then the impact of the water, the throbbing of his head...and sinking. His first really clear memory was thinking, swim, swim to the surface, yet when he tried, he felt the pull of the water, an invisible force wrapped around him trying to bring him down into the depths. Why is this so hard? he wondered, because he had tried swimming in the leather armor and had even dove underwater to do what he was doing now, and it had not seemed this difficult. It was, he quickly realized, because his strength had deserted him, and he remembered the other times this had happened, when the *thing* had taken over, and how once it had departed, it left him exhausted and barely able to lift his head. Titus, you're going to die if you don't swim, he told himself, and what frightened him was there was a voice, a tiny, barely audible voice that whispered, "So? Is that so bad?" He continued sinking, his eyes open and staring upward at the light of the shimmering surface, the bottoms of the two ships startlingly clear, and it surprised him to see how many of those tiny, foul-smelling creatures that they had spent so much time scraping from the hull of the *Viper* had already been replaced.

Isolde.

Whether it was the thought of her name that did it he would never know, but the next voice in his head was hers, saying simply, "Swim, Titus."

Somehow, he did, but the fire in his lungs was growing with such speed and intensity that it took every part of his willpower to keep from opening his mouth, knowing that it would spell his end. He was *so* close! Suddenly, the unbroken rippling was shattered by something, a dark shape that looked like a man, and Titus' first thought was that it was just another combatant falling overboard, except there was something different about the matter in which the man had entered the water. He did not see it plunging down towards him, but he certainly felt the strength of the hand that reached down, and because Titus had chosen to wear his hair longer than most Saxons, the pain of being literally yanked to the surface by the hair. His head breaking water and his mouth finally opening to suck in whatever substance surrounded his mouth no matter what it was occurred so that he sucked in equal parts air and seawater, half which his body gratefully accepted, the other half he promptly regurgitated in a gout of liquid.

"Use your legs!"

He knew that voice, Titus understood, but he was still groggy enough that he could not place it, yet he obeyed and began kicking, and now they were moving. As his head cleared, he could see they were in a patch of relatively open water, except they were moving away from the *Viper*!

"Let go of my hair!" he gasped, his voice strangled and not sounding like his own, but the man did not relent.

"Shut your mouth, *burlufotur*," the voice snarled.

"*Lord Einarr*?" Titus was incredulous, and in an unconscious reflex, he tried to twist his head, but Einarr's grip on his hair meant all he could do was yelp in pain and quickly desist.

"Listen to me," Einarr said urgently, although he was still kicking. "Do you want to live to see your home again?"

He felt a stab of guilt that it was not his sisters or his nephew that came to his mind's eye first, but he did not hesitate.

"Yes."

"Then you will keep your mouth shut, your eyes closed as if you are unconscious, and you will let me do the talking."

"How do I know you're telling the truth?" Titus asked instinctively.

"You do not," Einarr answered. "But if you choose, I will let you go, and you can try and swim back to that."

Even in what he was beginning to realize was a relatively short time in the water, since he was being pulled backward, Titus had a view of the *Viper*, and how another Danish ship had come alongside her starboard side from their bow, and while his view was obscured, he could see by the way the *Viper*'s mast began tilting in his direction that Danes were boarding the ship, his ship, and with a stab of shame, he made up his mind.

"No," he called over his shoulder, "I trust you."

Then he shut his eyes and surrendered himself to whatever came next by forcing his upper body to go limp, while still kicking under the surface. It was a supremely disconcerting and terrifying sensation, pretending that he was unconscious yet able to at least get a sense of what was happening when Einarr bellowed something. The answer came immediately, and from much closer than Titus expected, just a few feet behind him from the sound, and he tried to visualize the situation. Was that the ship the *Dragon's Fang* was supposed to attack? He instantly recalled seeing how the *Dragon's Fang* had dropped back, and while he had no way of knowing it, he experienced the same outrage and sense of betrayal that his comrades did at this sign of Centish cowardice...or worse. What happened did not matter in the moment, so he listened to the exchange, recognizing again Einarr's mention of Sigurd, and then his own name, but it was the tone that he listened to most intently, and he heard doubt in their voices. Maybe, he thought miserably, they'll just spear me so I won't have to go through drowning again. It was the impotence that was the most infuriating, and frightening, listening to an exchange that could end his days or give him the chance at seeing at least one more sunrise but not understanding any of it. And, as the back and forth continued, the voices on the ship seemed to get angrier, making the former fate seem the most likely to Titus. Then Einarr mentioned Guthrum's name, not his Christian name but his original name, and suddenly, the tone changed again; more importantly, he was suddenly yanked backward and he sensed that someone aboard had used a hooked pole to snag the back of his leather armor, signaling the first time Einarr released his grip on his hair, a blessed relief in itself, and it was when two pairs of hands reached down and grasped both arms that he risked a quick peek, hoping he could see something even with the water streaming down his face. He sensed more than saw that Einarr was clinging to an oar that had been dipped into the water, the rest pulled back and above the surface, then he quickly shut his eyes, and as he felt his lower body dragged up and over the side, he correctly guessed what was coming next, braced himself for the thudding impact with the bottom of the boat as he was dropped into it, with a bit of extra vigor added, forcing himself not to react, even as the breath was partially driven from his lungs. The hands released him, then he heard Einarr being pulled aboard, but then another voice, a new voice, suddenly bellowed in rage, unleashing a torrent of abuse of which Titus only picked out some of the epithets, but there was one word that chilled his blood...Saxon. Whatever was said, it seemed to equally enrage Einarr, then he felt the thudding of footsteps as who he assumed was Einarr came and stood over him, straddling his torso as the two Danes bellowed at each other. There was no way to know how long it went on, but what mattered to Titus was hearing the steersman giving the orders in Danish to which he had become accustomed, then the ship beginning to move. And, to his dismay, it was clearly moving away from the fighting, the sounds of which carried over the water, even down into the bottom of this ship.

Back and forth they went, with Guthrum's name mentioned several times, Alfred's two or three, but it was the mention of Lunden (London) that caught Titus' attention. Was that where they would be going, and not land somewhere in Wessex, or even back to Frankia? For, as his mind had cleared and he was beginning to think about it, these seemed the most likely outcomes, with the worst being that this ship was going to return back from where it had come, because he knew that even if he lived, it would be as a slave. There was something else strange going on that took a moment for Titus to understand, and that was, while he could feel the ship moving away from the fight, the din did not seem to dissipate all that much, and he tried to concentrate on what that might mean, but it was proving to be extremely difficult. It was not just the argument raging above his body that made it hard; with every passing moment, the pounding in his head worsened, and whereas at first it was his entire head that hurt, the pain was becoming localized to the left side, just above his ear. This was when he remembered something else; he had been struck a mighty blow on his helmet, hard enough to knock him senseless, making him drop his sword and send him over the side of the Danish ship. Had he been...at the bow? Yes, that was it, and while he did not have a clear recollection of it, he reasoned that he had been in that small space between where the *Viper's* prow was resting on the side of the Danish ship and that craft's bow when he went overboard. And then, it finally came to him as a fact that could not be denied, Einarr had deliberately leapt in, feetfirst and not headfirst as he had, the image of the Dane's spread legs above the surface coming back to him. This was when he noticed that the yelling had stopped, but he was completely unprepared to be given a rough kick in the side, which made him jerk in pain and surprise, though he somehow managed to keep his eyes shut.

"It is all right, Titus," Einarr said. "We are safe. For now."

"We are going to Lunden," Einarr told him a few moments later.

They were seated on two crates lashed down next to the mainmast, after having been given water and hunks of moldy bread, as the ship, which Einarr said was named the *Sea Wolf* and was not one of Sigurd's original band, continued east. While Titus had surmised this from the lack of anything resembling plunder and prisoners, he did not say as much. He was more curious about the looks he was getting from the crew; he had expected hostility and hatred, but while the looks were not friendly, they seemed more curious than anything else, and he reminded himself to ask Einarr why when the opportunity arose.

"What did you tell them about me?" Titus asked, then it came to him, and he stiffened. "Did you tell him I'm your prisoner?"

"No," Einarr said, then after a pause. "I said you were a *hostage.*"

"A *hostage?*" Titus gasped. "But I'm not..."

"*Shut your mouth,*" Einarr hissed. "Do not assume these men do not speak your tongue, Saxon. If you were a prisoner, they would have stabbed you in the water and let your body feed the fishes! But as a hostage, you have value!"

It was, Titus acknowledged to himself, a good and sensible point, and he nodded his understanding.

"So who did you say I was?"

"You are Thegn Titus, sworn to Ealdorman Eadwig of Wiltun," Einarr informed him.

A Thegn? Despite himself, Titus felt a grin trying to turn his mouth up at the thought. Yes, there were Thegns his age, but it was because they inherited the title from their fathers, and Leofric was no Thegn. With some effort, he managed to maintain his demeanor, and now it was Einarr who looked, if not amused, then close to it.

"Besides," the Dane added as if it was no moment, "they

saw what you did on the *Viper*, and I did not think they would believe me if I told them the truth, that you are just a Saxon warrior of low birth." This surprised Titus, but Einarr shrugged. "Despite our different gods, Titus, we Danes and Saxons are not as different as your King and your priests would have you believe. Yes, we are...harsher," was how he chose to put it, "but we respect warriors, especially great warriors. And," Einarr hesitated, giving Titus the sense that he was struggling with something, and he learned why when he said, "now that I have seen it myself, I know why you are called Berserker. It was," the Dane shook his head, sending droplets of water cascading away from his head, "something I have never seen before."

"Is that why you saved me?" Titus asked bluntly, but now Einarr looked over at him, sitting up straight as he stared at Titus, giving the young Saxon the impression he was trying to determine if Titus was being truthful, which prompted Titus to say softly, "I don't remember anything after seeing Willmar die, Einarr. That..." he struggled for the words to describe it, settling on saying simply, "...is what happens when whatever *this* is comes over me."

Einarr studied him for a long moment, and there was not just respect, but sympathy in the Dane's eyes that was gratifying and unsettling, in equal measure, to Titus.

"If you were a Dane, Titus, we would see that you are one of the gods' chosen ones," Einarr said seriously. "That they had given you a great gift. But," he sighed, and there was quality that made Titus wonder if Einarr was still talking about him, "being a Christian, I can see why your priests would not like that. Your God is a God of peace and love, is he not?"

"He is," Titus replied, though not with any conviction; it was just what he was supposed to say, but he was not thrown off, and he repeated, "I don't remember, Einarr."

The Dane returned to his posture of elbows on knees; they were now far enough away but within sight of the coast that there were neither the sights nor the sounds of the fight, and he did not answer immediately.

Staring down at the deck, he finally replied, "I went in to save you because you had just saved my life, Titus. I was about to get a spear...in the back," he said bitterly. "And you were fighting a man with an ax, and you shoved your shield in between me and the *huglausi* (cowardly) *oskilgetinn* and blocked his thrust, but it left you exposed. And your opponent tried to take your head off with his ax. I believe he was aiming for your neck, but the ship rolled and spoiled his aim and the edge hit you high enough that the helmet took the blow."

Before Einarr was finished, this part came back to Titus. It had been a completely spontaneous thing; out of the corner of his vision, he had seen Einarr cut down a Dane who had his back against the high prow of their ship, but in doing so, he had exposed himself to the spear thrust of another Danish warrior standing next to Titus' own opponent. And, he recalled, what Einarr said was true; he had seen the ax blow coming and knew his foe was going to try and decapitate him, yet he had nevertheless pivoted, not much but just enough to thrust his shield out in time to catch the spear thrust, then the blow to his head had come. The memory made his hand go back up once again to feel the wound, still finding it hard to believe that, while there was a cut, and it had swollen into a hard lump that ran horizontally above his ear, he did not think it would need to be stitched, which made him wonder if the Danes even did things like that. It was followed by the realization of how little he really knew about his foes.

Aloud, and not knowing what else to say, Titus decided to go with a mixture of humor and honesty, admitting ruefully, "If I had to do it over again, Einarr, you'd be dead."

For the first time, Einarr laughed, really laughed, then slapped Titus on the back so hard that it made him cough, although he joined in. Not surprisingly, the crew of the *Sea Wolf* wanted to know the jest, and after Einarr repeated it in Danish, they were joined by the men, with one notable exception, a tall but surprisingly thin Dane, his status proclaimed by the arm rings, six on each arm, and while most of them were silver, three of them were of gold, and the rich cloak lined with what appeared to be wolf fur, which was fitting given the name of the ship. He was in the prow, arms folded, wearing mail and a sword belted to his hip, although he was helmetless now, but the most striking thing about him was the length of his golden hair, which extended down to the middle of his back, although it was braided. However, it was the poisonous stare he aimed directly at Titus that was the most potent sign that Titus was not out of danger by any means.

Einarr saw where Titus was gazing, and he lowered his voice. "I see you've noticed Lord Leif."

"Who is he? I mean," Titus added hastily, "this is clearly his ship, but was he the leader of this *viking* that came to join Sigurd?"

"Yes," Einarr answered, but with a terseness that forewarned Titus more was coming. "He was invited by Sigurd. They are...were close friends."

God preserve me, Titus thought.

Aloud, he asked, "I assume he knows that Sigurd is dead?" Einarr nodded. Swallowing, he asked, "Did you tell him I'm the man who slew him?"

Einarr regarded him with sour amusement.

"Do you think you would be sitting next to me if I had? It would not have mattered how valuable you are, you would be fish food by now. If," he added heavily, "your God smiled on you and made it so. Otherwise, your last hours would have been filled with an agony you cannot possibly imagine."

Titus did not know what else to say other than, "Thank you, Einarr."

This clearly embarrassed the Dane, who shrugged but said nothing.

There was a silence, then Titus asked, "What's Lunden like?"

The purpose in requiring the men of Alfred's small navy staying in Romney was not just for the purpose of allowing the wounded to recover, but to give his messengers time to spread the official story, that a small raiding party of four Danish ships and originating from across the sea separating Wessex and Frankia, after a few weeks of raiding, had been trapped, destroyed, and while not all of the unfortunate souls who had been snapped up by the heathen marauders had been recovered, and much of their plunder had gone to the bottom of the sea, more than two dozen souls destined for a life of slavery were saved, and two Danish ships were captured, meaning that it was still a resounding victory. It was left to the youngest of the Wiltun nobles to explain, when Ceadda demanded to know why this was so important on the second night in Romney.

The young lord and his two Thegns had left the ship, putting Uhtric in command of keeping the Wiltun men on the *Viper* and were now back at The Merry Widow, where Eadward explained, "Because the King has to think of the larger situation, Ceadda. If he let it be known that they were joined by more ships, what kind of questions would it raise, such as 'where did they come from'?" He raised a finger. "Frankia?" A second, "From the Danish homeland?" The third. "Or maybe they sailed from Dyflinn and around Cornwallum?"

Ceadda did not know it, but the young lord had thrown this last possibility out as bait, because he immediately shook his head as he countered, "That would mean they would have been approaching from the west, Lord, and they were coming from the east."

Eadward smiled and nodded.

"Yes, you're right, of course, so that means it wasn't them. Now where else would Danish ships be coming from, in that direction?"

This was when Ceadda saw, if not the entire situation, but a glimmer of it, breathing the word, "Danelaw."

Again, Eadward nodded, and he lowered his voice as he went on, "And I don't have to tell you that there is more than one powerful man who believe the King made a serious error with the Treaty he signed with Guthrum in Wessex, and in Mercia...and Cent. Word that there were more ships than were originally reported will give credence to those men who want to agitate against the treaty, and this the King will not allow."

It was the mention of Cent that prompted Otha to ask, "What did the King say to your request?"

"It's denied," Eadward answered flatly, but before Otha could press for details, he said, "but that's all I can say about it. I swore to the King I wouldn't speak of it."

Otha was obviously tempted to pressure his pupil, but he discarded the idea. The lad had already shown more resolve and backbone than he had anticipated when he announced that he had decided to make a petition to the King to rescind his order to keep the Wiltun men aboard the *Viper*, especially while the crews from the other ships had been given the liberty of the town, including the men of the *Dragon's Fang*, although when the men, with Uhtric as their spokesman, had approached Eadward, Otha, and Ceadda to complain about the treatment, pointing out that the Centishmen who had fled from the fight were, in their words, "strutting" about Romney, when Eadward had pointed out that they were, in fact, *in* Cent, this made no impression on the crew.

"They abandoned us, Lord," Uhtric had summed it up. "We should at least be told what their reason was in leaving us. If the King had arrived when he was supposed to and not when he did, none of us would be alive, and with all respect, Lord, I think we deserve to know why."

This was the genesis of Eadward's request for a private audience with the King, which Alfred had granted, but when Otha made to go with him, the young lord had stopped him.

"This is my responsibility, Otha," Eadward told the Thegn, and it marked the first time, ever, where Otha heard Eadward's father's voice in the youngster, and while he was not happy about it, he had demurred.

Still, sitting in the alehouse, neither Otha nor Ceadda were through, and Otha pressed, "What did he say about the reason those Centish bastards gave for leaving us?"

"Nothing," Eadward replied unhappily. "He refused to talk about it. And," he warned, "he forbade me, or anyone from Wiltun to bring it up with him again."

For Alfred's part, it was not a decision he had made lightly, because the truth was that he shared the outrage of his Wiltun subjects, and it had been made even worse by the explanation offered by Beorhtweald, such as it was.

"Lord King," he had tried to sound deferential, yet commanding at the same time, failing miserably at both, "as you know, those deceitful dogs tried one of their heathen tricks by appearing earlier than they had for several days previously."

"Yes, Beorhtweald," Alfred had replied dryly, "I am aware." Before the Centish Thegn could say anything, he also pointed out, "But thanks to God, my part of the fleet also began moving back east earlier."

"That is true, Lord King," Beorhtweald had replied immediately, "but we had no way of knowing this. From my judgment, because of their early hour, I deemed that an attack would be not just wasteful, but suicidal."

And there was the rub, Alfred thought unhappily as he sat on the chair under the awning of the *Redeemer*. It was not an unreasonable assumption to make; still, there was more to question, and he moved on.

"And, did you let the crew of the *Sea Viper* know this, Lord Beorhtweald? That you would not attack?" Alfred asked quietly.

"We tried, Lord King," Beorhtweald answered immediately, "but to no avail. They were either unable," he paused, "or *unwilling* to hear or see our signal to them. I made no secret of my objection that young Lord Eadward be the commander of the *Sea Viper*, Lord King. Nothing against the boy, but that is what he is, a boy. And as old as we may be," he offered Alfred an ingratiating smile, "I know that we both remember what it was like to be young, and so eager to prove yourself in battle."

It was, Alfred knew with certainty, a lie, and not just because not Eadward, nor Otha, nor Ceadda had said there was a signal of any kind by the Centish ship, but in an odd way, the real confirmation came from the sudden and mysterious disappearance of Sigmund and Torbjorn from the *Dragon's Fang*, the two Danes having waited until darkness fell then vanishing into the night that confirmed the lie for Alfred...if they had indeed left of their own accord. And yet, it was not in his long-term interests to make this an issue with Sigeræd, at least not now; later, perhaps, when it could be useful. Consequently, he had curtly dismissed the Centish Thegn, and while he was not surprised that the Wiltun men requested an audience, he was surprised that it was just Eadward, with Otha nowhere to be seen. A second surprise had been how, despite his youth, Eadward's demeanor had been that of a man several years older, and while he had been forceful, he had correctly sensed when Alfred declared the matter closed that he meant it. Now, on the day after the battle, he would be returning to Wintanceaster, where he would undoubtedly be greeted with all manner of nasty surprises, and since the Wiltun men were on his mind, he called to Father Aethelred.

"Remind me to light a candle in my chapel for young Titus of Cissanbyrig as I promised them," he instructed the priest. He said nothing for a moment, then added, "It is a shame to lose such a promising warrior so young. And," he sighed heavily, "I believe we are going to need many more men like him before we can have peace." Then he turned his mind to other matters. "Have we received word back from Mercia yet?"

"No, Lord King," but Alfred was already moving on to something else.

It was a four-day journey to Lunden, and by the second day and to the surprise of both the older and younger man, Titus and Einarr were forming a friendship, although there were certainly strained moments, neither of them forgetting that the only thing binding them at this moment was a parchment and the promises of their respective leaders, but now there was another element that, fortunately, was stronger than any scrap of parchment; they had saved each other's lives in battle. It helped they had the same sense of humor, although there were some translational issues, but it also was informative for both men, although because of his age and exposure, Einarr already knew quite a bit about Saxon customs, whereas, as Titus was learning, much of what the young Saxon knew was superstitious nonsense, or more often, highly exaggerated. Their savagery, Titus began to understand, although dimly, came more from how they viewed their world, and the harsh existence of life in Daneland as compared to Wessex, where every day was a fight for survival against the elements. Of course it snowed in Cissanbyrig, but what Einarr described to Titus was beyond imagining, of snowfalls taller than he was, and the constant battle to keep their dwellings cleared so they could leave them; of winter days much shorter and nights much longer than he experienced, of bears, and packs of wolves, yet he could tell that Einarr missed it, despite scoffing at the idea of ever going back.

"Now that I have seen your lands, so green, so fat, so...soft and easy," he had said, "why would I ever go back?"

This angered Titus, and he was about to snarl a reminder about Ethantun, but fortunately, he saw the glint of humor in the Dane's eyes, and he realized that while Einarr was taunting him, it was in a good-natured manner, for the most part.

"We weren't that soft at Ethantun," he answered, and now it was Einarr's turn to be angered, but he surprised Titus when he admitted, "No, you were not soft at Ethantun."

After a moment, Einarr asked, "Is it true what I heard about you? When some of our men ambushed your baggage train, that you had never held a sword before, and you killed four men, all on your own?"

It had become a common question over the previous four years, and during that time, he had developed a standard answer that he gave, how things became exaggerated over time, and how God had watched over him and he deserved no credit. With Einarr, it was different; after all, he had now seen Titus on the ship, and there was now that bond between them having saved each other's lives, so he did not answer immediately.

Finally, he said, "I still don't remember that much of it. Because, I was..." he searched for the right words, then said, "...like I was on the ship. But," he turned to look Einarr in the eye, "yes, I was told by several men who were there that I killed four Danes."

"And you were fourteen?"

"Well," Titus said lightly, "since I'm eighteen now, and it was four years ago, yes."

"*Bacraut*," Einarr growled, Danish for "asshole," and Titus laughed.

Not all the subjects were light, because it became clear that Leif, his full name Leif Longhair, which was appropriate, did not approve of the budding friendship between Dane and Saxon, but it went beyond that.

"He suspects I am not telling him something about Sigurd's death," Einarr muttered after returning to what had become their spot on the *Sea Wolf* after a conversation that turned increasingly animated and heated by the moment between the pair at the stern of the ship. "And," he added, "I finally told him that you are not a Thegn, but you *are* the best warrior of Thegn Otha's men, and he will be willing to pay."

"He clearly didn't take it well," Titus commented, trying not to sound concerned, but he was surprised when Einarr shook his head.

"He saw what you did on the *Corpse Maker*," this was how Titus learned the name of the Danish ship, "so he believes me. He was not happy about it, no, but he is angrier about the thought that there is something about Sigurd's death that I am not telling him, and he believes I should be angry as well since he was my kin."

Titus had sat and watched the exchange, growing increasingly nervous, armed only with his eating knife, his sword either in the sea, or perhaps if he was fortunate, and there had been a Saxon victory and it was left on the Danish ship, had been recovered by Uhtric, who would recognize it as his...if Uhtric survived. He had done everything he could to avoid dwelling on the fate of the crew of the *Viper* and particularly Otha's men. He knew Willmar was dead, because he recalled the sight of his dying body slumping to the deck and how it had been what unleashed his fury, and he recalled snatches of memory, like glimpsing Eadward, his own sword in hand standing in the prow of the *Viper* and facing a line of Danes, but nothing beyond that. All he could do was pray, and while he never spoke of it later, Titus of Cissanbyrig prayed more during that four-day voyage than at any time in his life to that point.

As they rowed up the Temese (Thames) estuary, Titus finally asked Einarr, "How does this hostage business work?"

Einarr's reaction puzzled Titus, because he glanced about, but Leif was standing in the stern with his steersman and talking about something that, for once, did not seem to concern either Titus or Einarr.

"We," he said just loudly enough so that only Titus could hear, "have a treaty with King Alfred, but the Danes that you defeated, and," he nodded in the direction of Leif, "this *oskilegetinn* and his men are not sworn to serve King Guthrum, and my King wants war no more than yours does."

Einarr looked disappointed at this, but as Titus had discerned, the Dane was thoroughly loyal to his Lord; Titus refused to think of Guthrum as a King, but he had stopped needling Einarr by correcting him with Guthrum's Christian name a couple days earlier, and he knew that Einarr was being sincere.

"Where it gets...complicated," Einarr had to search for the English word, "is that in order to secure your release from the *Sea Wolf*, Leif must be paid, and what I do not know is whether my King will be willing to part with the payment to a man who owes him no allegiance, but I do not believe he will."

There were several questions Titus wanted to ask, but he started with, "How much is the ransom?"

"Ten pounds of silver," Einarr answered.

"Ten *pounds*?" Titus gasped, unable to conceive of a sum that, given the wage he earned from Otha, would take him years to accrue. "That's the *wergild* for a *ceorl* if he's killed by another Saxon and the man is found at fault!"

"That is the standard for a warrior sworn to one of your Thegns," Einarr assured Titus, but this was a lie; like all things in their world, no price was fixed and it was all subject to negotiation, although it was not unheard of, and this was a very high price for a lowly warrior.

"Lord Otha isn't going to pay ten pounds for me!" Titus exclaimed. Ruefully, he added, "*I* wouldn't pay ten pounds for myself."

This made Einarr laugh, but he asked seriously, "What about the Ealdorman Lord Otha serves? Lord Eadward's father? What is his name?"

"Ealdorman Eadwig," Titus answered, and despite himself, he felt a flicker of hope.

He *had* saved Eadward's life the day of the ambush, when Titus had gone from being the stableboy for the grotesquely fat, and now gone Dudda, to serving Lord Otha as a warrior. Would he be willing to part with that much money? he wondered.

Deciding that this was one of those problems that would have to be confronted further down the road, he asked, "What happens when we get to Lunden?"

"We will go to King Guthrum so that I can tell him what has happened," Einarr answered. "Although I suspect, knowing King Alfred, your King has already sent a messenger. And," his tone turned somber, "I believe that your King is going to demand to know where those Danish ships came from, which is why I need to tell him they were not any of our men."

This made sense, so Titus moved on.

"Is that when a message will be sent to Wiltun?"

"I cannot say, but I believe so," Einarr agreed. He hesitated for a moment, then said, "You need to know that this ten pounds of silver is not likely to come from us, not even as a loan from King Guthrum."

Titus did not understand the point, although he did allow to himself that it would be a bit much to expect that a Danish King, even if he was now a Christian, would deign to spend a shilling on some Wessex warrior.

"I didn't expect you to," Titus answered, "but what are you talking about?"

"That it is very unlikely you are going to be leaving Lunden as quickly as I believe you may think you will," Einarr replied, and he saw by Titus' expression that he had in fact thought that very thing. Going on, Einarr explained, "Titus, an exchange of a hostage for a ransom takes time. First, a message has to be sent to your lord with the price, and your lord will refuse to pay the price at first, even if it is just one of your shillings."

"Why?" Titus asked, baffled, but all Einarr could do was shrug.

"It is just the way I have always seen it happen, even when it is between Danes," he answered. Continuing, "Then we will send a message saying that, unless your lord pays, we will start chopping off body pieces. Usually," Einarr lifted his left hand, pointing to the littlest finger, "this is the first thing we send."

At first, Titus thought Einarr was jesting, but he saw no humor in the Dane's eye, and he felt the blood drain from his face. While he was tempted to do so, he decided not to ask Einarr how far this kind of tactic could go.

"I hope," he finally managed bleakly, "my Lord likes me as much as I think he does."

A cry from the bow interrupted their conversation, the tone alone indicating something important was taking place, and they both stood to get a better view, and for the first time, Titus saw Lunden, albeit in the form of a huge, dirty brown cloud of smoke. Suddenly, Titus' dilemma was forgotten as he realized that the men who had been to Lunden and spoke of its size had not been exaggerating; it was *huge*. The docks of Lunden were nothing like Hamtun, not only in the number of berths, but how far they extended. A long wooden pier lined one side of the river, but as striking as this was, Titus was staring at the rooftops of buildings peeking above the walls that, he was sure, were in numbers beyond counting. He also recognized there were buildings, or remnants of them, of the style he recognized from Bathanceaster, that he knew came from the Romans, completely unaware of his own connection to the vanished Empire that had once ruled his entire world. More than anything, it was the people thronging the pier, and he was certain that the entire population of the city was present. Certainly, a horde of Danes, but he saw men in Saxon and Frankish attire; what drew his eye and curiosity were men wearing clothes of a type he had never seen before, wearing looser-fitting robes and with the darkest skin on a man than he had ever seen before in his life, of the color of a chestnut.

The *Sea Wolf* drifted as Leif engaged in an exchange with another Dane standing on the dock, and after what sounded like haggling, the Dane on the dock pointed to an empty berth. With a skill that spoke of much practice, the *Sea Wolf*'s steersman, an old man by Titus' standards, meaning he was perhaps forty, barked out the orders that enabled the vessel to slip into its spot, whereupon two of the crew leapt up onto the dock, lines in their hands, a maneuver to which Titus had become accustomed seeing done but had never done it himself, and they snugged the lines, pulling the ship close to the pier so that it was just a matter of a step up. Titus was struck by the thought that this had been the longest period of time he had been at sea without ever touching foot ashore, and he turned to tell Einarr this. Even if he had turned his head sooner, and seen Einarr's eyes go wide as they were looking over Titus' shoulder, it would not have made any difference, and the simultaneous blows, with what felt like one spar across the back of his knees and one applied to the back of his head, brought him down, just as Leif had intended. He was not unconscious, but he was stunned, barely aware as rough hands grabbed his wrists and wrenched them behind him. This did rouse him, and even in a stupor, he put up a mighty struggle, breaking free from the grasp of the Dane holding his right hand to launch a wild swing at the Dane, a man with blonde hair who normally sat on the bench immediately behind the mast and had never exhibited any hostility towards Titus, and he was rewarded by the jarring thud as his fist struck the Dane in the stomach, the second-most vulnerable spot Titus could aim for from his kneeling position, doubling the Dane over, although he managed to maintain his grip on Titus' wrist with one hand, and for the briefest moment, he held out hope. Then the second blow landed, and everything went black.

When Titus came to consciousness, it was almost dark, and he was bound hand and foot, with a rope looped around his neck that was attached to something that he could not see because it was behind him, but in such a way that, when he moved, the rope tightened and cut off his air. Lying on his side, the right side of his face was in the customary inch of water that was always present in even the best-built ships, and he realized it was the sound of water running that caused him to open his eyes, just in time to see the blond Dane standing over him and pissing into the boat, but moving his prick so that the piss was making its way to Titus' face. Without thinking, he opened his mouth to shout something, which was a grievous mistake, and for a panicked instant as he coughed, spat the Dane's urine out of his mouth then instantly began retching, he wondered if he would be killed this way, a line of Danes pissing in the bottom of their own ship until he drowned. The Dane thought this was the funniest thing he had ever seen, and judging from the roars of laughter, so did his crewmates, and while it was humiliating, the question plaguing Titus was *why*? He was a hostage; he knew he could not expect to be treated well, but to be beaten, and judging from how his body felt, he had been savagely beaten after he had been unconscious, then be degraded like this? Hard on the heels of that thought came a second one; had Einarr betrayed him? Had the Dane been lying the whole time, and this was the plan all along? Then why not just kill him? he wondered. Fortunately for Titus, the blond Dane had finished, and he could not deny the deep sense of relief when none of the other crew within his range of vision stepped in to take his place. If anything, they seemed to have immediately lost interest, and had already turned away from him as they talked excitedly to each other, giving Titus an indication of it when he felt the boat gently rocking under his body as men leapt up onto the pier, then vanished from view. They're talking about getting drunk and finding whores, he realized, not recognizing the words, perhaps, but completely comprehending the demeanor of the crew as they eagerly hurried away. Which, he thought miserably, I had been doing too; I wasn't paying attention, and now this happened, and he returned to the pertinent question. If Einarr wanted to betray me, why wait? Why not either kill me himself, or if that violated the Danish code of honor since Titus had saved his life, have Leif do it? The longhaired Dane made no secret he wanted to do that very thing, yet he was alive...for now. Following that came another, and in almost every way worse thought; are they going to try and sell me as a slave? The recognition of this possibility struck Titus with almost as much force as he had exerted when he punched the blond Dane in the stomach, and with almost the same effect as he gasped at the idea, struggling to contain the despair, and the panic, that stemmed from it. It was a struggle, but he managed to keep from thrashing about; even as he had moved his head back to its original position, the rope had not loosened completely, and his breathing was slightly constricted. There were still Danes aboard, he could tell by the vibration through the planks of the ship as they walked about, but it was impossible to tell how many there were, or even in what part of the ship they were located, other than the fact that they were out of the range of his very limited vision. Night was coming, his head was throbbing, he was growing uncomfortable in the same position...and he was scared. Truly, deeply scared.

While Titus had been betrayed, it had not been by Einarr, but by Leif Longhair, and while the Dane was not treated as roughly as Titus, he was seized and held at sword point, while Titus was knocked unconscious, secured, then beaten and kicked.

"What are you doing, you ass-licking spawn of a pox-

ridden whore?" Einarr roared.

As enraged as Einarr was, Leif was the picture of composure, and he replied calmly, "Since you promised to pay me his ransom, as far as I am concerned, that makes him my hostage, to do with as I please. And," now his face twisted, "he is a *Saxon*!"

"Who we have a treaty with," Einarr retorted, but Leif was completely unimpressed.

"Who *you* have a treaty with," Leif shot back. "I am not sworn to Guthrum. I," he thumped his chest, "am Leif Longhair, and I have sworn to Thor and Odin that I will slay every Saxon I come across! So I piss on your treaty!"

This was when Einarr realized something; Leif was a young, prideful fool, and engaging in a shouting match with him, especially in front of his crew, who were standing around watching with an eager anticipation, would only end badly.

Forcing himself to remain calm, Einarr turned towards the dock, announcing his intentions to leave the ship, but when another of Leif's men stepped in his path, hand on the hilt of his sword, Einarr looked over his shoulder and sneered, "Are you saying that I cannot leave your ship...Lord?"

Leif's reaction was instructive, because it was clear to Einarr that he had not thought that far ahead and considered the ramifications of his actions, and the lean Dane shifted uneasily, licked his lips, then gave a jerk of his head that instructed his man to step aside.

Einarr leapt up onto the dock, turned so that he was looking down on Leif to warn, "You had your fun beating him, but you are not to harm him any further until after I return with instructions from my King."

"As I said," Leif shrugged, "he is my hostage. I may tire of him."

"*Vitsketkr*," Einarr's tone was lacerating, "do you have boiled sheep shit for brains, is that it? Did your mother drop you onto your head when you were a baby? How far do you think you will get?" Without waiting for a response, Einarr scanned the men in the area, most of whom had been drawn to the disruption aboard the *Sea Wolf*, and were standing watching with curiosity, and some anticipation of excitement. Spotting the Dane Guthrum had appointed as harbormaster, and who had been the man Titus had seen Leif negotiating with, Einarr shouted, "Olaf!" He had to shout twice more, but when the man looked in his direction, he beckoned to him, and Olaf came, and he did so quickly.

"Yes, Lord Einarr?" Olaf asked, and Einarr indicated the *Sea Wolf.*

"I am going to see our King, Olaf. This ship is from Frankia, it is the *Sea Wolf*, and it belongs to," he pointed to Leif, "Leif Longhair here. He is *not* one of ours, Olaf, and he does *not* have permission to leave until the King decides what to do. Get some men to guard this ship; it is not to leave before then. Is this understood?"

Now, Einarr thought, let's see just how much of a fool Leif is, while Olaf bowed and replied immediately, "Yes, Lord. I will make sure it is done."

Then he turned and, while not at a run, it was at a quick walk, leaving Einarr to stare down at Leif who, while furious, turned out to be not as foolish as he appeared. The position of harbormaster, especially for a port the size of Lunden, was the kind of position only a very high-ranking nobleman in their world could appoint, but it was the manner in which Olaf had instantly obeyed Einarr that told Leif that he was in considerable peril if he decided to flaunt his own authority, such as it was.

"As I said," Einarr broke the tense silence, "I am going to see King Guthrum now. And, as you heard, you are not to leave. And," he finished, and while he did not shout this, "if that Saxon is harmed any further, I will use my ax to open your chest, tear your heart out...and eat it in front of your dying eyes. Do you understand me?"

There was another silence, but this one stretched much longer, and Einarr was beginning to think that Leif would refuse, but while he did not say anything, he gave a curt nod, then, in a deliberate insult, turned away from Einarr. This angered the Dane, but there would be time for Leif later. Now he had to find the King and let him know all that had transpired.

Their first day in Lunden ended up being the worst Titus

was treated, although it was only marginally better after that. He had been unconscious during the exchange between Einarr and Leif, so he was unaware of what had transpired concerning his fate, and it was almost midnight when Einarr had returned. He heard him before he saw him, and again there was another acrimonious exchange of words, then Einarr appeared in his vision, standing on the dock, accompanied by six men, all armed and armored, as was Einarr, except now he was wearing mail. Understandably, fire and wooden ships were not a good combination, so the fact that two of Einarr's companions were carrying torches told Titus that this was considered important enough to risk it, but the two men were not allowed on the *Sea Wolf*, and he wondered if that was what the angry words had been about. While he was glad to see Einarr by virtue of the torchlight, he watched with a mixture of apprehension and anger as Einarr, alone, dropped down into the boat and crossed to the starboard side, where Titus was, kneeling down next to him.

"You have been like this the entire time?" Einarr demanded, and to Titus, it sounded as if he thought it was somehow Titus' fault, causing him to snap, "No, I was uncomfortable untied and sitting up and asked them to put me back like this."

Despite the tension, this made Einarr laugh, and he helped Titus up to a sitting position which, while it was a relief in some ways, meant that the blood that had been cut off to the entire right side of his body came rushing back, and Titus had to fight the groan of pain that began with a tingling, then turned to what he was sure being burned would feel like. Einarr loosened the noose and lifted it over Titus' head, but when he began to untie the bonds around his wrists, Leif appeared as if by magic, hand on sword hilt, shouting down at Einarr as he emphatically shook his head.

After more back and forth, Einarr informed Titus, "Leif will not allow me to untie your hands now, but when you need to shit and piss, and eat, they will untie you, and your legs will remain untied."

While it was nothing near what he wanted, Titus calculated that this was probably the best that he could hope for at the moment, but it still grated on him to say, "Tell him I thank him."

"No," Einarr answered firmly. "Not only is he wrong to do this, it will make you look weak if you thank him."

This suited Titus perfectly, and he glared up at Leif over Einarr's shoulder as the Dane removed the rope from around his feet, then helped Titus up. Interposing himself between Titus and Leif, Einarr helped Titus over to the mast and sat him down on the crate that had become his accustomed place over the previous three days.

"Titus," Einarr whispered, "you must trust me, I had nothing to do with this." After a span of a heartbeat, Titus nodded, but he was unprepared for what Einarr said next. "And while you will be allowed to stand and have your hands untied, I am afraid I cannot stop Leif from what is coming."

Before Titus could ask, the answer was provided by a length of chain, but when he began to twist away, Leif appeared, sword out and pointed at Titus' throat, while one of his crew, Titus could not see who, looped a heavy iron chain around his waist, snugly enough that there was no way he could slide it down past his hips, then fastened with a huge lock. The other end was wrapped around the mast, which was also secured with a lock, with about five feet of slack that gave him a bit of room to move, though not enough to make it up to the dock.

Once this was done, Einarr explained, "As I said, I have spoken to the King, and he has agreed to send a messenger at first light to Wiltun."

"But how?" Titus asked. "Danes aren't allowed outside the Danelaw, just like we're not allowed across into Danelaw."

Einarr laughed at this.

"Titus, there is still trade going on between us. Saxons come here, and Danes go there all the time...as long as they are merchants or their men delivering and bringing back goods."

Suddenly, Titus was reminded of Hakon, the Danish slave who was married to a Saxon woman, also a slave, after being sold to Lord Eadwig by a Dane, which was the first time he got a sense of how commerce, even between enemies, continued. Over the intervening four years, he had long stopped counting the examples of where the two warring entities conveniently ignored their hostility in an exchange of goods, and even services, especially all along the border between the Danelaw and Saxon lands.

As Hakon had put it to him once when Titus, who had come to like, and trust, the Danish slave, "It is hard for people who live next to someone to hate them when they see them doing the same work in the fields they are doing." He had grinned. "Danish cow shit smells the same as Saxon."

Now, when Titus nodded his understanding, Einarr warned, "That means that it will take longer than just a man on horseback carrying a message can make the journey. It may take some time."

It was, Titus would think back ruefully, a prophetic statement.

Days passed, then weeks, where Titus of Cissanbyrig's entire world was what he could see from the *Sea Wolf* as it bobbed at its berth, but if it wore on him, it was nothing compared to the growing tension among the Danes of the *Sea Wolf*. The prospect of enjoying Lunden, while eagerly anticipated as Titus had witnessed when they first arrived, had been replaced by the realization that every day they spent there deprived them of the chance for plunder, or so Titus assumed since what little interaction he had with his guards came in the form of epithets, most of which he understood by this point. Einarr came at least once a day, if only to tell him there was no news, while Leif, now that Titus was secured, had vanished, leaving two men behind to watch Titus at all times. For the most part, he was left alone, aside from the occasional rough shove as he was escorted to the side to relieve himself. He did fantasize about escape, but that was more to pass the time than anything; the only human being in Lunden he knew was a Dane, making his chances of escape, even if he managed to kill his two guards, nonexistent. He was fed once a day, but it quickly became obvious that what constituted "food" was debatable, and it actually reminded him of his childhood of moldy breads, usually with weevils wriggling about, worm-infested apples, and soup that was mostly water. This lasted for four days, until Einarr happened to ask how much he was fed, whereupon Einarr stalked down the dock, obviously heading for wherever Leif was staying in the town. Things changed then, and while it was still not enough, the quality was better and Titus was able to keep up his strength. His guards continued to ignore him, and he quickly became part of the cargo, and once Titus thought about it, he realized it made sense to think of himself that way. He was something that would fetch a price, and at first, the prospect of ten pounds of silver was enough to keep the crew content, but now, as the summer passed, tempers were beginning to fray. The pair of Danes always on the ship rotated, and very rarely in the same combination of men, telling Titus that Leif was being careful that he did not become too familiar with the crew, but what did not change was that, at some point during their time aboard, they would begin to quarrel with each other about something. When it happened the first time, he thought nothing of it, but it became a regular occurrence, and he braced himself for them to turn their attention on him, yet while he was cursed regularly, and spat at often, and every so often was shoved harder than necessary, he was more of a spectator than anything.

Finally, on one of his daily visits, Titus told Einarr, "Leif's men are unhappy."

"I have heard," Einarr commented. "There is a split between them."

"About me?" Titus guessed.

"Partly," Einarr admitted, "but not completely. I have spread some silver around the alehouses where they like to drink, and there has been trouble coming for some time. Leif and Sigurd were very close, and Sigurd had gone against the orders of his lord to come raiding in Wessex, and when Leif decided to come join him, many of his men did not want to go against their lord."

"Who is it?"

Einarr gave the name of the Danish lord in Frankia, but Titus had never heard of him, and Einarr went on, "Now there are men who think that the reason Leif is so set on getting your ransom is because he will give half of it to his lord now that all of Sigurd's ships were destroyed, and all but the *Sea Wolf* and one other ship escaped. And while they do not know with any certainty, many of Leif's crew assume that the other ship is returning to Frankia and they will be able to tell their side of the story to their lord first, and blame Leif for talking them into joining with Sigurd, using their closeness as the cause."

While this was interesting, it was the first part of Einarr's words that caused Titus to stare at Einarr in bafflement.

"What are you talking about?"

"Ah," Einarr did look embarrassed. "You did not know. I did not either until a few days ago," he lied, then hurried to explain to cover the fact that he had seen Titus in that intervening time but this was the first time he mentioned it, "but the plan worked because someone with your King's ships ordered them to begin sailing west earlier than the plan called for, and they arrived in time to spring the trap."

Titus stared, hard, into Einarr's eyes, looking for some sort of dissembling or that the Dane might be playing a cruel trick for his own amusement, but he saw no signs there. So, he thought as his heart began to pound, Uhtric and the rest of the *Viper* may be alive! It had been a thought he refused to allow his mind to go to, but he could not stop the more rational part of his mind that coldly pointed out to him what he had witnessed the last time he looked at the *Viper* as he was being pulled aboard the *Sea Wolf*. Slowly, something else came to him, and he felt chagrined that he had not thought to ask before this.

"Is that why Leif ordered the *Sea Wolf* to sail away when he did?"

"Yes." Einarr nodded. "He spotted the sails of Alfred's ships and realized that it had been a trap."

"Clever," Titus said, not liking to offer Leif any kind of a compliment.

"Cunning as well," Einarr replied. "But now his men are growing tired of Lunden, and they are worried that Leif is going to give half of your ransom to Leif's lord to win his way back into favor."

"Then," it was all Titus could think to say, "the sooner my ransom arrives, the better for everyone."

Eadward was in the training yard outside his father's hall sparring with Otha when Beohrtic came running through the open gate, panting from his effort.

"Lord Eadward!"

Rather than be alarmed, Eadward was irritated because it broke his concentration and gave Otha the chance to strike him in the ribs with his blunted wooden sword when Eadward allowed his shield to drift out from his body, opening him up for the blow. It knocked the wind from him, but he knew better than to complain that he had been distracted and Otha had not won fairly, because Otha would counter that there was all manner of surprises in battle, which, as he had learned, was a fundamental truth. They had been back in Wiltun for a bit more than a month, and life had returned to the normal rhythms of their world. Eadward's scar was now an angry pink, and as he had been assured by the warriors of his band, the women he encountered found it as attractive as knowing the fact that he was a young lord, which he had learned in Hamtun, and at every inn on the way home.

Now, however, he was wearing a scowl as he limped over to Beohrtic, who was bent over, hands on knees and trying to catch his breath, and he snapped, "Why aren't you still in Wiltun with Hakon?" Suddenly, he realized there *might* be a reason for concern, and he asked, "Is everything all right? Is there something happening? What is it?"

It took a heartbeat for the servant to answer the first question, "Yes, Lord," then corrected himself, confused, "I mean, no, Lord, there is no sort of problem in town. And Hakon is with the cart, Lord, but there is a messenger, and he said..."

"Messenger?" Eadward interrupted. "Who is the message for?"

"Your father, Lord," Beohrtic answered.

Eadward returned to his earlier state of irritation, "Then why did he send you here and not come here himself?"

"He can't, Lord," Beohrtic explained. "Because he's with a merchant traveling from Lunden, and this is just one of his stops. He will be leaving soon for the next town."

By this time, Otha had joined him, but when Eadward glanced over at the Thegn, all he got was a shake of the head, further irritating the young lord at this lack of help, though he said nothing.

Turning his mind to the matter at hand, Eadward thought that this was odd. Normally, anyone bearing a message was either from one of the other nobility, or from the Reeve, or perhaps even from the King, but no matter from whom the message came, they all had one thing in common; if they had a dispatch for his father, they would be standing here and not refusing to come the three-quarters of a mile from Wiltun. Also, as far as he knew, his father did not know anyone in Lunden, and anyway, it was infested with Danes at the moment and was from where Guthrum was ruling.

He was inclined to dismiss it as something not worthy of his attention and had even begun to turn away as he said over his shoulder, "If the message is important enough for my father, he can make the effort to come here."

"Lord!" Beohrtic blurted out, in a tone that arrested Eadward's return to his sparring. "He also said that I should tell you something so you would know it was worth your father's time. He said," Beohrtic closed his eyes, trying to recall what turned out to be all of two words. Remembering, he opened them and said triumphantly, "Berserker lives."

As one, Eadward and Otha sprinted to the barn to get their horses.

"Father?"

Eadwig was in his hall, shoving a rich stew into his mouth with a wooden spoon, so that when he looked up in irritation at his meal being interrupted, his clean-shaven chin was dripping with stew remnants and glistening from the grease, making for a rather unlordly appearance. The Ealdorman of Wiltun treasured his mealtimes, and his slaves, servants, and his children had learned that he was to be interrupted during his meals for only the most important business; one look at his son's expression told him that this was likely to qualify as important. Beckoning him to approach, as Eadward fully entered into the hall from the doorway, he saw Otha behind his son, and one look at the Thegn's face erased any doubt that this was something significant. He saw Eadward was holding a scrap of parchment, although in and of itself, it would have been meaningless for Eadward to hand him the message; he could not read. Thankfully, albeit in hindsight, Eadwig's wife, the Lady Leofe, had urged, at the time he would have said hounded, him to engage a tutor from a nearby monastery to tutor young Eadward in his letters. It had proven to be a wise decision when serving a King such as Alfred, who, while he did not make it a decree, strongly "encouraged" his highest-ranking noblemen to be literate, or at least have someone close at hand to them who was, and while Eadwig's steward was literate as well, he was off somewhere about the estate.

Pointing to the scrap, Eadwig asked, "What does it say?"

"That Titus is alive," Eadward answered, then broke into a wide grin, as his sister Eadburga gave such a high-pitched squeal of delight that it made Eadwig wince, and even Leofe, normally reserved and very conscious of her dignity as the Lady of Wiltun, clapped her hands.

And, for a moment, even Eadwig felt his mouth curl up into a smile, but then he saw Otha, still standing next to the long table, and his grim expression that stopped it from ever reaching its full bloom.

"What is it, Otha?" Eadwig asked, but the Thegn shook his head, and addressing Eadward, said quietly, "Tell him the rest, Lord Eadward."

So Eadward did, although there was not much to add. "He wasn't slain; he was knocked senseless and fell into the water. And," Eadward turned and offered Otha a look that the Thegn correctly interpreted as a silent rebuke, "it was as I said. Lord Einarr didn't desert us; he went in after Titus because Titus had just saved his life."

This version had unleashed a rancorous debate among the Wiltun men, and it still raged, with the men roughly evenly divided between those who could countenance the idea that a Dane would risk his life for a Saxon, during a fight against fellow Danes, and those who could not. And, to Eadward's surprise, Otha had been in the latter camp; what Otha had never explained to the young lord, for a number of reasons, was that on the subject of Titus, he preferred not to think of the young warrior at all. And now that he knew he was not dead, but what would be required to free him, Otha was all but certain that the youth would likely have been better off dead.

In a sign that, deep down, Eadward understood the reality of the situation, he hesitated before he went on, "And now he's being ransomed."

"*Ransomed*!" Eadwig exclaimed in astonishment.

"He is a warrior sworn to Thegn Otha, who is sworn to you, Father," Eadward replied with a calmness he was not feeling. "Such things are done all the time."

This, Eadwig acknowledged, was true. What was also true was that, even now, four years later, and despite not being in daily contact with the youth, he had seen the progression in Titus' skills, he still thought of him as a raw, bumptious teenager who had been blessed by God with enormous size, strength, and as he had seen, the kind of fury few warriors possessed...but not as a full-fledged Saxon warrior. Eadward was almost eighteen months younger than Titus, and, especially on his return from serving the King at sea, his son had changed; more mature certainly, but once again, he had sung Titus' praises, both at Stanmer and during the fight for their ship.

After a long silence, Eadwig allowed, "That is true. So," he sighed, "how much?"

Looking back, the Ealdorman realized there was no way that he could have prepared himself for Eadward to say, "Ten pounds of silver."

He heard someone gasp and recognized it as Leofe, while his jaw dropped so far that the remnants of the stew smeared his tunic.

It took him a moment to find his voice, which came out sounding as if he was being strangled as he repeated, "Ten *pounds*? As a ransom? Are they *mad*?"

He stood then, shaking his head vigorously, knowing he needed to nip this in the bud and instantly quell any wasting of time in discussion of such a preposterous thing. Nevertheless, he also understood that he was essentially passing a sentence of death on this young warrior, and that was if God was kind, because someone like Titus was likely to end up fighting in a pit against other men or beasts, until he made that one mistake that would cost him his life...and that would be the kindest fate.

Consequently, he tried to be kind but firm as he said, "I'm sorry, to both of you, especially you, Otha. I know how much you've invested in him, but I will not pay ten pounds for a warrior. That," he echoed Titus' reaction, "is the *wergild* for a *ceorl*'s life!"

He was prepared for Otha's look of resignation; the Thegn was experienced in such matters, but he expected a disagreement from Eadward, which meant he was completely unprepared for Eadward to, rather than argue, ask quietly and in an emotionless tone, "How much *would* you pay for a warrior, Father?"

Surprised, Eadwig considered for a moment, then said, "Two pounds." Then, after a moment, he did allow, "For a man like Titus? Three. But," he said emphatically, "not a shilling more than that."

"Then," Eadward rose, "I will find a way to raise the rest."

"*You will do no such thing!*" Eadwig thundered, leaping to his feet. "You will not incur a debt of that size, boy! You may be my heir, but you will *not*," he pounded the table, with enough force to knock over a cup, spilling its contents onto the table, which Leofe hurried to contain from spreading, "take on a debt that will threaten to ruin all that this family has built!"

Eadward endured his father's tirade silently, and even as Eadwig was bellowing, the Ealdorman noticed, with equal parts respect, anger, and unease that, unlike in the past, Eadward was not quaking in his boots and instead just regarded his sire steadily, and seemingly without any fear. Has he already become a man?

Once Eadwig's breath ran out, Eadward did not speak immediately, but he did stand up so that he was at eye level with his father to say quietly, "He saved my life, Father. And not just four years ago. He saved me, and," he turned and pointed at Otha, "Otha, and every man who came home from the *Sea Viper*, Father. If he had not...done what he did, we would have lost too many of us to hold out for King Alfred and the rest of the fleet once the Centishmen betrayed us."

While they had certainly talked about what had taken place, this was the first time Eadwig had heard this more explicit version of it, and he looked at Otha, asking sharply, "Is this true, Otha?"

Otha hesitated, torn between being completely honest because, like Eadwig, he knew that the Ealdorman was right, at least in how ruinous such a ransom would be to all of them, and what, whether it was true or not, had become accepted as a testament of fact by not just Otha's men, but those sworn to Ceadda and the dead Aelfnod as well, that the only reason they were upright and breathing was because of Titus.

Clearing his throat, Otha said, "It's impossible to know, Lord. But," he was suddenly inspired, "what I can say without any hesitation is that less than half of us would have returned...if that many."

"You already need to name a Thegn to replace Aelfnod," Eadward pointed out, which was true, and was becoming an urgent matter.

Aelfnod's holding was the smallest of the three held by the men sworn to Eadwig, but it also produced most of the wheat consumed by all of Eadwig's people, the rest being produced on Ceadda's hides, with the surplus being sold in Wiltun for the ever-precious cash money that was so vital to the daily running of his estate. Without Aelfnod's leadership, there had already been trouble with his men because, unlike Otha with his horses and various projects, Aelfnod did not make them work; that was for *ceorls*, not fighting men, and they had begun to quarrel among themselves. There had already been two incidents at the alehouses in Wiltun that had required Eadwig's intervention, and both of them had been with Aelfnod's men.

"Let me think on it," Eadwig finally said. "I need to consider the matter more fully." Looking at his son, he said quietly and grudgingly, "You have shown commendable loyalty to young Titus, my son."

Another sign of Eadward's maturity was in how, sensing that he had won a small victory, he bowed his head and said, with feeling, "Thank you, Father."

As was Eadwig's custom, this was met with a grunt, an irritated wave of dismissal, then he fell back down in his heavy wooden chair, staring down at the half-eaten bowl of stew, his appetite completely gone, and he shoved the bowl away from him, some of it slopping over onto the table, creating another mess, but this time, a servant hurried to clean it up.

"Lord husband," Leofe said quietly as she reached out to place her hand over his, "our son has become a man."

"I know," Eadwig admitted ruefully. Then, only half in

jest, he asked, "When did *that* happen?"

Outside, another, very different conversation was taking place.

"We have four pounds now," Eadward said, counting in the pound that Otha had also agreed to provide before they entered the hall. "Now, where do we find the other six?"

"I'm going to ask my men," Otha replied, "but while I know they're going to give everything they have, if we get a pound out of them, it will be a blessing from God."

"Should I go talk to Ceadda and his men?" Eadward asked, and Otha looked at him in surprise; he had been certain that Eadward would delegate this to him, but he could tell that Eadward was not only willing to go, but that it should be him and not Otha.

"It would save us time, Lord," Otha agreed. Then, "Let me go back to my hall, then I'll ride to Ceadda's and meet you there, and from there, we'll go to Aelfnod's together."

"We have seven days," Eadward said grimly, for that was when the merchant who had been carrying the message from Lunden was returning through Wiltun back to the Danish-controlled city. "I just hope we can come close enough that those Danish bastards' greed takes over and they're willing to take perhaps eight pounds instead of ten."

Privately, Otha did not think it likely.

Chapter Seven

Titus was dozing in what had become his spot on the *Sea Wolf* when he was jerked awake by the sound of pounding footsteps running down the dock, accompanied by shouts of protest or alarm, and he leapt to his feet, heart pounding as he tried to get an idea of what was happening. By this point in his captivity, he had become accustomed to the rhythms of the port; the comings and goings of ships, the curses, bellowed orders, and laughter of men working as they loaded and unloaded their cargoes. Men running up and down the dock had only happened a few times, but Titus was completely unprepared to see that it was Einarr who was leading a line of Danes running in his direction. While he saw Einarr was not alone, it took another heartbeat for him to recognize the Dane immediately behind him, and he felt his face split into a grin; it was Dagfinn! And, he quickly saw, Dagfinn's brother Sigmund, and Torbjorn, but it was the last man in the group who, while he was moving at a more sedate trot and seemed to be the most reluctant, Knut One-Eye, that sent Titus' hopes soaring; the ransom had arrived! What else could it be? he thought, but this sudden rush of happiness was destined last as long as it took for Einarr to get close enough so Titus could read his expression, which was grim. Leif's men had leapt to their feet as well, but they immediately moved down the ship to Titus' spot, interposing themselves between him and the pier, and while the one guard with a sword did not draw it, he had his hand on the hilt, while the second had picked up a spear and was holding it vertically, but in such a way he could quickly employ it.

Reaching the *Sea Wolf*, Einarr came to a stop, but his tone was urgent. "Titus! Something has happened, and I need to warn you..."

Before he got any further, there was another commotion farther up the dock in the direction of the gate into the city, similar in nature to the disturbance Einarr had caused, but much larger and, to Titus' ears, with an undertone of real anger, and looking in that direction, he saw a much larger group of men, throwing and shoving men aside, at least two of whom were flung into the water in a large spray of brown water. It was not as chaotic as a battle, but it was close, and then Titus saw the cause was Leif, leading this larger group, who burst out of the small knot of men on the dock who had returned to working, and he did not need the lean Dane to get any closer to see the rage that radiated from him.

"Somehow," Einarr spoke urgently, "Leif learned the truth about what happened at Stanmer, and that you are the man who slew Sigurd! He is coming to kill you!"

Titus did not really have time to digest or react to the news before Leif reached the *Sea Wolf*, where he was met by Dagfinn and the Danes who had come with Einarr and who had arrayed themselves across the dock, blocking Leif and his men. For the span of a couple of heartbeats, it appeared as if Leif had no intention of slowing down, his long hair, no longer braided but flying free behind him, streaming in the wind as he sprinted the last few paces, yet somehow he skidded to a stop inches from Dagfinn, who, wisely in Titus' opinion, had not drawn his ax. Everyone, on both sides, Titus saw, was armed with ax or sword, and while Leif did stop just inches from Dagfinn, he thrust one arm in between the Dane and his brother to point down at Titus as he screamed, face contorted in rage and with spittle flying, something that, while he did not understand, Titus instantly understood. He was scared, there was no denying it, nor did he try, but he also felt the stirring of anger there, a buildup of resentment over his treatment, and it was with some surprise that he realized something; he wanted to fight this arrogant Dane, and he wanted it badly.

Nevertheless, it took an effort for him to keep his voice calm as he asked Einarr, "What is he saying? Or," he forced himself to grin, "do I even need to know? Something," at this, he turned to look up at Leif, directly in his eyes, which were wide with the kind of battle fury that Titus had last seen on the deck of a Danish ship now several weeks before, "about ripping out my guts? Or how he's going to cut off my head and shit down my neck? Or is he just going to piss on my corpse?"

He did his best to sound as contemptuous as he could, and

while, like himself, Leif did not understand the words, he understood the tone, and it sent him into an even greater frenzy of fury, yet Titus noticed something. For all the rage and dramatic gestures, while Leif was certainly pressing up against Dagfinn and Sigmund, their bodies were not moving all that much, telling Titus that Leif was not making a serious effort to break through to get to him. It came to him suddenly; this is for his men. This is for show, to reinforce his leadership over the crew, and he recalled his conversation with Einarr and his own observation of the growing tension.

Finally, Leif relented in his ranting enough for Einarr to first say to Titus, "I am going to try and reason with him," then turn and walk the couple of steps so that he was standing just behind Sigmund and Dagfinn, but Titus noticed, just far enough away to draw his sword.

Titus was a silent witness for the exchange, which consisted of Einarr speaking calmly, almost soothingly, which as Titus expected, had absolutely no effect on Leif, but he still made no attempt to shove himself past Titus' protectors. As they went back and forth, Titus took the time to scan the faces of the crew of the *Sea Wolf* behind Leif, and he was heartened to see that, while there was clearly anger in their faces, most of them were staring directly at Leif's back. They're worried that he's going to kill me and they'll return to Frankia emptyhanded, Titus realized; they may not like me, but they *hate* him, at least right now. If this had been even a few months earlier, Titus would have been certain that one or more of Leif's crew would have simply stabbed Leif in the back and thrown his corpse into the Temese, but he had learned a great deal about the Danes during his captivity, and that they did have a sense of honor and loyalty, symbolized by their arm rings, which was a form of money but meant so much more than that. They considered an oath to be more than mere words, just like Saxons; well, Titus reminded himself, *most* Saxons, and he assumed that if there were men like that in the Saxon ranks, then it stood to reason there were Danes that way as well. If there were such men in Leif's crew, they had chosen to remain loyal, for the moment. Regardless, it was a nerve-wracking several moments before, while it could not be said that Leif calmed down, he at least subsided in his manic raging, at least temporarily. The whole time, Einarr had used much the same tone of voice that Titus used with the horses on Otha's holding, although he did raise his voice and speak in a sharp tone a couple of times, and both of those times Titus heard Guthrum's name mentioned.

Finally, Leif subsided enough that Einarr felt it was safe to address Titus, "As I said, he was in an alehouse and somehow heard about what happened at that monastery. And," Einarr said dryly, "it made him angry."

Despite knowing he was not out of danger, Titus chuckled at the understatement; and, he had gotten an idea, so he asked, "And?"

"And I believe I have managed to explain to him how...unwise it would be to kill the man who he has been waiting for so that he does not return to Frankia emptyhanded, because," Einarr's voice hardened, "he and his men *are* returning to Frankia, by order of my King. The only reason they have been allowed to remain as long as they have is because of your ransom."

"Tell him I want to fight him." Einarr behaved as if he did not hear Titus, and he was opening his mouth when Titus repeated, "*Tell* him I want to fight him, Lord Einarr."

Rather than act surprised, Einarr sighed, but he did look directly at Titus as he said, "I am not going to do that, Titus. Not now that he is calm...for him." He did smile slightly. Going on, "But I am going to leave Dagfinn here just in case Leif decides to be stupid. Although," he turned and scanned the crewmen arrayed behind the Longhair, "I do not think Dagfinn would even have to draw his ax before one of his own men chopped him down to size."

Titus replied, but not to Einarr; turning to look directly at Leif, he called out, "You were going to kill me because I slew Sigurd?" As he expected, it was the mention of the name that made Leif stiffen, and created a ripple of murmurs from his men. "But you were going to slaughter me like a pig!" Titus' voice was not only raising in volume, it was hardening as he felt the anger that he had been struggling to contain surging against that barrier, battering at it as it tried to come bursting forth. Not yet, he thought; he extended his bound hands from behind his back as he shouted scornfully, "You were going to kill me while I'm bound and unable to defend myself?" Turning his head, and with an effort to collect enough moisture so it could be seen, Titus spat on the deck. "You are a coward, Leif! You are pig shit! Your mother was a whore and you are an *oskilgetinn*!" He made sure to use the Danish words for the curses he knew, and for mother, although it was not all that different from the English, but to make his point, he thrust his hips obscenely, as he bellowed, "If she were here, I would fuck her right now! Right in front of you! And then, I would make *you* pay her! And then I'd shit on her face!"

To his surprise, this actually elicited a roar of laughter from the Danes who understood what Titus was saying, which baffled and enraged Leif in equal measure, and he screamed into Dagfinn's face, Titus assuming it being a demand to know what Titus had said.

"What are you doing, boy?" Einarr called down, yet to Titus, he did not seem altogether surprised, and Titus wondered if the Dane had divined Titus' intent.

"I'm getting off this poxed ship," Titus shot back angrily, but his eyes never left Leif as he renewed his assault. "Are you scared of me, Leif? Is that why the only way you will face me is if I am bound and chained to this mast? Is that it?"

By now, a large crowd had gathered, and Titus heard from among the throng a heavily accented voice translating Titus' words to Leif, and he was rewarded by a resurgence of the rage as the tall Dane resumed thrusting his finger past Dagfinn as he screamed imprecations.

"You do not know what you are doing, Titus," Einarr said, but Titus thought he heard a note of resignation in his voice, as if the Dane understood that neither man, the young Saxon or the frothing, screaming Dane, would be deterred. "Leif will kill you if you face him."

"And then," Titus was surprised how calm his voice sounded, "his crew will kill him. So, either way, he dies."

Now Einarr *was* surprised, and he regarded Titus with a shrewd graze, but he pointed out, "But you would still be dead."

To that, Titus just shrugged.

"I'm bored out of my mind," he answered, yet his gaze had

never wavered from Leif. "If it gets me off this ship and onto land, then that's fine with me. Besides," he shrugged, "if I'm going to die, I'd rather die on land." Returning his vocal attention to Leif, he resumed, "Well, Leif?" He thrust his hands out again. "Have one of your men," he thrust his chin out to the two guards who, of all of the onlookers, seemed the most bemused, "cut my bonds, give me time to get feeling back in my hands. And then," he paused, "I will kill you."

The translation was shouted to Leif, and suddenly, it became silent, the challenge unmistakable, and all eyes went to Leif, who, Titus noticed with a stirring of what might have been optimism, suddenly looked as if he did not want to be there. It might have been his imagination, but Titus thought it took a longer span of time than necessary before, for the first time, Leif turned his gaze from Titus and called out to the guard with the spear, giving his answer when the guard stepped behind Titus, drew his knife, and sliced through his bonds. Titus was prepared for the pain as the sensation returned to his hands by now, and as soon as he was able, began flexing his hands.

He was completely unprepared for the Dane to whisper just before he stepped away, in heavily accented but understandable English, "Kill him for us, Saxon. We want to go home." More urgently, he added, "And he is *very* quick, Saxon, but not strong. Catch him, you will kill him."

Then he stepped away, his bearded face revealing nothing, and Titus did not see any sign that Leif had noticed the exchange. Suddenly, Titus realized he had no idea what came next.

"Where will we fight?" Titus asked Einarr, then added, "And what do we fight with?"

Einarr's initial response was to shake his head in disgust, and he asked sarcastically, "So you challenge Leif Longhair to a fight, but you do not know what that means?" He muttered something in Danish, and Titus caught a word he knew meant half-wit in Danish, but in English, he said, "We will form a square, Titus. The two of you will fight with either sword or ax and a shield. And," he shrugged, "only the Spinners know which one of you will step out of the square. But," Einarr finished grimly, "only one of you will."

"I already knew that part," Titus said lightly, lifting his arms as the sword-wearing guard produced the key suspended around his neck and kept under his tunic on a leather thong, meant for the heavy lock around his waist, while Einarr just shook his head again.

The feeling of the chain dropping from around his waist made Titus feel noticeably lighter, and he wondered if his incessant pacing, which had been a regular source of irritation to all of his guards, had helped him in some way, making him lighter on his feet without the extra weight. Any sense of optimism he felt promptly evaporated when, crossing confidently to the side, he leapt up onto the pier...and promptly sat down, hard, on the wooden dock. Every man present, Saxon and Dane, free and slave, erupted in roars of laughter, even Einarr, as Titus experienced the same transition that every person who had been aboard a rocking vessel learned when coming into contact with solid, unmoving land for the first time. It was humiliating, especially when he saw that even Leif, while not laughing, was smiling down contemptuously at him, his eyes glittering with malicious humor. Titus had experienced the transition before, but never to this degree, and Einarr thrust his hand down.

Looking up, he could see even Einarr was grinning as the Dane said, "You have been on your sea legs for too long, Saxon!" Titus accepted the help up, and Einarr quickly turned sober, urging, "You need to get your land legs under you quick now, boy. Because you can wager an arm ring Leif will take advantage of that."

It was sound advice, Titus knew, yet it quickly became apparent that it was easier said than done as he stood for a moment, willing his body to make whatever adjustment it needed to make to make him trust that what he was standing on would not move. He took a wobbly step, but he angrily shook Einarr's hand off of his arm, not wanting the help.

"I can do it," he muttered tersely as the laughter died down and became something else, an excited buzzing in anticipation of what was coming.

"What now?" Titus asked.

"We will go inside the walls," Einarr explained. With

heavy humor, he went on, "These sorts of things happen quite often here, so there is a place we use that is suitable."

This was how Titus finally entered Lunden for the first time, on wobbly legs and as part of what was now a small parade of Danes, and a smattering of Saxons who were eking out an existence in the city rather than fleeing. While it did not matter in the moment, it would be another instructive moment for Titus, how the conquering Danes, recognizing they did not have the manpower to run a city the size of Lunden, had lessened the brutality and harsh treatment that had characterized the first months of the Danish occupation, with the two peoples settling into an uneasy, volatile, yet workable relationship. While it was not as far as he would have liked, every step there helped Titus, but he was also surrounded by the Danes of Alfred's fleet in a protective cordon, although he had managed to share an embrace with Dagfinn, the only Dane present near Titus' age, sharing a grin.

"How long have you known I was alive?" Titus asked as they made their way down the dock.

"When we returned to Lunden, you and Einarr had been here a week," Dagfinn explained.

Despite what was in his immediate future, Titus blurted out the question that had been tormenting him for the entirety of his captivity, "What about Uhtric? And Lord Otha? What happened to them?"

"Both of them are fine," Dagfinn assured him, and every so often for the rest of his life, Titus would recall the sensation created by the flood of relief that flowed through him with such an intensity that he almost collapsed again, which Dagfinn had fortunately anticipated, surreptitiously grabbing Titus' arm to keep him upright and moving. "Uhtric took an ax blow on his thigh and was limping for a bit, but while it was a bad bruise, by the time we returned to Hamtun, he was fine. Lord Otha was also bruised and two or three minor cuts, but that is all."

"That doesn't surprise me," Titus replied, but he was still savoring the relief knowing that young Wiglaf's father was still alive and, presumably, back at Wiltun being nagged by his sister for something.

Forcing his mind back to the moment, he was so occupied

questioning Dagfinn in the basics of fighting in the Danish square that he barely noticed their entrance into the city, but what mattered was that by the time they arrived at the place, not surprisingly in front of the partial ruins of a Roman building that had been converted into what Dagfinn informed Titus was King Guthrum's palace and that served for what passed for the Danish government of all of Danelaw, Titus had at least an idea of what to expect. Supporting Einarr's statement, the men accompanying the two parties had rushed ahead to claim premium spots for what was coming, and they were waiting for the combatants, the crowd already loud and boisterous. Once they entered the city, without anything being said that Titus heard, Knut and the other Danes had tightened around Titus, and he felt a stab of unease, wondering if in fact this all had been sort of an elaborate ruse. He quickly dismissed it as nonsense, and he learned fairly quickly that, while the Danes in Lunden tolerated Saxons in their midst who were of the lower class and performing their mundane tasks, a Saxon warrior was a target of hatred and derision. They were quickly surrounded by a crowd, a surprising number of them women, who screamed imprecations at Titus, and he was hit in the face by a rotten apple core once and his tunic was spattered with what he hoped was cow or horse dung, while his Danish escorts shoved the onlookers aside to clear a path. It was almost as noisy as a battle, Titus thought, yet for some reason, he barely noticed what was going on, and he realized that, on an unconscious level, he had placed his trust in Einarr and the Danes of Alfred's navy to protect him. They arrived at the square where, not surprisingly, the men who had rushed to see the upcoming fight were willing, even eager to step aside to let them enter, stopping on the side opposite from where Leif, with his crew making up most of one side of the square, were waiting.

"What do you want to use?" Einarr had to shout this in Titus' ear.

"Sword," Titus answered immediately, and Dagfinn pushed his way through the men, while, with snarls and curses, Knut, Sigmund, and the other Danes claimed a spot on the opposite side of the square.

"If you need to fall back," Einarr was speaking urgently

now, leaning close to Titus' ear, "to get your breath, come to this side where it will be safe. Otherwise," he used his hand to indicate the other three, "one of these *oskilgetinn* might jab you with his dagger to help Leif."

Before he could reply, Dagfinn returned, carrying a round shield, naturally the smaller Danish style, battered and chipped but usable, along with three swords, and Titus saw one of them was a *seaxe*, and with a mail vest draped over his shoulder. Dagfinn set the shield down, while Titus examined the three offerings, dismayed at the pitted iron, nicked edges, and the overall neglect, but when he glanced at Einarr, all he got was a shrug in return.

"This is the best that we have to offer," he said shortly. "Choose one."

He briefly considered the *seaxe*, but Titus chose the sword that most closely resembled the one he had been carrying for four years, taken from the Dane he had slain during their flight from Ethantun. It was, he instantly saw, a couple inches shorter, and the handle moved, not much but enough to notice, and while one edge was at least not nicked, it was dull, but it was the point Titus examined, relieved to see that it had not broken off, a very common occurrence in blades of indifferent quality.

Indicating this was the weapon he preferred, Dagfinn offered the mail shirt, saying, "It might be tight, but this was the biggest one I could find."

To their shock, Titus did not even glance at the mail.

"I'm not wearing it," he said.

"What?" Einarr exclaimed, suddenly wondering if Titus had decided he wanted to die this day. "You have the right to be armed the same way Leif is, and he is wearing his! So," he gestured to the vest, "put it on!"

Titus shook his head, and while he did not feel like it, wanting to spend the rest of what time he had to prepare himself, he saw in their expressions that he owed them some sort of explanation.

"Leif is fast," Titus explained. "The guard who cut my bonds told me. So I need to do something that helps me match his speed. And," he nodded at the mail, "that won't help."

Once explained, it made sense, though he could tell they

both had their doubts, for which he did not blame them; he understood, to a degree, the risk he was running, and honestly, he would have preferred at least leather armor, but his had been stripped from him as soon as he was pulled aboard and had been claimed by one of Leif's men, who spent the first day strutting about the ship where Titus could see him, until he realized Titus did not care. But, he thought as he bent down to snatch up the shield, blocking out the growing roaring of the crowd as he got closer to the moment when he turned about to face Leif, it's all in God's hands now; if He wants me to prevail, I will. Dagfinn had told him that as long as he kept his back turned to Leif, the fight could not begin, though the Dane did warn him that the spectators' patience was limited, but he had one more thing he needed to do. Two, actually; the first was to summon the image of Isolde, the way she looked on the night she had come to Titus before they left for Hamtun, and while it was for just a heartbeat, he felt the rush of warmth at the image in his mind, reminding him of his promise to himself that, even if she was married by now, which was almost a certainty, he would at least tell her how he truly felt, and offer the apology she deserved. Then, just as one would do when dousing a campfire, he summoned another image, that of Willmar, slumping to the deck, the life draining from his body, and he felt *it* come rushing up from deep within himself, rushing up through his body, searching for a release, intent on destruction, a towering, hate-filled rage that consumed him once more. When Titus turned, shield in one hand and sword in the other, while Einarr and Dagfinn were at least somewhat prepared for what they were about to witness, none of the other Danes howling for Saxon blood were...especially Leif.

It was, Titus thought that night, not that different from a Saxon hall, just a lot louder and maybe a bit more vulgar. His back and shoulders were extremely sore, though not from his fight with Leif who, from what he knew, was being prepared for his funeral rites, not that he cared. No, it was from a seemingly unending line of Danes who pounded him on the back as they bellowed in his face, leaving either Einarr or Dagfinn to translate what they were shouting, inches from his face. There was an unreal quality to it all that made Titus wonder if, perhaps, he had actually been vanquished by Leif, yet somehow had not gone to the Christian heaven, but to Valhalla, the fabled hall of warriors where, from what he had been told, what was taking place right now here in Lunden was repeated every night, but for eternity. Essentially, what Titus learned was that, despite being a pox-ridden son of a whore and bastard who ate pig shit to break his fast, he was a passable warrior...for a Saxon. It was not lost on him that, even as he stood panting over Leif's body, Einarr had gently but firmly removed his sword from his hand, and once more all he was left with was his eating knife, nor was he ever left alone. Otherwise, aside from the language barrier, it really was not all that different from a feast at Lord Eadwig's once enough ale had flowed.

Not for the first, or fifth time, Einarr, who had consumed more ale, and mead, than Titus had ever seen one man drink before, declare, "It was not like what you did on the *Viper*, but it was not a bad show. Although," Titus tried not to wince from the meaty arm Einarr dropped across his shoulders as he leaned close to blast Titus with his breath, "I do wish you had made it last a little longer and made that *oskilgetinn* suffer."

"Yes." Titus laughed. "You have mentioned that." Turning to Dagfinn, sitting on his other side, Titus asked, "Does he always get like this?"

"Get like what?" Dagfinn asked innocently, but there was a humorous glint in his eye.

Before Titus could respond, they were interrupted, but this time by a young, female slave who brought a wooden platter, piled with steaming meat, which she placed on the battered and scarred wooden table.

"Food for you, Lord." She had to raise her voice to be heard, and Titus heard the accent.

Without thinking about all that this meant, Titus laughed and assured her, "I'm not a Lord, girl."

"You are to me...Lord," she answered with expressionless eyes that seemed to stare through Titus.

As she was turning away, Titus, feeling flustered and guilty, called out, "Wait, girl. What's your name?"

Her back was to him, but she did stop. Turning completely around, she kept her eyes on the floor as she answered, "My name is slave, Lord."

Then, without another word, she turned back around and vanished through the crowd, dodging and ducking the pawing hands of the men seated around her with an ease that spoke of long practice. Suddenly, Titus lost his appetite. His Danish companions on either side had no such compunctions, and both Einarr and Dagfinn reached out and snatched hunks of what smelled like roasted boar, emptying the platter as they shoved the greasy chunks into their mouths, chewing with relish, leaving Titus to sit in a moment of relative peace. Einarr was right, he thought, no matter how many times he said it, because his fight with Leif had not been like the fight at sea; he remembered most of what happened with Leif, despite that familiar feeling of molten rage that usually blotted out his memory, and for reasons he could not define, he found that the most unsettling aspect of the entire fight. He had allowed Leif to make the first move, which the Dane had done by seeming to commit to a headlong attack, similar to how he had behaved on the dock, yet while he could not be certain, Titus believed that it was his noticing how Leif had seemingly charged into Dagfinn but had not even moved his Danish friend back a step that warned him, so when at the last instant Leif dodged aside, he did not make the thrust that would have hit empty air and, if Leif's plan had worked, would leave him off-balance and vulnerable. His Danish foe had dodged to his right, to Titus' shield side, making it difficult for Titus to pivot in time to score some sort of blow as Leif rushed past him. Difficult, but not impossible, and with this, Titus *was* certain that his eschewing wearing mail enabled him to pivot about rapidly enough to score a slashing blow to Leif's unprotected hamstring. It was a slight wound, but Leif bellowed with pain and it brought him up short and he spun about, his eyes blazing with fury...and something else.

When he thought about it, Titus decided this was the moment he knew he would emerge from this square victorious, yet in another sign of his growing maturity, in the moment it did not affect his behavior. Leif was more cautious after that, but while he *was* very quick, the few times he did make a hard thrust or slash, when Titus blocked it on his shield, there was not much power behind it and certainly nothing near the amount of force he could unleash, confirming the advice Leif's Dane had given him. When he did move, it was with devastating effectiveness, and while he used his superior strength, he also exhibited a calculation that had always been missing before, or if it had, he did not remember employing it. It took some time to maneuver Leif around the square, so that when Titus did rush at the Dane, it was at the corner of the square where Einarr, Dagfinn, and the rest of the Danes from Alfred's navy were standing. He held no illusions that they would do what Einarr had warned Titus about and try to hurt Leif in some way, but he did gamble that they would not protect him in any way either, and as he expected, Leif's response to Titus' sudden rush at him was to dodge to his right, again towards Titus' shield, signaling his intention to skirt around the shield and escape back out into the square. Titus had been watching Leif carefully, measuring how quickly he moved, but he himself had yet to move at full speed, so that when Leif did exactly as Titus expected, he reacted quickly enough and, taking advantage of his longer legs, made what under other circumstances would have been a wider sideways step than considered wise that opened his stance, counting on the strength in his arm to be enough to, if not stop Leif altogether, slow him enough to accomplish what he aimed.

By moving to his right, Leif placed his sword next to the onlookers on the side perpendicular to where Einarr and the others were standing, making him unable to parry or even avoid what was coming. Titus could have ended it then by plunging his blade into Leif's unprotected back as their shields collided with a terrific impact, which actually aided him by the momentum it created that allowed him to pivot on his left foot even more quickly, but instead, he performed another slashing blow in roughly the same spot as the first, just under the edge of Leif's mail. This time, however, he felt the blade bite deeply into Leif's hamstring, and while the momentum created by Leif's bodyweight finished shoving Titus' shield out of the way and he freed himself from the corner, he went hopping away on one leg, screaming in pain, his superior mobility gone, although he did manage to make it to his side of the square, only because Titus allowed it. After that, it was only a matter of time, and it was over within what Einarr said later was perhaps thirty heartbeats, when Titus performed another rush, and with the Dane now unable to dodge out of the way, he knocked Leif flat with his shield, the impact with the ground loosening the Dane's grip on his shield, which Titus kicked aside, sending it flying a few feet away. He had intended to savor the moment, looking down into Leif's eyes and seeing the despair there, the recognition that he was breathing his last breath or two, and while Titus did as he intended, to his disappointment, there was not the kind of ferocious joy there. Satisfaction, yes, but even as he thrust the pitted blade down, through the mail and bone and down through Leif Longhair's heart and felt the shuddering vibration up through the iron, he realized that, somehow, Leif Longhair had managed to convince the men who followed him he was a great warrior when he was not. That, at least, had been explained shortly afterward, although it did not make Titus feel all that much better.

"You remember that Danish lord I mentioned? Who Sigurd disobeyed?" Einarr asked as they made their way to what turned out to be this place, another old Roman building that had been turned into a feasting hall, and Titus nodded. "That lord is Leif's father." When this brought Titus up short, a look of horror on his face as he realized that he might have to face a blood feud with an angry Danish nobleman, even if he was in Frankia, Einarr laughed. "Do not worry. Leif was a third son, and his father hated him, and he hated his father. Now," he allowed, "if you had slain Bjorn, his *first* son..."

Rather than continue, he just drew a finger across his throat and mimed being dead, which Dagfinn thought was funny; Titus was not as amused. That had been hours earlier, and while he had drunk ale, he had been sparing in his consumption, remaining relatively clear-headed. The Danes around him had no such compunctions, and he found himself grinning at the sight of a man and woman humping on a bench as the Dane seated next to them was engaged in an animated conversation with his companion across the table, his upper body rocking in rhythm to the motion of the fucking couple. Games were being played, conversations that evolved into debate, that escalated into argument and, almost inevitably ended up in a brawl; all in all, it was a Saxon feast, just in a different tongue, and, Titus acknowledged, more raucous and vulgar.

Turning to Dagfinn, Titus asked, "And you do this every night?"

"Most." Dagfinn shrugged, then leaned away from Titus to regard him for a moment in surprise. "Why? Do you Saxons not?"

"By the Rood, no." Titus laughed. "Our priests would shit themselves if this happened every night. As it is, after a good feast, we spend the next week hearing from them about what sinners we are, and how we need to repent and do penance for all the wicked things we did that night."

Dagfinn did not share Titus' humor, which was partially explained when he said seriously, "I think the problem with you Saxons is your priests, and that God you worship."

Secretly, Titus agreed wholeheartedly, at least about the priests; the amount of time he contemplated the nature of Father, Son, and Holy Spirit over the previous year would not have filled an hour of his time. Outwardly, he felt compelled to offer some sort of defense.

"Some priests aren't bad," he allowed, albeit unenthusiastically. Then, with a shrug, he said, "But they're not going anywhere, so I suppose we just have to live with them."

"Unless we take the rest of your land." Dagfinn said this lightheartedly, and with a grin, but Titus saw by Dagfinn's eyes that he was deadly serious, at least in intent.

"You won't," Titus replied, not boastfully, not as a young, strong teenage warrior, but matter-of-factly, and while Dagfinn did not like it, he also took the young Saxon's words seriously.

Besides, it was not in Dagfinn's nature to be angry, at least when not in battle, and for any length of time, but he was curious enough to ask, "Why do you say that, Titus? What is it the Saxons have that will keep us Danes from doing what we have done to dozens of other places?"

It was without any conscious thought, said completely spontaneously, a single word, a name.

"Alfred."

The name surprised Titus almost as much as it had Dagfinn; he had not even been thinking of his King at the moment, so he had no idea why that was what came out of his mouth, yet as soon as it did, he felt certain he had spoken the truth, that the fate of not just Wessex, but the entire Saxon lands relied on King Alfred of Wessex. Now, he thought, I just have to hope that Lord Eadwig thinks I'm worth ten pounds so that I can help.

Lord Eadwig did not, although he did, very grudgingly, provide four pounds of silver, which, added to the pound Otha was able to provide, and the pound-and-a-half from every man sworn to Otha, Ceadda, and the deceased Aelfnod, they were still three-and-a-half short. Nevertheless, when Otha and Eadward sat in the alehouse in Wiltun twenty-one days later and the merchant, actually his slave, finally arrived, Eadward assured him that they had the required amount, handing the man a scrap of parchment stating such and a request for instructions for the next step. Despite his heart thudding so heavily against his ribs as he told the falsehood, the slave gave no sign that he sensed Eadward was lying, and it did not occur to Eadward that this slave might not have cared enough to pay attention. Arrangements were made for a reply, with Eadward agreeing to be in The Boar's Head every seven days at noon, and they returned to their respective homes, where the work continued, the seasons not concerned about the cares and worries of a relative handful of people. There was one inhabitant of Wiltun for whom this period of time in the year of our Lord 882 was especially excruciating, in more ways than one. It started about three weeks after the Wiltun warriors, their Thegn and young Lord Eadward had departed when, to his utter delight, and considerable surprise, Isolde had informed Hereweald that she was not only ready to wed but wanted to be joined as soon as possible. Because of his status as the village smith, and the fact that young Hereweald was such a likable young man, the entire village turned out, and Lord Eadwig had graciously allowed them the use of his hall for the wedding feast. Hereweald's wedding night would rank as the best night of his young life, and Isolde was everything he could have dreamed of in his life;

if, sometimes, he caught her standing in the doorway of their small house at the outskirts of the village that his father had provided for them, seemingly staring off in the distance at nothing, he supposed that was just something women did from time to time. Even better, she got pregnant *very* quickly, coming to Hereweald two weeks after their wedding night to inform him that her flow, which had always been as regular as the moon, had not come. He endured the lewd jokes and ribald banter with as much grace as he could muster, even his father getting in on the fun, causing young Hereweald to blush to the roots of his hair while secretly loving joining the world of men in this ritual. Then, the Wiltun men had returned, bringing all of their dead save one, but it was the absence of Titus, which was relayed to her by her father Cenric, who had been informed by Uhtric the day after their return, that cast a pall over his household with which Hereweald found it hard to deal. Yes, he knew that Isolde had had feelings for Titus, who he secretly loathed, so he tried to be understanding, but when it stretched through a week, then two, where she moved about her daily chores with red, swollen eyes, and he would come home to find her sitting at their table, head on it and weeping, he began to lose his patience.

"I am sorry he's dead, Isolde," during his first attempt to set his wife aright, "and I know you...." he could not bring himself to use the proper word, so he said, "...had strong feelings for him, but he is never coming back, and all we can do is move on."

That, he congratulated himself in the moment, is well-put, but his reward was to send Isolde into another bout of weeping that, if anything, was more intense than before he started. Nothing he said seemed right, and in desperation, he went to his mother for advice.

What he got was a scolding, a fierce one, as his mother snapped, "She's pregnant, you foolish boy. That's what pregnant women do! They weep when they should be happy, they laugh when they should weep! You," she had sniffed, "are a typical man, and just like your father."

Still baffled, he had gone then to his father and asked for advice, and the elder Hereweald's counsel was succinct.

"Keep your mouth shut and stay away from her as much as you can."

This did not seem right to Hereweald, but then he recalled how, when his mother had been carrying his three younger siblings, although only his sister survived, his father had spent extra time at his forge. It was attached to the home, yet the elder Hereweald would spend from dawn to well past dark without setting foot inside the home itself, so he supposed that his father must be right. Then, a few weeks later, he had been at the forge, which opened out onto the main street of Wiltun, when the young Lord Eadward and Lord Otha had come pounding up the street at a gallop, yet he was completely mystified when they did not draw up at one of the alehouses, but in front of a heavily laden wagon, spraying dirt all over the slave who was guarding it. This was strange enough, but when Eadward let out a whoop of joy, and even the normally dour Otha bellowed and they embraced, he considered that perhaps they had been possessed. In a town the size of Wiltun, it did not take long for Hereweald to learn the cause of their celebration, and setting aside his personal feelings, he left the forge and rushed home to inform Isolde that, in fact, Titus was alive but being held for ransom in Lunden, and that the young lord had loudly announced to all within hearing that he had every intention of paying the ransom. Whereupon Isolde burst into tears, and Hereweald reached a conclusion; that a woman carrying a child was at least temporarily mad, and he began following his father's advice.

It took another month before, at last, the instructions for the delivery of the ransom were delivered to Eadward, and preparations began for the journey. Because of the amount of money involved, Lord Eadwig had informed Eadward that he could pick eight of the Wiltun warriors as an escort for the eighty-mile journey to Lunden, although they would not be making the exchange in the city, but at a small hamlet just west of the city called Lambehitha, though not even Eadwig had ever heard of it.

"Any more men than that and getting that close to the Danelaw is an invitation to some Dane accusing you of raiding across Watling Street," Eadwig had said as his explanation, which made sense.

"Have you informed the King about what we're doing?" Eadward asked his father, because this had been a topic of conversation, with Leofe, Eadward, and Otha urging him to make the King aware that, in the event he received reports of a heavily armed party heading for the Danelaw, it was for the purpose of retrieving a man who had fought for the King. Eadward had gone as far to suggest that he should mention Titus by name, remembering the three occasions that their monarch had deigned to speak to the large youngster, including in Hamtun, and as Eadward had pointed out at the time, even remembered Titus' name.

Now, Eadward's question caused his father to shift uncomfortably, although he did answer, "I did not."

Sensing it would be unwise, Eadward did not press any further; if he had, he might have learned that his father's reluctance stemmed from not wanting to be accused of sentimentality for ransoming a lowly warrior, no matter how promising he was, especially for the sum he had been coerced into supplying. Better, Eadwig, had thought, not to bother the King with such things.

Finally, all was made ready for the eighty-mile journey. A single wagon hauling the ransom, supplies, and food for what would be, weather holding, a five or perhaps six-day journey, with Eadward as the leader, Otha as Titus' Thegn, and the other men drawn from the remaining warriors sworn to Eadwig. Not surprisingly, Uhtric was one of them, along with Hrothgar, Ealdwolf, and Leofsige. Of Ceadda's men, Aelfnod's cousin, also named Leofsige and Aedelstan were in the party, while the dead Aelfnod's men Seawine and Willibald completed it. They assembled at Eadwig's hall in the predawn darkness in the first week of September on the Day of the Feast of Saint Augustine, so there was a chill in the air that portended that autumn was arriving, which also meant it was not the best time for them to be leaving since it was harvest time, but while these men did perform manual labor for their lords, and participated in the myriad tasks required during harvesting season, Lord Eadwig had shrugged and said his *ceorls* would simply have to work themselves and their slaves harder in their absence.

Since the road led through Wiltun, there was no way for the townspeople to miss them as they passed through, but the party was met by mostly silence, and it reminded Otha that, in the town, Titus' reputation was decidedly mixed. There were men who thought highly of him; that they were all men of the *fyrd* who had marched to Ethantun back when Titus was an anonymous stableboy and had seen him in action was no coincidence. However, Otha could not deny that his young warrior had not endeared himself to another group of townspeople, who, before his beating Hrodulf to death, they viewed as something of a swaggering bully who was looking for the slightest excuse for a fight. Once he had killed Hrodulf, to these people, he elevated himself into being a *dangerous,* swaggering bully, but what struck Otha was the thought; had it *really* only been a few months earlier that the killing of Hrodulf had transpired? When they passed Wulfnod's combination house and business, it was the cloth maker's bad fortune to have stepped outside just as Eadward and Otha, riding ahead of the wagon, rode by.

"*Wes hal*, Lord Eadward," he bowed to the young lord first, then to Otha, "*Wes hal,* Lord Otha."

"*Wes hal*," Eadward replied with a flat tone that conveyed his feelings about Wulfnod and his disappeared daughter more than anything else he could have said, while Otha fixed him with a cold stare, and it was left to Uhtric, from just behind the wagon to call out with a lacerating sarcasm, "Have you heard from your daughter lately, Wulfnod?"

This enraged and shamed Wulfnod, but as he, Uhtric, and every other spectator present to this little drama knew, there was nothing he could say in response that might be perceived as defiant or defending his wayward daughter without risking a beating...or worse. The fact that he was glad to be rid of the girl did not matter, not to these men who viewed her as the source of all the uproar that resulted in Hrodulf's death at their comrade's hand. There was one other townsperson who had just opened the door to her house at the end of one of the two streets that intersected with the main one that ran through Wiltun, and despite the distance and the dawn light, the townsperson recognized both Eadward and Otha, sitting tall and straight in their saddle, but it was the extra horse, tied to the back of the wagon, that made Isolde go weak in the knees, recognizing the animal even from this distance.

"Thunor." She breathed the name of Titus' horse. "They are going to go bring Titus home."

Forgetting what she had wanted to do, she shut the door, laid her head against the rough wood, and began to weep.

Not surprisingly, the closer Lunden became, the higher the tension grew with Eadward and the men. After the second day, and with a bit of grumbling, Eadward had ordered that they wear their armor along with their weapons, their shields strapped to their saddles in the Saxon manner.

"There's no Danes this far east, Lord," Willibald had argued. "And there are no bandits mad enough to try and attack us."

"I would rather be ready than not," Eadward had replied, although the truth was that he had given the order impulsively and was not looking forward to a day in the saddle in mail any more than the others, but he also knew that reversing himself would be a mistake.

He was also aware of Otha eyeing him, but ever since the *Viper*, he had become, if not reticent, then more willing to let Eadward give orders without offering any advice or criticism. If he had been asked, as he had been by Lord Eadwig, Otha would have said that Eadward's sudden maturity was nothing short of astonishing, and in some ways, paralleled Titus' rapid development in his skills as a warrior. While he had not spent much time on the matter, he had wondered on occasion if their mutual blossoming had been aided by the friendship between the young Lord of Wiltun and the only warrior close to his own age. Whatever it was, it had been an astonishingly rapid development, which was why, when Otha had been asked by Eadwig if he thought Eadward was up to what was a potentially dangerous task, he had been unequivocal in his assurance that, yes, he trusted Eadward in this endeavor.

Although he did qualify, "Since Titus is sworn to me, Lord, I'll be there as well, but I have every confidence in Lord Eadward."

The one worry, and it was a substantial one, was that they did not have the full ransom, but while it was a risk, it was a calculated one, and in a rare moment of optimism that he would have blamed on young Eadward and his youth, he was hopeful that the Danes' well-known lust for silver would prevail, and he had almost convinced himself that they would thank their gods that a lowly warrior fetched six-and-a-half pounds. Never, in his wildest dreams, would he have been prepared for what was coming.

"Get up."

When Titus did not stir, Einarr muttered a curse, and using a foot, gave Titus a shove that sent him rolling from the fur-covered benches that he had been sleeping on and onto the rush-covered dirt floor, upon which Titus landed with a satisfying thud, although it was the cry of surprise that was most gratifying to the Dane. For Titus, there was nothing to like in how he had been awakened, because he hit the hard-packed dirt face first, which was a terrible way to wake up.

Rolling onto his back, he had to blink several times before he demanded, "What did you do that for?"

"It is time."

It was all Einarr said, yet because of what had taken place the night before, it still took Titus a moment to recall through a pounding headache the meaning of the Dane's statement. The realization did more to clear the cobwebs away as his heart began racing, though it did not do anything for his head, but he leapt to his feet, making a half-hearted swipe to brush the dirt off of his tunic, which, thankfully, had been washed upon his release from the *Sea Wolf*, although it was now filthy again. There was nothing he could do about his hair or the shaggy beard that had grown to the point that he thought, with a mixture of amusement and unease, that he looked more like a Dane than a Saxon. Einarr had already turned around and walked over to the table in the house that, from the looks of it, had belonged to a moderately prosperous merchant that now served as Einarr's residence. Over the intervening four years, any resemblance to a Saxon Christian home had been erased, and he had been assured by Einarr that, aside from the different kind of construction, it resembled a pagan hall as closely as possible, which meant there were skulls and carvings made of wood and bone, all of them dedicated to one of the dizzying array of Danish gods, of which Titus had learned only a few, all of those the major deities like Odin and Thor. Dropping down across from Einarr, Titus waited for the man who was both his host and his guard to pour a cup of ale, which he shoved across to him, poured one for himself, then they drank in silence. Dagfinn lived with Sigmund, but the brothers appeared shortly after, and sensing the mood, they accepted their own cups, and the four sat there in silence, while the members of Einarr's household, consisting of a half-dozen warriors and their women, sat at the other two tables. For Titus, he had no idea what to say because his feelings were hopelessly confused by now. From the first night he spent under Einarr's roof the night of the feast, long after Einarr and the men and women who were attached to him had fallen asleep, Titus had lain there, wide awake, trying to make sense of what, for him, was a cascade of conflicting emotions. He had attributed that first night to the residual of the nerves and the subsequent, rapid change in his circumstances for being unable to stop his mind from racing. By the third night, when he had gotten no more than a few hours' worth of sleep over the intervening time, he broke his self-imposed rule against drinking enough ale, or mead, to alter his senses, and while a part of his mind screamed at him he was being foolish, that Danes could not be trusted, he ignored it, the need for sleep, no matter how it came, overriding his innate distrust of the Danes. And, thanks to the Danes' own love for debauchery, unencumbered by sour-faced priests and monks hovering about to remind everyone with ears of the perils of Hell that seemingly came from just about everything in life that felt good, Titus found it easy to slide into the never-ending festivities that needed no special occasion or Saint's Day. What made him most uncomfortable was that, in his heart, the Danes' belief that life was to be enjoyed to the fullest, precisely because life in their world was so uncertain and seeing a new day was never guaranteed appealed to him far more than the way of life in any land that was Christian. His solution to this dilemma was to drink himself insensible, even after he was informed by Einarr that they had received a message that Lord Eadwig had agreed to the terms and setting a date for delivery, which was supposed to be today. This, he had been told, was the plan at least, but Einarr had been blunt.

"Do not be surprised if they are not there in Lambehitha today," he had warned, "or even the day after or the day after that." Shrugging, he said, "We will be there at the agreed time as promised. After that, it is up to the gods."

Some bread was brought, though baked in the Danish manner, which Titus found tasteless, but he tore off a hunk, chewing it as he tried to decide when he should say what he had decided he needed to say to Einarr, deciding it could wait. After all, he reasoned, as Einarr had said, they might not be there today, then he would feel like a fool for what he was certain the Dane would view as a display of mawkish sentimentality.

Instead, he broke the silence by saying, with a grin, "Did I forget to thank Gunna for last night?"

As he hoped, this made all three Danes at the table laugh, but it was Einarr who assured Titus, "Oh no, you did not forget. In fact," he winked at Dagfinn, "as I recall, I heard you boast that you...thanked her three times!"

Now Titus joined in the laughter, and while it was heartfelt, at the same time, he felt a twinge of the same problem that had been plaguing him from the beginning of this period of captivity, hopefully coming to an end, and it was never lost on Titus that, despite the comfort, he was still a captive. While he was allowed out into Lunden, and even taken on a tour of sorts, he was never alone, and whoever was with him was always armed, but what was undeniably true was that, especially early on, it was as much for his protection as it was to keep him from trying to escape, although as his beard grew out, the hostility from other Danes lessened. That the most vehement came exclusively from the Danish women was explained by Dagfinn.

"Every one of these women has lost someone," he had patiently explained when Titus complained that he was tired of being spat on. "Maybe it was their husband, or a brother...or a son," Dagfinn said in Titus' ear as they pushed their way down an especially crowded street. "So is it any surprise that when they see a Saxon, especially one like you who is obviously a warrior, that they would behave in this way?"

When put that way, Titus could not bring himself to complain anymore, so he bore it in silence, for the most part. Otherwise, Titus' memories of Lunden would be of the awe he felt seeing this many people gathered in one place. Never in his life, even at Ethantun, had he seen this many people, he was certain; that they were all crammed within the walls of a dirty, teeming city made it even more impactful. At the core of what was tormenting Titus was his knowledge that these people were his enemy, that he should hate them with an abiding passion, yet when he saw them in the streets, and in Einarr's hall, laughing at a jest, enjoying eating a meat pie, or simply talking to each other as they passed by, it was becoming exceedingly more difficult to think of them that way. They were, after all, people, and once one got past their gods, and some of their customs that even Titus still found barbarous and cruel, they were not all that different from his own Saxons. And yet, according to the priests, these people were the enemy of not just the Saxon people, trying to take their homes and land, but an enemy of God Himself. The former Titus completely understood, and in fact he had begun to cling to that thought to remind himself that, while Einarr, Dagfinn, and their fellow Danes may have been friendly, they were *not* friends because, to his credit, Einarr had never pretended that, if the circumstances changed, he would be happy to resume trying to take Saxon lands. For a young warrior facing his nineteenth year, it was surprising that it was the latter aspect of what he had begun to think of as his "Dane problem" that had troubled him the most. Like most of his fellow Saxons, and Christians in that time, he accepted what the priests said about God and His heavens as fact, yet with all the idle time he had on his hands, it gave Titus the time to think about these things that he had previously always believed as factual and true. God, he had been told, created everything around him; the land, the sea, the sun, the sky, the moon...and every man and woman under that sun, and using rudimentary but sound logic, Titus concluded that God must have made the Danes. Now, the priests talked about "free will," which they used to explain how, if all of this was true, there were people who refused to accept what was, after all, fact, that there was only one God, and the Danes had made the choice to reject the one true God in favor of paganism. It was an explanation that satisfied every Saxon he knew, and before he sat on the *Sea Wolf*, gently bobbing in the water and watching the tide that Einarr had told him came all the way from the sea and pushed the river water up and down, it satisfied Titus. But, with nothing else to do, he continued to think, and he also recalled how the priests said that God was an all-knowing God, that he knew what was in the hearts and minds of each and every soul in the entire world, and how He had a plan for their world that ended up in a glorious time when there would be no such thing as war, or pain, or hunger. If that was true, he had reasoned one afternoon, then did that not mean that the Danes and their constant marauding, raids, and greed for more land and all the bountiful things that came from it was part of His plan? It happened gradually, but by this day of his possible release, Titus had far more questions than answers, and he could be forgiven, at least in his mind, for wanting to drink himself insensible so that he was not plagued by them for a few precious hours.

"What is wrong with you?"

Titus jerked in surprise, looking up from the cup he had been frowning into to see Einarr had risen, and the Dane said jokingly, "I have said three times that it is time to go. But if you enjoy our company so much, I will be happy to tell Lord Eadwig and your friends to turn around and go home. Although," he finished with a shrug, "that would mean no ransom for us, and then we would have to kill you."

It was said lightly, but there was also something in Einarr's voice that made it least a partial question about whether this was one of his barbed jokes. Still, Titus got to his feet, then followed Einarr and the others outside; it was the sight of the fourth horse, saddled and ready to go that hit Titus with the force of a blow the reality that, at last, he might be going home. It also reminded him of Thunor, and the thought of being reunited with his horse brought a lump up from his chest and into his throat, the horse that Einarr indicated was his to ride beginning to shimmer a little in his vision. Hoping they did not notice, and with the impish thought of giving the Danes something else to remember, he disdained the use of the stirrup, or using his hands, leaping up into the saddle with them behind his back, a maneuver that he had practiced countless times in preparation for a day where he might be bound and was trying to escape.

This did impress the Danes, who were indifferent horsemen, viewing them in more utilitarian terms, but Titus felt compelled to admit, "I won't tell you how many times I had to do that before I landed in the saddle the first time."

Einarr chuckled, while Dagfinn guessed, "Ten?"

"No," Titus replied, then after a pause, he grinned. "More than that."

They set out through the streets of Lunden then, as the Danes took turns guessing the number of times Titus had failed before he succeeded, crossing over the bridge over the Fleet River and out of the Roman part of the town and into the newer part of Lunden. It was not until they reached the western gate before it was Sigmund who guessed the right number, at least according to Titus.

"Thirty?" This came in a ragged unison from the three Danes, and Dagfinn gave a snort of disbelief.

"I do not believe you." He shook his head. "I do not believe you have enough patience to try that many times."

It served to remind Titus that Dagfinn and Einarr had been with Titus for several months by this point, in close proximity, and especially after the rocky beginning of their relationship, he could not blame them for their skepticism.

"It's true," he insisted, then felt compelled to explain, "Sometimes it wasn't my fault. Thunor would move just as I made my leap, and a couple of times, he threw me off when I did."

They roared with laughter at the thought, and it was Einarr who gasped, "Even your horse does not like you!"

It was a lighthearted moment, certainly, but once outside the gate, the levity left, because they could see Lambehitha, just on the other side of the one spot where the Temese could be forded, although it was just a cluster of huts scattered on either side of the road, hardly enough to be called a village, although there was one stone building that, while it did not have a cross atop it, had at least at one time functioned as a church. The fact that it did not have a cross was a testament to the precarious situation in which the people of Lambehitha found themselves, because the Temese at this point was considered by the Treaty signed at Wedmore to be the border between Saxon lands and the Danelaw. And, as Titus thought about it on their approach, he could see how the Danes would view a cross, the most potent symbol of the God that they hated because it was a threat to their way of life, sitting within plain view from the walls of Lunden. There was a ramshackle building that, once they got close enough, he identified as an inn or perhaps alehouse by virtue of the tables next to it, protected by an awning attached to the hut. When they drew up, Titus saw that there were tables on the other side of the inn as well, which was explained by Einarr.

"This is a meeting place, so depending on who is meeting who, you can sit and see them coming from either direction."

Not surprisingly, after they dismounted and wrapped their horses' reins around the vertical pole used for that purpose, they chose a table on the western side of the inn.

Glancing up at the sun, Einarr said, "We are a bit early. So," he dropped onto a bench, "now we wait."

Ordering ale from the thin, sallow man Titus assumed was the owner of the inn and who kept his eyes on the ground to avoid giving offense, they engaged in light conversation, but their hearts were not in it, and they soon gave up. Try as he might, Titus could not keep his eyes from straying up the western road, but while there was traffic in both directions, it was not particularly heavy, and none of the travelers could conceivably fit what he imagined would be the traveling party from Wiltun. They would need a wagon, he reasoned, to haul that much silver, and he could not imagine Lord Eadwig sending that much money without a heavily armed escort. Once he had learned that it was on its way, much of Titus' inner time had been spent wondering who would be coming. Naturally, Lord Eadwig; it never occurred to him that Eadward would be entrusted with such a heavy responsibility, and Otha certainly, and probably Uhtric. Beyond that, it was pure speculation because, as he knew, it was also harvesting season, and aside from the reaping itself, there were literally dozens of jobs to do.

It was the one time of the year that even warriors were supposed to contribute, although those tasks were usually things like chopping wood, or even digging and clearing out ditches because these were tasks that could translate to their real job of protecting the *ceorls*, freedmen, and slaves who performed the lion's share of the work. It was cool, with the kind of a bite that warned of a hard winter, but the sun was out in a cloudless sky.

"Watching the sun will not make it move any faster," Einarr noted with amusement, and Titus felt his face redden, but he only shrugged in reply, mainly because he knew that it was true.

Time passed, and as Einarr said, the sun did not move any faster or slower on its progress through the sky, but if you had asked one young warrior sitting at a table in a hamlet outside of Lunden, he would have argued the point.

They saw Lunden from several miles away, in the form of a dirty brown cloud that, in and of itself, was impressive.

Eadward had never been to Lunden, and when his eyes took in the sight after they emerged from a heavy wood about three miles west, he drew up, his mouth dropping open from the sight.

"How many people would it take to create that much smoke?" he asked Otha, who, while he had visited Lunden before, it had been years earlier, and he could see it had grown in that time.

"I don't think anyone knows, Lord." Otha shrugged. "Especially now that the Danes have infested it." He leaned over and spat on the ground as if clearing his mouth of a foul taste. "I've heard men say that it's at least twenty thousand people, and a few say that it's bigger than that."

"Twenty *thousand*?" Eadward gasped, accepting the lower number because thirty thousand was simply too ludicrous to ponder.

Wintanceaster was the largest city Eadward had ever seen, and he had heard its population put at perhaps five thousand souls, which meant Lunden was four times the size, and he struggled with the concept.

"Lord," Otha spoke gently, and marked the first time he

had offered the young lord anything resembling what might be called advice, "since we had to repair that wheel, we're already late as it is. It's possible the Danes have gone back into the city by now."

Eadward reddened slightly, but he took the rebuke as it was meant, and nodded, kicking his horse back into motion. The wagon resumed a heartbeat later, and they continued their progress. With agonizing slowness, the thin dark line on the horizon resolved itself into the walls of Lunden, but it took a bit more time before they were close enough to distinguish the huts of Lambehitha, just this side of the small river that flowed into the Temese as it ran along the wall of the city. They got not much farther when, once again, Eadward thrust his hand into the air, calling a halt, ignoring the groans of the warriors, while Otha made an effort to curb his impatience now that their destination was within sight.

"What is it, Lord?" he asked with as much patience as he could manage.

"We're stopping," Eadward answered, but his eyes were on the cluster of buildings, now perhaps a half-mile away.

"Yes, so I gathered," Otha answered dryly, "but can you tell me why?"

Pointing at what they were about to discover was the inn, Eadward asked, "Do you see those four men sitting at the table?" Silently cursing young eyes, Otha squinted until his eyes watered, but after a moment, he answered that he did. "They all look like Danes," Eadward explained, "and while there's one who's large enough to be Titus, he's got a beard."

"It has been a few months," Otha replied, still not convinced. "And I doubt the Danes were much concerned that Titus look like us rather than them."

Eadward shook his head, and he sounded impatient as he added, "It's not just that. Does that man look like he's been held prisoner? He looks like he's just one of four Danes and not held captive for months." It took a few heartbeats for Otha to watch the four men, then when the largest one threw his head back in a manner that suggested laughter, the Thegn was forced to admit that Eadward was not being unduly cautious. The young lord solidified Otha's belief that Eadward was right to be wary when he pointed again, not at the inn but across the road to three huts aligned directly across from the larger inn. "See those three huts? If I intended to ambush someone, I'd have men inside them. Then, while the men at the table who are acting as bait engage us in talk, I'd attack from behind." Jerking a thumb over his shoulder, he said flatly, "And there's no way that we could turn the wagon and get away without them surrounding us if they're on foot." Finally, he pointed to what they could identify as a barn for livestock. "And I'd have mounted men in there. Yes, they're farther away, but in all the confusion, they would be on us too quickly to do anything about it."

Otha, to put it mildly, was impressed, and he realized that, while he tried not to show it, he had gotten distracted at the prospect of being reunited with Titus, leaving it to the youngest member of their group to retain a clear head and view the situation as a commander should.

"You're right, Lord," he said, but only so Eadward could hear, "and you might have saved our lives."

This pleased Eadward, but he covered it with a grin as he turned to Otha and said in mock surprise, "Lives? Who cares about your lives? I'm worried about the silver."

As Otha laughed, Eadward spun his horse about to trot to the wagon, ordering Hakon, "Hand me the branch." Raising his voice, he informed the men, "Lord Otha and I are going to approach while you stay here and guard the wagon. If God wills it, this will be an unnecessary precaution, but we're dealing with Danes, and we're at the edge of the Danelaw. If," he hardened his voice, "there *is* treachery, I order you in the name of my father that you do *not* try to come to the aid of Lord Otha and me, and instead, escort the wagon back to Wiltun. Is that understood?"

The response was ragged, but it was firm and unhesitating, a chorus of "Yes, Lord's" that Eadward savored for some time to come, though he did not show it.

"Uhtric," he nodded to Titus' brother-in-law, "if that happens, you are in command."

"Yes, Lord," Uhtric replied, though Eadward was sure he saw disappointment on the warrior's face, understanding it, certain that Uhtric wanted to come with them.

Returning to Otha, he hesitated for the briefest moment, then glanced over at the Thegn, who nodded in readiness.

Nudging his horse forward, he said more to himself than to Otha, "Let's see what the day holds for us."

It was actually Dagfinn, who, while he was seated with his back to the west, had glanced over his shoulder but immediately picked up movement, warned Einarr in a low voice, who twisted around on the bench. As he had been doing for the past hour now that it was well past noon, Titus was moodily staring into his cup, trying to hide his disappointment and consoling himself that this was just the first day and they would probably come tomorrow. Consequently, the first indication something was happening was when the three Danes suddenly stood up, shading their eyes against the glare of the lowering sun as they stared westward. With his heart in his throat, Titus stood as well, and it took his eyes a moment to take in what he was seeing, and most importantly, what it meant for him. At first, he just saw a wagon, and then a pair of mounted men ahead of it, not all that different from the kind of traffic that had been going back and forth all day. Then he saw how, behind the wagon, there were pairs of horsemen, but it was the glint of the sun off something metal on the body of one of the leading riders that could only mean the man was wearing armor of some sort that gave him his first dawning hope. With an agonizing slowness, the figures resolved themselves, but then he was forced to endure another wait when the wagon suddenly stopped.

"What are they doing?" He did not realize he had asked this aloud, but Einarr answered readily enough.

"The same thing that I would be doing in their position. They are trying to decide if this is a trap."

The words seemed to freeze Titus' blood as he realized that it had never occurred to him that Einarr had some sort of ruse in mind, and he spun about, looking at this seemingly random collection of huts and outbuildings with different eyes. Surely, he thought, I would have noticed something if Einarr had an ambush in mind; just as quickly, the sobering question popped into his mind. Would you? How closely have you been paying attention? You've been more worried about the possibility of going home than whether there's some sort of treachery planned, and you forgot that they're Danes. Turning his attention away from his surroundings, he studied Einarr, still standing across the table, and while his back was partially turned, the Dane noticed the scrutiny.

"No," he broke the silence, though he did not take his eyes off the party up the road, "I do not have a trap laid for your friends."

Now Titus felt a stab of shame for considering it, and he moved slightly so he could have an unobstructed view, and he saw the moment when the leading rider, who was indeed wearing mail, trotted back to the wagon, paused there for a moment, then returned to the other rider. He was carrying something, but Titus could not see what it was, and there was another brief pause before the pair began moving towards them.

It was when they were within perhaps a quarter-mile that Titus saw the large, leafy branch that was held aloft by the mailed rider, which in turn prompted Einarr to say, "It is time to get our horses, I think."

They walked to the post, and this time when Titus mounted, he did so normally, mainly because his legs were shaking so badly that he was certain he would have humiliated himself at the worst possible moment. However, when he started to nudge his horse next to Einarr, the Dane shook his head, pointing behind him.

"You ride behind Dagfinn and me," he ordered, then added, "and ahead of Sigmund."

For a heartbeat, Titus thought about not complying, but for one last time, he decided he had to trust this Dane, and while he was scowling his displeasure, he reined in to give the pair a few paces before falling in behind. He heard Sigmund do the same, and they went to the trot.

Because of Einarr and Dagfinn, Titus' view was obscured, so he heard the reaction from one of the approaching riders, though his heart leapt when he determined just by the manner in which they sat their mounts that it was Lord Eadward and Lord Otha, yet it was not a cry of happiness but one of surprise, and worryingly, anger.

The mystery was soon solved when he heard Otha

bellowing across the quickly closing space, "You! Einarr! You're the one? I should have known it was you, you treacherous bastard!"

This was when Titus realized that, for reasons that would only become clear in the next few heartbeats, Otha and the Wiltun men had not known the identity of the Danes demanding ransom.

"I should gut you where you stand, you pig spawn!" Otha bellowed, but Einarr was strangely silent, although Titus saw his stiff posture in the saddle, his body radiating anger and readiness, his free hand on his sword.

Without thinking, from behind them, Titus shouted, "Lord! It's not what you think, I swear it!"

Whether it was the words or just the sound of his voice, it did cause Otha to subside, then a few paces later, Einarr slowed to a walk, then drew up, beginning what was an exceedingly awkward silence before Einarr broke it.

"Lord Eadward," he said formally, "Lord Otha, I believe I have something of yours."

This was when he gestured to Titus, who took it as the signal to come forward, and despite having identified the pair, the sight of Otha and Eadward, now separated by no more than ten paces, made his vision blur, and he expelled the breath he had been holding in a great sigh.

"You," Otha said without expression, "look like a Dane."

"Yes," Einarr agreed, "we have improved his looks a great deal."

"Maybe for fucking pigs," Otha shot back. "I know that's your favorite animal."

The men glared for a long moment, but it was Eadward who spoke next with a cold tone, and to Titus, it sounded as if his friend had aged years instead of months. "Lord Einarr, why didn't you tell us that it was you demanding the ransom in your messages?"

"Because it was not me, Lord," Einarr answered evenly, and Titus waited for him to explain, but he said nothing more, and it prompted a disbelieving snort from Otha, who retorted, "Yet here you are, with our man!"

Without thinking, Titus spoke up, "It's true, Lords. Lord

Einarr wasn't the one who was demanding ransom. That was...another Dane."

"And," Eadward asked reasonably enough, "where is this other Dane?"

The fact that this elicited chuckles from the Danes, while Titus looked, if not sheepish then uncomfortable, was quite confusing, but it was not helped when Einarr said only, "I will let Titus explain it to you."

Puzzled, Eadward glanced over at Otha, but the Thegn looked as mystified as Eadward felt, then when he glanced over at Titus, all he received was a shrug, and a lame, "It's...complicated, Lord."

Equally frustrated and irritated, Eadward snapped, "So what happens now? Do I signal the wagon to come forward?" Then, something else occurred to him, and he leaned to look past the Danes and Titus, looking back up the road. "Did you bring a scale?"

Apparently, Einarr had decided he had enjoyed the Saxons' confusion enough, because in answer, he replied, "No, Lord Eadward, I did not bring a scale. I did not bring one because there is no ransom to be paid." When this was met by disbelieving stares from the pair of Saxons, he shrugged and said, "It is true. As I said, the man who was demanding the ransom no longer has any need of it." He paused, then he felt it was right to explain, "The reason that I did not put my name on any of the messages is because, while they do get through regularly, they are also intercepted regularly. And as I told you many times when we were together on the *Sea Viper*, I am as loyal to my King as you are to yours, and he has deemed that keeping the peace with you Saxons is in our best interests. If my message had been intercepted, it would have created..."

"Complications," Eadward supplied the word, and Einarr nodded.

"Well, not every Dane under your King Aethelstan," Titus winced at Otha's use of the Christian name, and he saw Einarr's knuckles whiten, "wants peace clearly, if they're demanding ransom from us!"

"Leif Longhair wasn't sworn to their King, Lord," Titus spoke up. "He was part of the raiding force. He was in one of the ships that escaped." Turning to indicate Einarr, "And you should know that when Einarr went into the water, he wasn't trying to escape, he was saving me. He," Titus said forcefully, "saved my life."

"Only after he saved my own," Einarr put in quickly. "I was repaying a debt, no more."

Titus was slightly confused by Eadward's reaction, who behaved as if this confirmed something he suspected; it would not be until they talked later that he learned that Eadward had been a matter of a couple paces away, albeit on the part of the deck of the *Viper* that was lodged on the side of the Danish ship, Titus having no memory of that. On some unseen signal, Einarr suddenly lifted his leg and swung down from his saddle, which Dagfinn and Sigmund immediately copied, followed by Titus, so that the four of them were dismounted. After a heartbeat, Eadward copied them, followed by Otha, and Titus could feel the tension draining from the scene.

"Then you have our thanks, Lord Einarr," Eadward said once they were all dismounted, and while his voice was not warm, it did not hold any hostility. Clearing his throat, "So, how do we do this, then? You said the ransom is no longer necessary..."

Einarr did not answer immediately, but when he spoke, none of them were prepared for him to ask Eadward bluntly, "What punishment did Lord Beorhtweald and his Centishmen receive from King Alfred?"

Once again, Otha growled in anger, but this time, it was not aimed at the Danes, although he allowed Eadward to answer flatly, "As far as I know, Lord Einarr, nothing has been decided, but when I left Wiltun, neither Lord Beorhtweald nor Ealdorman Sigeræd had been punished." Then, he thought to add with what could be called a bitter smile, "As with your messages, I suppose that for King Alfred, it's...complicated."

Titus heard Dagfinn mutter a Danish phrase under his breath of which he had learned the meaning, and normally what he said would have made him laugh, but since this was the first he had heard about the Centishmen seemingly escaping any kind of punishment for not following through with their part of the attack, he was as angry as the Danes. He was also sufficiently distracted not to make an issue of it, and an awkward silence settled on the six of them, Saxon and Dane, who, through a quirk of fate, had been allies on behalf of their kings.

Einarr broke it by saying, with some humor, "Because of my...exit from the *Sea Viper*, I never had the chance to tell your men something." He paused, then with an exaggerated shake of his head he said, almost sadly, "They were *terrible* seamen." After another pause, he added, with an intensity that Titus had not heard from the Dane during their time together before this, "But they are *great* warriors, and I would stand *with* them in battle again if your God and my gods will it."

Neither Saxon knew what to say, but finally, Eadward managed, "Thank you, Lord Einarr, and I will tell them that." More to change the subject and lighten the mood, he said, "Normally, I would suggest that we retire to that inn so that we can drink some ale and swap stories about our time together, but..." His voice trailed off.

"But," Einarr agreed, "you would be seen by other Danes, and not everyone in Lunden is happy with our King and the treaty."

"So, is Titus free to go?" Otha asked in what passed for a reasonable tone for the Thegn.

Einarr hesitated, and Titus stiffened, but the Dane's hesitation was explained when he answered, "Yes, but I would like a word in private with him, if I may, Lord?"

It was, they all agreed later, a highly unusual moment, but this whole situation was unusual, and while Eadward agreed, he was clearly reluctant.

"Lord, it's all right," Titus assured the pair. "I'd like to talk to Lord Einarr and Dagfinn as well."

Eadward nodded his assent, then turned and mounted his horse, though Otha hesitated for a moment, but none of them were prepared for the Thegn to suddenly cross the distance to thrust out his hand and offer it to Einarr.

"You," he said, and while there was not a hint of a smile, Titus heard the humor, "are not all that bad for a pig-fucking Dane."

"And you," Einarr matched Otha's demeanor, but he took

a step and accepted the Saxon's offer, and they clasped hands, "are not all that bad for a big Saxon turd."

They broke their clasp, both of them seemingly embarrassed, then Otha turned, strode to his horse, and leapt aboard.

"We'll be at the wagon," Eadward said, and they returned to where the rest of the Wiltun party was waiting, dying of curiosity.

Although Einarr had asked to speak to Titus, the young warrior beat him to it, blurting out, "I just wanted to thank you for all that you have done, Lord Einarr."

"I owed you a debt," Einarr answered honestly, but his face was grim. "But what I wanted to tell you, not in front of them, is that I do not believe you belong with the Saxons, Titus. You," he said forcefully, "are too much of a warrior for those people with their God! You belong with people who are like *you*!" He jabbed a finger at Titus, which he did not mind in this instance. "Warriors! Men who love the battle joy, who love to vanquish their foes and see them flee before you!"

Titus stood there, silent, although he was not altogether surprised, thanks to Dagfinn's warning that Einarr was seriously considering this. And, he could not deny that, deep within his soul, he was attracted to the idea. Before he had become the Berserker, he had been Titus of Cissanbyrig, son of a one-hide *ceorl*, despised by his father, and because of his size, strength, and temper, feared and hated by his peers around the village. But then, the ambush on the way to Ethantun had happened, followed by the great battle that was responsible for the fact that he was now standing in front of a Dane and they were not trying to kill each other and all that he had done that had given him an opportunity to become more than just Titus of Cissanbyrig, destined to toil for the rest of what he knew would be a short life with little joy. And now? Here was Einarr essentially promising him a chance to do more of the very thing that had given him his chance to elevate himself in the first place, and that he was very good at doing.

Titus was honest with himself enough to admit that a part of him was tempted, but there was little hesitation when he replied quietly, "I could never turn against my people, Lord.

Never. I am a Saxon."

Einarr did not look surprised, and he sighed, "Well, I tried." His voice hardened then, and he went on, "But, Titus, the other thing I want to tell you now that you have made your choice is that our debt to each other has been paid, and we owe each other nothing. Do you know what that means?"

The question was put almost gently, but Titus was not fooled, nor did he flinch as he looked Einarr in the eye and answered coolly, "It means that if we meet in battle, we'll do our best to kill each other." He paused, not liking the words but knowing they needed to be said. "Without hesitation, Lord Einarr. That's what it means."

He was surprised that Einarr actually looked relieved, but then the Dane reached into the pouch at his belt, and he removed an arm ring, of the style that Danes wore in abundance. But *this* arm ring made Titus gasp.

"I am giving you this arm ring," Einarr said, "so that, even if we do meet in battle, you will remember our time together, and that we Danes are not what you think we are."

It was hard for Titus to concentrate on what Einarr was saying because he could not take his eyes off the arm ring. Like the one that had belonged to Sigurd that Eadward had given him, it was made of solid gold, but of intertwined gold wires so that it looked like a rope, while both ends had bulbous ends shaped a bit like acorns, and Titus had no way to estimate its value but it had to be very expensive.

"Lord Einarr, I...I can't accept this," Titus gasped, then thought of something else. "Besides, I don't have anything at all to give you in return!"

"You already did," Einarr insisted, and when Titus looked at him mystified, for the first time, the Dane admitted, "I was not lying when I said that Sigurd the Bold was my cousin, Titus, but I did not tell you the whole story." Something came over his expression then, a pain, and an anger that Titus would only understand shortly. "Sigurd's father was my father's brother, and before I was born, they were very close, but then there was a woman who they both wanted, and they began quarreling. It got so bitter that their lord had to intervene, and he decided that my father's case was stronger to take this woman as his own.

His brother, my uncle, was very angry, but over time, he said he got over it, and two or three years later, he found another woman, who was Sigurd's mother. I was born, and another brother, but he died when he was only months old, and life went on, and it was forgotten, or so my father and mother believed. Then, one day Sigurd's father invited my father to go hunting, just the two of them. And," he shrugged, but there was no mistaking the anger, bitterness, and hurt in the Dane's expression, "my father did not return. His brother claimed that they had been set upon by a bear, and when they were trying to escape, my father slipped as they were using a narrow trail high above a river in the mountains near where we lived, and he fell down into the gorge. His body was never found, and because he did not die in battle, my father is in Niflheimr."

Titus had heard the word, but he did not know what it meant, and when he asked, it was Dagfinn who explained, "It is what you Christians call Hell, except that rather than being very hot and full of fire, Niflheimr is the opposite, a world of nothing but ice."

This made sense once explained, but Titus still did not understand completely, and he asked, "But was it ever proven that your uncle killed your father?"

"Proven?" Einarr echoed, then offered a bitter smile. "No, it was not proven since it was the two of them, but I *know* that he either pushed my father in the back or killed him then threw him into the gorge so that his body would never be found. And you," Einarr pointed at him, "sent Sigurd to Niflheimr." Titus stared at him, still uncomprehending, until Einarr reminded him, "Do you remember when I asked you about the fight you had at Stanmer? And if he had his ax in his hand?"

"And," Titus remembered, speaking slowly and telling a partial lie, "I kicked it away from him."

"Yes," Einarr nodded, and there was a savage satisfaction in his voice as he pointed at the arm ring, "and *that* is what that arm ring is for, because I *hated* Sigurd the Bold. He was as arrogant as his father, and while I cannot touch the father, knowing that his son is in Niflheimr is worth it."

"His father is still alive?" Titus asked, and when Einarr nodded, he tried not to sound troubled at the thought as he asked, "Is he here?"

"No, he is back across the sea," Einarr assured Titus. "He has grown too fat to go to war. But I do look forward in letting him know what happened to his beloved Sigurd."

Not knowing what else to say, Titus copied Otha by extending his arm, but when Einarr grabbed it, it was to pull Titus to him, and they embraced, slapping each other on the back hard enough to make them both wince, then grin at each other, then Titus repeated this with Dagfinn.

When they parted, Titus asked lightly, "So will you try to kill me too, Dagfinn? If we meet in battle?"

Dagfinn's eyes went wide in mock surprise at being asked such a silly question, replying, "Of *course* I will, Titus! I am just as much of a Dane as Einarr!"

Titus laughed, but then he turned sober, and he meant it when he said, "When I go home, I am going to go to our church, light a candle, and offer a prayer that, even if we do go to war against each other again, I never see either of you across from me."

Then he turned and walked off, while Einarr and Dagfinn watched him stride away, and they could tell he was examining the arm ring.

"I notice," Dagfinn kept his eyes on Titus as he spoke in Danish, "you decided not to tell him that you were the one who told Leif Longhair that Titus had slain Sigurd."

Einarr's gaze did not waver from Titus, and he acknowledged, "No, I did not. I thought about it, then I decided that this was something he did not really need to know. Besides," at this, he turned and made for his horse, clapping Dagfinn on the back as he did, "I knew that Titus would kill Leif. We both saw what he did on the *Viper*."

"It is shame we did not keep the money," Dagfinn rebuked Einarr gently, but the older man shrugged it off.

"I believe," he did not look at Dagfinn as he spoke, "that there will be plenty of chances to get more Saxon silver in the future."

Dagfinn smiled, but he did not move for a moment, still watching Titus' receding figure, nor did he say what he was thinking, that Einarr had decided it was not worth the risk of rousing the ire of Titus the Berserker by telling him this.

"So...you killed the Danish bastard who was holding you for ransom?" Hrothgar asked for the third time.

"Yes, Hrothgar," Titus answered again, although he was grinning widely, knowing that it was because of the copious amount of ale that his comrade had consumed. "He challenged me because he found out that I had killed Sigurd."

They were seated at a long table in an alehouse in a village a dozen miles west of Lambehitha, where Lord Eadward had ordered they stop for the night.

"It has been an...exciting day," he had said with considerable understatement, "so I believe it warrants stopping a bit early."

This was meant with immediate approval, but in another sign of his growing maturity, while he rotated them, Eadward had ordered that the wagon be guarded by one of the warriors at all times, along with Hakon and Beohrtic, although he did have the guard relieved more often than was normal to enable each of them to participate in the festivities. It was well past dark now, and to say it was celebratory would have been an understatement, and now that ale had been flowing for a few hours, it had become boisterous, yet Eadward did not seem concerned. If anything, he was one of the leaders of this debauchery and, Otha allowed, he had reason to be happy, not just because he had accomplished the mission of rescuing Titus, but he would also be returning every shilling of the ransom to those who had supplied it. That he was most concerned with his father Lord Eadwig Otha did not begrudge in the slightest; besides, he was happy to have his own pound of silver back since it had constituted almost his entire reserve of hard cash. Naturally, the men were happy as well for that reason, though Uhtric was clearly the happiest of all, and he had been the man who led Titus' horse Thunor to him, resulting in an emotional reunion that, while it was touching, was also the kind of thing that under normal circumstances would have resulted in days of teasing for Titus, but Otha suspected that he would be exempt from this, given all that had transpired.

In the immediate aftermath of the fight, it had been widely

accepted by the Wiltun men that Titus' actions had bought them enough time for Alfred's fleet to arrive without suffering even more grievous losses, although there were a few exceptions, one of them notable because he was the only one of Otha's men to be among those few skeptics, and that was Snorri. Now, in the intervening time, the belief that Titus had been the man responsible for their salvation had hardened into a conviction, and Snorri had become a problem for Otha, who had already begun harboring doubts about the warrior during their time in Hamtun, and he was very close to realizing that the man was a mistake that needed addressing. Shoving that thought aside for the moment, he was content to watch the younger men swapping their own stories about all that they had done, but in the center of it was Titus. While he still thought of him as a youth, as he had already observed with Eadward, their time at sea and his own ordeal had changed Titus in a way that was undefinable yet also unmistakable, but what was most striking was in how he did not boast about what he had done as he would have in the past, although he certainly told the tale of his fight with the Dane Longhair with considerable relish. Still, there was...something different about him, and if Otha had learned about Einarr's offer for Titus to join the Danes, he would not have been that surprised, though not because he suspected Titus' loyalty to the Saxon cause. Titus was Saxon through and through, yet he was also something else, and not just because of his size and strength, or his growing prowess as a warrior. He doesn't think he fits in here, not anymore; it came to Otha suddenly, and as soon as the thought crossed his mind, he was certain he had put his finger on it. Now, he wondered, what does that mean? Because, as God as his witness, he had no intention of releasing Titus from his oath to serve him as his Thegn, and it was not entirely out of selfish motives, because a warrior without a lord far too often became an outlaw, especially in a Wessex under Alfred. Deciding this was a problem for another day, he shoved it aside and decided to participate in what was a cause for celebration; Titus was back where he belonged.

For Titus, much in the same way his first night of freedom away from the *Sea Wolf* had a dream-like quality to it, that first night back among his own, and honestly, the next day as well, had an unreal air about it, where his mind would begin to wander, then he would come back to himself, startled that the rocking motion under him was not from a ship, but from being astride Thunor. As Otha and his comrades had witnessed, his reunion with his horse had been a powerful moment for him, unleashing a set of swirling emotions that caused him to stand, motionless, his forehead against Thunor's for several long moments as his horse thrust his soft nose against his torso, snuffling through his huge nostrils, taking in Titus' scent, while he did the same, savoring the smell of horse that, while the same, was still subtly different with each animal, something Titus had learned during his time with Otha. This feeling extended through the rest of the ride that first day, followed by a night that, save for the different tongue being spoken, was essentially identical to his last night, and many of his previous nights in Lunden. Which meant that, when the dawn came, he had a sore head, sour stomach, and the need to vomit, though he was far from alone. If anything, Lord Eadward was in even worse shape, and they got a late start that morning, while Eadward, pale as death, clung to his saddle, leaning over to retch every mile or so.

"Our young lord doesn't have the head for ale." Uhtric had laughed, after perhaps the fourth or fifth time they watched him lean over and begin dry heaving before sitting back up.

"I don't feel much better," Titus admitted ruefully, though he did allow, "but I've had more practice these last months. Otherwise, I think I'd be doing the same thing."

"They really drink that much?" Leofsige, riding on the other side of Titus from Uhtric, asked.

"More," Titus replied honestly. "I've never seen men who drink that much then are able to function the next day. Then," he sighed, "they do it all over again the next night."

"Do they do any kind of work?" Uhtric asked, and Titus shrugged.

"Some do," he answered, then reconsidered. "Maybe even most of them do, but I was only around men like Lord Einarr and Dagfinn, and they're sword Danes, so what work they do is more or less the same as ours."

"For war," Uhtric said tersely, and Titus nodded.

"Do you think they'll break the treaty?" Leofsige asked Titus, who was beginning to realize that he was now being viewed as an expert on all things Dane, which made him uncomfortable.

He surprised Leofsige by saying, "No." But then, after a heartbeat, he turned to look down at Leofsige and gave him a direct gaze. "I *know* they'll break the treaty. But Guthrum isn't ready yet."

This led to a few miles where the men around him speculated on when the Danish king might be ready, a conversation in which Titus did not participate much, offering noncommittal answers when pressed, insisting that he had no special insight into the question. The topic also provided the opening that Otha needed, Eadward delegating this task to him because of his poor condition, with the Thegn informing Titus of the official story that the King had been assiduous in spreading, that there had only been four Danish ships and not nine, that the raiders had not come from the Danelaw but from Frankia, and that two of the ships were sunk and two captured, but with no ships escaping. Not surprisingly, Titus was of a like mind as his comrades, but when he began arguing that this was not what had really happened, it had been Lord Eadward who had taken Titus aside, ignoring the monstrous headache and sour stomach that still plagued him, well after midday. Rather than explaining the reasoning behind King Alfred's fabrication, the young lord had simply asked that Titus go along with this fiction, as a personal favor to Eadward and his father. Given the circumstances and that he had just been rescued, despite his dislike of what he viewed as a lie, Titus nonetheless swore his oath to never divulge the truth, telling himself that it was not a complete fabrication of what had happened; the ships *had* come from Frankia, and he had been told that two of the ships had been captured, including the one left behind at Hamsey.

As the party returned to Wiltun, aside from being informed about Leofflaed, grieving with Uhtric when he informed Titus that she had lost the babe she had been carrying shortly after their departure from Wiltun, Wiglaf, and Eadgyd, who, finally, had accepted a marriage proposal from a *ceorl* with four hides of land, making him far more prosperous than their father, Titus had not asked about anyone else. This was not lost on Uhtric, or the others for that matter, although it was his brother-in-law upon whose shoulders it fell to break the news that he knew Titus was interested in the most, even as he refused to ask about Isolde. Deciding that, if Titus did not broach the subject by the day they were to arrive back in Wiltun, he would do so, Uhtric was content to let the matter lie, and Titus seemed to be disposed to do the same. In fact, when one of the others came close, like talking about something her father Cenric had said at The Boar's Head before their departure, it was not lost on any of them that Titus changed the subject; the fact that it was to relate a tale about one of the feasts he had attended and what he had seen, and he would relate with a grin, things he himself had done, Uhtric had observed, worked every time. After all, talking about rutting with a woman was more interesting than some witticism Cenric had uttered. However, like Otha, Uhtric had noticed the change in Titus, and if anything, he was more disquieted than the Thegn by what he saw. Outwardly, it was the same Titus; boisterous, laughing and joking with his comrades as he always had, yet there was a separation there, as if his brother-in-law was playing a role to which he was not fully committed, and there was a watchful air about him that had been missing before. Most striking, however, was how he seemed to consider what he was about to say before he opened his mouth, whereas the Titus of before could be counted on to blurt out whatever came into his head without any thought of what it might mean to his listeners. It was on their fourth day back that, as he was ruminating on this, with a sudden shrewd insight, it came to Uhtric; it's as if he realizes how his words might hurt someone, and he immediately thought of Isolde, which in turn led him back to the recognition that, unless it was tomorrow, Titus had no intention of bringing her up, and Leofflaed had pressed upon him the importance of warning Titus.

"You know what happens when something bad happens to him that surprises him," she had reminded him the day of their departure. "And seeing her in her condition without warning will be bad for everyone."

Tomorrow then, Uhtric thought, even as he was laughing at something Hrothgar had said; I'm going to have to tell him tomorrow if he doesn't bring it up when we stop tonight. Whereupon he began praying that Titus would do that very thing.

Titus did not, and time was running out, which Otha pressed on Uhtric in no uncertain terms.

Pulling him aside to let the procession pass at the beginning of the final day, then waiting until Titus, still riding just behind the wagon, was out of earshot, he said harshly, "Uhtric, we're arriving in Wiltun by noon! I don't know what you've been waiting for to tell him about Hereweald and Isolde and that she's pregnant, but your time has run out!"

"I know, Lord," Uhtric replied miserably. "I confess I've been waiting for him to bring it up, but so far..."

"I don't want to hear your excuses," Otha cut him off harshly. In a slightly softer tone, though not much, he went on, "Do I have to remind you what he's capable of if he loses his head? You've seen it as many times as I have! What do you think will happen if we come through Wiltun and she's standing there in the market? She's showing now!" As hardened as he was, Otha shuddered at the thought. "If he has one of his...fits, it will be bloody, Uhtric. And, you know as well as I, there are already people set against him because of Hrodulf."

"You're right, Lord," Uhtric sighed, then promised, "I'll tell him now."

They spurred their horses into a trot, whereupon Uhtric returned to the spot next to Titus he had claimed when the day's journey began on Titus' left side...just in case.

He did not get the chance to begin speaking because, while Titus still looked straight ahead, he asked tonelessly, "Was that Lord Otha ordering you to tell me about Isolde?"

Seeing no reason to lie or to prolong it anymore, Uhtric answered simply, "Yes."

Nodding, Titus said softly, "I thought so. Which means," he did turn to regard Uhtric, giving him a look that did not betray his thoughts or his feelings, "they've been married."

Uhtric nodded, but then he continued looking up at Titus,

and for the first time, he saw a glimmer of his friend's thoughts in the sudden widening of his eyes; whether Titus took pity on him, he would never know because they never spoke of it, but it was Titus who murmured, "And she's pregnant already." Trying to hide his relief that Titus had divined this on his own, Uhtric nodded, praying that Titus would not ask the next, obvious question that usually followed this type of news; his prayers went unanswered. "When do the women say the babe will be due?"

Swallowing, Uhtric answered in as even, and slightly disinterested, a tone as he could manage, knowing that while they were pretending not to, the other men were all listening avidly, "Shortly after the beginning of the year is what they're saying."

Titus frowned, doing the arithmetic in his head, and while his stomach was now twisting and turning and his mouth had gone dry, he heard his voice and thought it sounded, if not indifferent, at least dispassionate as he tried to sound casual. "They must have wed soon after we left, then, and she got pregnant almost immediately."

"A month after we left," Uhtric confirmed, again attempting to sound as if he was simply relaying information, the kind of thing people in a community shared, but he was certain Titus was not fooled.

As far as Titus was concerned, he tried, unsuccessfully, to quell the rush of feelings that, in their own way, were every bit as powerful as the thing inside him, yet try as he might, his mind kept shouting the same message.

"That's my child!"

Consequently, he said nothing for an interminable period of time, knowing that he could not betray his real emotions, but Uhtric knew him too well.

"Titus," he drew nearer so that their thighs were touching and allowed Uhtric to keep his voice low so that only his friend could hear him, "I know what you're thinking right now, but the truth is that you may *think* the babe is yours, but only God knows the truth of it, and if you make a claim, it will shame Isolde and ruin her life. And," he added what would be the most salient point, "the babe would be condemned as a bastard for the rest of its days."

Thankfully, even before Uhtric had begun speaking, Titus' mind had run through the events that would cascade inevitably from his claim to be the father of the child of a woman married to another man. It would, in simple terms, create chaos in Wiltun, although this was a minor consideration for Titus because, as wary as many of the townspeople were of Titus, he held those same people in just as much disdain. When they need men like me, he had often thought, even before they left for Hamtun, they sing our praises and buy us ale and pound us on the back, but once the threat is over, they treat us like mad dogs who need to be avoided, or even worse, chained up. But, he could not deny, there would be one townsperson who would bear the brunt of the inevitable backlash, led by the town priest Father Cerdic, who unfortunately was the type of priest that Titus loathed, a pinch-faced, sour cleric who saw sin everywhere he looked, and was not shy about pointing it out while excoriating the sinner for glancing lustfully at a passing woman in the market, and that would be Isolde. It was maddening, it was frustrating, and it was painful, but even before Uhtric had finished his warning, Titus had already arrived at the inevitable conclusion.

Consequently, he assured Uhtric, "I'm not going to say anything that might get Isolde in trouble, Uhtric. I swear on the Cross I won't." Sighing, he admitted something that surprised Uhtric simply because it was such an unusual thing for a man to say in their world. "Besides, it's as much my fault as hers. I could have refused her that night."

Uhtric covered his shock, as he usually did, with humor, "And if you had, I would have said you had gone truly mad, Titus." Without thinking, he added, "I love Leofflaed, but I don't know if *I* could say no to Isolde."

Despite the subject, and the twinge of jealousy Titus felt at the very thought of Uhtric, who had been renowned among Otha's men for his romantic conquests, laying with Isolde, he could not resist the opportunity for fun, and he looked over at Uhtric with a raised eyebrow.

"I'm sure my sister will be *very* happy to hear that, Uhtric...when I tell her." He looked away so that he could maintain a sober demeanor.

He felt Uhtric's eye on him, and he could sense that his friend was trying to determine if he was jesting.

Obviously, he was unsure, because he said, "Titus, you're joking...aren't you?"

Enjoying himself, Titus shrugged and asked blandly, "Am I? I may be." He paused, drawing out the tension, then furrowed his brow as if he was trying to remember something. "But I seem to recall you telling me that you had no secrets from Leofflaed, Uhtric. Wouldn't this qualify as a secret?" Before Uhtric could respond, he went, as if arguing with himself, "So, if I were to keep this secret for you, that you lust after another woman..."

"I didn't say I lusted after Isolde!" Uhtric squawked in protest, and he heard their comrades beginning to chuckle.

"Oh? I'm certain I heard you say something about not being able to resist Isolde and tell her no," Titus countered, then twisted to where Hrothgar, Leofsige, and the others were all grinning broadly, "Is that what you heard, Leofsige?"

"I did!" Leofsige answered cheerfully, and he was joined by Hrothgar, and Ceadda's Leofsige added his voice in a ragged chorus.

"See?" Titus asked. "They heard it too." Deciding he had had enough fun, he grinned at Uhtric as he allowed, "But I don't want to see my sister dragged to the hundred court because she broke her husband's skull with a bucket. So," he said loftily, "I have decided to be merciful, and I will keep your secret."

"Oh, lick my ass," Uhtric growled, realizing that Titus had been tormenting him and ignoring the laughter of their comrades, but he was still deeply relieved.

As happy as he was with his wife and the life they shared, while Leofflaed did not have the kind of fits that her brother did, her anger was still a formidable weapon, and he had learned early on that it was unwise to rouse it unnecessarily. It was a lighthearted moment, and one that he would think back to in the near future, as the Wiltun men approached home.

Chapter Eight

Just as Uhtric had predicted, Isolde was in the market, haggling over the price of a cheese when, from the eastern side of the large area used as the market, someone shouted that a mounted party was approaching. Her first reaction was a sudden weakness in her legs, because through her husband Hereweald, she had heard about the attempt to retrieve Titus, and that they had departed more than a week before, meaning that they were due back soon. Wracked with guilt, Isolde was in a miserable state, and had been for days, straining her already tense relationship with her husband, whose patience had worn thin, even further. She understood that it did not help that she refused to discuss anything either directly related to, or could lead to the subject of Titus, which only fueled Hereweald's ire, but she was every bit as stubborn in her own way as Titus. Hereweald had not harmed her physically; in this she had been fortunate in her husband, since it was simply not in Hereweald's nature, but he had taken to spending more time at the alehouse, coming home later than normal and weaving, not much, but noticeably. More importantly, the ale seemed to make him more prone to angry outbursts, and once he had grabbed her arm more roughly than he intended, she knew, because when she had winced, he immediately let go of it and apologized. Still, it was a tense and largely unhappy time. It did not help that she was so uncomfortable all the time, but what was worse was that she did not miss the looks exchanged by some of the women in town, and she knew it was because of her size, which as she was informed in the way only women can communicate, was much larger than one would expect with a babe supposedly due in four months. She bore these small comments and petty slights with a dignity that, after she walked away, left some of her tormenters feeling smaller than before...but not all of them. Her only confidant was Leofflaed, but since they lived closer to Lord Otha's holding than Wiltun, and on the opposite side of Otha's, she did not get to talk to her friend as often as she would have liked. And now, while she tried to pretend it was of no moment; after all, people either came to Wiltun, or more often, passed through it on a daily basis, once she had concluded her transaction, she could not avoid turning and looking east through the open gate, wondering how she would feel if she saw they had been successful and Titus was with them, and how she would feel if he was not.

The approaching party had been moving at a walk, but now the pair of riders in front of the lone cart, with mounted men behind them, suddenly began moving at a trot, as if they could no longer hold themselves back, and by the time they were within a hundred paces of the gate, Isolde had her answer. He was unmistakable, sitting a half-head taller in his saddle than the next tallest Saxon warrior of Lord Eadwig, who she knew was Hrothgar, and broader across the shoulders as well. Despite knowing it was unwise, given the gossip, she could not seem to tear her eyes away from the approaching party, with Lords Eadward and Otha leading the wagon as they slowed back down to a walk just before they reached the gate, when Eadward turned and said something, whereupon Titus moved from behind the wagon at the canter and joined the two noblemen. Eadward pointed to a spot ahead of them, so that it was Titus of Cissanbyrig, although now that his exploits aboard the ship the *Sea Viper* had been spread through the three alehouses now in Wiltun, he was almost exclusively called the Berserker, who led them through the gate. She could not tell who started it, but it was a man's voice that suddenly raised a cheer that was immediately joined by the other onlookers, drawing other townspeople from their daily tasks, where they formed a ragged line on either side, turning the moment into an impromptu parade. He looks like a Dane, and that he'd rather be anywhere else, she thought, and despite her turmoil, she felt her lips turn up in a smile at the sight of Titus' obvious discomfort, oblivious to the eyes of some of the other women in the town on her, who exchanged knowing looks and murmured their disapproval. Then he was less than twenty paces away...then ten...then he was passing by, and not once in that time did he even glance in her direction. Yes, she was standing a short distance away from the muddy strip that served as the street, still at the stall of the woman who sold cheeses, but he was at least acknowledging the cheers and calls to him by the people of Wiltun who were lining the street, even speaking to some of them, like Wigmund, owner of The Boar's Head, and the woodworker Burgred, and even her friend Cyneburga's father Cynebald, and while he smiled at what they were saying, which she could not hear over the shouts and cheers of the other people, he did not laugh, nor did he seem all that happy, and she wondered if it was because of her presence. Despite knowing that ignoring each other was for the best, she could not help the sudden welling of sadness and despair that she experienced, wanting desperately to call to him, to run through the small crowd to stand in front of Thunor and force him to look at her, yet she stood there, silent and unmoving, simply watching the small procession reach the western gate, which they would exit before turning north to Lord Eadwig's hall and which had to be where they were going. When the last pair of riders disappeared from view, now that the excitement was over, the crowd began to disperse, drifting back to their chores and daily routine, and Isolde turned away, her day's shopping completed, yet she remained standing there, seemingly staring into the distance as people moved around her.

"Hrothgar told me that when they were on that ship, that giant killed a dozen Danes on his own!"

"Ceadda's man Sigeweard said it was more than a dozen, and that he chopped their heads off with a single stroke!"

"That half-Dane Snorri says that he didn't kill that many men! Snorri reckons he slew at least four of those Danes they're giving Titus credit for!"

"I just hope killing Danes satisfies him! We don't need another dead *ceorl* like Hrodulf just because he gets angry that his ale tastes like piss!"

This was considered quite witty, but the men in the small knot stopped laughing abruptly when they saw Isolde standing there, holding her basket, her cheeks colored a flaming red that, as those who knew her had learned, signaled that she was outraged.

"Er, *wes hal*, Isolde," Eardwulf, one of the two tanners in the town and the man who had made the last comment offered, but when he tried to pass, she stepped in front of him and blocked his path.

His companions, taking one glance at Isolde, made the silent but collective decision to leave Eardwulf to his fate, mumbling their own greetings before hurrying past, leaving the two standing, facing each other.

"Who," Isolde's voice was quiet, but there was no mistaking the fury, "do you think you are, Eardwulf, to say that about Titus? Everyone in Wiltun who was at The Boar's Head all told the same story, that Hrodulf was the one who started that fight! How *dare* you imply that Titus just killed him because," her tone turned mocking as she did a passably fair imitation of Eardwulf's nasal drone, "'his ale tasted like piss'!"

Eardwulf held his hands out, permanently stained a dark brown from the dyes he used for some of his leathers, while Isolde was suddenly reminded of why most people tried to stand downwind of the tanner because of the especially acrid stench from the piss that was, next to the hides themselves, the most important component for a tanner.

"I didn't mean anything by it Isolde," his original intention was to mollify her, but as he was speaking, he noticed that there were others now paying attention, which prompted him to say, in a slightly louder voice, "but it's no secret that your...I mean," he hurried on, mainly because that was a place he was unwilling to go because of Hereweald, "that Titus has a nasty temper." He saw out of the corner of his vision that some heads were nodding, and he heard a low murmur of agreement, which emboldened him to continue, "And he has a...reputation here in Wiltun, Isolde. Surely you know that. He's beaten a dozen men, some of them badly, and one near to death *before* he killed Hrodulf!"

She *did* know that, because she had seen the aftermath, not with the losers, but with the victor of every one of those brawls, because Isolde was the first person Titus sought out afterward, so she had seen, if not the remorse, then at the very least the regret he felt for letting his temper get the better of him.

More than once he had told her, as they sat outside Cenric's farmhouse, or perhaps as they walked across the communal fields surrounding the town where Lord Eadwig allowed the people to graze their animals, "I don't want to lose my head,

Isolde, I really don't. It's just that, when someone challenges me, it makes me angry, and I just get...." he searched for a word that would come close to describing the sensation, but despite knowing how weak it sounded, repeated, "...angry."

She had mostly listened, not trying to scold him, or challenge him, although she had been honest with him about it.

"I know that you don't *start* trouble, Titus," she had told him once, "but honestly, how often have you avoided it?"

She had uttered this shortly before the incident with Aslaug, so they never had a chance to speak of it again, but her words had stayed with Titus. In this moment, however, all she saw was him being blamed, unfairly in her opinion, for Hrodulf's death.

Aloud, she said coldly, "What I know, from my father, and from the men who were there, that Titus' temper saved Lord Eadwig's only son and heir when he was just fourteen years old. And," she had not intended this, but she felt the anger building even more, "he stood in the shield wall at Ethantun, alongside my father, who saw what Titus did."

"I was there as well!" Eardwulf shot back. "I answered the *fyrd* that day as well!"

"And you volunteered to watch the camp in case one of those sneaky Danes slipped away from the fight to plunder," a new voice sounded, although it was quickly drowned out by a roar of laughter.

Isolde recognized Cynebald's voice, but while the handful of people who, as some people tend to do, drifted over at the sight of a potentially interesting development they could share with others, laughed at his jibe, Isolde was still too angry.

"And now," she had to raise her voice, "he returns from being held *hostage* because once again he fought for us and for the King. *Now*," her tone turned scornful as she pointed at him, "you cheer for him and call his name because he fought well, and from everything I've heard from Uhtric and Leofflaed, he's the reason the men who came back are alive! But as soon as he passes by, you insult him! You essentially call him a murderer of Hrodulf!" She was shouting now, and she knew she should not, but she could not help herself. "Titus is a good man! He is a *great* warrior! I thank God and all of His Saints that at least

Lord Eadwig knows his value to Wiltun and Wiltscir, even if you don't!"

She spun about and, still holding her basket against her hip, tried to walk away in as dignified a manner as she could muster given her condition, breathing as if she had just run across a meadow and feeling lightheaded from the effort. Less than a half-dozen paces later, she became aware that Hereweald, not her father-in-law but her husband, had been standing outside the smith, arms folded, a silent witness to what had just transpired. She braced for his anger; what she was unprepared for was the expression of hurt and sadness on his face as she passed the smith by, and a part of her longed for him to call to her, while another part did not, but it never occurred to her to change her direction to go to him. In her mind, if she did that, it would be a tacit admission that she had been in the wrong, and while she did not show it often, Isolde had her own pride to consider, and as far as she was concerned, she had done nothing wrong. With every step, she waited for Hereweald to call her name, but he remained silent, just watching her walk back to their home. Waiting until she shut their door, only then did he turn back to the forge, where his father was intent on his work, while Hereweald picked up where he had left off, and they labored in silence.

Not surprisingly, Lord Eadwig was astounded and pleased to learn that, not only had Titus been recovered, but it had cost him nothing other than some missing labor for ten days.

Equally unsurprising was his reaction when Titus entered the hall, behind Eadward and Otha, but by now, Titus was accustomed to receiving, "God's blood, boy! I thought you were a Dane at first, with that hair and beard!"

Titus made sure to bow first, then gave a polite laugh. "No, Lord, I'm still Saxon through and through."

"I'm glad to hear it," Eadwig replied, but now that the surprise had passed, the rough geniality was no longer present, and he said, "but you cost me a great deal of money, boy. A *great* deal of money. I hope Eadward here made you aware of that."

"He did, Lord," Titus replied humbly, and he was sincere

when he said, "and there is no way I can ever express my appreciation for your efforts, Lord, truly. It's an honor to serve a lord who is willing to do that for someone like me."

So far, Titus thought, it was going exactly as Eadward had predicted, that Eadwig would immediately bring up the ransom. Most of the last day before their arrival had been spent discussing exactly how to give Eadward's father what could only be described as good news, and, with an impishness that is the province of the young, Eadward had proposed having a bit of fun with his father.

The only man who objected was Otha, and it was only half-hearted, pointing out, "You know your father doesn't like surprises, Lord."

"No, Otha, he does not," Eadward seemingly agreed, but then added with a grin, "yet somehow, I think this will be one that he rather enjoys once the shock wears off."

Now that the subject had been brought up, Titus deferred to Eadward, who was standing next to Titus in front of Eadwig, who was seated in his chair on the slightly raised platform, the signal that he was acting in his capacity as Ealdorman of Wiltun. Otha flanked Titus on the other side, and now it was Eadward's show.

Clearing his throat, a habit that his father abhorred because he said that his son always did that when he was about to broach a potentially sensitive or upsetting topic, which this time had been by design on the son's part as part of his ruse, Eadward began, "Father, about the ransom. There's something I need to tell you."

Eadwig's eyes narrowed, not liking where he saw this heading because the boy had cleared his throat, and the last time that had happened, he had brought up this whole endeavor.

Sitting up, Eadwig asked tersely, "What about the ransom?"

"Yes," Eadward seemingly prevaricated, deliberately fumbling his words, "er, yes, about the ransom." He took a visible breath. "Well, as you know, we did not raise the entire amount demanded."

"Yes, I am aware of that. But," Eadwig pointed at Titus, "here he is." Suddenly, he felt a lurch in his stomach as a thought struck him, and he repeated, "And yet, here he is." Turning to Eadward, he growled, "What did you do, boy?" He did not give Eadward a chance to answer, leaping to his feet, the likely explanation coming to him, as he gasped, "Please tell me that you didn't go to Wintanceaster and petition the King!"

He was not yelling, yet, and to forestall him, Eadward hurried to assure him, "No, Father, I didn't, I swear it on holy relics!" Eadwig subsided, and Eadward waited until he sat back down before he repeated, "No, we didn't go to Wintanceaster. Although," he admitted, "I thought about it. But," at this, he turned and signaled to where Hrothgar was standing at the entrance into the hall, and the large Saxon turned and disappeared, "there *is* something you need to know concerning the ransom, but I think it's better to show you rather than tell you."

Totally confused now, Eadwig leaned over slightly to look past the three men standing in front of him, and he saw, framed in the doorway and outlined by the sun, Hrothgar returning, carrying the chest in which the ransom had been placed. It took him a moment to comprehend that the manner in which Hrothgar was carrying it was not what one would expect from a man carrying an empty chest, and he tore his gaze away to stare down at Eadward.

"Are you jesting, Eadward? Is that the ransom?"

"It is, Father," Eadward confirmed, and he broke into a broad smile, pointing to the table next to the chair, and Hrothgar dropped the chest onto it, the weight of it landing on the wooden surface making it creak a bit under the weight. Eadward walked to the chest, withdrew the key from the thong around his neck, used it to open the chest, then stepped aside so his father could see its contents as he said with what he felt was justifiable pride, "Every shilling, Father."

Suddenly, Otha coughed, and Eadward reddened slightly, as he hurried to amend slightly, "Well, not *every* shilling, Father. I hope you'll forgive me, but I used a few coins. I thought a...celebration was in order, and I used a few coins to pay for ale. And," he grinned, "other things."

Eadward felt a sudden stirring of unease, because Eadwig was no longer smiling, and in fact his father's face darkened, a sign he had learned usually meant that trouble was in the offing; his lord father's temper was not like Titus' when aroused, but it was formidable, and in its own way, just as dangerous.

"You used some of the money," Eadwig repeated evenly. He fixed Eadward with a cold stare, then in the same deceptively quiet voice, asked, "Who gave you the authority to make that decision, boy? Did you ask me before you left if, in the event that the ransom was no longer needed that you could use any of that silver?"

Eadward's heart seemed to freeze in his chest, but he answered without hesitation, "No, Father, I did not ask, nor did you give me the authority to do such a thing. I," he hesitated, then decided to be honest, "just thought that it was an appropriate gesture, given the circumstances."

For a long moment, Eadwig said nothing, just continued to sit and stare fixedly at Eadward. Then, he began to growl; at least, that was what it sounded like, but within a heartbeat, the Lord of Wiltun was roaring with laughter, and he pointed at Eadward as he hooted, "You should see your face! You look like you swallowed a turd!"

For an instant, a brief one, Eadward thought his father had gone mad, but then he heard the others, especially Otha, joining in; it was such an unusual way for his normally dour father to behave, but within a heartbeat, he joined in.

"Now," Eadwig roared after he caught his breath, "I want to hear how you managed this, Eadward. How did you bring Titus here back, and the ransom?"

The young lord turned and looked up at Titus as he answered his father, "I'm not the one who's responsible for that. Titus is."

Bellowing an order for ale to be brought, Eadwig rose from his chair, ordering the men to sit at the table, where he joined them, dropping into his customary seat.

Once the ale arrived, cups were filled, and Eadwig ordered Titus, "All right, boy. Let's hear this story. Why do I still have my money, but you're still in the land of the living?"

Because of their relatively late arrival, Lord Eadwig ordered that a welcoming feast be prepared for the next night, declaring that it would be an event people talked about for years.

"He's so happy that he didn't lose that four pounds to the Danes, he's willing to spend it on a feast," Eadward had laughed, which was an exaggeration.

They were outside Eadwig's hall; it was dusk, and Uhtric and Titus were now going to ride to Uhtric's small but neat home on Otha's holding for the last and, for Titus, most important reunion.

There was an awkward moment then, as Titus searched for the words.

"I can't thank you enough, Lord," he finally managed. "Truly, nobody has ever done anything like this for me before."

Eadward was as embarrassed as Titus, and he laughed as he said lightly, "I would hope not because it would mean you've been captured by Danes twice now. And," he added, only partially jesting, "I wouldn't make it a habit of it. I was surprised my father allowed this once, and I can promise he won't do it twice."

"I won't," Titus promised, then offered his hand. "But I'll never forget this, I swear it."

"Oh, don't worry," Eadward accepted the hand, trying not to wince from the crushing power of Titus' grip, "my father won't let you."

It was after he swung into Thunor's saddle that Titus said quietly but with an intensity that Eadward would never forget, "Lord, you're a worthy heir to Lord Eadwig, and I tell you this now; all you have need of is to call on me, and I'll come, no matter what I'm doing or where I'm at."

Eadward wanted to say something, but his throat had closed up, and all he could manage was a brief nod, then he spun about and went back into the hall; it was only later that he would have cause to wonder at the significance of Titus' words, words that might have indicated his future plans. Uhtric was a silent witness, but while he knew Titus' words were heartfelt, he was also troubled at his brother-in-law's wording, though he said nothing about it, and he turned his horse and kicked it into a trot, heading for their home. They rode in silence, which allowed Uhtric to ponder; what, he wondered, did Titus mean when he said, "no matter what I'm doing or where I'm at"? For a Saxon man in those times and of their class, it was an unusual thing to say, because it implied that Titus believed he might not always serve Lord Otha, and Lord Otha's heir, for the rest of his days, however long God deemed that would be, and by extension, Lord Eadwig, then Lord Eadward. The vast majority of people, both men and women, grew up, lived, and died in the place they were born, and rarely traveled more than twenty, or perhaps thirty miles from their birthplace. It was, Uhtric had always accepted, the way of their world, and it was why strangers were treated with such suspicion. Yes, he and the other Wiltun men had gone further afield, but that was because they were warriors; besides, going to war was different. Did Titus think that Lord Eadwig had ambitions that would see them leaving Wiltscir? Or was this connected to Titus' conviction that the Danes would break the truce? Deciding this was the most likely explanation, he put this thought away, and like Eadward, he would have cause to think back on it in the future. Besides, they were in sight of the home he and Leofflaed shared with Titus, the warm glow from the fire coming through the unshuttered windows having the same effect it always did, eliciting a feeling of a contentment that, frankly, Uhtric never expected to feel once he decided the warrior's way was for him. Even now, as Wiglaf was a bit more than four years old, having his birthday while Uhtric was with Alfred's navy, and despite Leofflaed's two miscarriages, he was hopeful for the future, even with Titus' dire prediction that the Danes would return, although deep down, he agreed with Titus. It was, he thought, a good life, all in all, and he was thankful for it, and Uhtric never lost sight of the fact that it would not have been possible if a fourteen-year-old from Cissanbyrig had not defied his worthless father and come to Wiltun when the *fyrd* was called. His train of thought was interrupted when, without warning, Titus kicked Thunor, going to the gallop as he raced towards home, pulling up in front of the thatched structure that, when he sat his horse, he could actually see over, spraying dirt everywhere, although this time, young Wiglaf was not there to watch it and squeal with delight while Leofflaed chided her brother for rushing up like a madman. Titus was already through the door by the time Uhtric drew up, and he heard rather than saw the reunion between brother and sister, Leofflaed's cry of relief and joy like an arrow to his heart, yet in a good way.

He did arrive in time to see Wiglaf, screaming at the top of his lungs, rush into his uncle's arms, Titus sweeping him up, and both of them having learned their lesson the hard way from the low roof, stepping back outside before throwing the boy up into the air, sending him a couple of feet up above Titus' outstretched arms as Wiglaf squealed in delight, then catching him in his arms, both of them laughing at what was Wiglaf's favorite game, while Leofflaed chided Titus like she always did. In the span of an eyeblink, Wiglaf's laughter turned to sobs as he wrapped his arms around Titus' neck, burying his head in his uncle's shoulder, and both Uhtric and Leofflaed watched, tears in their eyes as their son let out all of the fear and the intense relief that he had been holding in for what was a significant amount of his young life.

"It's all right, Wiglaf." Titus patted his nephew on the back as he reentered the house, trying to soothe the boy, but his own eyes were filled with tears and his voice was choked with the almost overpowering emotions he was experiencing just as much as Wiglaf. "I'm home now," he repeated this several times until, at last, Wiglaf subsided, though he was still hiccupping as he leaned back and, for the first time, examined his uncle.

"You," he hiccupped again before he finished, "look like a Dane, Uncle Titus. And," suddenly, his nose wrinkled and he grimaced, "you smell!"

The three adults laughed at this, and Titus admitted, "So I've been told, Wiglaf. About both things."

"I have a meal ready," Leofflaed announced, wiping the tears away, becoming once again the mistress of their house. "Go to the bucket outside, Titus, and at least wash your face and hands." She eyed him critically, "And tomorrow, you're going to have a thorough washing, and I might have to cut that tunic up for rags because it's *filthy*."

"Yes, Leofflaed," Titus said meekly, though he threw Wiglaf a wink, then went back outside as ordered.

As promised, the feast was held the next night, and as

322

Eadwig had invited all who could come, the hall was packed, but the honored guest, who for the first time in his life was given the place of honor for the common folk, at the table nearest to Lord Eadwig's chair across from Lord Otha, it was the absence of one guest that he noticed, though he was not surprised. Neither Isolde nor her husband were there, although the older Hereweald and his wife were, offering an excuse for his son and daughter-in-law's absence.

"It has been a difficult pregnancy for the girl, Lord," Hereweald had explained to Lord Eadwig during the formal welcoming. "And since this is their first child, my son doesn't want to leave her side."

Because of his status as the guest of honor, Titus heard the exchange from where he was standing, next to Lord Eadward, and he braced himself as the smith performed his obeisance to the Lady Leofe, the young Lady Eadburga, whose betrothal to the son of Lord Cuthred, Ealdorman of Hampscir had been announced while the Wiltun men were at sea, then Lord Eadward, then the smith was standing in front of Titus. In an overt insult, unlike the other townspeople, Hereweald said nothing to Titus, which did not surprise him given their last confrontation, but what did was the smith not even deigning to look him in the eye, choosing instead to greet Lord Otha, who was to Titus' left. Hereweald's wife held no such qualms, glaring up at Titus with a poisonous hatred, though like her husband, she said nothing, her mouth going from what could only be described as a grimace to a smile as she moved on to Otha.

"If looks could kill," Eadward murmured, though he did not finish.

There was no need; Titus was not only not surprised, he really did not blame the couple all that much, and the thought did cross his mind to wonder if he would have felt the same way if this was before his captivity, before he had so much time to think about his young but event-filled life. He put that thought away as the next guest stepped in front of him, and this time, he did smile, because it was Burgred, who had made his shield.

As they greeted each other, Titus said, "I'm afraid I lost your shield, Burgred. Can you make another?"

"I can," Burgred nodded, then gave him what passed for his grin, "as long as I have more time with it this time."

Titus promised that he would have all the time he needed, and the guests continued streaming into the hall while Titus tried to curb his impatience. He saw Cenric approaching, and he once more braced himself, although this time, there was a fluttering in his stomach that had been absent with Hereweald and his wife, because Cenric, while not a warrior, was a man whose opinion of him Titus cared about deeply, only dimly aware that the *ceorl* had served as something of a surrogate father figure, especially in the early days of Titus' new life here in Wiltun. When the moment came, unlike Hereweald, Cenric did look Titus in the eye and offered his hand, but his normally affable demeanor, and his habit of making some sort of joke was absent.

Instead, he said simply, "I'm glad to see you're alive, Titus. We heard of your exploits here when the other men came back." There was the slightest quirk of his mouth, as he continued, "And I can't say that I was surprised to hear about them. You always had a nose for trouble." Any sign of humor vanished, and he stepped closer, dropping his voice so that only Titus could hear him say, "Which is why I thank Almighty God that my daughter is married to Hereweald, because she doesn't deserve to be a young widow." Titus stiffened, but he said nothing, noticing that Cenric now looked, if anything, sad. "You're a good man, in your way, Titus," Cenric allowed, "but you have a...demon in you that I don't know will ever be conquered, and that's why I'm happy that Isolde chose Hereweald and not you."

Then he stepped away from Titus and turned to Otha who, despite Cenric's attempt at discretion, had heard every word, and the Thegn braced himself for some sort of outburst from the giant warrior next to him, but while he was a shade paler, Titus' expression was unreadable, and he was already turning away to greet the next man. For Titus' part, he felt as if he had been punched in the stomach, not because Cenric's words had been a surprise, but they had confirmed his worst expectations of what the *ceorl* might say to him. Before this, it would have angered Titus because, while he would not have admitted it to himself, he knew the words were true back then; the difference was that, now, Titus was no longer lying to himself about it. He *did* have a demon inside him, always lurking, always waiting, and until he could come to terms with that, Cenric's judgment was the correct one; Isolde had made the right choice for her. It did not make it any less painful, nor did it give him any sense of peace in recognizing this, and in some ways, it was worse, acknowledging this truth about himself, but now his greatest struggle was trying to work out a way to achieve some sort of balance within himself. None of these thoughts were evident to anyone, even Otha, and as he matured, Titus would come to appreciate the value of his time in captivity, sitting on the *Sea Wolf* without one moment of privacy, because it had taught him the value of hiding his thoughts and feelings from others. Whereas before, anyone nearby would know when he was happy, or more concerning to those around him, angry, now, he had developed the ability to maintain a demeanor that did not communicate his mood to others. That night at the feast, it proved to be the most valuable skill at his command.

During that first full day home, he had gone to the nearby stream to thoroughly wash himself, returning to find that Leofflaed had laid out a clean tunic, taken from his pack, which, thankfully, had been retrieved, although she had followed through with her threat about his old tunic, cutting it into strips of cloth for other uses. She offered to make him a new one, but he assured her that he had enough money to purchase one from the widow who made her living weaving in her cottage. Then, despite his protests, she had sat him down and, while she once again begged him to be allowed to cut his hair short in the Saxon style, he forbade it, although he did allow her to trim it a bit, then had her pull his hair back and weave it into a long braid.

"Why," she asked in exasperation, "do you want to look like a Dane?"

"Well," he had lied, "I *am* called the Berserker, after all. So," he shrugged, "I thought I should look the part."

The truth was more complicated, but he was not ready to discuss it, not even with Leofflaed, who had been his closest confidante for as long as he could remember. On the subject of his beard, however, he proved to be more flexible.

"Go ahead and shave it off," he told her, "but leave the mustache."

The truth was that he detested the beard because it made his face itch, and when she was through, Titus once more looked more Saxon than Dane, although his long braid would cause commentary wherever he went, which he did not mind all that much. For the feast, he donned the arm rings he had earned from Lord Eadwig along with those Lord Eadward had awarded him for slaying Sigurd, but whereas most Saxons eschewed wearing them and instead used them most often in trade, usually chopping them up for hacksilver, Titus had kept them intact. But, not surprisingly, it was the golden arm rings that had drawn the most attention, including from Lord Eadwig, and Titus was certain that he saw a covetous, greedy gleam in the nobleman's eyes, and he wondered uneasily if the Lord would somehow claim a right to one, or even both. Certainly, if the ransom had been paid, Titus would have handed all of them over immediately, and he supposed that, somewhere, there was probably some Saxon law written down somewhere that would have given Lord Eadwig the pretext for demanding it, but nothing came of it other than a covetous glance. No more than an hour passed at the feast that Titus began regretting wearing the one Einarr had given him, because it seemed as if everyone wanted to know the story behind what was, by any measure, an item of extreme value. As Uhtric had pointed out, with that arm ring alone, he could have purchased a fine mail vest, had a sword made for him, along with a helmet and shield, and still have a good deal of money left over, probably enough to buy another horse. It *was* tempting; he had been fortunate for the most part, losing only his leather armor that he had been wearing for the last fight, his shield, which he had been informed he flung overboard, though he had no memory of it, while his helmet was at the bottom of the sea, and although he had dropped his sword when he took the blow to his head, Uhtric had recovered it. Despite needing to replace these items, he never seriously considered using the arm ring Einarr had given him, nor did he use the two that he had been given by Lord Eadwig and the three from Lord Eadward, because sewn into a secret compartment in his pack that Leofflaed had made for him was the last of the gold coins that he had been allowed to keep when he had taken the spoils from the fleeing Dane. The subject of spoils was a sore one with the Wiltun men, as Titus had learned on the journey from Lunden, because of what turned out to be an extremely unpopular decree from King Alfred. Because everything recovered from the captured ships that did not sink had originally come from Saxons, the King had pronounced that it would be unjust and unchristian for the warriors to keep what they had recovered, ordering that, since it was impossible in most cases to determine ownership of most of the plundered items, anything clearly coming from a church or monastery be returned to the Church, with the rest of the items equally distributed among the recovered captives, save, of course, enough to cover the expenses incurred by the King during the campaign against the raiders.

"It's not right!" Hrothgar would declare whenever the subject came up, which was several times a day on the journey, and Uhtric had informed him this had been the case the entire time since their return from Hamtun. "It's not just! It's not the Saxon way! We earned that money, and it should be ours!"

While Hrothgar was the most persistent, he was far from alone; Snorri ran a close second, but while Titus had never trusted him, he was surprised at the thinly veiled animosity the rest of Otha's retainers showed towards the half-Dane warrior. Titus did not have strong feelings either way about the spoils, although he did understand his comrades' feelings; they had toiled at the oars, endured the misery that came from the harsh training they were forced to undergo, the discomfort of being aboard ship for long stretches of time, lived through a storm, and a fight aboard ship. To return to Wiltun without anything to show for it other than stories was a bitter blow for most of them, and Titus recognized that his lack of anger at the injustice stemmed from the golden and silver arm rings around his bicep that night. Consequently, when he heard Hrothgar, seated a few spots down the table on his side begin muttering what had become a refrain by this point, the only surprise was that it had taken two cups of ale instead of one. Otherwise, it was a festive occasion, and Titus' back became sore again from all the pounding on it as he repeated the same stories to men, and some women, who crowded around him. What surprised him was that, while some men wanted to hear his side of the stories that his comrades had already shared at The Boar's Head, The Bounding Stag, and the newest addition, known simply as Offa's, everyone was more interested about his time with the Danes.

"Do they really drink blood?"

"Do they really share their wives?"

"Are they as savage as people say?"

The questions were endless, not to mention repetitive, and Titus tried to be patient, but both Otha and Uhtric began growing nervous, waiting for an eruption of temper that, to their shock, never came.

Indeed, at one point during the night, Uhtric leaned over to Titus and asked with only partially feigned concern, "Did that blow to your head that knocked you off the *Viper* addle your wits?" Before Titus could answer, Uhtric made an exaggerated showing of touching Titus' forehead, frowning as he asked, "You don't seem feverish. Maybe your humors are out of balance."

Titus knocked Uhtric's hand aside, though he was smiling, but he was serious as he assured his friend, "I'm fine."

"I've been waiting for you to knock one of these *ceorls* on their ass for asking you the same question over and over," Uhtric laughed.

Titus' answer surprised Uhtric, saying with a touch of impatience, "It's not the same question for them, Uhtric. It's the first time they've asked it, and it's not their fault they didn't hear me answer it the first..." he grinned then, "...or the second or third time."

It was, Uhtric would reflect later, an almost astonishingly mature thing for a young man to say under any circumstances; in fact, it sounded to Uhtric like the kind of thing a young lord like Eadward would say, a politic statement uttered by a member of the noble class, and not a sword-wielding warrior. Whatever the cause, once explained this way, Uhtric could not deny the sense of it, so he consoled himself with becoming irritated on Titus' behalf, since, given his seat next to his brother-in-law, with Leofflaed on his other side, he was forced to endure the repetition as well. Like most of the smaller children, Wiglaf had been beside himself from the excitement of it, and while he was too young to understand the specifics, he was aware that this was for his uncle, and he had offered his parents a solemn vow that he would stay awake to listen to what Lord Eadwig had to say about his uncle Titus. By the time the moment came, Wiglaf was sound asleep, with his head in his mother's lap, and it was not Eadwig who spoke, although he did offer a few remarks of welcome. What became clear to the onlookers, and especially to his warriors, was that this feast was almost as much about Lord Eadward as it was Titus, as Eadwig told the story of how his son, just sixteen years old at the time, had not only distinguished himself serving their King repelling the Danish raiders from across the sea, but then had braved his father's ire on Titus' behalf, pressing Eadwig to make an attempt to save Titus from the heathen Danes, and a fate that would make any good Christian man shudder with fear. It was all true enough, but Otha and Ceadda bridled a bit at their lord's enthusiastic approbation of his son, muttering under their breath that they had had *something* to do with it, after all, but neither of them were inclined to do more than grumble, because they had been informed that, tonight, Lord Eadwig would be announcing his decision about who among his retainers he would be elevating to the status of Thegn...depending, of course, on the King's approval, although this was not usually an issue. The one person who might have taken exception to the casting of the young lord as the hero of this tale did not seem to mind all that much, and in fact, Titus did not. He was happy for Eadward, as even he had noticed the rapid maturation of the young lord during their time in Hamtun, deferring less and less to Otha, who, to his credit, did not fight it...much.

Although every person at the feast had heard about the fight aboard the *Viper* from Lord Eadwig's men in the alehouses, only Eadwig had heard Eadward's account of it, so the crowd sat, spellbound, as he described all that he saw. To his credit, he neither exaggerated nor did he minimize the role he himself had played, and he made sure to mention the Wiltun men by name, and offered an anecdote of something he had seen them do, although he reserved his most heartfelt praise for those men who were now interred in the growing cemetery outside the lone church of Wiltun, and if he embellished their exploits a bit, the only men who knew were seated at three tables, and none of them were inclined to argue. There was one, and only one man's name who was not mentioned at all, a fact that was not lost on Snorri, and more importantly, his comrades, because it had been a matter of intense speculation about whether young Lord Eadward had taken notice of the half-Dane's constant shirking, and more damningly, his habit of being in the rear when it came time for a fight. For his part, Snorri's first impulse was to blurt out a defense of his actions, but as he opened his mouth, his eye was caught by Lord Otha's, who was on the opposite end of the table, offering Snorri a cold gaze that, in its own way, sent an even more potent message than anything the Thegn might have said. The onlookers were enthralled, going completely silent as Eadward spoke of Willmar, Wilwulf, and the other men who had fallen, then erupting in roars and banging the table with hardened fists as he told of the desperate fight aboard the *Sea Viper*, whereupon attention turned back on Titus as Eadward spoke, though not in graphic terms in deference to the mixed company, of the events that Titus still only had a patchwork of memories about, skipping the part about Titus rushing at the Danes with the loops of a slain man's intestine wrapped around his ankle, which was always the most popular part of the story in the alehouses, and there was no missing the looks of disappointment on men's faces at this omission. Finally, he ended his story, then slowly, and deliberately, he turned and indicated that Titus stand up.

"What I have related," he was getting hoarse now, but he still spoke strongly, "should tell you why, when we learned of Titus' fate, that he had lived and was being held for ransom, I came to my lord Father and urged him to pay it, because I and," he waved an arm to indicate all three tables of warriors, "every one of these men owe him a blood debt, and honoring a blood debt is the Saxon way." Once again, the hall erupted at this proclamation of Saxon honor, loudly enough now to make the rafters tremble, shaking dust loose to drift down onto the crowd. Eadward waited for them to subside, before he continued, "But Titus' service to my lord Father did not end there. It was through his actions that we were able to return to Wiltun, not only with Titus, but with the ransom money!" More cheers, but Eadward held a hand up, a slight but noticeable change in his voice, and Titus understood why when the young lord continued, "But it wasn't just Titus' act of slaying the Dane who was demanding ransom, but the honor of one Dane, Lord Einarr Thorsten, who was the master of our ship, the *Sea Viper*, appointed there by King Alfred, in honor of the agreement between King Gut..." Eadward stumbled, but quickly corrected, "...Aethelstan to repel these Danish raiders who were *not* sworn to the Danish King, and came from across the sea. And it was Lord Einarr who protected Titus from other Danes while he was in Lunden, and who released him without ransom." The crowd had gone silent again, but this time, there was an undercurrent of, if not anger, then something close to it, which Eadward addressed directly. "I know that the Danes are pagans, and that they can be savages," he paused, "but there *is* honor among them, especially when they recognize courage and skill in battle, and those two things are something that," he indicated Titus, "Titus of Cissanbyrig, now better known as Titus the Berserker, has in abundance!" He snatched a cup and lifted it in the air, turning to Titus and bellowing, "To Titus the Berserker, slayer of Danes!"

The subject of this toast and the bellowing approbation of his fellow Saxons sat there, completely flummoxed, and in a state of equal parts, pride, embarrassment, and surprisingly, regret. Certainly, a large part of that regret came from the fact that, because of his own actions and behavior, the one person he most wanted to impress was not even there, but it was also because of his now seemingly hopelessly entwined feeling about the Saxons' mortal enemies, the Danes. While he had no way of knowing it in the moment and would only become dimly cognizant of over the years, what Titus was experiencing was something that many warriors faced, and that was the humanization of their enemies. As long as they were nothing more than bloodthirsty pagan fiends, it was of no moment for Titus, or any warrior, to thrust a blade into their guts, twisting and ripping and slaughtering another man, but now that illusion, that they were not really men but just demons in human form, had been stripped away, and he watched with a strange sense of detachment as these people, *his* people, howled and shouted their own imprecations at the Danes.

Gradually, the tumult died down, and Eadward, breaking his promise to Titus, turned and gestured to him to stand as he said, "And now, let's hear from Titus how he slew Leif Longhair, son of a Danish Lord who is in Frankia, in single combat!"

Titus glared up at his noble friend, but Eadward was completely unapologetic, evidenced by the broad grin on his face, although he was careful to keep arm's distance as he yielded his spot for Titus. When the young warrior turned to face his audience, with every eye on him, he was certain that he would have rather faced a thousand screaming Danes than do this. But, he told himself, there's nothing for it now, though he did decide to exact a small revenge of his own. The hall grew silent, with an expectant air now that their appetite for a good story had been whetted by Eadward's tale, which Titus acknowledged was very well told, and he was struck by yet another similarity between Saxon and Dane, how both of these people loved a good story, and the bloodier the better.

He began, "If I'm being honest, I challenged Leif Longhair because I *really* wanted to get off of that poxed ship." He thought he might have gotten a few chuckles, but the crowd exploded with laughter, and when he glanced over his shoulder, he saw Lord Eadwig sitting at his place, laughing as hard as the rest of the crowd. Once it subsided, he also admitted something that, if he had been a Dane, he would have taken with himself to Valhalla, but he was among fellow *burlofotur* Saxons now, and he knew they would understand, "But since I'd been on that fuck...cursed ship for so long, when I got up onto the pier, I fell flat on my ass." Another roar, and Titus began to warm to the telling, actually enjoying the laughter that, while aimed at him, was not mocking or derisive, but was appreciative.

"The Danes formed the square," he continued, then thought to add, "Lord Einarr told me that in Daneland, they use hazel rods, but here it's formed by men, and you have to be careful if the man you're facing has friends, because they will help their friend by stabbing you." He had not meant adding this to incite the crowd, but the Saxons began hissing and otherwise expressing their contempt for such dishonorable methods, and he felt compelled to add, raising his voice to make sure he was heard, "That's why Lord Einarr warned me, and he placed all of the Danes who served with us with King Alfred on one side of the square so that if I needed to catch my breath, I could come to that side and not worry about being stabbed in the back." Now, he did not try to disguise the pride in his voice, nor the contempt that he felt, although he stopped himself from spitting on the rush-covered floor. "But I didn't need to catch my breath to kill Leif Longhair. He was the third son of a Danish lord, and he was quick, but he was weak. He was a lord and had men at his command not because of his prowess as a warrior, but because of who he was. And," he finished simply, "he was the easiest Dane I've ever killed."

And with that, he sat down, and while men resumed cheering, he could tell they were disappointed that he had not told his tale with the kind of detail and bravado that was expected of a warrior winning a great victory, but he did not care all that much. The truth was that, mentioning Einarr had put him in a melancholy mood, but he did his best to appear as if he was happy, and now that the talking was over, he threw himself into the drinking, laughing at jokes, hooting at a witty insult, all the things that were expected of him, and he did a fair job of it as far as he was concerned. And, when morning came and he woke up in his bed at Uhtric's, he had a sore head, a sour stomach, and little memory of the night before, telling him that it had been a successful evening. Riding Thunor the short distance to Otha's, he was unsure what to expect, and he got his answer when, after taking Thunor to the barn, he came out into the yard, and Otha was waiting there, holding a spade.

Thrusting it out, Otha said only, "The ditch next to the eastern wall needs to be cleaned out again."

The Titus before Hamtun would have bristled at both the peremptory tone and being assigned what was, while better than mucking out the stables, a menial task, but this Titus, the Berserker, smiled as he took the spade, saying only, "Yes, Lord," then turned and strode away without another word, leaving Otha to stare at his back and thinking that, perhaps, that blow to the head on the *Viper had* scrambled his brains after all.

September ended, October coming with the first frosts, and while it took some time, soon Titus fell back into the routine of life serving Otha. His time was evenly split between working with the horses, resuming his spot as Leofsige's top assistant, which he thoroughly enjoyed, and training for what was, after all, the reason Otha had taken him into service. There was one change, and it was a gradual, but subtle one, and that was Lord Otha began relying on Titus to take on the role as teacher to the other men, which did not sit well with some of them, until he put them on their ass. It was not just the other warriors, all of them older than Titus and some by several years, who felt awkward about this arrangement, but as Titus pointed out several times, Lord Otha had not asked his feelings on the matter. One day, without any warning, he had simply announced he had other things to do, turned to Titus and ordered him to take over the training, which on that cold afternoon had been working on the stakes. To be fair to the others, the only complaint that first day had been from Snorri, but he was completely isolated by this point, barely acknowledged by his comrades, and Titus ignored him, at first. The biggest change came in Lord Eadwig's decision about who to replace the dead Aelfnod, although it was not by elevating a man to replace Aelfnod, but in the form of equally dividing Aelfnod's holding between Otha and Ceadda, including dividing his warriors between the two Thegns, a decision that caught everyone by surprise but for which Eadwig offered no explanation. For a span of a week, there was turmoil and acrimony between Aelfnod's former men as they tried to flatter the Thegn they preferred to serve, and because the ten remaining men were to be evenly divided but six men declared they wanted to serve Otha and only four with Ceadda, all of Lord Eadwig's warriors finally learned why Aelfnod's own cousin had chosen to serve Ceadda. And, as they all unanimously agreed later at The Boar's Head, it should not have surprised any of them that it was over a woman, although it was not as straightforward as it had appeared. The man who refused to serve with Ceadda was Eoforwine, the warrior who had served Aelfnod the longest, and next to Theobald, who was now a cripple but had been retained by Otha because of his skill with wounds, was the oldest man of all of them. He was forty-two, old for their kind of life, and the brutal truth was that the only reason that neither Otha nor Ceadda had refused to allow him to continue to serve as a warrior was because of Lord Eadwig; he and Eoforwine had grown up together, and had been boon companions, and in another show of sentimentality, when Otha and Ceadda had approached their lord to suggest that perhaps it was time to give Eoforwine a patch of land, a couple of pigs, and a stipend, Eadwig, while he said he understood why, refused.

"I can't take this away from him," Eadwig had said. "It's all he knows. I don't expect you to put him in the front of a shield wall, and I know that his best days are behind him, but," his eyes took on a faraway look then, staring past the pair out through the open doorway of his hall, "he and I have shared too many adventures and seen too much blood spilled for me to put him behind a plow now, not at his age."

Otha and Ceadda had drawn lots over Eoforwine, and Ceadda had drawn the short straw, but then Eoforwine had balked at serving Ceadda; when asked why, he had spat the name.

"Leofsige."

While it was well known that there was bad blood between Aelfnod and his cousin, neither man would speak on the reason why, and as it turned out, Eoforwine was the only man whose relationship with the dead Thegn extended back long enough to know the cause.

"Aelfnod was all set to marry a girl," Eoforwine had told the two Thegns and Lord Eadwig when he had been summoned to the Ealdorman's hall to resolve the situation, which, privately, both Thegns hoped would end up forcing Eadwig's hand in sending Eoforwine into retirement. "My Lord was very happy, because he had long sought her as a wife. She was the daughter of a merchant from Wintanceaster. Wassa," he almost sighed the name, and the other three men exchanged a glance, sharing their amusement, "*was* a beautiful girl, she truly was. And her father had told Lord Aelfnod that, should he become a Thegn, that was when he could marry his daughter." Eoforwine was staring into his cup, lost in time, so he missed their reaction, "My Lord was *so* happy. But then," his mouth twisted, "*he* came to visit, Leofsige. And he whispered sweet words into Wassa's ear, and she fell in *love* with him!" He leaned over and spat on the floor. "He was nothing but a sword warrior, not a Thegn, not like Lord Aelfnod. But they ran off and were married in secret by some priest," pronouncing the title as an epithet, "who married them for a handful of hacksilver." He looked up then, and there was a pleading quality to his tone as he said, "I can't serve alongside a man like Leofsige, Lords, I just can't. You know this to be true, Lord Eadwig, but Lord Aelfnod was never the same man after that. And then, when his brother Aelfgar died at Stanmer, he just...gave up."

"What happened to Wassa?" Ceadda asked. "Because Leofsige's woman is named..." he had to search his memory, "Ebba."

"She died bearing him a child," Eoforwine said with a tone of satisfaction that was notable for its vehemence. "I told the bastard then that it was God's punishment for what he did to his cousin!"

Ultimately, the two Thegns struck a bargain after some intense negotiations, during which Otha tried to offer Snorri in exchange for Eoforwine, arguing that Snorri was younger, but Ceadda flatly refused. With Lord Eadwig's permission, Otha agreed to take on Eoforwine, but he would be paid and supported by Ceadda, who, while he was not happy about it, viewed a lighter purse as the lesser of two evils. There was friction at first, but this was to be expected, as the new additions sought to align themselves in the informal hierarchy under their Thegns, who, at least in Otha's case, was willing to let the men work it out for themselves. And, as Otha's new additions learned, no matter how experienced they were, they all had to face Titus in a sparring session as a sort of initiation, even Eoforwine, and it was after their bout that Titus approached Otha, catching him when the Thegn was in the barn and alone.

"Lord," Titus spoke bluntly, "Eoforwine isn't fit to fight with us."

Otha did not answer immediately; he had witnessed their bout himself, and he had seen it as well. The problem for the

Thegn was that, if Eoforwine could no longer be counted on to fight, he would have to fulfill other tasks about the holding, but while Aelfnod's land had been added, the truth was that, as Wulfgifu continually reminded him, he already had enough mouths to feed. Osric, who had lost his right arm at Ethantun, performed a number of menial tasks around the holding and was competent enough at them, and Otha had more than enough help with the horses, although now he was thinking of expanding further with the addition of more grazing land. The problem was that Eoforwine was not suited for working with horses, having too heavy a hand and, unlike Otha, and as the Thegn had observed, Titus, he did not have an affinity for the animals.

To Titus, he said shortly, "I know. I saw."

However, even with this admission, Otha did not dismiss Eoforwine and refused to give his reason for his decision, which of course became one of the dominant topics of conversation among the other warriors. Aside from this disruption in the normal practice, the new additions to Otha's men soon settled into the routine that, while subtly different under Otha, was essentially the same as their former Thegn. November came, and the first snow fell, a presage to what the *ceorls*, who were tied to this land through untold generations, had been predicting, a hard winter that year. Short days meant short work hours, which in turn meant that the warriors spent more time in their favored alehouse, with one notable exception. Even men with families like Uhtric made an appearance at least one or two times a week, but every time he walked into The Boar's Head, it was alone, and now that the men had grudgingly accepted that Eoforwine was one of their band, the dominant topic of conversation became Titus' absence. Everyone knew why he refused to come into Wiltun in a general sense, that it concerned Isolde, who was now so large that the women in the town were speculating that she was destined to bear twins. While only Uhtric, thanks to Leofflaed, knew the truth, and their comrades, knowing how close Leofflaed and Isolde were, continually pressed him, the one-eyed warrior refused to give any indication that he knew anything more than they did.

"When they start talking," he said more than once, "I stop

listening." As was his habit, he made a joke of it. "That's why I have a happy life. When the women talk, I stop listening."

For Titus, his self-imposed exile was torture, but the sight of a pregnant Isolde once had proven to be almost too painful to bear, although it was more than that. He knew himself well enough by this time to understand that, even if he prepared himself to see her, if he went into Wiltun and he saw her there in the market as he had on his return to Wiltun, he might not be able to stop himself from approaching her and demanding to know if the child was his. And, as much as he wanted to know, he knew that it would destroy Isolde's life. Consequently, he stayed with Leofflaed and Wiglaf, contenting himself with playing with his nephew and trying not to think about what it would be like if he had a son of his own. Only once did he speak to Leofflaed about it, waiting for the one night a week Uhtric went into Wiltun, giving what had become a ritual answer to his brother-in-law's invitation to join him, saying that Wiglaf was much better company than any of those misbegotten bastards, and Uhtric would laugh and pretend to believe him. And, somewhat to his surprise, Titus found that, while he did miss sitting in The Boar's Head with his comrades, swapping stories and telling jokes that they had all heard before, he did enjoy this quiet time, watching Leofflaed, who was always busy with something, usually sewing but sometimes repairing some piece of household equipment, her head bowed in the firelight as she frowned in concentration, while listening to Wiglaf spin some fantastic tale out of the stag he had seen crossing the field that day, and how he believed he was ready for a puppy, his latest fixation.

Without thinking, one night, he asked the question that had been haunting his thoughts, "Do you think Isolde would survive bearing a child of mine, Leofflaed?"

His sister froze, needle poised just above the pair of trousers she was mending, but she did not answer immediately; it was a question she had prayed to God that Titus would never ask, if only because it was a question she had been asking herself ever since she had last seen Isolde and seen her size. What, she thought miserably, can I tell him?

Finally, she lifted her head and turned to give her brother a direct gaze, though she had to swallow twice before she said, "Only God truly knows the answer to that question, Titus." This did not satisfy him, as she had known it would not, but she was searching for something she could say that might bring her brother some comfort. More than anyone else who knew him, Leofflaed had seen the deep change in her brother, and like Uhtric, Lord Otha, and his comrades, she was happy to see that he was not as prone to angry outbursts as he had been before, but she also was deeply disturbed, worried that, instead of losing his temper over seemingly inconsequential things as had been his habit, he was smothering that anger deep within himself. She knew nothing of volcanoes, but if she had, she would have instantly understood that her brother was like a volcano. Yes, right now he was seemingly dormant, but she worried about the pressure that was building inside her brother, with no outlet, and the truth was, she feared for Isolde just as much as her brother. Aloud, she continued, "Isolde is young, and this is her first child, Titus. Our mother had already had me, Eadgyd, and two other babes, one stillborn and one who died within weeks before you came along. She was older, and she had been ailing the last two months before you were born." Suddenly, she dropped her sewing to lean across the table to grasp Titus' arm, squeezing it to emphasize her words. "Childbirth is dangerous for a woman, Titus, you know this. But *if* something happens to Isolde, that doesn't make it your fault now, any more than it was your fault when you were born. It's..." she searched for the words, but all she could offer, despite knowing how unsatisfactory they were, "...God's will."

To her despair, she saw in her brother's eyes that her words did not console him in the manner in which she hoped, although aloud, he said, "Thank you, sister."

Then he gently took her hand, kissed the back of it, then turned about on the bench to stare into the fire. This was the only conversation they ever had about Isolde and her fate.

Yule came, with Titus helping with the task of going into one of the forests that was within Lord Eadwig's lands, with Lord Eadward leading, and selecting the Yule log that would be dragged to the hall to burn for the twelve days. It was bitterly cold, and an unusually strong storm that dumped three feet of snow created difficult conditions for the people of Wiltun, no matter their status, and it was made even more difficult because of Alfred's law decreeing a strict observance of the Yule traditions as prescribed by the Church. Yes, there was nothing but the most necessary labor allowed, such as feeding the animals and cleaning up after them, giving the normally hardworking people the chance to rest, but it was the fasting required of them that was most wearing. And, for Titus, who was always hungry, Yule was his least favorite time of the year, and it was even worse this year because he could not avoid going into Wiltun to attend church, although he resisted it until Leofflaed lost her patience.

"People already are whispering that you've become a Dane," she had snapped. "So you're coming with us and you're going to listen to Father Cerdic say the Mass and give his sermon. Now, make yourself presentable."

Somewhat to her surprise, Titus had meekly obeyed, but it was on the ride to Wiltun, with Wiglaf riding in front of Titus on Thunor as he always insisted, while she rode her own mare that Uhtric had bought for her as a wedding gift, that Leofflaed began to wonder if, perhaps, she had been hasty in insisting on her brother attending. Yes, his absence would be noticed, and tongues would wag, but as the wooden walls of the town, which had been constructed two years earlier by order of Lord Eadwig, came into view, she began having second thoughts. Gossip, while pernicious and as irritating as it could be, would pass over time when someone else did something that those prone to do such things found a worthy subject. Titus, seeing Isolde, who Leofflaed had last seen a week before when she had gone into Wiltun, would see the same thing she had, a woman who was very near her time, no matter that the calendar said that she was still three or four weeks away. Then what would happen? she worried. Would he be able to control himself, and avoid doing or saying something rash, the consequences of which would, ultimately, fall on Isolde's shoulders far more than it would on her brother's? It may have been the way of her world, that men were never blamed as heavily by the clergy, and the more pious of their peers, when they succumbed to sin, and there was no greater sin of the flesh than lying with a man to whom a woman was not bound by God and law, and even worse if the woman was married to another man, but it did not infuriate Leofflaed any less, and she knew she was far from alone. She even opened her mouth to suggest that, perhaps, Titus should just return home, but the words would not come, although as they passed through the gate, she offered a prayer to God that her brother would control himself. Her fears, to her intense relief, were unfounded, because Isolde nor her mother-in-law were present, sending the message to Father Cerdic that Isolde's time was close at hand, and in fact she had been bedridden for the previous four days. Not surprisingly, her brother went pale when she quietly relayed the news inside the church as other townspeople were still filing in, and while she did not say anything to him, Leofflaed reached out, took her brother's hand and held it, hoping that it would bring him some comfort as it had when he was a child. His face was unreadable as they stood, in the back, almost a full head taller than everyone around him, with his long braid that people still stared at, which he always ignored, and while weapons were strictly forbidden inside the church, he had worn his sword, which was now hanging from Thunor's saddle outside. Rather than try and dissuade him; wearing weapons *to* church was not forbidden although it was discouraged, Uhtric had chosen to do the same, in a tacit statement of support for his friend. At Father Cerdic's signal, relayed to him by Lord Eadwig, who was at his rightful place in front, the doors were closed, and the Mass began. Titus barely noticed, his mind occupied with who was not there and not who was present, and he had pressed Leofflaed who, reluctantly, relayed the information she had been given by Cyneburga about Isolde's condition. Going through the motions, mouthing the ritual responses to the Mass, while Titus was praying, it had nothing to do with the birth of the Savior, Our Lord Jesus Christ, but the birth of a mortal soul who, even now, might be coming into the world. The service concluded, and the worshipers filed outside, talking excitedly about the coming feast and the end of what, while they would never say as much, was as much of an ordeal as a celebration.

"I expect to see you at the feast tonight, Titus."

Titus was standing with his back to the church, facing Thunor as he strapped on his sword, but he turned, and in the same motion, bowed to Lord Eadward.

"I'll be there, Lord," he assured his noble friend. "And I'm looking forward to it."

"Liar," Eadward said, but he was smiling. "I'd wager you'd rather be anywhere else than in my father's hall." Glancing over his shoulder, Eadward stepped closer so that only Titus could hear to say, "And I know why, Titus. Remember, I've known you ever since you came to Wiltun. And," he added with a quiet intensity, "I've known Isolde all of my life. I understand your worry, my friend, but it's in God's hands now."

"I know, Lord," Titus replied, experiencing a mixture of comfort and apprehension as he wondered, if Eadward knows, does everyone else? But he trusted Eadward enough to say, "But it's just...hard. Not knowing, I mean," he added hastily, "whether she's going to be all right or not."

If Eadward knew, or suspected he knew Titus' real cause for concern, to his credit, he gave no indication of it, saying only, "Know that I'm praying for her as well, Titus."

"Thank you, Lord," Titus answered, and meant it.

Eadward returned to where his family was waiting, and they mounted and moved at the trot, leaving Wiltun to return to the hall, where the servants and slaves were working through the day to prepare the feast. They had time to kill before going to the feast, and Leofflaed announced that she and Wiglaf were going to visit some of her friends in Wiltun, and while Uhtric invited Titus to come to The Boar's Head with him, he expected the same answer from Titus as always.

To his surprise, Titus, though he hesitated, shrugged and said, "All right. It's been awhile."

Husband and wife exchanged a look that communicated their mutual surprise, and Leofflaed pulled Uhtric aside to whisper, "Make sure he doesn't drink too much ale. We still have the feast, and with Isolde and her time, we need to make sure he's under control."

While Uhtric understood and agreed with the sentiment, he was under no illusion that he, or anyone, could control Titus if his temper was roused, but he also knew that saying as much to his wife was not wise, so he promised he would. The alehouse was already full, those men who, for a variety of reasons, did not attend the Mass already there, which included a fair number of Lord Eadwig's warriors, and Titus' appearance was greeted with raucous cheers and jokes about a Yule miracle, which he bore with good grace, knowing that he deserved it. After all, he *had* avoided The Boar's Head, and despite his preoccupation, he slowly began to relax, though he had overheard part of Leofflaed's warning to her husband, and he was moderate in his consumption of ale. Perhaps an hour passed, and to his surprise, he found that he was not only relaxed but was enjoying himself immensely, and he realized just how much he had missed this time with his comrades. It was undeniably true that many of the stories being told were the same, yet they were also subtly different, depending on who was telling them, and if he did not completely forget, he was able to put Isolde and whatever she was going through away in a corner of his mind, so that after another hour, it was almost as if he had never been absent from this gathering. Roars of laughter, bellows of mock anger over a disagreement, all very raucous yet good-natured, the smell of ale almost overpowering the other odors, and best of all, the feeling of belonging that had been eluding him, making Titus realize that, as much as the fighting, and the training for fighting, these moments were every bit as important in forming the bond between warriors. He was even getting accustomed to hearing the story of how he attacked the Danes with a man's guts wrapped around his ankle, though he still could not quite laugh about it, not because of any squeamishness but because he still had no memory of it. Meanwhile, men were coming and going, opening the door to let a blast of icy air into the snug warmth of the alehouse that was always met by protests and curses at the arrivals, and jeers at the departures for not being able to handle their ale. It was nearing dark and time to leave for the feast when the door opened again, except this time, it was thrown open so violently that it swung inward and banged against the wall, instantly arresting men in mid-story as they all turned in surprise, more than one hand dropping to the hilt of a *seaxe*. Normally, Titus sat so that he could face the door, but on this occasion, his and Uhtric's late arrival had placed them side by side with their backs to it, and when they both twisted around, they saw a man, framed in the doorway but clad only in a tunic, with no cloak despite the cold.

"*Where is he? Where is that bastard?*" Hereweald the Younger roared, then stepped into the alehouse as the men closest to the door scrambled to their feet, shocked into silence, but while the other occupants came to their feet, there was one exception. The young smith stepped inside, scanning the crowd, and because of the standing men, it took him a moment to spot where Titus was still sitting, although he had swung his legs around on the bench but otherwise was not moving.

"He's got a *seaxe*!" a man shouted, and now the men in his path scrambled out of the way, although a couple of them were not quite quick enough, and with his left hand, the smith shoved them, hard, sending one man reeling into another and taking them both off of their feet.

Hereweald, now that he had seen Titus, strode towards him, not taking his eyes off the warrior, and still Titus did not rise, but when Uhtric, who was on his feet, began to sidestep to block Hereweald, Titus reached out and stopped him. When Uhtric looked over his shoulder in surprise, he saw Titus shake his head, but he still did not step aside.

"It's all right, Uhtric," Titus said quietly, but while he was expressionless, his face was extremely pale. "Let him say what he has to say."

"It's not what he wants to say that I'm worried about," Uhtric snapped, pointing to the *seaxe* in the smith's hand. "It's what he plans on doing with that."

"Do you think I can't handle it?" Titus asked, still not raising his voice, but what concerned Uhtric was that he had still not come to his feet.

By this time, Hereweald had reached a spot a pace away, with only Uhtric between him and Titus, and he snarled, "You need to listen to the bastard, Uhtric!" In only a slightly less hostile tone, he allowed, "My quarrel isn't with you."

Uhtric had not drawn his own weapon, also a *seaxe*, but while he kept his hand on the hilt, he reluctantly stepped aside, and suddenly, Hereweald seemed at a loss what to do, and another emotion began to compete with his rage, his eyes beginning to fill with tears.

"Isolde," he managed, his voice now hoarse, "is dead." There was a chorus of gasps and muttering that bore the cadence of prayers from the men, yet Titus said nothing. "Did you not hear me, you arrogant bastard? You turd? *You pig-fucking son of a whore?*" Hereweald bellowed, beginning to raise the *seaxe* in a manner that suggested he intended to thrust it into Titus' body.

And yet, Titus still did not move, still sat with his hands on his knees and returning Hereweald's hate-filled glare, but Uhtric and Hrothgar, who had been on Titus' other side, saw his chin quivering, a sign that he was struggling to control his own grief. The fact was that, in the span of a heartbeat after Titus had spun about on his bench, seen the figure, then identified it as Hereweald, he had known why the smith was there, and that Isolde was dead.

His voice sounded as if it belonged to someone else, answering, "I...I heard you, Hereweald." He was numb, and it was as if he was watching the scene from just above, disembodied and detached from what was happening. "What...what about the child?"

"Dead!" Hereweald spat, then cried out, "And it's the babe that killed her!"

There it is, Titus thought; this is God's punishment, and there was a part of him that wanted Hereweald to plunge the *seaxe* into his chest, to end the sudden, monstrous agony that was suddenly consuming him now that his worst fears were confirmed.

"Hereweald," Uhtric spoke quietly, and with genuine sympathy, "I know that you're grieving, and know that I grieve with you. I was very fond of Isolde, and I've known her as long as you have."

Hereweald did not even glance at Uhtric, his eyes still on Titus, his face twisted into a mask of grief and hatred, but when Titus still did not come to his feet, he shouted, "Stand up, you bastard! Stand up so that I can kill you! I won't kill you when you're sitting down!" When Titus still did not move, he took a step closer, and there was a hissing sound as Uhtric partially drew his *seaxe* in a warning. Nobody else was moving, no man wanting to be responsible for the kind of bloodshed that seemed to be in the offing, even if some of them were eager to see it. Frustrated at Titus' immobility, he bellowed, "Stand up, you *coward*! I'm not afraid of you," his mouth twisting, as with lacerating scorn, he mocked, "Titus the *Berserker*, and I'll prove it if you get to your feet!"

Now Titus did stir, and while none of the onlookers thought it could have gotten more tense, they understood they were wrong as Titus came, slowly and carefully, with both hands out from his sides, to his feet.

"I'm not going to fight you, Hereweald," Titus said in an eerily calm voice, particularly since, never before in their association, had Uhtric seen his friend like this, refusing a challenge. He did notice that Titus used his left hand to point at the *seaxe* in Hereweald's hand. "If you want to kill me, you're going to have to thrust that into my body. And," he promised, "I won't stop you."

"Titus!" Uhtric gasped. "What are you saying?" Turning back to Hereweald, the one-eyed warrior spoke harshly. "If you do that, Hereweald, you'll be a murderer. We're all witnesses! Titus said he won't fight you. And," he finished, his voice turned flat and matter-of-fact, "if you do it, I'll kill you where you stand, Hereweald. Do you understand?"

For the first time, the young smith took his eyes off of Titus, giving Uhtric a scornful glance.

"Do you think I care?" he asked bitterly. "Do you think I'm afraid to die?" Turning back to Titus, he screamed, *"Draw your sword, you coward! Fight me!"*

"I will not," Titus replied, making it clear by keeping his hand away from anywhere near the hilt of his sword.

Then Hereweald took another step closer, and now Uhtric's blade was all the way out, while Hrothgar was only a heartbeat behind him, but while he was within striking distance, Hereweald kept the point of his own blade pointed at the floor. Instead, he made a hawking sound, then spat the contents fully into Titus' face, eliciting a chorus of gasps and murmured exclamations, and for the first time, the huge Saxon warrior reacted, his hand instinctively starting towards his sword, as the onlookers braced themselves for what they now viewed as inevitable. And, whereas there might have been some sentiment in favor of the dead Hrodulf, not one man among them would have faulted Titus for avenging what was the most mortal offense one man could perpetrate against another in their world. Titus' hand stopped, though he did reach up with his left hand, but instead of wiping his face with the sleeve of his tunic and thereby obscuring his vision, he used his hand to wipe the expectorant from his face, his eyes never leaving Hereweald.

"It's not so easy, is it, Hereweald?" Titus asked, still not raising his voice. "Killing a man? But," he moved his hands out from his side, "you'll never make an easier kill than right now, because I swear by the Rood, I will not stop you."

Then, shocking everyone, it was Titus who moved next, taking a single step so there was less than an arm's length between them, and he indicated Hereweald's *seaxe*. "Go on, lift it." As if in a trance, though his eyes were still fixed on Titus' and still blazing with the hatred he felt, Hereweald did until it was parallel to the floor, only a couple of inches from Titus' body. Because of their height difference, the point was aimed just above Titus' navel, and all Hereweald had to do was thrust it into Titus' body, which was protected only by his tunic. He did not move, though anyone with a view could see the tip of the *seaxe* trembling violently, but Titus did, just a couple of inches so that the point was pressing against his body. "Now," Titus said, still quiet, "all you have to do is lean forward, but be sure and put your weight behind it." Still, Hereweald did not, and when the men who were present told the tale, while as always happened, the accounts would vary wildly, there was one thing they all agreed on, that the alehouse was deadly quiet, as quiet as any of them had ever heard it. With a touch of impatience, Titus urged, "Go ahead, Hereweald. Do it. Plunge your blade into my body. And then, be sure and twist the blade. That's an important thing to do if you want to kill me."

For the first time, Hereweald made a noise, a low moaning sound; at least this was how it began, but it gradually increased in volume and intensity until he was screaming, nothing intelligible, just a long, drawn-out shriek of unimaginable pain, rage, and impotent fury until finally, he was out of breath. Suddenly, he dropped the point of his *seaxe* back to the floor, his shoulders slumped, and without a word, he turned and raced from the alehouse and out into the growing dusk, leaving men who suddenly were no longer in a festive mood. With Hereweald's absence, it was natural that all eyes turned to Titus, who, only now, did he use the sleeve of his tunic to clean his face, then, ignoring the stares of the others, turned and sat back down at the table.

"Are you all right?" Uhtric asked, realizing what a foolish question it was, but he was concerned by what he saw in his friend's face.

Titus did not answer immediately, but when he did, it was to ask, "Isn't it about time to collect Leofflaed and Wiglaf and head to Lord Eadwig's?"

In fact, it was still a bit early, but Uhtric understood, lying, "Yes, it is. No doubt she's waiting for us."

Their comrades pretended to believe the lie, and while men had begun talking again, it was in low tones, the kind when they did not want to be overheard, but it was the way in which they all avoided Titus' gaze as he stood, then followed Uhtric out of the alehouse that spoke most eloquently. Not surprisingly, what happened in The Boar's Head that Yule night would be the talk of Wiltun for weeks, especially after what was still to come.

Uhtric was not surprised when, as soon as they exited, Titus announced that he would not be attending the feast and would return to their home.

"Please tell Lord Eadwig I apologize for being absent," Titus said, using a tone that Uhtric had never heard before, dispassionate and distracted, but more alarmingly, he did not look his brother-in-law in the eye. "I'm going home. I...need to be alone."

Not knowing what to say, Uhtric cursed himself for uttering the kind of platitudes one did at such a moment. "Titus, I am sorry, and I grieve for Isolde. And, for the babe. Sometimes," he concluded sadly, "it's impossible for us to understand why God does what He does. All we can do is accept it and offer our prayers for their ascension to Heaven." Titus acted as if he had not heard Uhtric, swinging up onto Thunor, and with a sense of a growing desperation, Uhtric reached out

348

and grasped Titus' thigh, looking up at his friend, whose face was still unreadable, and he said urgently, "Titus, you do *not* know whether that babe was yours, and you don't know what happened! It may have had nothing to do with...with what you think."

"No," Titus shook his head, sounding weary, "I do know. It was my boy, and he killed Isolde just like I killed my mother. And now," he finished bleakly, "I'm damned for eternity...and I deserve it."

"That's not true!" Uhtric replied, with a touch of anger now. "I don't care what a poxed priest tells us! You and Isolde loved each other, and they tell us that our God is a God of love! You didn't rut with her like you do with Frida," this was the name of the Danish slave that Wigmund offered customers for a penny, "or even when you were with Aslaug. You two loved each other, and I know that, while she may have married Hereweald, she *never* stopped loving you!"

Uhtric would never forget the look that Titus gave him then, in the fading winter daylight, looking so much older than his almost nineteen years, as if a much older soul was peering through his eyes, and there was an unutterable sadness in them, which was matched by his voice as he replied, "And I'll never stop loving her. But it doesn't make her any less dead."

Gently but firmly removing Uhtric's hand from his leg, Titus turned Thunor's head and went to the trot, heading for the gate that led home, leaving Uhtric to wonder how he was going to tell his wife as he began heading to the home of Cynebald the baker, and whether they should hurry home after Titus.

He wanted to cry, yet he could not, even when he was alone in the growing darkness as he guided Thunor to the home that he shared with Uhtric and Leofflaed, barely noticing the biting wind. It was a full moon, and it was low in the sky now, making the snow shine with a silver tint that, under other circumstances, he would have found beautiful, but now he barely noticed. When the young Danish slave Gunni came running out of the house, hearing the hoofbeats, Titus told him to go back to his spot in the corner of the barn that was his spot and go back to sleep. Unsaddling Thunor, he took extra time rubbing him down, feeling comfort from the solid bulk of his horse, hearing him blowing in the darkness, every so often offering Titus a gentle nicker as he worked. Finished, he entered the house, where the fire had been banked, with only smoldering coals as was the custom when there was nobody home, and he quickly got it going, the room filling with the warm, orange light of the fire from which he normally took comfort, yet now the coldness he was feeling within himself would not go away. He had taken off his cloak, and unbuckled his sword, laying it on his bed, then went and sat on the bench nearest to the fire to gaze into the flames, the numbness slowly wearing off and the reality of his world, that all the things he had planned to say to Isolde would now go to the grave with him unsaid, because Isolde was dead. Yet he still could not summon the tears, only a bone-deep, painful weariness as now, for the first time in his life, he felt a sense of sympathy for his father, finally understanding the pain he must have felt, and while he had not thought it would be the case that he would ever understand, why Leofric hated his son so much, blaming him for the death of what was clearly the only person Leofric had ever loved in his mean, bitter existence. *Would I hate my son like he hates me, if he had survived?* Titus could not seem to banish this thought because, while he did not think he would, he could not say so with any certainty. He was sad, yes, but he was also angry, so angry, but this time, it was at himself. These were his thoughts for the entire time he sat there in a seemingly endless repetition, staring into the fire, moving only to add wood, until, with some surprise, he realized he needed to piss. He had no idea how long he had been sitting there, but when he went outside, he saw the moon high in the sky, judging that it was close to midnight, meaning that either Uhtric, Leofflaed, and Wiglaf were close to making their way home, or as he thought more likely, would be spending the night in Lord Eadwig's hall. Thankfully, he only had to piss; the idea of sitting on the wooden bench of the privy, even after he brushed the snow off of it, did not appeal to him in the slightest, and since Leofflaed was not there to nag him about it, he just walked around to the back of the house a few paces away.

It was the sudden, rapid crunching sound of running footsteps on the snow that warned Titus, and if Hereweald had waited for Titus to pull out his cock then approached more stealthily and attacked Titus when he was in midstream, the outcome would have been different. But clearly, just seeing Titus from where Hereweald had been crouched, shivering in the cold, was too much for the young smith, and to his credit, when he burst from his hiding spot in a clump of bushes twenty paces from Uhtric's hut, there was no hesitation this time, charging at Titus at an all-out sprint, *seaxe* in hand. Titus heard the crunching of snow, spinning about and, thanks to the moonlight, clearly recognized his attacker as he charged at him, and once they were facing each other and there was no need for silence any longer, Hereweald roared a single word challenge.

"*DIE!!!!!*"

Hereweald was strong, there was no doubt about it, but while he had received some training as part of his obligation to Lord Eadwig as a member of the fyrd, it was only with a spear, and he was still wielding the *seaxe*, which he held raised above his head as he rushed at Titus, signaling his intention to smite Titus with a mighty, overhand blow with the aim of splitting his skull. As happened with these moments, everything happened quickly, so before having any conscious thought, Titus' body reacted from the cumulative months of training in Otha's yard. An overhead blow was a favorite of those warriors who favored the ax, and while they were trained to block it with a shield, Lord Otha had required them to train without one, meaning that Titus reacted by taking a single step forward with his left foot while raising his left arm up and across his body just as Hereweald, slowing his charge, swung the *seaxe* down, and because of that step, instead of the blade cutting into flesh, their forearms collided. The force was terrific, and while he had never seen it himself, Titus had been told stories of warriors whose arm had been broken from a block such as this, although he would only come away with a deep bruise. While Hereweald had been forced to slow his headlong charge to launch his attack with his blade, his momentum was still enough that he was within Titus' reach, and again without thinking, the young warrior's right fist shot out, catching Hereweald flush on his cheek, the force of the blow multiplied by the young smith's momentum. It was a devastating blow, especially from Titus, and every other time when he had hit another man with that much force, his opponent was almost always knocked flat on his back and was usually unconscious. But this time, while it did send Hereweald reeling backward several steps, somehow the young smith managed to keep his feet, and his grip on the *seaxe*, as he waved both arms in an instinctive move to remain on his feet, and while he knew it was a foolish thing to do, Titus did not press his advantage, choosing instead to let the smith regain his balance, whereupon he stood there, panting, but still holding the *seaxe*, his face pale in the moonlight but still blazing with hatred that was impossible to miss.

"Go home, Hereweald," Titus said tiredly. "I don't want to fight you."

"'Go home'?" Hereweald asked incredulously, his hatred momentarily in abeyance as he stared at Titus, and he repeated, "'*Go home?* What home? I don't have a home anymore without Isolde!" It was the mention of her name that brought the hatred rushing back, and with his free hand, he pointed an accusing finger. "And it's because of you that she's dead! I'm not stupid! I know that you lay with her! And you killed her!"

"You think I don't know that, Hereweald?" Titus asked quietly, and for a brief moment, just one, they stood there, sharing their pain.

Then, without another word, Hereweald charged, and this time, he did not raise the *seaxe* but held it out low, albeit awkwardly. Now, however, Titus was ready, and correctly anticipated that the smith would overextend on his thrust, which Titus avoided by twisting his torso while leaning to his right as his left hand clamped down on Hereweald's wrist, and with all of his strength, he gave a tremendous yank in the same direction of the smith's headlong attack that sent Hereweald careening past him, his own momentum sending him shooting past Titus. This time, he was unable to remain on his feet, going sprawling face first in a spray of snow as Titus pivoted and, in what proved to be a mistake, when he walked over to the smith, instead of striking Hereweald, kicked the *seaxe* from his hand, sending it several paces away in a smaller shower before settling into the soft snow. He did not see Hereweald's kick coming that struck him behind his left knee, buckling it and bringing him down to the ground on that knee, then before he could react, Hereweald scrambled to a crouch then launched himself at Titus with a low, almost feral growl, their bodies colliding and knocking Titus flat. It was an extremely unusual situation for Titus, being on the ground, and even more so to be the man pinned as Hereweald immediately straddled his chest, so he was slow to react as he felt the smith's hands go to his throat, the pain from the grasp of a man whose grip was every bit as strong as Titus' feeling as if someone had shoved a lit torch down his throat. The pain was horrific, even worse than when Sigurd the Bold had tried to choke him and was compounded by the fact that he had had the wind knocked out of him and now could not draw a breath. For the first time in his life, Titus of Cissanbyrig felt the beginning of what he dimly understood was panic, a wild, unreasoning fear that was so overwhelming that he seemed unable to defend himself other than to try and wrench Hereweald's grip from his throat. Is this really so bad? The pain will be over soon, and if Uhtric is right, that God is about love, wouldn't He make sure that he was reunited with Isolde? Titus knew he was dying, was on the verge of surrendering, and had even stopped trying to pry Hereweald's hands from his throat, though he was still grasping his wrists, when the smith made his mistake and sealed his own fate.

"She was a *whore*!" Hereweald hissed, straddling Titus' chest and leaning forward to put all of his weight and strength into choking the life from Titus, spraying Titus in a shower of saliva for a second time. "Nothing but a filthy, poxed whore!"

Suddenly, Titus' hands left Hereweald's wrists, shooting straight up to grasp the smith's head in his hands, but Hereweald, out of his mind with rage, did not recognize Titus' intent, although he did bellow in pain as Titus began squeezing as if he was trying to bring his hands together with Hereweald's skull in between them. No human was strong enough to crush a man's skull, no matter how painful it might have been; this was Hereweald's thought so he made no attempt to wrench his head from Titus' grasp, intent on choking the life from his foe despite the crushing agony. Too late did he understand that this was not the warrior's intent as he felt Titus' thumbs sliding upward along his cheeks towards his eyes, but when he did try to yank his head free, or even move it violently from side to side, he could not, held in place by a grip made of iron. He had less than a heartbeat of time to understand, instantly relinquishing his grip on Titus' throat to reach up to grab Titus' wrists, but it was too late to stop Titus' thumbs from plunging into his eyes, rendering him instantly blind and in an overwhelming pain so consuming that he threw himself backward, off of Titus' body to clutch his ruined eyes, writhing and shrieking in agony, while Titus rolled over, came to his hands and knees and began retching, as much from what he had just done and the sensation of turning a man's eyes into a pulped jelly as from the throbbing pain of his throat. It took a tremendous effort for him to draw enough air into his lungs for the roaring sound in his ears to fade away and his head to at least partially clear, and he only became gradually aware of Hereweald's screams: shrill, piercing and never-ending. With an effort, he slowly turned his head to where the smith was rolling on the snow, blood spattering all around his head even as he clutched his ruined eyes as he shook his head back and forth from the pain, his legs kicking and thrashing in a spray of snow. Any sympathy and pity he had felt for the smith had vanished in the time it took for Hereweald to curse Isolde, and he climbed slowly to his feet, then stumbled over to where the *seaxe* lay partially buried in the snow. Briefly, he considered going into the house to retrieve his own sword, thinking that he should use his own weapon to finish this, but he did not, unsure whether he would have the strength to return and kill his foe. Staggering over to Hereweald, whose shrieks had begun to subside into a low, guttural moan, although he kept shaking his head back and forth as if in denial about what had just happened to him, the blood and matter that had welled out from between his fingers black in the moonlight, it made Titus think of standing over Sigurd the Bold at Stanmer and seeing the Dane's blood, gleaming black in the same way. Our blood looks the same in the moonlight; this was the thought that went through his mind as he stood, still weaving slightly.

When he finally spoke, his voice came out as a croak, so he was not even certain that Hereweald understood him when he said, "You shouldn't have called Isolde a whore, Hereweald."

The sound of Titus' voice stopped Hereweald's head from moving back and forth, and in what was an unconscious reaction, he turned his head towards the sound of it, and he even dropped his hands, perhaps in a hope that, somehow, he would be able to see his enemy standing over him, but there was only darkness, and Hereweald began sobbing, making a low, keening moan of agony and despair that aroused not a flicker of emotion in Titus as he stared down at the smith.

"I know," he rasped, "we're both going to Hell, Hereweald. But," he took a couple steps closer so that he was standing directly over the smith, "at least this way, you will never see me when I come to kill you again. And again. And again," he said, then thrust the *seaxe* down into the base of Hereweald's throat, feeling the grating as the point cut through the bones of the neck, followed by the vibration as Hereweald's body spasmed, his back arching off the ground for less than a heartbeat before collapsing back with the limpness of death.

Out of habit, Titus wrenched the *seaxe* from Hereweald's body, then without thinking, dropped it next to the smith's body, near his outstretched hand. Bending down, he scooped up a handful of snow and used it to clean the blood and bits of gore that had once been Hereweald's eyes from his thumbs, dropping the remnants of the snow and leaving a mound of pink slush. Then, a bit more steadily, he walked a few paces away to take the piss that he had been holding, watching the steam rise from the hole in the snow. Then he returned back to the hut, where the door was still open, making it cold inside, and he closed it, but instead of adding wood to the fire or returning to his spot on the bench, he went to the corner of the main room that was his and began packing. He thought that if Uhtric, Leofflaed, and Wiglaf had not returned by now that it was likely they would be spending the night in Eadwig's hall, but he did not want to take the chance, so he worked quickly, gathering all of his possessions, realizing what he had to do. Carrying his pack, he returned to the stable, where he dimly saw Gunni, huddled in the corner of the barn with his knees pulled to his chest, the thick blanket that was part of his pallet pulled up so that only the upper part of his face was showing, and even in the gloom, Titus could see the youngster's eyes wide with fright.

"Don't worry, boy," Titus rasped. "I won't hurt you. Just stay there."

Not surprisingly, the young slave did as Titus commanded, nor did he say anything, just watching as Titus led the horse that he and Uhtric shared as their packhorse outside. Technically speaking, the horse belonged to Uhtric, and Titus felt badly about taking it, but he decided he would leave one of his arm rings as payment. Once the horse was loaded, he saddled Thunor, then led both of them out of the barn and around to the front of the house, then returned inside. While he knew it was not necessary, he chose to wear his mail vest before strapping on his sword belt, then donned the fur-lined cloak that he had saved to buy a year earlier. Placing one of the silver arm rings from Sigurd on the table, Titus' deepest regret was that he did not know his letters so that he could have left some sort of message behind explaining his actions. Of course, neither Uhtric nor Leofflaed were literate either, but they could have taken the message to Lord Eadwig's steward to read it for them, which was a fairly common occurrence. He was also aware that he would be leaving without the permission of Lord Otha, which would be a violation of his oath of loyalty, not to mention that, no matter the cause, there would be a hearing over Hereweald's death in the hundred court, and a decision would be made about the *wergild*, although he did not think he would be found at fault, especially after what he had done to avoid trouble at The Boar's Head, but there was nothing for Titus here in Wiltun, not anymore. It was not that he had a plan; he did not, aside from this driving urge to leave this place, which he had begun to think of as more his home than the village to the north where he had spent his first fourteen years. Wiglaf would be heartbroken, he knew, but even this was not enough to make him stay, and with one last look at the small but tidy hut, he exited, closing the door behind him. Swinging up into the saddle, Titus leaned down and picked up the lead rope attached to the packhorse's halter, then nudged his horse into a walk, pointing him north, leaving the hut, and Hereweald's corpse with a halo of blood around his head to tell the story, behind. He did not look back, and within a matter of moments, Titus of Cissanbyrig, better known now as the Berserker...was gone.

Made in the USA
Las Vegas, NV
08 January 2022